I0727530

PHYSIO DEPT.
4
BEARS
CUBBY SEASON

Copy & Proof edits by Callie - CJ Editing

Cover art by Luisa Sipia-Luyco

Formatting by Love Bug Romance Covers

Published by Bindi K Publishing

In the interests of a good tale, the locations in and geographical features of Boston have been fictionalized.
This novel's story and characters are wholly fictitious creations of my imagination. Certain long-standing institutions, public offices & agencies, celebrities, works of literature, film, T.V. & songs are mentioned.

Likewise, all references to Boston College, Boston University, the teams mentioned, the NCAA and NHL have been created in my mind. Creative licenses have been applied liberally, and none of the rules, regulations or actions in Kitty Season are representative those of the real organizations.

For the carers
The burnout is real and you're fucking incredible

CUBBY SEASON

P eople are perplexing. I don't enjoy them. One could even say I hate them. And for someone like me, someone who chose to build their life around healing and educating people, *that* is an issue. Come to think of it, all that healing and educating may be the reason *why* I hate people. They're just too needy, with too many nuances. Too many layers. Too many ways to say one thing, and not enough of saying what they mean.

There are exceptions, of course.

Within ten minutes of meeting David Harris, coach of the Boston College men's hockey team, I deduced not only that he was strikingly handsome, but he also possessed many qualities I seek in those I'm forced to interact with. Assertiveness, brutal honesty, and methodicalness being of utmost importance.

Perhaps predictably, the same cannot be said for his young charges. And it's them, his players, who will consume the majority of my final twelve weeks of clinical training.

At the side of the man I'd spent a week practice-smiling at in my vanity mirror, I'm witnessing their first pre-season practice after summer break. Though it feels like I've been here for hours, one glance at my watch tells me it's been fifteen minutes.

Fifteen.

That's it?

The arena's harsh lighting isn't helping, but there is one, or twenty odd, reasons all the paracetamol in the world would fail to nullify the headache brewing.

"They're a good group," Coach Harris says, confidence

briefly faltering as two forwards slam into each other, peel apart like two halves of a banana skin, then fall onto their backs. "Utter morons, but good."

"So I hear. Faith mentioned you've created quite the NHL factory. What was it? Three Bears players that went on to the majors?"

"Five." He nods, with a proud puffing of his chest.

Ugh, straight men are so easily fluffed.

"Two were drafted at eighteen," adds his assistant—and my clinical supervisor—Coach White. "And three were picked up as free agents. This year is looking just as promising. Again we've got plenty of talent and two more draftees, Malkovich and Bailey. Both are at their respective team camps, but should be back— "

"Ah, Basse. Glad you decided to join us," Coach Harris cuts off his 2IC and gives an un-enthused grin to a hulk of man more suited to the set of a Baywatch reboot than a hockey rink, approaching us from the right

"Hey Coach. Sorry 'bout the time. Quinny was—"

"Running late? Well, there's a shock," David huffs, looking at me like I'm supposed to know who Quinn is. "I know you two are attached at the hip, but maybe you should make your way to campus independent of each other."

Blushing, he rubs one hand over the back of his neck and shoves the other in his pocket, fingers clearly fiddling with something inside. No one else seems disturbed by this, so I presume it's not as suspicious as it looks. "Yeah, nah, that wouldn't work. Troye has the other car. I could catch the Green Line, I suppose. Or Quinny could get Lotte to–"

"I lost interest before you started, Basse." *And* there's that refreshing brutal honesty. Exasperated by the ten second conversation, he points to the two goalies laughing hysterically as they whack each other's pads with their sticks. "For God's sake, go and do something with Larsson and Nurse before I send them back to their mommies."

"Sure thing." He flashes us a quick smile and wink, then hits the ice, slipping his helmet on as he goes.

"He's your goalie, Coach?" I ask. Trying, but likely failing to keep the skepticism from my tone. "He looks young to hold such a position." As I say that, I notice the manner in which Larsson and Nurse stand to attention as he approaches. There's a level of respect. An eagerness to impress in their movements missing mere seconds beforehand.

Observing the trio, David Harris nods and pops a piece of gum in his mouth.

Great.

He's a chewer.

No matter what he says now, that sloppy, gnawing of polyisobutylene will be all I notice.

"He's one of them, yes. We have a full-time coach, but Basse will be helping out a few times a week. He was our starting goalie last season, but two concussions within weeks of each other put an end to his career."

My stomach twists. "Poor kid."

"Yeah. It's a crying shame. He was a rare talent. And weird as fuck. The NHL would have loved him." I'm not one that would usually be described as a giggler, but the last half of that sentence shocks one out of me.

"As a former tender myself, I should probably be offended." I pause, waiting for the reaction. Types such as Coach Harris are normally surprised by my—ugh, I hate this term—*jock* history. David Harris doesn't bat an eyelid at my revelation, which means one of two things. He's not listening, or Faith already blabbed.

"But you can't be, because I'm right. Right?"

"Right."

Again, I wait for the inevitable follow-ups. *You don't seem like the type. Why did you quit? Was it because you're a talent-less hack, or because you're a raging homosexual?* I'm mildly disappointed when that, too, fails to eventualize. When I follow his line of sight, I see why. His junior coach is skating on one foot and attempting to juggle four pucks.

"You're supposed to be teaching them, Basse, not applying for head clown." Ridiculously, I find myself chuckling again. It's over suddenly though, when the mood shifts, and I sense a disturbance in the force.

"Oh, you're here, Jamie." Cool. Sterile. Monotone. My sister has arrived.

"As you see," I reply flatly before leaning closer and whisper, "And it's James, please and thank you."

"Sorry Jamie. I mean James. I mean Jamie."

"Really. Here? Aren't we above this?"

"You're a child."

"I know I am, but what are you?"

Most of my free time is spent with Faith, who is the team's psych consultant, and I do love her. I do. But as Mum always said, the only things we have in common is our surname, autism, and a severe superiority complex, which means much of that time is spent in conflict rather than comfort.

True to form, Faith merely scoffs, then turns and speaks to Coach Harris as though I'm not there. "Since *he* is my brother, and not my sister, I trust Jamie's received a more ... respectful reception than the one I was afforded?"

David stops scowling at his players, and joins me with a huffed laugh. "Well, we've had no wolf whistles, baying at the moon, or marriage proposals, *but* the day is young." Since we're neck deep in the world of hockey, the day could be as long as time itself and I should think myself safe from unwanted advances.

In my experience, queer and hockey don't mix.

Taking my iPad from the satchel I placed on the bench, I shift my focus back onto the ice, doing my best to forget my sibling's presence, and the touch of melancholy slowly sinking in. Immediately, I note the goalies are sorely in need of core and hip strengthening. If Larsson is anything to go by, some basic breathing bio-mechanics wouldn't hurt, either. I need to speak to this ... Basse. My hockey history means I understand the propensity for sportsmen to refer to each other by their surnames, but as an independent thinker—not a sheep—I prefer to address others by their given names.

"Sorry to interrupt, David, but what is Basse's first name?"

"Brady," Coach and Faith answer in unison.

No way. I grip Faith's arm and spin her to face me. "That's *your* Brady?"

Eyes wide, Faith emits a pained peep, slaps her hand over mine, and drags me towards the players tunnel, not an easy task since I'm well over two hundred and fifty pounds of man-flesh.

"David, excuse us for a minute." Now just the two of us, the fancy accent we both adopted when we moved to the States is forgotten. "What the hell, Jamie? He is not *my* Brady. I told you there was nothing going on between us and I meant it."

"Relax, sis. I was just teasing. I know you're not stupid enough to get involved with a student." She nods, but it's premature. "You were definitely close though." I really shouldn't tease her. Like me, Faith has obsessive behaviors, meaning once we care about someone we can easily become fixated and overly protective, which is exactly what happened with Brady. She also has a wickedly sharp sense of humor, and for those that don't know how she ticks, that's a lethal combination.

As is her right-left jab.

"Shut your face, Jamie." She gives me a perfect one-two combo, then sashays back to the open rink. I follow, but decide it might be wise to give her some space. With a glance toward David, I motion towards my intended destination and head out to the goals, sliding to a halt alongside the trio, earning a dimple-popping smile from Brady.

"Nice moves, Doc." Great, thirty minutes here and I have a nickname.

"Mr. Plum would suffice."

"Plum!" he squawks. "Your last name is Plum? Plum as in Professor Plum? You're related to Faith?"

"I am. She is my sister, and coincidentally, I am her brother. She never mentioned me? I thought you two were quite the bosom buddies."

"Bosom." Larsson and Nurse snort.

"We are mates, yeah," Brady replies, eyes narrowing in warning towards his juniors. "But she never let slip that she had a bro. Actually, 'part from growing up in Sydney, she's never spoken about her family at all."

This shouldn't come as a surprise, but still, I'm slightly wounded. "Too busy regaling the world with stories of herself, I suspect."

"No way." He smiles. He seems to do that a lot. "Faith is amazing. She's been great for the team. Kept our heads screwed on right throughout the finals, and kept the boys humble after the win. She was a great support when I had to quit, too." The grin drops, and so does my stomach. The poor kid can't be more than twenty-one or two, and he's already lost his dream. Having endured a life filled with the same sharp pang of grief and regret, I fight the urge to engage in pointless trauma sharing.

Some may believe this appropriate, but some are also fools. I know myself, my list of flaws is as jam-packed as my Rolodex of annoying human traits. Having fallen victim to my own weaknesses one too many times, I can't let myself again. I can't get bogged down with other people's business. I must control my emotions. There's just too much at stake to let that happen now.

With that in mind, I move on, perhaps coldly.

"Glad to hear it, but there's a new variety of Plum in town, and this one is less concerned with the emotions clogging that giant muscle in your head, and more with oxygenating it. Now, let's get to work."

It's the last day of development camp in Montreal and I still can't believe I'm here, training my childhood dream team. It should have registered by now. I mean, I'm almost twenty-one, and I was drafted just before I turned eighteen. But nope. My future with the Mounties is as unbelievable to me as it was the day they called my name and slid that red and white that jersey over my head.

Since I head home tomorrow, I've arrived at the stadium a little early, and am just chilling in my stall, soaking it all in. Oh, and sneaking around, taking photos for my sister, Cherry. As many twins are, we're super close—when we're not fighting or trying to humiliate the other and have both loved the Mounties since the first game we watched together, huddled up on our living room floor in Boston—AKA Mounties Enemy Territory.

Scrolling through my phone, I send her a shot of the hockey sticks lining the property manager walls, and wait for the reply.

I don't have to wait long.

Holy shit! Just think how much money is sitting in that room. How many do you think you can fit in your bag?

Smiling like a fool, I'm typing my reply, when my fellow rookies begin piling in.

"Hey, *Cubby*. Who's got you grinning like that? Got a hot girl waiting for you back home?"

Cubby? For the love of Mary Jane.

I thought I made it. After two blissful weeks of no jeering, minimal patronizing 'little guy' quips, and pretty much nothing but hockey, someone's blabbed. I ignore the hot-girl mention, and go straight to the nickname.

"Who told you!" I demand, pointing toward Dylan Prescott, the Cubby-caller. After laughing for a solid minute, he and the rest of the Montreal rookie brains trust—White, Coleman and McKinney—unfold themselves and regain enough motor-control to speak.

"My buddy Jax has a girlfriend who hooked up with some guy who knows your sister. She told him, he told her and she ... no he ... wait."

Fucking, Cherry.

Sighing, I rub my hand over my face to hide my blush. "Not sure I needed that detail, but thanks."

"I still like Mr. Ripley," Coleman, a hulking redhead from Georgia chimes in with the name he christened me with on day one. "You really do look like baby Matt Damon." He considers me, then holds out his hand and with his thumb and index finger an inch apart. "But then again, Cubby suits 'cause you're so tiny."

I should just ignore this, too. After all, feeding a beast only serves to make it hungrier. But I can't.

"I'm not tiny, I'm five feet, eight and a bit inches." Of course, this sees their laughter become hysteria. Way to go, Dickhead.

"See," Coleman wheezes. "Like I said, tiny."

"Kind of cute, too." That's McKinney. NOT checking him out has been the hardest thing about camp. *Cute* from him is intriguing. *Cute* from him has me preening. "And hairy," he adds.

Hairy? Silently, I look down to the three hairs on my chest.

"On your head." He sweetly taps his own to demonstrate. "Your hair. It's lush, and all soft and fluffy looking."

Lush? Hmm. Maybe I'm not the only one NOT checking teammates out.

No one else seems to notice the way he's licking his lip as he studies my locks, then mouth. And that's a good thing. I'm a baby gay, and I haven't known these guys long enough to ascertain how safe a space this is. Still, I know what I want, and it's all about the D.

And I don't mean defense.

All in high spirits for our last session, the boys wrap up their taunting, kit up, and leave the room en masse. But it's Nate McKinney who waits for me. Nate who looks over his shoulder and shoots me a wink that has my dick twitching uncomfortably in my cup.

Yeah. I know what I want.

"WHY DID I wait 'til the last night? And where have you been hiding those glasses?" McKinney's voice cracks as I lick the pre-cum from his glistening pink tip.

Conversation is not what I'm here for, so I shrug, then splay one hand over his toned abs. With the other, I grip his ass and pull until his dark, mass of curly hair tickles my face, and his dick hits the back of my throat.

Fuck I love this.

The smell. The feel. The taste.

I work him over, bobbing up and down on my knees for as long as I can before I relent to the need for air. "Probably for the best though," I pant, nuzzling into his balls. "You're so hot, had we hooked up on day one, my constant boner may have hindered my performance."

His dick swells before my eyes. "You think I'm hot?"

"What do you think?" I lean back, palming my erection that thickens with the widening of his eyes. "You're so big and brawny. Those arms and hands are huge. Bet you could toss me around if you wanted."

"Reckon I could." He nods. "Pity, we don't have time to find out."

"Real pity."

"Guess we'll just have to make up for–" Out in the hall, a door slams, and we both jump then still, listening for any further noises. No one should walk in on us. After flirting all day at practice, playing footsies under the table at lunch, and dinner at the hotel, we waited for the guys to get to bed, then crept into a storage closet. But still. That door is a reminder of the risk we're taking, and fuck it if that doesn't make this a whole lot hotter.

I palm myself a little rougher. Man I need to come.

Impatient to get this done, I fist McKinney's dick, and look up at him with a sly smile. "You still good to go?"

"So good." He smiles, taps his dick against my cheek a few times, and that's all I need.

Wetting my lips, I open up and take him deep again, using my tongue to massage the delicious velvety underside. He grumbles, weaves his hand through my hair and begins to thrust.

Guess I'm not the only one in a hurry.

I keep my eyes on him as I work him over, soaking up the quiver in his lip, the rush I get from reducing a big guy like this to a bubbling mess. Make no mistake, I may be the one on my knees with a dick in my mouth, but I am Superman. I hold all the power.

Proving just that, I hollow out my cheeks and suck. He spasms, leaking onto my tongue and shit, he really does taste amazing. "Close," he grunts. "Take it out, please, I wanna watch you."

He hasn't said it in so many words, but I know what he wants, and thank fuck. I release my grip on his ass, push my glasses back up my nose, then drop my hand back down, tugging at my sweats until my cock pops free. "Knew it," he chuckles. "So big for such a little, glasses wearing, cutie. So hot."

Christ, I better get this over with before he proposes.

Being so new to this, I'm far from an expert, but the few bumbled bj's I've given and received have taught me a few tricks. As has OF.

My dick throbs in my hand as I slide my free hand back between his cheeks. He realizes my intended target, and spreads his shaking legs a little wider, just enough for me to breach his sweet little hole. Should it be an iPad security lock, I don't think it would even have had time to register my fingerprint, but it does the job. Instantly he stiffens, convulses, and unloads streams of sweet, hot cum in my mouth.

"Fuck, those fucking glasses," he mumbles, running his thumb down my cheekbone, tugging my bottom lip. I'm so close, still swallowing his load, still jacking myself off when I turn my head and suck it into my mouth. His still hard dick, his thumb fucking over my tongue, is too much.

"Fuck." I cough and come so hard I fall forward and end up head-butting against his stomach. While I'm busy painting floor and fist with my release, McKinney's muttering sweet praise and affectionately sweeping his hand through my hair. As soon as I'm with it enough to register what he's doing, I freak out, pull back, and tuck myself and my mess back into my sweats.

"Do you have to go straight away?" He pouts, tugging me to him with a fist in my shirt the second I'm on my feet. Staying for round two is tempting. Like I said, he's big, we had fun hanging out today, and that secret sexual tension feels close to the high I get scoring a goal. I could easily see myself exploring a little more with him.

And that's exactly why I can't.

"You know I do. Don't make this more than it is, man."

There's a flicker of hurt in his eyes that I pretend I don't recognize. He's new to this too, he told me as much when he first dragged me in here. But he reeks of clingy, and that tells me to cut my losses and run. Just like I have all my other hook-ups this summer. "Well, maybe we can hang out when our teams play in October."

"Yeah, sure, maybe." Sated by that, he leans down to give me a kiss, but I turn my head and slap my palm into his chest. "See ya round, McKinney."

I feel like a dick, but I have to protect myself. As my hero Spider-Man says, 'someone's got to look out for the little guy.'

Who better than the little guy himself.

Heavy-hearted and already missing NHL life, I'm at a gas station in the middle of nowhere, filling up my sister's crappy car when my phone dings again, and grimace. McKinney has sent me three messages before I've even hit the border.

The hockey fuckboy lurking inside of me loves knowing I rocked his world so hard that he can't wait for more. But there's an even bigger part that wants to run to whichever government department processes name changes and beg for immediate assistance. I could probably just block his number, I guess, but that seems a bit extreme.

There's other messages waiting for attention, too. Several masterpieces from Cherry :

CHERRY

Where are you Numbnuts?

CHERRY

UGGHHH. Billie didn't sleep again last night. I think I might fall asleep standing up.

CHERRY

There's a new nurse on my ward and he's hot AF. I think he's bi. Fight you for him.

CHERRY

I'm bored. Where are you?

CHERRY

Will you be home when I finish my shift?

> CHERRY
>
> OMG mom keeps messaging me. Get a life, woman.

Then there's the non-stop group chat our new idiot captain started. I'm that idiot. A well meaning one, but an idiot all the same.

> EVAN
>
> Who's up for O'Reilly's tonight?
>
> TOM
>
> Stupid question, bro. You know we're all up.
>
> SAM
>
> I should be back from NYC by 5. See you there, boys. Cubby, you in?

I glance at the time, hoping it will be too late to head out when I get home, but no such luck. Even allowing for unpacking and a nap, I'll have loads of time.

Dammit.

It's important I do this. Big league call-ups, graduation, and Brady's long term injury, means we'll be starting this season without five of our best players. Bonding with the new guys in a relaxed, Coach-free zone seemed like a good idea. It wasn't. Not for Cory the introvert, anyway.

When I'm at the rink, it's easy to forget who I am. Maybe it's the endorphin and dopamine high, or the Zamboni fumes, but on-ice or locker room Cory is confident to the point of obnoxious, and always up for post-game partying.

Normally, by the time I've showered and dressed, my interest in heading out wanes. Edginess hits me in the parking lot, and roughly five minutes after arriving at our teams hang out, O'Reilly's, all enthusiasm to *bro it up* has vanished.

Most erosion is due to the intense pressure to get smashed and take home the first consenting blonde. I don't mind a beer, and obviously, hook-up culture isn't something I'm adverse to. It's more *who* I'm expected to hook up *with* that is.

Bunnies. Bunnies, and more Bunnies.

In not coming out, I am contributing to my own misery. I do know that. But it's a new season. A new team. And 'til I suss everyone out, the closet is where I will stay.

Loaded up with gas and snacks I will not tell the team dietitians about, I jump back in the car and merge back onto the A 35 with Boston in my sights.

MIFFY, my mom's long-haired dachshund, is at my feet, loudly protesting my return as I carefully make my way through the screen door hanging by one hinge. It's been like this for maybe two years and I've offered to fix it several times, but Mom says it adds character.

"Is that my baby boy?"

"Yes, it's me, but no, I'm not your baby. I'm almost twenty-one, Mom." Much to Miffy's disgust, I drop my bag on the floor, toe off my shoes and sloth my way to the sofa.

Why is driving so exhausting? I can play hockey for hours and not feel this beat. There's no time to get cozy though, Mom's on me in a second, practically leaping into my lap and throwing her arms around my neck. "Oxygen, Mom. Need oxygen."

Giggling into my shoulder, she squeezes tighter like she thinks I'm kidding. "How am I going to cope when you leave for real?" And here comes the guilt trip. "Your sister's always at work, and Billie just sits there and drools at me."

"She's a baby, Mom. That's kind of what they do."

"Don't talk back. You know, maybe you should just quit hockey and stay home to care for your aging Mom."

"You're fifty, Mom. Pretty sure you're a few years off needing a full-time carer."

With a gasp, she pulls back and glares. "Are you trying to curse me? What if I fell down the stairs and broke my head tomorrow? Would you care for me then?"

"Yes, Mom. Should you fall down the stairs and break your head, I promise I will care for you. Or pay someone a shit-load to do it for me."

In the same breath, I'm rebuked with a slap to the side of my head, and rewarded by her releasing me from her death-grip. Growling, she rushes off into the kitchen only to return a second later with a glass of OJ, a serve of potato chips and three way sandwich so loaded with roast beef, cheese, mayonnaise, and barbecue sauce that it's dripping from the plate onto the step.

I'm still digesting the gas station snacks. There's not one part of me that wants to eat this, but I do, 'cause she's my mom, and she made it for me.

Eager as I am to leave, the woman raised me and Cherry alone while my dad ran around the country chasing get-rich-quick schemes, and anything in a short skirt. His only contribution to our upbringing, was the occasional chunk of cash deposited into her bank account. Now she fusses over me and cares for Billie while Cherry works. She's the best.

Watching me chew, her smile grows with every bite I take. "Cherry will be home for dinner, and I'm making your favorite, mac and cheese." The sandwich curdles in my stomach.

"Mac and cheese? Mom, it's almost six. I can't eat this now, *and* mac and cheese in an hour."

"Nonsense, you eat that much all the time."

"Yeah, after a day of school and practice, or a game. Besides, I'm heading to O'Reilly's."

"Out. You're going out? I've been alone for weeks. Pacing the halls, cleaning your room over and over—" Oh, shit—"Waiting everyday for your calls, and you're going out five minutes after walking in the door. Screw the old folks home, Cory. Why don't I save us all some time and money and die now."

With a sigh, I drop my sandwich onto the chipped plate and sit it on the coffee table. Reminding Mom she's rarely alone because she lives with my sister and her grandbaby is pointless. This is a contested puck I'm never winning.

"Trust me Mom, I'd love to stay with you so we can crochet and watch SVU reruns all night... But I'm the captain now and it was the first practice today. I missed it, so I have to make an appearance. The team needs to b–"

"Bond, yes I know. What about me, though? How about you

make some time to bond with the walking vagina, your massive head ruined with an eighteen hour labor."

It's right as Mom drops the vagina bomb, that Cherry walks through the door, Billie babbling as she sucks on her hair. "Jesus Christ, Deidre, what are you guilting the kid into now? Let me guess." She slams the door, and barrels into me like we spent two years, not two weeks apart. "You have to go out and she's complaining that she's been all alone without you."

"Got it in one, sis." As I affectionately kiss the top of her head, then Billie's rosy cheeks, I have a flashback to the locker room. To that guy's cousins, brother, sister-wife or whoever it was, she told about Cubby, take Billie from her and push her away. "Oh, by the way. Thanks for telling whoever you told about my stupid nickname. One place, Cherry. All I wanted was one place I could just be me. Just Cory."

"Cubby's not stupid. It's cute and snuggly, like you. Also, when you're a famous NHL player, you should totally have a cologne named Just Cory."

Exasperated, my glasses fog. "I am not cute. Cute and snuggly doesn't do what I did with a team mate in the hotel closet—sorry Mom. Also, there will be no cologne."

"I dunno, kid. You are pretty cute." Pop, Mom's dad who may as well live here too, nods to me in greeting then smiles to Mom. "Remember when the store had to special order his widdle skates , as they had none to fit his teeny widdle footsies."

The room erupts into laughter and I've had enough. "You know what. I am sick of being the butt of the joke. You can all go get fuc–" Mom raises a single finger. "Freaked. I'll be in my room napping, then I'm going to join my friends who appreciate me."

Ignoring their continuing giggles that follow me upstairs and into my room, I draw the blinds, flop onto my bed and sulk with posters of Canadian hockey greats staring back at me.

I know they are joking, my family, not the posters—and I know they love me. But God dammit. I expect this at the rink. Chirping is part of hockey. With my contacts in and cocky attitude on, I can take it on the chin, and bro it up with the best of them—for the most part. Outside of that, I need a break. Luckily, as they did for Clark Kent, my glasses, a backwards cap or hoodie afford me one. It's disturbing how well it works. The same sycophants that hang off me at games and the bar, walk straight by me without so much as a glance. People really do see what they want.

I'm so successful at my dual life, Coach Harris once called me 'the boy who disappears.' "*All these other clowns are causing me grief at frat parties or shirtless all over Til Tak, or whatever the hell you call it. And then there's you, Malkovich. Hell. I wouldn't even know you went here if you weren't the best little winger I've got.*"

Now that I think about it, even in his praise, my height gets brought into it. Fuck.

There is only one place I'll ever play up to the size thing—dating apps. The whole nerdy-twink thing does surprisingly well, especially when it comes to my favorite big boy bottoms.

Speaking of which.

Rolling to my side, I pull my phone from my pocket, and open Grindr. Maybe after O'Reilly's, I can find someone to appreciate me a little.

Or a lot.

G ood lord, was I *like this?* I'm beginning to think I've made a terrible mistake. Scratch that. I know I have made a terrible mistake.

My life is stressful enough as it is. These men. These ... boys ... are going to break me. And it's not because they're living out my dream. Not at all.

It's because, as their coach described on day one. They're morons.

"Pilates. You want us to do Pilates?" Judging by their sulky, slack jawed expressions, you'd think I'd asked them to skate on their faces while naked. Actually, they'd probably enjoy that.

"Pilates works every muscle in your body. Strengthens your core. Increases your pulmonary function ... Lung capac—how you breathe," I add, dumbing it down after they stare back at me blankly. "Think of what that could do for your game."

"Screw our games, imagine sex!" They rise as one, cheering and high five-ing Evan Drummond as though he just scored a hat trick instead of making a lame-ass gag. I should probably reprimand him. Try and gain some kind of control, but his observation seems to have garnered the team's interest. Several players have even sat. Yes it's on the table or floor, not a chair, but it's something.

"You can do all that with Pilates?" Evan doubles down. "I thought it was a girlie thing ... like Zumba."

"Zumba is killer," inserts Larsson. "I went to a class with my sister and nearly died." And now they've moved onto Zumba and hot girl outfits worn to Zumba.

For fuck's sake.

Not for the first time today, I long for the century old equipment and musty carpets of the practice I began my physio training within. I had a future there. Regular patients, predictable hours that left me time to indulge my secret hobby of writing Spider-Man/Hulk fan fiction. But then I remember the scandal that saw it shut its doors after thirty years. My ever compounding student loan my brother, and the day Faith and I moved back into our parents house to care for him, then promptly blink those memories away.

WHAT AN ABSOLUTE CLUSTERFUCK OF A DAY. Weary, bitter, hungry beyond belief, I unlock my dungeon door, plod my way towards the too-small sofa and flop myself onto the well worn cushion.

Clutching my chest, I wonder how I got here. Not here as in a dank basement, but *here* metaphorically. I'm too young to hoard so many regrets this close to my heart. Too old to be doing so with my dad's civil war reenactment costume hanging from the makeshift clothesline on my ceiling. It can't be healthy, living like this. So knotted up that I can't sit straight.

Now that I think of it, I have been sweating a lot lately. Especially at night. Lots of chest pain too. I've been putting it down to a poor diet and indigestion, but maybe it's more. Maybe I'm one bean burrito with extra jalapenos away from full blown heart disease.

Maybe I should call Doctor Lappin?

Shit, too late. Here comes the sweat.

Everything's gone black.

Yup. I'm definitely dying.

I don't think I'm going to make it.

A harsh meow makes my eyes pop to find Cleo sitting on the foot on my bed.

Oh. I *can* see. So, maybe not dead ... yet.

As you might expect a half-deaf thirteen-year-old sphinx cat with diabetes and a traditionally female name would do, Cleo considers me with his usual utter contempt. After a heady, uncomfortable stare off, I break—he wins and promptly decides *against* blessing me with any affection and proceeds to lick his ass.

Shame. I could have done with the cuddles today. Lucky I'll get plenty from Dyl.

Speaking of which. Pushing off the couch, I climb the stairs, push the door that sticks open with my shoulder, and enter the kitchen.

"Manny? Dyl, are you here?"

When there's no reply, I make my way into the lounge, rubbing self-comforting circles into my chest. Finding it empty, I circle back and head for the wine rack tucked beside the fridge. That's when I spot a note on the counter.

Hi Faith & Jamie. We've had a rough afternoon, so we decided to go to the beach and chill for a bit. Should be back before dinner—we made a lasagna, it's in the fridge. If we're not back and you're hungry, just pop it in the oven to reheat.

See you soon,
Manny & Dyl

"Manny, I could kiss you." I drop the note and watch it float back and forth towards the bench.

"Probably best if you don't. We can't afford to lose him." Faith, looking as exhausted as I feel, shuffles rather than walks to my side, dropping her bag and keys on the floor then flopping her head onto my shoulder. "Please tell me this is going to get easier."

The *this* she's referring to is balancing work, and our new life as support providers for my big brother, Dylan. He's on the spectrum too, but he's non-verbal and has full-time, high support needs. Needs we are struggling to fill.

"I'd love to Faithy, but I don't think I can." What I can do though, is grab two wine glasses, fill them a touch generously, and offer her one even though she's going to turn her nose at the vintage. Tears clinging to her lashes like dewdrops on a leaf, she accepts the offered glass, aerating the crimson liquid with a swirl as she picks up and reads the note I just dropped.

"How did Dad do this by himself, Jamie? There's two of us, and we're more than half his age."

"Honestly, I have no idea. But it won't always be like this, sweetheart." I say this for myself as much as Faith. I wonder if she believes it as little as I do? "Once the insurance is sorted, we'll be able to get more help." There it goes. Another stabbing pain in my chest. Tightening of lungs to the point of uncomfortableness. Gripping the bench to keep me upright, I count to ten, once, then twice, hoping it settles. If I was alone, I would go lay down, pull a blanket over my head and stay there. But I'm not and I can't say anything to Faith, either. She'll just call me a hypochondriac. Which I am.

This time feels different, though.

This time *could* be it.

Of course, she notices the tensing of my body, wiping her tears away and sliding that Doctor mask back on. "It's not a heart attack, Jamie," she says, with zero compassion, "You're holding your breath, and since you're a person and not a fish, you can't breathe when you hold your breath. You know this."

Fuck. My lips flop like a horse neighing as I exhale. "I didn't even say anything."

"No, but you were turning purple before my eyes, because again—not a fish."

"Not a fish," muttering to myself, I fold forward until my head crunches against the paper, noticing Cleo purring while cutting figure-eights between my legs. All this talk of fish has him excited. Vibrations from his gentle hum are more soothing than my deep breathing, Faith's half-assed there-there pats to my back and any fucking mantra my therapist could ever provide.

Like so many on the spectrum, anxiety, depression and I are

well-acquainted. Back in my teens, I would have periods of situational mutism, and yes, I call it situational not selective on purpose. I never selected or chose to shut down. My brain just decided the situation called for it. Anyway, I haven't had an episode like that for a long time, but every day that passes since Dad died, I feel myself inching closer. Guess that's what happens when your life erodes before your eyes.

Those damn hockey boys will probably be the ones to get me there.

Faith keeps nattering until she's satisfied my hyperventilation is over, and after slipping an apron over her neatly pressed shirt and pencil skirt, we get to work on dinner. Wordlessly shifting around each other, she heads to the fridge and takes out the lasagna and some salad ingredients, while I switch on the oven then start chopping.

"You know what, Jamie? You need to get laid."

Before I slice one off, my brain orders my fingers to drop the knife. "Who are you and what have you done with my prudish, demi-sexual sister?"

"Oh," she scoffs, taking another swill. "Don't be mistaken. My beliefs surrounding humanities over reliance on intercourse remain unchanged. I'm simply repeating what I hear from the masses. Anytime someone has a problem, sex is the universal first suggestion. Especially by men."

"Men like your Brady?"

Faith's at my side, so I don't see the slice of tomato coming for me. I feel it though. Sliding down my neck, it nestles in the collar of my white polo. That's going to stain. "One, he is not *my* Brady, and two, no, he wouldn't say anything of the sort. He's a gentleman. Unlike that boyfriend of his."

"Boyfriend? He has a boyfriend?" Reaching around, I pull the tomato from my shirt and fling it into the sink. "Are you sure we're talking about the same Brady?"

"We are, and he does. They, as in Brady and Troye, have a girlfriend too. David Harris' daughter Quinn. They live together in Back Bay. It was quite the scandal."

I'm desperate, no, gagging, for more gossip, unfortunately

Faith holds a similar contempt towards spilling tea as she does fornication. I have to tread carefully.

"A queer, poly-relationship blooming in one of the highest realms of toxic masculinity. That's highly ... irregular."

"Normally I would agree, but change is inevitable, Jamie. Even in the world of hockey. Maybe queer acceptance has improved since you fell out of love with the game."

Fell out of love with the game? Hockey was the first, and only thing I have ever loved. Being part of a team. Having actual friends. Working out together. Goalie hugs. I didn't fall out of love with hockey. The world just forced us apart.

None of this torture is displayed though. All is swallowed down in order to maintain the unaffected facade. "Within this team, maybe. But that's a huge, massive, maybe."

Faith slides open the cutlery drawer, knives and forks rattling. "It's been years. Are you ready to tell me the real reason you quit?"

Damn that sibling intuition.

Of the myriad of excuses pulled from my ass, none have ever convinced Faith. The truth, I quit so Dad could pay for Dyl's therapy, and your college is one she will never hear. Not if I can help it. "Nope."

"Jamie–"

"Honey, we're home!" *Perfect timing.*

Echoing down the hall, and saving my day is Manny's cheerful, yet tired voice and Dylan's clomping footprints. *Check his orthotics,* I remind myself. *His gait sounds off.*

As his voice predicted, Manny looks exhausted. Smiling, but exhausted. "Sorry we're so late. The traffic was a nightmare. We had a great time at the beach though. Didn't we Dyl? He even had a little splash in the water."

Faith and I exchange concerned glances. Dylan having fun in the water is great, but he and stagnant traffic don't mix, and when his lanky frame appears in the kitchen, there's no need to ask how he coped. His face is blotchy and red, bottom lip bleeding. As is the tender skin just beneath the cuticles of his right hand, his favorite place to gnaw when heightened. I wince as his raw looking fingers grip Dad's chair.

It's been three months since we lost Dad, but Dyl still walks straight to it, pointing between it and the back door, like he does each morning and night. Each time as heartbreaking as the last. Faith's bottom lip trembles, so even though she is far and above his favorite sibling, I take the question.

"No. Dad's not outside, Dyl. He's in heaven, remember?"

We all wait, eyes flitting. The way he handles the daily reminder that Dad's gone varies. Swollen, dark circles beneath his eyes tell the tale of a tough day, so tonight's reaction will depend on if he is on the right or wrong side of over-tired.

With a desolate little grunt, he rocks on heels and toes then nods, repeating the noise over and over. He's stimming, processing, and when he sits at his spot and begins to shred the paper we always leave there for him, we know he's accepting.

Sighing in relief, Manny turns to me and Faith, "We've brought half the sand on the beach home, so he'll need a good scrub down. I tried to wash his legs and feet, at that faucet near the parking lot, but he wasn't having it."

"I don't blame him," I huff. "Those taps are disgusting."

"They are," Manny laughs, but soon sombers. "I'd love to stay and help you out, but Louisa has her first dance class. I can't—"

"Manny, it's fine." Faith smiles as warmly as she can, and nods towards the door. "You're amazing, and you've done more than enough. Go see your little girl dance, and make sure you take some photos. I want to see her in that tutu."

"I will, Faith. See you tomorrow at eight guys." He waves over his shoulder, before calling out to Dylan, "Bye Dyl."

And, that's why I love Manny. We all know there's a ninety percent chance that Dyl won't acknowledge his departure, yet he *always* acknowledges Dylan's presence.

Always. Even when he's worked almost an hour over his shift end time. So many support staff over the years have been the opposite, taking Dylan's lack of interaction as a sign of disengagement, when that's not the case at all. He's just moved on to the next phase of his routine.

I wish there were a million more Manny's in the world. I wish I was more like him. Dylan deserves no less.

Some night's it's a battle for Dyl to eat anything, especially when he's tired. But tonight, he's in rare form, and covered head to toe in red sauce after polishing off two slices of lasagna and three of Manny's homemade garlic bread.

"He looks the happiest I've seen him since ..." Faith stops, eyes darting between Dyl and I. We both know what she means. Neither can bear to say it, so as usual, we just move on.

"It's 'cause you are happy, aren't you, bud?" Rocking in his chair, Dylan nods, and hums around the last bite of pasta. "And why wouldn't you be? An afternoon at the beach, the sun on your skin, water lapping at your feet, sounds infinitely more appealing than the frozen version I was dealing with. And those boys. Faith. What the hell?"

"You'll get used to them. And don't forget, you were one of them a decade ago."

"Hey, I was never that bad. Was I Dyl?" Another cheeky smile and nod comes my way. "Oh, that's lovely. Gang up on me after I slaved over dinner for you both."

"Really, James. Reheating is hardly slaving, but since you feel so hard done by, why don't I take kitchen clean up, and you tackle showering Pasta Face over there."

I'm not sure I'm getting the deal Faith seems to think I am, but it doesn't matter. Dylan, a massive fan of all things water, is up and out of his chair in a beat, stripping off as he heads upstairs. Laughing, I give chase, and overtake him just before he reaches the bathroom.

It's there, as steam fills the room, and bubbles cover Dyl's full head of curls, that his fatigue kicks in. At six-five and well over two hundred and fifty pounds, I'm no lightweight—and no match for a heightened Dylan. With one nudge, I'm slammed into the glass shower wall, and left wondering again how the hell Dad, who was half my size, managed this alone.

Dyl grips my wrist and tugs. He's not trying to hurt me, he just wants out. That's clear. What's not, is his hair.

"Dyl, mate, we have to wash your hair first. Then you can get out. Just ten more seconds, okay. Come on, count it with me. One ... two ..." Counting out loud is a technique Manny taught us when we first moved in, and it's one of the best tools we have. Dylan can count, he just can't count out loud. Rather he nods and hums along with me.

At five, I angle the shower head, then gently edge him towards me. I'm not trying to get him all the way in, rather just enough for the water to reach his soapy locks. It takes to the count of forty, but the bubbles are out, Dyl's eyes are soap free, and he's ready for bed.

So am I.

DYLAN IS dry and dressed and Faith's getting him settled. As much as I want to be doing the same with my own exhausted frame, I'm back in the car, heading to my old apartment to get more of my belongings. An itemized list of said belongings is not what's on my brain, though.

A thousand and one things have happened tonight, but Faith's, *You need to get laid,* is all I can think of. Why? Because honestly, she wasn't wrong. It's been at least a year since I split with my ex, Brandon, the breakup leaving a bitter aftertaste, I haven't wanted to so much as look at a man sexually. But tonight? I dunno. Maybe it's all the testosterone I've inhaled today at the rink, but losing myself in someone, having them take the lead and give me what I need does sound appealing.

Ghosts of hook-ups past whisper into my ear, as I glance at my phone. *Dooo ittt. Dooo ittt.*

Hmm. Should I?

An aggressive series of beeps from the car at my rear let me know the light is now green. With an apologetic wave in the mirror I take off, eyes constantly flicking to my phone on the passenger seat. Barely cognizant of how I got here, I park in my prime space right out front of my building, and head up the stoop, my stomach twisting with each step.

It's been two weeks since I was here—one because I have such limited free time these days, and two because just seeing the post-card perfect streetlights, and the little garden with its hydrangeas beginning to bloom, it hurts like hell.

I fucking love this apartment.

It's a ridiculously large three-bedder in Chestnut Hill, with high ceilings, exposed brick walls and the walk-in closet of my fantasies. And since it's the last in a neat row of brownstones, every room is bathed in light that never failed to lift my spirits. The day Brandon and I moved in, heads full of dreams, hearts with hope of the family we would create here, was one of the happiest of my life. The day he left for Florida, weeks after moving in was one of the worst.

So yeah, I love it, and I hate having to let it go ... if I ever can find someone to let, or buy it, that is. And I need to. Desperately. Brandon did a job not only on my heart but on my bank balance. He came from money, and together we could easily afford the mortgage. But apparently, there were *issues*. The majority of his cash was tied into a family trust, so he paid the deposit but the mortgage was in my name with my dad as a guarantor. With Brandon and Dad gone it's my responsibility. The entirety of my savings, mere monthly income and then some, is gone only to have the place sit empty.

Anxiety claws at my throat, as I make my way up the stairs, wave to my neighbor Mrs. T, then unlock the door, the knife lodged in my heart turning in sync with the key. Boston city lights up the black sky as I step inside, wander over to the window, dropping my keys on the dust-covered coffee table, and flicking on light switches as I go.

"God dammit, this sucks." Instead of closing the blinds like I should have done the last time I was here, I stand there like a loser, taking in the torturous view for what may be the last time.

AFTER MOPING, crying and lecturing myself to snap the fuck out of it, I get busy packing and ferrying boxes down to the car, until all that's left is the sofa Brandon loved but I hated, the small dining and coffee tables, my old bed, and the spare in the second bedroom, oh, and of course my youth, hope and chance of any future happiness. Exhausted, I slide down the living room wall until I slump against the floor and bury my head in my hands. "What an utterly fucking, cluster fuck miserable life this is."

Out of no where, I hear Faith's voice. *"Jamie, you need to get laid."*

Now, I'm not normally one to take sex advice from my big sister, but maybe invisible Faith's right. Maybe it's time to dust the cobwebs off and have some fun.

If I can remember what that is.

Like it can sense action is coming, my dick swells against my zipper. It wants in. Fuck it.

I raise my ass, slide my phone from my pocket, and scroll. When I swore off men months ago, I deleted all my apps, so I re-download Grindr and am up and running in a disturbingly short time. Which is a good thing, I tell myself, because intellectually I know using one of society's most potent dopamine providers is morally repugnant, and the longer it takes the more chance there is of me wimping out.

Which I'm close to doing as I flick by the first dozen or so profiles. I am a terrible person. Judging people by photo-shopped mug and junk shots is – *Ooh, a twink. Ooff, he's a swimmer. That explains the bod.*

Normally go for guys like me, big, burly. Strong. But a long lean body, with two perfect plump cherry nipples, sparks something inside me.

Something called horniness. I scope the rest of his pics, see that he's close by, and of legal age. Before I can overthink this, I tap, type, and send the lamest message ever.

HANDYRUB04

Hi. Hello. How are you? You're cute.

I'm googling how to unsend Grindr messages when I hear the infamous blip-blip.

TWINKIEBEARBEAR21

Hey. I like your tattoo. I struggle with finding that. Is that why you got it?

"What the fuck is he talking about?" Then it clicks. I pull out the collar of my polo and see the lame ass BALANCE tattoo on my right pec. At nineteen it felt super deep. Now. Well. I dunno.

Hey yourself. Thanks. It's …

I pause, trying to think of something sexy

permanent.

What the actual fuck, James?

TWINKIEBEARBEAR21

You don't say. I don't have any tatts, but I'd love to get one. Maybe a tiny one on my pec like yours.

No, don't do that. Not there anyway. Maybe your arm?

TWINKIEBEARBEAR21

Arms are hot, but why not my pec??

It would be a waste: You get a tattoo to be seen and admired, but no one will be looking at anything on your chest other than those pretty pink nipples.

TWINKIEBEARBEAR21

You like my nipples?

That's weird, sorry.

TWINKIEBEARBEAR21

No it's not. It's kinda hot. No one's ever just put it out there like that, which is kind of surprising considering.

There's a short delay, enough for me to worry that I've ruined it already, and then...

TWINKIEBEARBEAR2

So you're a nip guy?

Am I? I glance at the pic again, zooming in on the light dusting of hair above them and the tight toned muscle beneath. My cock is weeping from a freaking nip pic.

Not normally, but in this case yes. It would appear so.

TWINKIEBEARBEAR21

Would you like to see them in person?

I should probably say something hot and flirty to seal the deal, but I have no idea what.

So I say just that.

Yes. I would. Very much so. Sorry I know I should say something sexy, but I'm no good at this.

TWINKIEBEARBEAR21

No, you're direct. No games. I like it. That and you're fucking massive.

In return, I'm going to make this real easy.

I want to straddle your thick neck, watch you suck my dick and go to town on my nipples until I blow my load all over that big furry chest. Then, I'll return the favor.

That or you can fuck me. Or vice-versa. I'm
easy.

Holy shit. That sounds ... yeah. That sounds ... good.

I glance at my watch. I told Faith I'd be home by eleven. That gives me two hours.

Normally, I would feel weird about having a stranger in my house, but after tonight it won't be my house. If he did decide to come back and murder me, I won't be here.

I'm aware that he *could* also murder me while he's here, but with my dick aching the way it is, that's a risk I'm willing to take.

TWINKIEBEARBEAR2

You still there? Did I freak you out?

Nope, just figuring out logistics. How soon
could you be here? I have to be home by 11.

TWINKIEBEARBEAR21

I can leave now. Gives us plenty of time

> I want to straddle your thick neck, watch you suck my dick and go to town on my nipples until I blow my load all over that big furry chest.

Sometimes, I shock myself with my sluttery.

If me-of-a-year-ago witnessed the me-of-now type those words, he would never have believed such filth would shoot from my brain, and out my fingers.

But it did, so I guess he'd have to.

Palming my cock as discreetly as I can, I check out Handyrub04's pics again while we wait for a light to change. We've just exited O'Reilly's, and even though a hook-up with no face shots can be risky, it really is the best excuse I've ever had to get the hell out of there.

Ten minutes of feigning interest in bunnies, and fake laughing at the boy's disgusting jokes regarding them, was all it took to reinforce that I hate bars. Another fifteen and my face was buried into my phone, escaping it all in the fanfic world of a queer, kinky Spider-Man. But the potential of spending my night wrapped around a brawny man has turned that frown upside down.

Big boys are my thing, but normally they are pumped and ripped-big. This guy's got some muscle, his arms in particular. But he's not cut. There's a layer or three of meat on those bones, and I am ready to chow down.

First, I need to lose my goalie coach.

My friends Quinn and Troye, the latter who's now playing

for the Boston B's, always joked that their boy Brady was a light-weight drinker. I just didn't realize they meant featherweight.

"I thought you Aussies were big beer fans, Brades. You finished one IPA, and you're rambling more than the orange-ass we call President."

Blushing profusely, Brady sinks deeper into the passenger seat. "Sorry, Cubs. I was so nervous for my first official week of practice ... and for Troye's first NHL practices ... and for Quinn's first day using the proper coffee maker machine thingy at Beanz and Bookz, I couldn't eat all afternoon, and I eat a lot." He rubs his belly to demonstrate, and my own stomach twists in guilt. The guy is the best, the ultimate golden retriever, and genuinely worried. In contrast, here's me, thinking only of me, my dick and getting it wet.

Do better, Captain Cory. I think, giving myself a verbal slap.

"How is Troye doing with the big boys? Are they playing nice with the rookie?"

A dull thud accompanies Brady's snort as his head bumps against the window. "Is he playing nice, is more the question. First day there, he lined up against Aiki Heikkinen in a scrim-mage, nudged him and said, "My left ball sack dangles better than you."

"Hart Memorial trophy winner, Aiki Heikkinen?"

"Yep," he hiccups. "Aiki called him a cheeky shit then spent the next hour whooping his ass. They're buds now. Even had lunch together yesterday. Troye tried to be all cool about it, but he was so excited." Pausing, he looks at me and rubs his belly like a toddler would. "Speaking of lunch, can we stop for—"

"NO STOPPING," I yell, empathy eroding. "The drive-thru will be jammed this time of night, and I don't have enough gas to keep the car running." I really hope he's drunk enough to miss that I'm driving a Prius. When he glances around, I think he's onto me, but his eyes quickly go glassy and his head falls back against the headrest.

"Can't we stop and get petrol too?"

"Petrol? You mean gas?"

"Gas, yeah."

"No. This is a Prius."

"Oh. Yeah. Right." From the corner of my eye I see his blush spread as he nods again. Then he's silent, there's a little grunt, and yep, he's asleep.

Occasionally emitting a cute as hell snore, he remains that way 'til we reach his place, where I don't push him out the door, but absolutely nudge him. "There ya go big fella. One foot in front of the other. That's it."

Loyally, his girlfriend Quinn is waiting for him at the door, a besotted smirk firmly fixed as she plods towards her rubbing his eyes. "Hi, Quinny, I think I drank too much beers."

As sweet as I'm sure it will be, I don't hang around for her response. Instead, I type Handyrub04's address into my GPS and floor it. It's time to make my big bear roar.

OTHER THAN MY HEIGHT, my glasses and well ... me in general, there are only a few things I'm insecure about. Money, as in I don't got none, is one of them. Sure, that's going to change once I'm in the NHL, but for now, I'm broke af. So when I pull up to a row of brownstones, in a snooty part of town folks like me only venture too to get somewhere else, I'm a little ... edgy.

"This can't be right." I check the address again, and yep. This is it.

Shit.

Obviously, fancy people, or Toffs, as Brady called them, have sex too. But I always figured they would be having it with other fancy people while eating caviar and oysters.

I look down at my faded tee and sweats. wondering if I reek of 'penniless student'.

I'm contemplating turning around, going home and ghosting this dude, but decide to take another look at his profile. I won't regret ignoring the hard-on weighing me down since that first message if the pic's are marginally less impressive than my brain's telling me.

"Okay, one look. Bet he wasn't as hot as I—"

Fuck. That furry belly. That big, broad chest. Those tree trunk legs.

Before I can talk my broke ass out of it, I leap from the car, bolt up the stairs two at a time and press the buzzer for 3C.

I am not prepared for what comes next.

"Hello, this is Jam… I mean, Jammy, … I mean. Shit. This is … shit." Not only is this guy's voice so deep I can feel the vibrations in my balls, he sounds nervous and cute and *ugh*. He also seems unfamiliar with using a buzzer, as I can hear him mumbling and calling himself a buffoon.

Why is that so adorable?

I lean into the speaker and force myself to stop smiling. "You know, I can forget I almost heard that if you like. Oh, and hey, it's me, Twinkiebearbear."

"I would appreciate that, thanks." He sighs, deep and rumbly. "Door's open. Come on up."

Pulling on the brass door handle does nothing, so I wait for a bit then realize he's still holding the intercom button down. Still mumbling, too. "This is a bad idea. You are going to get murdered and …" Eventually the penny drops must drop, he mutters something else incomprehensible and the door clicks.

Despite wanting to burst in like my ass is on fire, all I do is stick my foot in to keep it ajar, then buzz him again. "Hey, still me. Just wanted to reassure you that I'm not here to murder you. Are you sure you want me to come up?"

He grumbles again. "Sorry you heard that. I'm sure. Yes. I'm definitely sure … but thank you for checking, Twinkie."

That oddly polite, rough voice has my stomach doing an odd flip. *Jesus Christ Cory, he's going to fill you like a Twinkie, not marry you.*

Reminding myself what this is … and isn't, I kick the door the rest of the way open, and bound up the stairs. The interior is even fancier than the facade. There's rich people hall-runners under my feet, and those plaster flower things above my head. What are they called, ceiling daisies? Ceiling roses? I don't fucking know. But I do know that even when I make the big bucks, I will never feel comfortable in a place like this.

Heart pounding, I make it to 3C, and stand at the door. "You got this, Cory." I haven't even knocked when the door swings open, and all air is sucked from my lungs.

HOLY FUCKING GRETZKY.

This guy. This *Jam, Jammy*, is gorgeous. Like a Dolce and Gabbana cologne model, so far out of my league it's not funny—Zoolander really, really, really good looking—gorgeous. Falling into his eyes, and poking from behind his ears are light brown curls. A matching thick mustache covers what looks like a full top lip, and an even thicker neck sits atop a collarbone and clavicle so deep I could snuggle in and use it for a hammock.

I can smell him, too. We're a good two or three paces away, but he smells like ... money and honey. I don't actually think I've ever noticed the smell of honey, but that's all I can think of as I breathe him in, accidentally letting an elongated, "Wow," slips from my lips.

Hungry eyes, such a unique machine-amber brown, scan me head to toe. I stand tall, attempting to project confidence, even when it's currently wallowing around my ankles. "Wow your-self," he replies. "I didn't expect reality to beat that phone face and bod, but, yeah. Here you are."

"Here I am."

That's the end of the flirty exchange. Instead, we just stand there, eye-fucking each other on his door step. It's not even uncomfortable. In my mind, it's kind of how I'd picture myself at the Louvre in Paris. He's the Mona Lisa and I'm purely appreci-ating his beauty.

After a freakishly long time, it's my host that breaks first—my host that suddenly seems chill. "Thanks for coming over." He takes one tiny step to his side, then pauses. "Sorry, but I have to ask. Has anyone ever told you you look a little like–"

"Matt Damon in Mr. Ripley?"

"Yeah, that's right. Mr. Ripley." He laughs, and it's full and hearty and again, wow. He has dimples. "You get that a lot, I'm guessing?"

Normally, when I'm not tongue tied and out-hotted times a hundred, I would reply with something flirty and cheeky. Instead, I blink myself out of the dimple coma, and go with the unfortu-nate. "You could say that, yeah. I also get, why don't you come in and Ripley my clothes off? Or could you just Ripley that condom open. And the classic, I'm going to Ripley you a new assho…"

"Ahh, yeah. I think I get it." There's another chuckle, but this one seems forced. I'm screwing this up before screwing. This is not good. "Why don't you come in, have a drink and we'll talk about anything other than … that?"

Relieved as shit not to be sent packing, I nod. "Let's do it."

Standing to the side, he waves me in. "That's the plan."

F orget love at first sight. Is cum at first sight a thing? 'Cause this guy, this Twinkie Bear Bear, is unbelievably attractive.

A young, bespectacled Matt Damon was my first thought, and while there is a remarkable resemblance, a second name sits in the tip of my tongue as I stand aside and let this sexy stranger in.

It clicks as he passes, casually running his hand through his hair. Like many women her age, my sister was obsessed with The Gilmore Girls. Dean in particular. I, too, was a fan. Especially of his dreamy, floppy 90's boy band hair. So yeah, should Mr. Ripley and Dean have a love child, Twinkie Bear is him.

He's lean, but muscular, shortish, under six foot anyway. *Easy to toss around.*

I'm so lost in the contemplation of his finery, that I don't realize I'm still standing in the open doorway. Still staring. "Sorry. I ... um, you're distractingly beautiful ... In the most manly sense of the word, of course."

"Oh, of course. That goes without saying." His cheeks color, the confidence exuded in our messages all but vanishing in a puff of modesty. It's a shyness that has me overcome with a barbaric desire to get him all hot and bothered. Not only because I want to touch every inch of him, but to see if I can get those glasses fogging up. Only problem is I have no idea how to make the first move.

A myriad of things run through my mind, but then he drifts closer, eyes roaming over me as he licks his lip, and every intelligent thought I've ever had evaporates. All I can think of is getting naked and wet.

Oh. Liquid.

"Can I get you a drink?" I offer, motioning, then walking backwards to the kitchen, purely so I can keep watching him work that lip.

"That would be great, thanks." With a smile that takes my breath away, he turns and bends to remove his shoes. A good sign, I think to myself, he'd be unlikely to take them off if he was planning to run. Since it's mild out, he's only wearing a faded Red Sox tee and a pair of gray sweats stretched to the point of oblivion over his glorious ass and thighs.

I've worked on plenty of swimmers in my time, a fair amount of hockey players too, and this is no swimmer's body. I know a hockey butt when I see one.

For a moment, I simply watch that ass jiggle as he navigates his laces, then remember what I'm supposed to be doing, and turn away, reaching for a glass into an overhead cabinet. "I've only got water from the faucet. Hope that's okay?" Behind me I hear the gentle pad of his feet, then feel him warm against my back.

"Water's good. Can I give you a hand?" Exhaling a shuddering breath, the glass I'd just taken possession of, slips from my grasp when two fingertips brush over my hip. The old goalie reflexes kick in and I twist to catch it. "Nice save. Ever played hockey?"

Looking directly at him feels too daunting, so I remain facing the tiled splash back. They really are nice tiles. Good quality. "I've dabbled, yeah. And you're a swimmer? If I had to guess, I'd say you have a hockey build."

He huffs a laugh and steps closer, fingers brushing the sliver of exposed skin on my side. "I do enjoy swimming, yeah. And hockey, and lots of other things. Sex for instance."

"Oh ... that's a ... coincidence. I ... too ... enjoy sex." I pause and clear my throat, hopefully removing the robotic overlord that's possessed my voice box. "It's been a while for me, but you know what they say. It's like riding a—"

"Big, hard dick?"

"Something like that, yeah."

His grip tightens, nails digging into my skin as he attempts to twist me towards him. Being so much bigger, I could easily resist, but I don't.

"Hi." He smiles once our eyes meet. "I'm Cory, and since I heard nothing at all embarrassing through the buzzer, can I ask your name?"

"Jimmy," I say after regaining a little composure. "My name's Jimmy." Why I chose that, the name only my late dad ever called me, is a mystery. Judging by the breathtaking smile that lights his face, Cory approves.

"Like Jimmy Olsen. You're not a photographer for The Daily Planet are you?"

A DC comics joke. It's weird how much that turns me on. "Not the last time I checked, no."

"Well, Jimmy. Why don't we save the water for later. There's something else I'd rather swallow."

Hansel and Gretel would be proud of the trail of discarded clothing we leave behind us. Bumping off each wall we pass, when we make it to my old room I'm down to my briefs, and he's in his tee and a fetching pair of boxers featuring Spider-Man's face. Should this be a date-date I would be thrilled by the prospect of spending time with a fellow superhero nerd, but that's not what this is.

This is sex.

Just sex.

And I want it.

Having climbed me like a pole, apt analogy, Cory is in my arms, his insanely muscular legs wrapped around my waist, his perfectly plump ass in my hands. His roam my chest, tweaking my nipples as he sucks at my neck. "God dammit, Jimmy. You are such a man."

"A good thing, I hope."

"A very good thing." My dick throbs, goosebumps igniting as

he drags his tongue over my Adams apple, then up until he reaches my chin. "Can I kiss you, Jimmy? Please say yes. I think I might die if you don't."

In reply, I crash my mouth onto his, a heady moan escaping as my tongue traces his bottom lip, before forcing its way inside. His tongue is smooth, wet and warm. Lips plump and soft. I want them all over me. Sucking me. Drinking me down.

Mouths entwined, I'm only cognizant that we're in the bedroom when the back of my legs press against the mattress, causing me to lose balance. Rolling with it, with me, Cory presses his palms into my chest and we topple onto the freshly laid sheets. "Do you remember what I wanted to do to you," he pants between kisses.

"Are you kidding? I think I'll remember it 'til the day I die."

"So can I?" he asks, breathless. "Can I ride your face while you play with my nipples and suck me off?"

Before I can reply, he's reaching for the neck of his tee, tugging it over his head to reveal pale skin, a consolation of freckles dusting his shoulders, and the two prettiest, pinkest nipples I've ever seen. "Holy … Cory. They're even more perfect in real life." Wasting no time, I grip his waist and hoist him over my stomach, until his ass hovers above my pecs. While there, he obligingly lowers his boxers, freeing a disproportionately large, hard, weeping cock.

"Put me down, Jimmy. I need to ride you." I nod, 'cause what the hell do I say to that, and do as she pleads, lowering him until he straddles my chest. Once seated, he folds forward, lips ghosting over mine. "God, I'm so hard."

"I know. Let me take care of that for you."

Muscle shifts deliciously beneath flesh as he leans back, allowing me to run my hand over that patch of freckles before taking grip of his ass and shifting him forward, stopping only when his leaking dick taps my cheek. All it takes is a slight drop of my chin and, yes, that big hard dick is against my lips.

This. This is what I needed.

Cory blinks down at me, unfairly long lashes fluttering.

Fuck, he's stunning. "Suck me, Jimmy. Suck my fucking brains out." And needy.

I groan my agreement, nuzzling, breathing him in. "You smell so good."

As much as I want to take him hard and fast, it has been a while, so I start small, using my tongue to glide over the soft, velvety underside, teasing his slit, before wrapping lips around him and giving an exploratory suck. Seconds later, his hands are in my hair, he's rocking into me, my nails are digging into that ass, I'm opening wide, taking him all the way to the back of my throat.

"Jimmy. Your mouth." I'm already so lost in his panted, shaken breaths, and his filthy sounds, that when the sweet and salty taste of him hits my tongue and slides over my pallet, I lose it. I release my grip on his ass and slap my palms over his chest, molding the muscle before coasting my fingertips over those insane nipples. "Cory," I whine around his girth. "You're fucking perfect."

Of course, it's then, right as I apply my first moan inducing, cock pulsing nip-twist, that my phone rings. Discarded somewhere between here and the lounge, it rings then rings again. And again and again. Since I'm currently attached to a hot man like a 1950's phone operator, I'd rather not figure out its exact location, but then I remember.

Gone is the somewhat carefree James of a year ago. I'm now one half of a team responsible for the health and happiness of another human.

Fuck this.

I release Cory's nipple, slide my hands up his smooth chest, and allow myself a brief moment tracing shallows of his clavicle, before cupping his face. "Cory—"

"No, no, no," he whines. "You're kidding me right? Ignore it. Please."

"Sorry, I can't." Shaking my head, I grip his waist and roll him off my chest. "I'll just be a second."

On all four, I forage, the phone ringing out three more times before I feel it buried inside my jeans pocket, beneath his tee, behind the sofa. It's silent as my fingers slide inside the denim, but rings again as I pull it free. This isn't going to be good.

Head cast down, fingers pinching the bridge of my noise, I answer, "Faithy, what's wrong? Is Dyl okay?"

"No, he woke not long after you left and he's really heightened, Jamie. I've tried everything but I can't settle him. He just smashed a mirror. Can you come home?"

"Absolutely, sweetheart. Sit tight, I'll be home as soon as I can." Before I can even disconnect the call, a pillow lands squarely in the back of my head.

"Guys like you make me sick. You're fucking around in your rented sin-shack, when you've got a wife and kid at home."

"What?" I turn in the direction of the bedroom just as a shirtless Cory hops by, one leg in his sweats, my red hand prints visible on his pecs. "Sin-shack? What does that even mean?"

Clearly flustered, his waistband snaps against his abs as he hastily rushes to the door. "It means you should be ashamed of yourself, asshole. Consider yourself blocked."

Much to many a professor's disappointment, during today's lecture I was distracted, lethargic, a step behind on every move. It's not a good sign. Classes have just begun and are overwhelming me already. Now I'm at practice, my first as captain, and I'm afraid things haven't progressed. They may actually be worse, and it's all because of last night.

Because of Jimmy.

Jimmy who got my Superman reference, and didn't give me shit about it. Jimmy who touched like a man possessed, and nearly had me blowing my load the instant he tweaked my nipples.

As lame as it sounds, I was really into him.

Like, I may not have even blocked him after I left.

Overriding all the positives, though, is the silhouette of a cowardly, naked man clutching his phone to his head, promising to be home soon.

Should I have given him a chance to explain before storming out? Maybe. There's a ton of guys that have no issues hooking up with family men on the down low.

As for me, I am not, and will not ever be one of them.

You want to have a little down low fun while single hiding out in the closet? Who the fuck am I to judge when I'm not really out myself? Adding a third for fun? You do you. None of my business. But to go to the extent this guy did. Having a secret place to bring home his *beautiful* men? Ugh. No thanks.

Signaling it's time for a break, Coach blows his whistle and points to the bench, a severe scowl aimed squarely at me as he does so. I take a seat on the bench and bury my head in my hands.

"Cubby. Dude. I'm hungover as fuck, but you're as slow as a wet week out there. You okay?"

I raise my head and groan. "I don't know what that means, but I think I'm going to be sick."

Brady's cheeks flush and he hops from foot to foot like he needs to pee. "Oh, shit. Want me to get a trainer? Or a bucket? Or both?"

"Nope. Just a hot man with a moral compass."

His eyebrows rise then knit together. "Oh, I. Um, I dunno if I can help you there."

Despite being a year older than me, he grunts like an old man as he drops at my side, and slings his giant arm over my hunched back. It's not at all helpful for my nausea.

"Can I ask you something, Brades? It's kind of personal."

He tightens his grip. "Shoot, Little Guy."

Swallowing my pride, and the vomit he seems determined to squeeze out of me, I inhale. Exhale. "I'm gay, Brades. Gay and quickly discovering the worst thing about *being* gay is men, because men, including myself, are disgusting." I pause, waiting for a shocked, OH MY GOD NO WAY, reaction, but my grand coming out earns nothing more than a head nod and a cautious smile. It's both brilliant and anticlimactic. "So yeah. I'm new to it. Have been hitting the apps pretty hard, had some amazing sex, but have also met a few guys I feared may rob me blind or wear my skin as a jacket if given half the chance."

"Jesus, Cub."

"Yeah. Well, anyway, last night I met up with a guy at his apartment and things got weird."

"Since your guts aren't hanging out, I know it's not the skin thing, but he didn't actually like, rob or hurt you in another way did he?"

"What?" I rear upright, causing his hand to slide down my back. "No, nothing like that. I mean, maybe psychologically, 'cause I can't stop thinking about him, and his massive biceps I wanted to be sandwiched in ... or the fact that he was married."

That spurs a reaction I've been expecting. "He was married?"

"Yep. I think so. He didn't tell me as much, not directly. But we were in bed, and he was sucking my—"

"Don't need that level of detail, Cub," he whines, glancing over his shoulder.

"Right. Sorry, so yeah, we were fooling around and his phone rang and rang, and he ignored it at first 'cause he was doing this thing with his tongue. But eventually he answered it and, yeah. It was his wife. Pretty sure he had a kid, too."

"How do you know? You just said he didn't tell you."

"He didn't, and I didn't give him the chance to. It was obvious. You should have heard the affection in his voice when he called her, Faithy, and then he asked if Dyl was okay."

Brady rubs his hand over his chin. "Hmm. That does sound sus. But it might not have been his missus It could have been a friend or—"

"Nah. It was his wife. It all fits. He was fucking huge, and smoking hot, so I didn't pay much attention at first, but I should have known the second I walked in and saw the deal with his furniture. And by deal, I mean there was none. No photos or art or ugly plastic plants or any fucking thing other than a bed, coffee table and sofa. And there was a bucket of cleaning stuff—"

"Oh, maybe he was—"

"And it was fancy, too. Rent would have been a bomb. Who has a place like that with nothing in it?"

"Maybe—"

"Freaks, that's who."

"Maybe—"

"God, a weirdo like that. I bet the place was littered with cameras."

"Oi!" Brady's surprisingly soft hand clamps over my mouth. "Can I speak for a second?" I nod, and Brady releases his grip. "He could definitely have been married with a kid. Or, like I was trying to say, Faithy could have been anyone. A sister. A neighbor. And there's lots of reasons his apartment could be empty."

"Yeah, name one other than fuck house, or he just scrubbed the place down 'cause it was a crime scene."

"Maybe he was moving?"

"Or maybe it was his kinky-ass, sex dungeon hideaway ...." Don't roll your eyes at me, Basse."

Clenching then flattening his hands over his thighs, he pushes off the bench, then bends down to whisper, "Thank you for trusting me with your sexuality. I'm really proud and honored that you feel comfortable coming out to me, and hope you know it will stay between us until you tell me otherwise."

"Thanks, Brades"

"Don't thank me yet," he says firmly. "I'm not judging you at all when I say this, but you called this guy a freak, and there's worse than married men with kids out there, Cubs. I've heard lots of horror stories from Troye to prove it. Maybe casual hook-ups with strangers aren't right for you."

"Nooo," I whine. "I've just tasted them and they're so yummy."

"Look," he laughs. "I know you love your comics and fanfic, but this *isn't* fiction. Letting your imagination run riot on the regular could bring more trouble than it's worth. Skip the apps for a bit, and try old fashioned dating." He chuckles again when I roll my eyes, then ruffles my hair like a big brother style. I like it way too much. "Just think about it, okay?"

"I might die of boredom or boner-overload while I do, but sure. I'll think about it."

I DO NOT THINK about it.

I agonize.

But not about ditching the apps as Brady suggested. No. What's running through my mind more than Coach's plays, or sports psych theories, are those hands. Those arms, and the body they were attached to. I can't stop. The depravity of my thoughts matched only by the obscenity of *his* actions.

Maybe that's why I can think of nothing else. Because he's forbidden.

Yeah. Forbidden. Like that fic I was reading at O'Reilly's

where Spider-Man hooks up with Hulk, much to the chagrin of Daddy Stark.

At the most unfortuitous moment, my dick twitches, and chubs. We're not talking Iron Man hard here, but enough for me to be uncomfortable in, and grateful for my cup and hockey padding.

"Isn't that right, Cory? Cory–Cubby Malkovich!!"

"Huh?" A chorus of laughter follows, everyone finding my absentmindedness hilarious. Everyone except the coaching staff. Coach White is shaking his head. Brady is mouthing, *wake the fuck up,* his eyes almost popping out, and Coach Harris. Well, he looks as though he's regretting whatever life choices led him here.

Possibly making me captain, too.

"Sorry, Coach," I mumble, blush burning my cheeks. "I think my time in Montreal is catching up with me." It's a lame excuse. Knowing that, I avoid Brady's glare.

"It's been a chaotic time for you, Cory. I get that. But your transition from college to the NHL is a rough one, so if you can't handle a two week training camp, and a four hour car ride home, you may want to reconsider your future. Same goes for you, Bailey."

"What did I do?" Sam Bailey whines at my side.

Like he hadn't just kneecapped, and thrown Sam under the bus, Coach moves on.

"Unless you've already scared them off, the Plums will be back today, and I expect a better display during James' session than what I witnessed yesterday. You are not preschoolers. You are adults. Act like it."

Once he's done chewing our asses out, Coach calls out our next drill, splitting forwards and D-men for zone work. Still sulking, I slide on my helmet, and join the rest of the forwards at center ice, all the while, trying to figure out who the other Plum is. Does Professor Plum have a brother or sister? A second hit Plum would fit Coach's demand for better behavior. The boys are pigs, and would have squealed as much if there were two of her.

I've got no time to ask, though, because Coach White has set up for five-on-five drills, and the next hour is lost in a blur of sweat, not quite blood, and for the new guys, definite tears.

The first few weeks of preseason training are demonic. It's not so bad for me this year, as I started early in Montreal. But for the others, skating 'til you vomit is not unheard of. And should we fuck around, and really piss Coach off, bag skates are guaranteed. Judging by the hue his quickly balding head is taking, they're imminent.

Training and trying not to set him off has at least taken my mind off that dick Jimmy. I've hardly thought about him.

Not at all.

Okay so maybe I thought I've heard his name a few times, but in my defense, the guy's I want on my line this year, have names that make it really hard to stay focused. Fellow winger Tom Swallow's, for instance, unfortunate nickname is Spits. I mean, come on. How could I not go there?

The other is Sam Bailey, and when you're up against the boards fighting tooth and nail for the puck, Bailey can sound an awful lot like Jimmy.

After an hour of pain, Coach blows his whistle forty-seven times and calls it quits. "Listen up, men. James has a few words to say before he runs us through some new stretching routines. Give me respect or give me bag skates."

Called it.

A loud back-slap echoes across the ice, but with a crowd of players surrounding whoever it is, I can't see who's on the receiving end of Coach's not-so-gentle touch. Slowly, as the crowd disperses, I catch sight of a mop of brown curls, amber eyes and then that fucking mustache.

No fucking way. It can't be.

But it is. It's him. Jimmy. The married guy who blew me last night is standing beside Coach in a Goddamn BC hockey trainers' polo.

I tug on the sleeve of whoever is closest and point to the swine. "Who the fuck is that?"

"That's James Plum. Professor Plum's bro," Lucas replies with a snort that heavily implies I'm an idiot. "He's a physio student doing placement and he wants us to do Pilates," he scoffs again, voice dropping as James speaks.

"G'day boys. Sorry I missed most of the session, but I caught the last twenty minutes or so, and I can already see a big attitude shift from yesterday." Na uh. No way is this dick going to stand there and give us a pep talk. "That was some good, honest, hard work—"

"Honest? Honest?" I scoff. "Like you're in the position to lecture anyone on honesty."

Nervously, a few bodies around me still, but no one at the front of the gathering seems to have heard me. Which is probably a good thing.

But then again it could also be a very, terribly bad thing.

Who's to know?

James keeps talking, I keep fuming, and by the time he sends us off to get a drink before meeting back up in the gym, I'm practically levitating with rage. Who the fuck does this guy think he is?

The boys head off in varying directions, and I make a bee-line for trouble, skating way too fast and snowing the fuck out of him as I stop. "Who the fuck do you think you are?"

One eyebrow raises as he scans me, skate to helmet. If I was any less furious, I might think he looks sexy as hell in his polo and tight pants he must have painted on. That whistle hanging around his neck is doing things to me too. But I am so, no, it's not.

I don't think he smells fucking amazing either.

"I'm James Plum," he says, offering an extended hand. "New physiotherapist student. And you are?"

Taking advantage of my additional skate added height, I slip closer until I'm right in his face. "I'm your Kryptonite."

"I'm your Kryptonite."

It takes strength I didn't know I possessed not to laugh in this cocky little upstart's face. Instead, I return to my factory setting, sarcasm. Yes, it's the lowest form of humor, but at the rink, bottom dwelling is where I feel most comfortable. "Lex Luthor? Is that you?"

The cute number four snorts, and looks around for backup. "You have no idea who I am, do you?"

"Well since I'm guessing that's a no to bald billionaire industrialist, no. No, I don't. Should I?"

"Dunno. Should you?"

I am seriously not in the mood for this. After practicing my, 'I don't hate you, that's just my face-face', I was twenty minutes behind schedule. Then my car broke down on the way here. Since I'm a loser with zero dollars to his name, Faith had to leave campus, pick me up, then bring us both back. Meaning we were both late. Meaning she's pissed and I am even less ready to *people* than usual.

"Look, I have some stretching routines to fine-tune, so if you don't mind, maybe we can catch up later, and you can tell me exactly who it is you are."

"Sure thing, Jimmy."

Jimmy? That little fucker.

"I know it's hockey etiquette to designate nicknames, but my name is James. Just James. Now, as I said, this is not the time or place. If you have an issue, we can speak about it later. Perhaps

Professor Plum could join us and offer you some ... professional assistance."

The kid's chin hits the ice, and I take that as my cue to leave.

I hear him behind me, muttering to himself, skates clomping on the rubber matting lining the halls between the ice, locker room and gym. Though he doesn't shut up, he does gather the stragglers loitering outside once we're ready to start. The players seem to respect him, and it's only then I notice the C on his practice jersey.

Ahh, so this is the long lost Malkovich. His first name slips my mind, but I know they call him Cubby. Respect he may have, but I'm beginning to suspect he's not the brightest spark. I watch, trying hard not to laugh, as he furiously unties his laces, discards his skates, then plonks on the prepared yoga mats—all while still wearing his helmet. I should probably ask him to remove it, but it's more fun to see how long it takes him or one of his *boys* to notice.

"Right, now as we discussed yesterday, Coach Harris has brought me here to work on strengthening, flexibility, and improving respiratory endurance. You'll all be used to jumping on a bike or treadmill after a game, and we're still going to do that, but we're adding some other elements, too."

"Wow," Cubby moans. "Coach sure has a lot of *faith* in you to *tweak* our routine. Hope all that *trust* is warranted."

Shit.

Faith. Trust. Does this kid know what happened at my old practice? Were his parents caught up in the scandal?

On the outside, I keep my cool and continue running through my pre-prepared program, but memories and accusations I've tried to repress bubble beneath the surface.

Bryan Ferris, my first placement supervisor, and founding practitioner of Ferris Health Group, had been embezzling business funds, employees entitlements, and defrauding insurance companies for years. He took me under his wing, called me Son, and duped me into investing my savings into the practice he claimed would one day be mine. When accusations were eventually made, the business was investigated, and the man who had been my mentor laid the blame squarely at my feet. Ultimately, I was cleared of any and all wrongdoing, but it was too late for my bank account, and the practice's reputation. Mud sticks, and if it hadn't been for Faith vouching for me with Coach Harris, I don't know who else would have given me a chance.

Somehow, I get to the end of my rundown, and set the boys off to get to change and do their preferred cool down before we do some stretching.

Just how much my presence has skittered beneath Malkovich's skin is evident when he makes his way towards a row of spin bikes instead of going to change. With disarming ease, he slings one leg over, mounts and settles in the saddle, the sight sparking a memory I need to forget.

I want to straddle your thick neck, watch you suck my dick and go town on my nipples until I blow my load all over that big furry chest. Then, I'll return the favor.

I shake my head to clear the smut, and refocus on work—in particular the helmeted one with a broad back that tapers into narrow hips, I would find incredibly attractive should he not be who he is. He only does so maybe five or six full turns, hips gently rolling side to side, before he slows, turns and faces me. Someone's realized he's the only one still here. In full gear.

Lord, I wish I could see his face.

Peddling a little longer, the stubbornness I'm also afflicted with eventually subsides, and he relents, removing his helmet and slicking back his wet, dark blonde hair. Stray strands refusing to be tamed, are tucked behind his ears with huffs of disgust. I kind of feel bad for the kid. Maybe it's time for me to save him from himself.

"May I have a word, Mr. Malkovich?"

"Can it wait?" he grumbles, peddling resuming. "If I don't cool down, I won't be able to walk tomorrow, let alone skate. I know you don't care for such trivial things as disappointing or letting people down, but I do. I'm the captain."

Right then.

"See, that's what I want to speak to you about. I'm not sure if you have me confused with someone else, but I assure you, I care very much about my work and have no intention of letting anyone down."

"Pfft. Whatever."

"No, not whatever. Look, once our session is over, I insist that you come to my office so we can sort whatever this is out."

"Can't sorry," he huffs, voice barely audible over the noise of the bike. "No time."

"Make time, Mr. Malkovich."

On a heavy sigh, he looks up from his feet, sweat dripping from his nose. Familiar blue eyes meet mine, and just like the wheels on the damn bike, the world slows to a halt. "My name is Cory. Just Cory, thank you."

WHY THE HELL does the world hate me?

387 days. I waited 387 days without sex, not that I was counting, and out of all the men on Grindr in Boston, I chose him. The captain of the hockey team I've been hired to service.

No. Not service. Bad choice of words. Hired to provide care for. Yeah, that's it.

Those eyes never leave mine as I all but tear him from the bike by the back of his jersey. Like all hockey players are born to do, he curses a blue streak as I bustle him down out of the gym, down the hall, and into the joke of an office I've been assigned. I'm fairly certain it's a closet, but who am I to complain?

As much as I want to slam the door, I also don't want to garner any attention, so I lean my back against it, letting the cool surface calm me as it closes with a soft click.

"Mr. Malkovich."

"Cory." With the same brash confidence he wielded in my former bedroom, he deposits himself in my chair, legs spread wide enough for me to stand between them, should I feel the urge. "You had no problem calling me Cory last night. Although, you moaned it more than said it."

"I didn't moan." I whined like a pathetic, perverted old man. There's a difference. "About that."

"About what? About you undressing me, playing with my

nipples, molding my ass in those big strong hands. Sucking my—"

In a bid not to punch the wall, I clench my fists at my side. "That's enough. You're acting like a—"

"Student? Because I am. I mean, I am an almost twenty-one-year-old college student, but a student all the same. How do you think Coach would feel about you inviting college kids back to your secret lair? Do you think he'd be as pissed as say ... your wife?"

At first, the implied threat to my job consumes the majority of my cognitive power. But slowly, the full accusation slips through the cracks. "My wife?"

"Yeah. Your wife. The old ball and chain. The woman you're married to. The mother of your child, Dyl. You know, her."

In a bid to assert some kind of dominance, I want to remain standing, but the *mother of your child, Dyl,* bit has me staggering to the first sit-able surface, my desk. It's a dangerous spot, leaving me vulnerable. I'm not quite sure that he's sane, so I don't care to leave my back to him, but should I sit on the same side, we would be so close our bodies would likely touch, and I don't really want that either. Instead, I shuffle to the short side, my ass hanging precariously close to the edge.

"I mean this with all sincerity, Mr ... sorry, Cory, but what the fuck are you talking about? Unless you didn't notice last night, I am gay with a capital G. I've never even kissed a woman, let alone married and produced offspring with one."

"Sure," he huffs. "I know what I heard, *'Is everything okay, Faithy? Is Dyl okay? Sit tight, sweetheart.'*"

I freeze. What the hell was that? "Okay. There's a lot to unpack there, most important of all being, why does your impersonation of me sound like Daddy Pig?"

"Ahh, 'cause you're a Daddy, and you're English."

"No, I'm Australian. Even then, most people don't notice the accent.'"

"Yeah, well call me Cory, and a linguist genius. Can we get back to the daddy and wife and secret pad part now? I'm dying to hear this excuse."

Feeling slightly more at ease, I cross my arms over my chest and one foot over the other. "I will as long as you stop calling me Daddy."

"Why?" He snaps, replicating my pose. "Does it turn you on?"

"Yes. It does, and since we both know that's not good for either of us, I suggest you stop."

Ahh, finally, something that shuts him up.

"That call last night came from my sister, and was calling about Dylan, our brother."

"Ahh yeah, sure. I have a sister and I would rather plunge a knife in my eye than call her *sweetheart*."

"For the most part, I would be inclined to feel the same, but Faith, my sister, was distressed, and worried about our brother. Not that I owe you this much detail, but we lost our dad recently and we've had to step in as Dylan's primary caregivers. Faith needed reassurance, Dad called her sweetheart when she was upset, so I've begun too as well. Now, I know you're angry, and I must admit it's noble if not misplaced. But I need you to slow down, and think. My name is James Plum. My sister is Faith Pl—"

"Plum," he finishes. A new layer of shame washes over me watching the brash exterior of a young man full of swagger, yet naive to the harshness of the world at his feet, fades away. Suddenly, he appears every bit the young adult he is. "Faith Plum. Professor Faith Plum."

"Correct. Glad we're on the same page." I lean to my desk and grab an unopened bottle of water, handing it to him without meeting his eye. "Now, as for the apartment, it is mine, or was mine, but I have been forced to sublet or sell it in order to move back home."

"Oh."

"Yes. Oh. indeed. And as much as I enjoyed the short time we spent together, since we will now be in frequent, professional contact, I would greatly appreciate it if what occurred last night, and what I've told you today, could stay between us."

Thoroughly chastised, Cory lowers his head and nods. "Of course."

"Excellent. Perhaps it's best if we go do that cool down now?" Lord knows we both need it.

In the Amazing Spider-Man #141, a hangry Peter Parker, AKA Spider-Man, uses his web slinging ability to pluck a man's McDonald's right out of his hands as he strolls down the street. It was a low act, proving that even the greatest of heroes can be absolute jerks.

Is it comparable to what I did to James? I dunno. Probably not. But a week on, as I sit alone, reading fanfic and eating my un-stolen lunch, I feel weighed down with remorse. The pain in James' warm honey eyes, the aura of grief surrounding him as shared his family tragedy, hasn't left me.

I don't think it will anytime soon. Hmm. I wonder if Spidey felt the same way as he chowed down on that lifted sub?

Outside of cordial yes/no replies or directions at practice, the man that I accused of being the worst kind of person, hasn't spoken to me, let alone let me apologize. True, he's only with the Bears three days a week—more once the season starts—so there hasn't been a lot of opportunity to get him alone. But the awkwardness is still there. Even when I've seen him around campus.

Thanks to my trusty glasses-hoodie or cap combo, he hasn't seen me as I leapt into the closest available bush. But that uninter-rupted viewing time has given me perspective, a few boners, *and* forged a fierce curiosity that is now a burgeoning obsession.

Through observation and a little shady digging, I've discov-ered James Plum is indeed the brother of professor Faith *'Faithy'* Plum and seems just as uppity and seriously grumpy. Like all the time. No progress has been made in regards to his brother, so I can't say for sure if that was a bullshit excuse or not. Everyday he has his homemade lunch here with Faith, which he carries in a Marvel lunchbox. HOT. Normally it's a PB&J sandwich, sometimes with chips, sometimes with juice. And finally, according to our NYC-bound center, Sam Bailey, the man can loosen a hamstring with the flick of his wrist.

Other than that, I've got nothing. Hence the convenient position of my regular launch jaunt, which allows me to hide from people, and stake out his sister's office. I'm not sure what I think I'm going to get out of it, especially when I'll see him again at practice this afternoon. But all I can say with absolute certainty is that I need to know more about him, I'm borderline stalking, yet I can't seem to stay away.

Lucky for me, I'm Mr. Invisible.

"Cubby, is that you?"

Fuck.

A firm hand grips my shoulder, twisting me until two sets of blue eyes lock. "It is you. What's wrong? Are you okay?"

"Hey, Brades. Everything's fine, why wouldn't it be?"

"Ahh, because you're lurking outside the admin block that houses the scariest professors in BC. Most students avoid this place like the plague. Is everything okay with your grades? Are you in trouble? Are you ..." With each hypothetical, Brady's blush intensifies. "Shit, student health services are next door. Are you sick, or?" He pauses, glances around and leans in. "Do you have an STI?"

Looks like I'm not the only one with an active imagination.

"No, I don't have a STI." I don't think. "I'm just ... I don't have any friends, okay? I'm a loser who avoids social interactions by hiding in plain sight amongst the teachers. Happy now?" Shit. Where did that come from?

His eyes soften, then crinkle at the edges. "What do you mean you don't have friends? You have me and Quinn. And what about the team?"

"The team?" I scoff. "I guess friendship sign-ups for the new guys were held on day one, 'cause everyone's buddied up without me, and even when I am invited along, I feel ... out of place. And you're the last of last years crew, so unless I want to be the pathetic third wheel around you and Quinn—"

Brady's face contorts in concern. "Cubby, that's—"

"Not your fault. I get it. You're grossly in love and want to spend all your time together. I'm happy for you. I am. But it just means there's no one left for me." I know I could talk to him about James too, but make an impulsive decision to exclude it. While I'm more than happy to own my loser status, Brady knows about what went down at the apartment. I can't give more details and risk Brady putting two-and-two together. Outing James as the hook-up, is something I'm not prepared to do.

Seems my partial confession is enough anyway. Pity colors Brades' eyes. "Why didn't you say something before, ya duffa?"

I tilt my head to the side. "And a duffa is?"

"Oh, a silly sausage. A silly Billie, a—"

"A dickhead, right. Got it." I rub my hand down my face to buy some time … and conceal my embarrassment. "You're right. I should have said something but I'm supposed to be the captain. A leader of men. Life of the party. BC legends on and off the ice like Noah and Shane. When in reality, I'm this closeted queer nerd that hates socializing, and that no one recognizes without a stick in his hand. No pun intended." Hands on knees, I bend at the waist and pant like a dog. Holy shit! What started as bullshit, is ending with me almost hyperventilating.

Has all this crap been lurking inside me all along? "How can the team go from them to me? I don't think I can do it, Brades."

Dropping his backpack, Brady sighs and plops beside me. "Look, I know Noah and Shane left big shoes, and egos, to fill. But personally, I don't think being Mr. Big Guy on campus is a requirement. Coach made you captain because you're a leader where it counts—in the locker room and on the ice. If you want to change the friend situation, Quinn knows everyone and every-thing. She can totally hook you up with the right people. And you can always come sit with us between classes. But like I said, that's if you want it."

"What if I don't know what I want?"

With a huffed laugh, Brady slaps my back, almost sending me

hurtling off the bench. "Well, Cub. I guess that makes you like me, and ninety-nine percent of the student body."

At that very moment, looking like an absolute wet dream, the thing I wanted more than anything a few days ago appears. He's wearing one of those damn tight polos again. And that ass trapped inside the chinos that he definitely paints on. He's so ... beefy and bite-able. Not a snack. A whole freaking smorgasbord. Huh. Maybe the need pulsing under my skin, driving me to see him, isn't that complicated.

Hopefully unaware of my perving, Brady notices him the same time I do, nods in his direction and quickly stands. "Sorry to rush off in the middle of a D&M but I better go. I'm supposed to be meeting James and Faith. Remember what I said, Cub. If you want some company, give us a call."

Oh, I want some company alright. But I don't think it's the kind my team's goalie coach is offering.

I watch him break into a light jog that with his long legs allows him to catch James in a few strides. They shake hands, then Brady glances over his shoulder and waves. James' gaze follows, like so many others on campus he doesn't acknowledge me, but looks straight through me.

Utterly lost and confused, I lean into the student I sat beside in a few classes last year, and whisper, "Sarah, do you have any idea what he's talking about?"

Despite the fact that Sarah Appleblum from Mayfield, Wisconsin, and her friends, also regularly attend training, she glares at me like she's never seen me before. Then confirms it. "Do I know you?"

"Sarah it's me. Cory Malkovich. We had multiple classes together last year. I play hockey."

"Oh, yeah, Conan, right. Um. Professor Sharpener is explaining that there's evidence to support the theory that organelles were once free-living prokaryotes and ...."

On and on she goes about prokaryotic cells and eukaryotic

cells until I regret asking. I have no freaking clue what any of it means.

I have to pull my head from my ass and study. But when?

As always, I slip out of bio a little early, and run to practice, ensuring I'm the first one there. It's part routine, part need to de-dork before the boys arrive.

No matter what Brady Basse with his surfer dude good looks believes, being yourself isn't easy for everyone. I learned quickly in my first year on the team that me as 'me' doesn't fit in the hockey world. Should I be a goalie like him, my quirkiness would be expected, welcomed even. But I'm not. I'm a winger, the rock stars of hockey, and for us it's all about chirping, flows and bunnies.

Well, it's supposed to be anyway.

Squinting in the mirror, I've just finished popping in my contacts when booming laughter echoes outside the locker room. Perfect timing. I quickly pack everything up, making a note to refill my contact lens prescription, and am back at my locker changing when the hairs on the back of my neck raise.

"Why do you have to be such a dick all the time? Give me my stuff, you ass." Seconds later, a kit bag whizzes by the back of my head, landing with a thud at my feet. Without looking I know that voice was Lucas, second shortest and the youngest on the team, *and* who he's cussing at, Trent Hoffman.

I met his big brother, Connor, who already plays for the Mounties, at training camp. Unlike his little bro, Connor seemed like a really solid guy. Talented too. Last season, Trent was a fourth line with little ice time, something he's desperate to change. As such, he spent his summer improving his edge work and bulking up, but his attitude is the thing that needs the most improvement. The guy's a spoiled, rich bully, and in the time that I've been back, Lucas has been his frequent target.

That ends today.

When Trent finally saunters in, he spots me and that frat-boy stupid smile fades. "Captain." He nods.

My forced smile back pains my cheeks. "Nice to see you helping out your fellow teammates with their things, Hoffman.

I'll let Coach know. He's always looking for volunteers for cleanup." While Trent grumbles under his breath, I turn to Lucas and drop my voice. "Let me know if this continues. He would never pull this shit with Noah and Shane around, and he won't with me either."

Lucas blushes and runs his hand through his thick, dead-straight locks. "Thanks, Cap. Us little guys have to stick together, hey."

I want to enforce that height is not the reason I'm doing this, because neither of us are *little*. But then I notice his puffed chest, and that he's standing taller, and if having me in his corner gives him that, then great. So, instead of being defensive, I do what Noah would have done, I offer the stock standard fist bump and continue getting dressed.

THE SECOND COACH Harris strides out onto the ice I know practice is going to be brutal. Dude straight up looks like someone pissed in his coffee.

"Right, before we get started on what will be a painful day." Called it. "We need to have a little chat." A chorus of groans is quickly snuffed out by Professor Plum's appearance.

"Afternoon all." She smiles.

Preening, the guys chant, "Afternoon Professor," like kindergartners, which seems to piss Coach off even more. He's working his gum so hard I think his jaw might break.

"I've had a call from the manager of Balls'up, the pool hall over on Cambridge Street." In my periphery I spot a few of the boys sliding to the back of the pack. "Seems a few idiots while wearing BC hockey hoodies, decided to have a little drunken dance-off last night ... on three of their brand new, three thousand dollar pool tables."

Fuck.

"Now, I've been in this business a long time. I know what it's like to be young, dumb and full of ..." he pauses. "...at the top of your game. To think you're bullet proof. That your talent makes you untouchable. Well guess what? You're not and it doesn't. None of you are immune to the consequences of your actions. I've said it before and I'll say it again. I am not here to only produce great hockey players. I want to produce great men."

"Which is where I come in." Plum nods to Coach, who hands her the clipboard he's been white-knuckling. "Would any one care to take responsibility?" No one does, of course. It's disappointing, but like me, Plum and Coach don't seem surprised. "Right, you are all old enough to know the dangers of drinking to excess, especially for young athletes, so I'm not going to lecture you on that right now. But we will be running some drug and alcohol education sessions next week. In the mean time, if anyone would like to come and speak to me in private, my door is always open."

"What? That's it?" Lucas asks. "No punishment. No bag skates?"

"Coach Harris did suggest that, but since your actions affected a small business in the greater Boston community, we decided repaying that community via a variety of fundraising activities would have a more lasting, educational impact."

"That's right, boys," Coach snarks. "Your Sunday afternoons now belong to us. Since we don't have a lot of time to prepare for this weekend, we're starting with an old fashioned car wash here in the Conte parking lot. And don't think you can get out of it. This is considered an official team event, attendance is compulsory and staff will be onsite at all times to make sure no shenanigans are had."

Great. I barely have enough study time as it is. Losing the one free day we have is going to hurt.

While I have enough brains to internally moan mine, others aren't. Discontented grumbles are everywhere but Trent is the only one dumb enough to say the quiet part out loud. "Every Sunday? For how long?"

Ready for a fight, Coach crosses his arms over his chest. "Until you've raised enough to cover the repairs."

"What! That could take weeks."

"It could, Hoffman. But it could also end before it begins if the numbnuts responsible come forward." Accusatory glances are flying everywhere, but no one raises a hand. "Right then. Sunday it is. Don't forget your Speedos. Things are going to get wet."

The squad's been split into two groups, one remains here on the ice doing drills with coaches Harris and White, while the other is in the gym with Brady and James.

From the goodness of my own heart, I volunteered to hit the gym first, but Coach had a plan, and me thirsting over his physio wasn't it. Instead, I'm standing on the sidelines, giving my opinion on new lines for this season. Not a simple task, and not one I think I'm qualified in.

"Are you sure you want my input on this?" I say, handing the last of the red practice jerseys to Larsson. "I mean, I can tell you that Tom, Sam and I work great together, but wouldn't Brady or one of the other assistants be more knowledgeable?"

"In some things, sure. But you've got great hockey smarts, Cory. You're intuitive and read the play as well as anyone else here. You're also familiar with the after hours team dynamics, in a way we can't be. It's the beginning of a rebuild. Who's inclusive and supportive? Who's putting in the extra training? Who can be trusted? These things count more than you might think."

"Trust is everything." I nod. "If you can't trust someone to have your back in the locker room, how can you trust them on the ice?" My mind goes straight to Hoffman. Can the team rely on rich boy Trent when he bullies whoever he deems the weakest among them? Then, to me. I don't want them to know I wear glasses and love comics, for fucks sake. How can I be comfortable telling them I love dick? I don't even know James. He's practically a stranger. One who's seen me naked, but still. Right now, I have more faith in him than I do the men I'm supposed to be leading.

"Exactly. Among us right now, we have five clowns that will let all their teammates take the fall for something rather than take accountability. We can't have that. A center must trust his wingers. The goalie must trust the D-men. You all must trust your goalie. Coaches must feel they can trust toward their players, and vice-versa. Without that, we're not a team. Without that, we have nothing."

Man, captaining is hard.

The day that my leadership was announced, Noah was here, standing alongside Shane as the boys, half of whom are gone now, hooted and hollered their approval. "Call me whenever you need, Cubby." He'd whispered, tapping the golden C on the chest of my jersey. Maybe it's time to take him up on the offer.

"Okay three on three, red v black. Yellow vs Blue, and then the rest. Light contact." Harris yells at the top of his lungs . I was so zoned out, I almost fell on my ass. "We need to protect those hands, boys. Come Sunday, you've got a lot of scrubbing to do."

IT's days like these that make me appreciate the feel of bare feet on any surface. By the time Coach sends us to change, my legs are shaking so badly, my feet aching, I can hardly walk. The moan I release, the relief I feel to finally sit and take my skates off is damn near orgasmic. By the sounds around me, I'm not alone in that feeling. The space is giving a porno set, more than a locker room.

Lucas collapses beside me, so exhausted he just lets his head clunk against the wall with a dull thud. "Ow.'" He runs a hand through his hair. "That was the worst. I still don't get why we are all getting punished for something five of them did." Subtly, he points to the same faces I too suspect to be the culprits—Brodie Townsend, Trent Hoffman, Brad Smith, Dean Cole, and Robbie McAvoy. All D-men. All under Hoffman's thumb.

"Because we're a team, Lucas. When we win, it's a victory for all of us, even if only one line played well. Flip that and it's the same. No one taking responsibility, means the whole team takes the loss." I take my disgusting socks off and toss them in the giant laundry tub in the center of the room. As I celebrate my three-point landing, I look up, my heart skipping a beat to see James by the entry, leaning against the wall. That snooty, judgmental look souring his face as eyes scan the room. They settle on me, and I know we have to be all professional like, but I can't stop myself winking as I strip my shoulder pads off in record time.

"Look at it this way," I laugh, still watching James, but speaking to my neighbor, "at least we're washing cars, not stinky jerseys and jockstraps."

Almost despite himself, Lucas laughs too. "Not this weekend anyway."

For no reason other than offering anyone with a mustache a better view, I stand and peel off my long-sleeved base layer. Right as it reaches my ribs, I hear James clear his throat. "Don't get too cozy, gentlemen. You have fifteen minutes to change and then it's straight into the gym." He leaves in the few seconds where my face is covered, but I'd like to think he was sporting a blush. Maybe a touch of a chub, too.

ALL SIX-FOOT-FIVE of James Plum's deliciousness stands before us. Gone is the Bears sweatshirt he was wearing in the locker room. All that remains is a slutty sleeveless workout tee, gray sweats that highlight all those manly lumps, and a frown.

It's a killer combo.

"Afternoon, gentlemen. It's circuit time." There's a slight tremble to his voice. Is my big bear nervous?

Lucas, who appears to be my new shadow, elbows me in the ribs and does a shit job of whispering, "Why does he keep calling us gentlemen?"

"Because," James replies, standing taller, one eyebrow raised. "*He* is a gentleman and hopes by treating *you* as such, *you* will act as such."

I swear to god, I almost choke on nothing. Sir James

fucking Plum can be all Mr. Fancy Pants here, but the last thing he said before he stopped sucking on my dick like a candy cane was something like, *Cory, you're mouth is fucking perfect.*

Actually, as far as dirty talk goes, I guess that is kind of gentlemanly.

Brady writes our workout on the board, and mass groaning breaks out. "Boys, we want ten of the following, single-leg glute bridges, shoulder taps—times ten on each side. Next it's side planks for thirty seconds each side, and finally five hip flexor stretches. Let's see who can finish first, go!"

Given the level of whining and the workout we've already had, I'm surprised how quickly the boys start. But then again, we are all hockey players, which means we're all ridiculously competitive.

"You're not joining in, Brades?" I ask before beginning.

"Nope. See this?" With a huge grin, he dangles his COACHING STAFF lanyard in my face. "Means I get to sit on my soon to be fat ass and watch. It's brilliant." Laughing, he turns to James and offers a fist bump. Mr. Uppity 2000, or whenever the fuck he was born, stares at the offered fist like it's the first time he's seen such a thing. "Tap it, Jamie," Brady urges. "Tap it. Deep down I know you want to."

Reluctantly, almost painfully, James grimaces and does indeed 'tap it'. Not bending over and offering my ass as James' next tap-able item consumes every ounce of strength left within me. Like he's reading my thoughts, he shakes his head and frowns. "You're almost a set behind, Mr. Malkovich. Better get to it."

"Sure thing, Doc." I give him another indiscreet wink and drop onto all fours, arching my back and jutting out my ass for absolutely no reason. With my head full of James, I have no memory of what we are supposed to be doing, so I quickly read the instructions written on the whiteboard and as James said, get to it.

On our second rotation, James leans over a tiring Evan Drummond, whispering instructions in his ear, those massive hands and thick fingers spreading over his stomach to correct his positioning. Lust licks up and down my spine picturing James behind me, whispering in my ear. Touching me.

I want some of that.

Grunting and groaning, I let my muscles lax, drop my hips and start flopping like a dead fish. I do get the attention I seek, but from Brady, not James. "I see what you're doing, Cubby," he mutters through thinly pressed lips. "Knock it off."

I don't knock it off, I ramp it up.

As hard as it is to shake your ass doing side planks, I Cardi-B that shit up. And the shoulder taps, no one has ever performed more lewdly.

I'm not sure if all this sexiness will see me getting any action, but it does earn me a head shake, the briefest hint of a James' smile, and a rare and gorgeous rolling laugh.

I HAVE A PROBLEM.

Actually I have several, but unlike the boner that left me lying face down on a yoga mat for fifteen minutes after James's workout ended, this is happening in the semi-privacy of my room. Coach Harris is calling me at nine p.m.

"This can't be good," I say to Cherry, who's finally got Billie down, and is next to me on my bed watching Drag Race as we bitch about the unfairness of life. "Shut up, turn it down. It's Coach." Hoping it removes all traces of panic, I clear my throat. "Coach, hey how's it hanging?"

Kill me now.

Someone very not Coach sounding giggles, "Relax, Cubby. It's me, Quinn."

Confused, I pull the phone from my ear, yep, definitely says Coach Harris. "Quinn? Why are you on your dad's phone?"

"Well, the thing is, we've just had dinner at his place, but I left my phone in the pool house, and I can't be bothered walking all the way out there to get it. Anyway, we're escaping to O'Reilly's and—"

"Wait." I hold my palm out to tell her to stop like she can see it. "You can't be bothered walking to get your phone, but you can get in the car, drive across town and go to a bar?"

"Yup! Wanna come?"

I'm tempted to ask why the Queen of BC would be calling me in the first place. I mean, sure I was invited to her last birthday party, but that was down to Coach. Then I remember the little discussion I had with one of her boyfriends outside Plum's office, and it all makes sense.

"Brady made you ask me, didn't he." Quinn giggles, and I hear something shuffle in the background,

"Shit, he guessed. Say no, Quinny."

"Hi, Brady," I laugh.

"Oh, um, hey Cubby. So, you coming or what?"

There's a million excuses I could come up with—I have to study, I'm too tired, my leg fell off—but I don't use any. There was truth in what I blurted to Brady, so much so I was just repeating my woes to Cherry. I do want to be a great captain like Noah and Shane. I do need to come out of my shell off the ice and the apps. But how ready am I to do that?

"Sounds great, Quinn." It really doesn't. "See you soon."

The second I drop my phone, Cherry pounces.

"So, little bro. Where are we going?"

"We? I don't know what you're doing, but I'm going to O'Reilly's."

With ridiculously contagious enthusiasm, she commando rolls from the bed, landing on her feet and her arms above her head like she's about to bust out a star jump. "If you think I'm letting you go without me, you've got another thing coming. I haven't left this house except for work in months, and I haven't seen Quinn and Brady since he was discharged from the hospital. I'd like to check in on his progress."

"*And* you want to interrogate them about their throuple-ship?"

"Yes, and that." She follows me into the bathroom, peppering me with questions, and creepily watching as I reach for my contacts. "This is it, Cory. Our hard launch into Boston hockey society."

"Hard launch? I have been out with these people before. I was last week."

"Yeah, like twice, *both* without me. A*nd* you said you spent the whole time hiding in a booth reading before leaving to meet some guy."

"Oh, fuck off."

"What? It's true. You probably had bunnies all over you, but actually spoke to like three people–"

"No," I grumble, "not fuck off *you*. Fuck off this." I hold the contact lens box in Cherry's face. The empty box. "I forgot to pick my prescription up. Fuck."

Cherry groans and slams her head against the wall. So dramatic. "Cory. WEAR. YOUR. GLASSES! There is nothing wrong with being you. You is great ... are great ... You're great. If you can't handle being yourself, maybe you shouldn't go."

"Fine. Let's not go."

"Noooo," she whines. "We have to."

"Okay then, so should I ditch the specs, and rock the blurred-vision hockey fuckboy look? Or do I embrace the real me. The geek."

"Jesus, Cory. If you listened to anything I just said, the answer is fairly obvious."

"Yeah, you're right. Blind fuckboy it is." I pick up my comb, swipe a generous amount of hair gunk onto my fingers, and get to work.

"What's behind this, no glasses and slicked back hair back, will make the team fall at your feet-theory?"

I stare back at her in disbelief. "Um, obviously Clark Kent, but also Josie Grosie, Laney Boggs, Mia Thermopolis, and every other bookish girlie in like, *every* high school movie ever made?"

"God, you are so gay."

"Yeah, no shit." I laugh. "That's part of the problem. I can keep changing before everyone arrives, and dressing before they wake on away games, but I can't keep avoiding partying with the team, or the bunnies. Even if it means staying in the closet a little longer, using this time to make friends and earn the respect of my teammates will be worth it when I do come out."

I hope.

I 've said it before and I'll say it again.

The world hates me. Case in point. Ryan Fink.

Ryan is the only person I could tolerate from my old workplace. To this day, one of the only people I could remotely call a friend and, for some time, the only other gay man in my acquaintance. He's also kind of a jerk, and chews gum so frequently and loudly that it drives me insane, but beggars can't be choosers.

Like most people our age, we keep in touch with intermittent texts, shared memes on Instagram, and that's about it. Out of the blue, he called me today and asked me to join him for a beer. Since it had been a particularly rough day at home with Dylan, I accepted.

That's how I found myself at an off campus Irish bar, three tables away from Cory Malkovich. More of the team are with him, Quinn Harris too. But it's Cory and Cory alone I can't take my eyes off.

Primarily due to his absurdity.

Gone is the grace he displays on the ice. He tripped on a chair leg upon entering, again on absolutely nothing when strutting from the bar back to the table, and he squinted at an upside down menu for a good fifteen minutes before the girl next to him angrily tore it from his hands and replaced it with glasses, which he refused to put on ... Until she also put him in a headlock.

He's ... odd.

From what I've observed from my booth, at practice, and while maturely hiding behind the corners of buildings at BC, there's three different versions of Cory Malkovich. None of which seem to be *out*.

Hockey Cory, with his hair slicked back and contacts in, is all swagger, arrogance, and whether he knows it or not, commander of respect. Around campus, he seems the total antithesis. Walking with his head down, a backwards cap, that floppy Dean hair hanging randomly over the frames of his sexy glasses. At my apartment, and here tonight, he seems a mixture of the two, glasses with slicked back locks, cocky, but moving clumsily. He's adorable. Should he not be on the team, I would be on him so fast—buying him a drink and asking if I could take him home.

Well, the old pre-Brandon me would have.

Now I just watch wistfully from afar, wishing he was someone different, and that I was too.

"James." Wriggling his hand, Ryan bobs around before me as though he's been trying to catch my attention for some time. Reluctantly, I unglue my eyes from where they shouldn't be, to where they should.

"Sorry, you were saying?"

He waves it off like me ignoring him is nothing, and smiles. "I was just asking how things are going at home with Dylan?" With no conscious decision to do so, I release a slow, deep, indicative of my mood, breath. "That good, huh?"

Nodding, I take a drink. "It's good and bad, rewarding and defeating all within the same hour. Today, he was heightened as it's Monday. Mondays are a Manny day, but today, Manny was off sick."

"Manny's a carer?"

"Yep. A brilliant one at that. He worked with Dylan at his old day service, and agreed to take on private work for us while we sort out the insurance. With Dad gone, and Faith and I moving in, Manny has been his one constant." The weight of it all settles over me, and I physically sink in my seat. I need to change the subject before I end up on the floor like Cory's drinks. "God, I'm so fucking depressing. That's enough about me, how are you and Kane doing? Still renovating?"

"Divorcing, actually."

"What!" The generous sip of red wine I just took flies from

my mouth and all over Ryan's shirt. His crisp white shirt. "Shit, I'm so sorry." Jumping to my feet, I rush at him with a stack of napkins, and squat at his feet, patting and rubbing his chest.

He stills for a moment, then chuckles and takes hold of one of my wrists. "Don't worry about it, it's Kane's shirt. Fuck him."

"Oh." Slightly relieved, I move to return to a non-crouched, almost in his lap position, but he grips me tighter, holding me in place.

"I know another way we could get to him that might be fun." I feel the pad of his thumb swipe over my pulse point.

This is not good.

I force myself to laugh, feigning cluelessness as to where this is heading, and make my way back to my seat. "What, are the pants his? Want me to ruin them as well?"

"No, they're not. But technically what's inside them is. Since you already fucked his shirt, why don't you fuck his husband, too?"

"Umm. Well. I. Umm."

In my mind, I count the days since someone, not on an app, propositioned me. I lose count at around eighteen months. Ryan is a good looking guy. Very good looking. In fact, when I first met him, I harbored a tiny crush.

That was a long time ago.

A lifetime ago.

Ryan's marriage has begun and ended. As did my time with Brandon, and Dad's gone. I've lost everything, and am trying to carve out some semblance of an existence in a world where nothing feels the same.

Through no fault of my own my gaze lands on Cory as he takes a sip from Sam Bailey's beer, leaving a thin layer of foam on his top lip.

Huh.

In general, I don't fancy beer, but I suddenly have an unquenchable thirst for it. Those lips curl into a hint of a smile, causing a tiny crinkling of his eyes. They really are the most alarming shade of blue. *Not remotely appealing though*, I tell myself.

Remembering I still haven't replied to Ryan, I force myself to look away.

"Thanks for the offer, but I don't think that would be wise."

"Oh, it's not." Reaching out, Ryan cups my jaw in his palm, caressing his thumb over my bottom lip and dragging it down. "But fuck it. I've been through hell and back in the last twelve months. I know my shit is nothing compared to yours, but maybe it's time we don't think and just ..."

"Fuck?"

"Exactly."

At the most fortuitous time blonde man mountain, Brady Basse, and Quinn Harris approach the table. "Ah, it is you, Plummy." Smirking, Ryan raises a brow on my behalf. He knows I hate nicknames. I've told Brady this too, but Faith and he are tight and I'm sure she's told him to do it regardless.

"We told Cubby it was you," Quinn adds, a mischievous twinkle in her eyes. "Would you and your friend like to join us?"

"Thanks, Quinn, Coach Basse, but—"

"It's Brady, remember. None of that Coach rubbish. Makes me sound like an old fart. So, you coming?"

I pause, and glance around Brady to their table. There's a flash of Cory's face, teeth piercing a bottom lip. Two glimmering blue eyes widening, taunting, daring me to accept, before he ducks behind a menu. The pretty young woman with her arm draped around his neck, laughs and squeezes tighter, and an irrational burn, indigestion on steroids, scolds my insides. "I'd love to, guys, but my friend, Ryan and I were just leaving."

Before Brady and Quinn can react, Ryan is on his feet, a hand reaching out to pull me into mine. I take it, then sling my arm around his shoulder. Given the circumstances, his waist would have made for a better show, but he's much shorter than me, and has always been sensitive about his height.

Tossing a twenty on the table even though we hadn't ordered food, I say goodnight to the loved-up duo and drag Ryan towards the exit. If I yell, 'your place or mine', over my shoulder as we pass a certain table, it's purely by accident.

WHAT THE FUCK is wrong with me?

In a life littered with monumental errors in judgment, this is surely the most reckless. I'm almost twenty-five years old, and have just used the only friend I have to make someone I can never have, jealous.

Marching to the car like a man possessed, each individual, minuscule piece of gravel I tread on sends a dull throb through my brain. Losing enthusiasm, my march becomes walking, walking slows to plodding, plodding to stopping. Ryan, who's been silent since we exited the bar, halts beside me, tugging on the hem of my shirt, a wide smile making me feel even worse.

"What's up, big guy? Are you nervous about me ravishing you?"

"What? Nervous. No way. I'm ... pumped."

"Pumped, hey? I'm glad to hear it, because I have this new harness and whip and I've been dying to try it out. The old one snapped in half on the swing. I think I was a little too rough." For that last bit, the little too rough bit, Ryan leaned in to whisper, then lick the shell of my ear. Kinky or not, the prospect of taking an attractive man home should be exciting. I'm young. Supposed to be dumb and full of ... stuff. But blood rushing south is not going to my groin, it's going lower. Draining down my legs, oozing from my toes.

I think I might faint.

All the while, Ryan maintains that smile, teeth glowing under the street lights.

The glow isn't helping, but now that I think of it, he does look a bit psychotic. Maniacal even. I don't think he's blinked this whole time.

"Oh. Whips, hey. Wow."

"Gags too. The whole basement is decked out."

"Oh. Wow."

"Do you want to leave your car here and I can drop you back in the morning ? You probably won't be able to sit, let alone drive once we're done." Without waiting for a response, he takes off, striding towards his car, a rather hearse-looking black station wagon, looking back at me once he makes it to the driver's side door. "You have medical insurance, with that new job, right?"

Still no blinking.

"Oh. I. Um."

Without moving my head, I scan the parking lot. My car is hard to spot, it's in the darkest section on the other side of the lot, right beside the fence that separates O'Reilly's from a Green Line train stop. It's a run-able distance but with the blood loss and my hot girl fitness, I'm pretty sure he'd catch me.

Fuck, this is just so typical of me. First guy I go home with in eons and he's a gay, less hot Christian Grey. I still haven't moved, but Ryan has. He has both hands cupped around his eyes blocking the reflection as he peers into the back of the wagon. Maybe I should make a break for it now while he's distracted.

"Looking for something?" I ask instead, because I am a stupid nosy bitch.

"Just my rope."

"Oh. Rope. Wow."

Ryan straightens, his head turning like a possessed Chucky doll. "How do you feel about asphyxiation?"

McJesus dreams about skating as fast as I run. He would probably leave out the wailing, but who's to say. All I hear is the thundering of my feet, my heavy panting, the cry of terror, and riotous laughter. "James, I was kidding. Stop running, you fucking idiot."

It takes a few strides for his words to sink in, but when they do I come skidding to a halt, dropping onto my haunches. "Thank God. I'm so unfit."

Still by his car, Ryan's bent over too, he's laughing though, not struggling to breath. "Anyone ever told you that you run like Kermit the Frog?"

Yes. Frequently. "No. I just run on the balls of my feet like a lot of autistic people do. I also have hyper-mobile joints. Flexibility is what made me a great goalie."

"Ooohhhh, sexy. Maybe we should reconsider the harness." Though I would like to head in the opposite direction and never stop, once I regain the ability to breathe I amble back over to the comedian I wish I never befriended. As soon as I'm within reach, he pulls me in by the shirt and wraps his arms around me. "Who's the kid?" The first thing he says when he stops slapping my back.

"What kid?"

"The kid you kept looking at over my shoulder. The one that made your face contort whenever he touched the girl attached to his side. The kid that—" Fucking hell. Shoving my palms onto Ryan's chest, I push him away then fix my twisted shirt, then pants then hair. Am I stalling? Absolutely. It fails. The second I look up. "The kid with the glasses that looked like he wanted to stab me in the eyes with a tooth pic when you touched me."

"He's not a kid," I say, feeling the tips of my ears burning. "He'll be twenty-one soon."

"Oh, you're right. He's practically geriatric."

"See. And I wasn't watching him. I was … monitoring. He's on the team and I was just making sure he didn't drink too much. We have an early practice tomorrow." The last part is true. The start is not.

"Wasn't aware a team physio's role was to babysit. But I do know a way you can ease your mind."

"One, I wasn't babysitting, and two, how?"

Ryan tilts his head to the side then nods in the direction of something over my shoulder. "Why don't you ask him? He's been staring at us since we walked out, and oh, look, here he is now."

Apparently my circulatory system is back up and running, heating my face as I turn. Like a man on a mission, Cory is advancing on us, that girl still hanging off him. The closer they come the more familiar she seems. Maybe she's a BC student?

They're within earshot now, Ryan appears delighted, me not so much. The kitchen arrhythmia I narrowly survived is regrouping, the rib crushing, heart adjacent spasms doubling me over.

"Not a fish. Not a fish. Not a fish." I unfortunately repeat out loud. "Breathe. James. Breathe. Not a fish." Oh shit he's so close, I need to do something. "This is very inappropriate, Mr. Malkovich," I holler, while for some reason standing on my tip toes, my voice three octaves higher. "You cannot accost me in this manner."

BEEP BEEP. An ominous glow is emitted from the silver Prius to my right. Holy shit. Ryan is cackling, and again, I am not. "Oh my God. He's parked next to us. This is so embarrassing for you."

What I'm also not, is close enough to Cory's car for him to rub against me the way he does while moving between the two cars. "Excuse me." He smirks, his hand running over my hip and stomach, slowing now that we're chest to chest. Should he be taller, or I shorter, we'd be eye to eye.

How unfortunate that would be. *Side note, his hair smells like mint.*

"Not a fish. Not a fish. Not a fish."

Cory's face shines brighter than the street lights, the stars, and the almost full moon above us. "Not a, what?"

"Not a Finn." Suddenly at my side, Ryan knocks his shoulder into mine, pushing me closer to Cory. "I was asking if the surname Plum is Finnish. It's not, apparently."

"English," I blurt. "Or north German. Not a Finnish ... name."

"Huh, ya don't say. Malkovich is the Americanized version of the Slavic Matković, but my family is from Ukraine."

"Right, of course." There is no need for me to extend this conversation, but I can't seem to help myself. "And your friend?"

Confusion clouds those baby blues, until Cory glances over his shoulder to the blonde. "Oh, my *friend*," he giggles, she doesn't. "She's Ukrainian-American, too."

"Huh. Small world."

"You know what they say, sexy things *come* in small packages." He leans in, and I lean back to the point of almost toppling. "And on big furry chests. Guess you'll never find out, though." Observing me wobble, he pokes my pec, right where my tattoo lies. "What's wrong? Having trouble with your *balance*?"

Cocky little fucker.

Before I can collect myself and reply, a grumble comes from the blonde behind him. "Good God, Cory. Can you please take me home now? I have to get out of these pants."

"Sure thing ... *sweetheart*." He winks, then steps back which is both a relief and a crying shame. "See you round, Doc."

What's the difference between a hockey player and a one year old baby? The baby would have more teeth. Noah *'Dad Joke'* Petterson, told me that one, and never has the comparison between my teammates and infants felt more apt. Teeth, it seems, aren't the only things babies come out on top in. They're infinitely more mature, too.

Although O'Reilly's was nothing more than clinking glasses, familiar voices and blurred shadows for the first twenty minutes or so, the boys were in fine form, a little too flirty with my sister, but other than that, everything was going well. But as soon as I tried to drink from the ketchup bottle, and Cherry hounded me into wearing my glasses, it started.

Four-eyes, poindexter, Stuart Little, Chicken Little, the taunts were harmless enough, and of course I sat there, taking it all in good humor as I have been trained to do all my life. But for a guy who is one hundred percent faking it 'til he makes it, busting his ass to earn the respect of his team, all the mockery does is reaffirm my belief that the real me has no place in the hockey world.

Luckily, sex, AKA the hypnotic twitch of James Plum's furry top lip, and the frequent licking of his red wine-stained bottom one, served as a distraction. At school, he made it pretty clear nothing would happen between us, but the eye-fucking across the room, even as his hands roamed all over the guy who licked his ear, the same one who's taking him home, says different.

I've never taken such risks, been so obviously, overtly and

publicly flirty as I am with him, but the rush I get when he's all flustered—mumbling about fish for instance—is addictive. Even in the dimly lit parking lot, I could see his blush. He was horrified.

Speaking of which.

"Ugh, most of your team are horrific and so immature to pick on you because of your glasses. You're not much better." My sister complains, as I pull out into the still-busy traffic. I remind her that, technically, they aren't my friends, but that's disregarded with a huff. "You ignore me half the night. Drag me away from Quinn, Brady and that hottie Sam—the one decent guy there—just so you can follow some other guy and his date, then creepily refer to me as a *sweetheart* to make him jealous. I'm not your '*sweetheart.*' I'm your sister."

"I did nothing of the sort." I one hundred percent did. "Sam isn't hot." Sam is hot. "And you are sweet, and my friend. Probably my best friend." Sadly, that is truer than I would like it to be. It also plays to my sister's one true weakness. Herself.

"Aww, you're my bestie, too. And I *am* pretty sweet." She reaches over the center console, to hug me. Real safe.

"Driving here, sis."

"Oh, right, sorry." After a tiny squeeze, she slides back to her seat but doesn't shut up. "Now that you've declared your brotherly love for me, tell me in great detail who that slab of beef you wanna pound is."

Now there's a mental image. "That was James Plum, the Bear's new physio, the mountain I'm busting to climb, the quest I'm planning to conquer, the beast to my beauty."

"Plum." Cherry scoffs. "That was no plum, that was a peach. Did you see his ass?"

"Did I see?" I snort so hard I set myself into a coughing fit. "Did I ... No, baby girl, I didn't see the plumpest ass in the greater Boston area. I'm gay you twit, of course I saw."

Determined to kill us, Cherry whacks my arm, almost sending the car veering into the wrong lane. "Some way to speak to your bestie, the one who stopped you making an even bigger fool of yourself than you already had. You wouldn't have seen shit if I didn't bring your glasses."

"Yes, well some of us are blessed with beauty, some with brains. Guess which one you are."

"We're twins, idiot. We're both hot, vibrant and young. You know who didn't look young? The astonishing-ass guy. He's a bit old for you. And what's with that mustache?"

Ahh, the mustache. "Hey, leave the 'stache out of it. That thing's hot as fuck, just like the rest of him. And he's not old, he's not even thirty, plus with age comes experience, and with experience comes me … frequently and substantially."

Slapping her hand over her mouth, Cherry makes an exaggerated gag. "Ugh, you are proof that homosexuality is not a choice. I'd be a lesbian so hard if it meant never dealing with disgusting, slutty men."

"Hey, for a dork like me, slutty is a life goal. I choose to take that as a compliment."

"Yeah, well maybe you should choose to take my advice. I'm serious about Old Man Plum. Playing Hide the Cubby may seem like all shits and giggles, but fun for you could mean trouble for him."

"Please, I am nothing if not discreet." I don't have to look at Cherry to know she's rolling her eyes. "Not that there's an immediate need for discretion, Mr. Plum seems to have all the company he desires right now."

"That's a great thing, Cory. Trust me. No good has ever come from a student-teacher relationship."

"Not a teacher." I remind her. "And something good will come of it–"

Cherry folds herself into her sweater like a turtle. "Please don't say it."

"Me."

IT'S after eleven when Cherry and I stumble into the house, stilling almost immediately.

"It's quiet," she whispers. "Why is it quiet?" Many homes would be at this time of night, but in this house, a relaxed noise-free evening means trouble. Mom and Pop—who comes over for dinner every day—are night owls, their games of Crazy Eights often lasting 'til the wee hours.

Linking arms, we leave the darkness of the lounge and shuffle our way towards the soft light emanating from the dining room where hushed conversation can be heard. There we find Mom and Pop, sitting at the dining table. Paperwork covers a good portion of its surface, frowns mar their faces, turning two of the most un-serious people I know, solemn.

A dread-flavored lump forms in my throat, the Plum-fueled high I was riding instantly evaporates.

Pop's chronic kidney condition had him in the hospital for two weeks last month, and I fear this is a result of that. If it is a money thing, Cherry and I need to be delicate. Mom's as proud as she is loud. The slightest sign of us interfering in potential financial problems will see her deny, deny, deny.

Relying on our twin tuition to explain just that, I give Cherry a wink and drop into the empty seat beside Mom, eyes discreetly scanning. "No cards tonight, Pops? Did you finally concede that your daughter is a superior card shark?" What starts as a laugh turns into a wet, rolling cough that rattles his lungs, and my nerves.

"Never. Your mom and I were—" Before he can finish, Mom jumps to her feet, hands swiping the paperwork into a pile.

"Just heading to bed. Night, kids. See you tomorrow, Dad." Cherry and I exchange glances, one waiting for the other to speak but neither doing so. Pops remains seated, looking so glum it hurts to witness.

"What's going on?" Cherry asks the second Mom is out of earshot. Pops leans back in his chair, squinting into the dark lounge to make sure she's not hiding.

"It's not my place to say, but ..." He scratches his chin, then exhales. "Cory, I know you have a pretty tight schedule with school and practice, but do you think you might be able to pick up a few hours work here and there? Maybe something to do with hockey, or in a store or—" Right. So it is money.

"Absolutely I can, if ... if I have to, yeah. I'll start asking around tomorrow." With a faint smile, he rustles my hair before pushing off the table and saying good night.

Internally panicking and suddenly exhausted I slide down in my chair, waiting for Pops' shuffled steps to fade and Cherry's opinion.

"What the hell, Cory! How—"

As I do what I do, I know she's going to lick my palm. I know it. Regardless, I raise my hand and slap it over her mouth. "I don't know, okay," is all I can get out before her tongue makes its first pass. "You can lick it all you like, but the hand stays until you promise to shut up."

"Prwomise," she mumbles, licks again then says something so muffled it's unrecognizable as English. As tempted as I am to smother her, I yank my hand free. Surprisingly, Cherry sticks to her word, saying nothing verbally, but everything with her eyes that are wider than I've ever seen and boring holes into my forehead.

"If Mom can work and help you with Billie, run the household and care for us, I can manage a few hours work on top of hockey." There's not a single, tiny, teeny, weenie spec of me that knows how, but I will. I have too. "Lotte and Brady are running some skate and hockey programs over at Green Line Ice, maybe I can see if they need some help."

"Brady has a boyfriend and a girlfriend. I don't think he needs the kind of help you want to give him."

"And I don't think it's fair of you to accuse me of wanting every man with a dick, but here we are." It's hard to keep a straight face as I say this, because while it's true, I'm not attracted to all men the same that she's not, Brady Basse is a delicious piece of ass, and I absolutely would go there should he be single and interested. Since he's not, Cherry doesn't need to know how on the money she is. "I'm a hockey player. He's running a camp. That's it."

"Keep your wig on, Bro. I'm just kidding. I think it's a great idea, the kids will love having you there. You can teach them everything you know, and give them the chance to be taller than someone."

Again with the gags. Puffing out my cheeks, I exhale slowly, rise to my feet and say, "Fuck you and good night."

14

JAMES

Hairspray, the once loved classic starring Nikki Blonski, John Travolta, Zac Efron, has rapidly morphed from my autistic comfort movie, to the most hated, dreaded, nausea inducing thing in my life.

Apart from gum chewers.

When my Australian Mom died and my American Dad decided to relocate us kids back to Boston, *Hairspray* was my first thought. And possibly the first indicator of my sexuality, but that's a whole other conversation. Poor Dad must have reinforced that Boston and Baltimore weren't the same place a hundred times, but I refused to listen. As far as I was concerned, I was going to live in the same city as Tracy Turnblad, and I couldn't wait to catch the bus and sing *Good Morning* to my adopted city.

Like me, Dylan is a big '*Spray* fan. Watching and dancing to the musical with Dad was one of his favorite things, and since we lost him, there have been days where he would do nothing but sit in Dad's chair and watch or listen to the soundtrack on repeat. The color, the music ... I think all of it provides Dyl with a sense of safety—predictability—when the person who once bought him those things in abundance suddenly disappeared.

Hence why, on the third day Manny has been off ill, possibly vanishing like Dad in Dyl's mind, we've done nothing but listen to that not-so-brand-new beat.

Our morning started well enough. Dylan had a rare full night's sleep and woke happy and seemingly content. Breakfast was eaten with minimal fuss. We showered, brushed teeth and dressed, then went for our regular walk to the nearby dog park where Dylan met up with three of his neighborhood friends, Maria, Jose and Lyle. I sat with their moms while the four of them laughed and cuddled the pups, before coming home to wait for Manny. That's when we got the call.

So yeah, *Hairspray* is on repeat and loud because Dyl's been so distressed that he's snapped both pairs of his headphones; the feel of them over his ears just too much when he is so heightened and hypersensitive.

It breaks my heart seeing him like this ... So vulnerable. So voiceless. So trapped in his fear and entirely debilitated. It also demonstrates my absolute ineptitude to support my brother the way he deserves.

It's almost six p.m. now ... I am exhausted, frustrated and overwhelmed, so I leave Dyl in the kitchen and call Maria's mom, Sue. "I'm sorry," I whimper, hello barely having passed her lips. "I don't know what to do. Dyl's smashed another mirror, his headphones, and he's crying, Sue. He can't stop crying. I ... I don't know how to help him."

"It's Alexithymia, James. His routine's fucked, and he's having trouble regulating his emotions. Have you put on—"

"Hairspray, yep. It's been on all day and it's helped I think, but he's been picking at his skin and I can't seem to make him stop." Through the phone, I hear footsteps, the distinct jingling of keys and then Sue's muffled voice.

"Maria," she sing-songs, "you up for a trip to the park with Charlie? Awesome. James, honey, I'm back. Do me a favor, okay? Play the soundtrack on your phone, take as long as you need, we'll be waiting for you by the swings."

It takes almost twenty-five minutes for me to get Dylan out the door, another ten to walk the two blocks to the park, Boston's pink-hued dusk darkening on each step. I hear, rather than see, Maria as we approach the hedge row fence, the effect of her squeals of glee immediately visible in the upturn of Dylan's lips.

Charlie, the mildly psychotic Cavalier King Charles Spaniel, is the first to greet us after we unlock the gate, her excitable, high-pitched yap infinitely worse than her non-existent bite.

"James, Dylan, over here!" Waving her arms is Sue. "You made it, well done." There's no patronization in her praise, just genuine understanding and heartfelt acceptance. "Rough day, huh?"

"Understatement of the decade." Like a sack of spent shit, I drop onto the damp grass and verbalize the panic that has my insides twisted in a knot. "Remember how Manny's been away? Well, he has strep, so he'll be off 'til Saturday. Faith's in New York until Friday, so I've had to call in sick at the paid placement I've only just started. I'll probably get fired, and if I do we're fucked. I don't know how I am going to cope by myself for another three days. I'm not built for this, Sue. I'm the absolute fucking worst person to be left responsible for another human. I can hardly regulate myself, just ask my ex. How the fuck am I supposed to help him?"

I don't realize I'm flat on my back until I feel the press of Sue's shoulder against mine. She's beside me, her graying blonde curls splayed out on the grass like a paint brush. "Yesterday I hid in the pantry and ate a whole jar of peanut butter. The day before that I got into the shower with my socks and glasses on, and that night went to bed at seven when Maria did, and laid in there listening to *Folklore* for four hours."

"It is a great album."

"It really is."

"My point is. None of us know what we are doing all the time. All of our kids, or siblings cope with stressors differently, and we do too."

I squeeze my eyes closed to stop a fresh wave of tears. "I know, but it feels like I can't cope."

"Oh really." Sue sits and points to Dyl who's sitting on the swing next to Maria, not swinging as such, more rocking. "Did Dylan eat today?"

"Yeah, yeah he did. Mainly just toast and bananas but he ate."

"And did he drink?"

"Yeah. Some water and juice."

"Did you make sure he hadn't hurt himself when he smashed the mirror or the headphones?"

"Of course, but—"

"And did you try to distract him from picking his skin by dancing and singing to Hairspray even though you never want to hear Travolta say 'stricken chicken' again?"

Pinching the bridge of my noise, a huffed laugh escapes me. "I did. Yeah. Think I might have popped a hip I boogied so hard."

"And is Dylan safe, and smiling at my daughter right now?"

Joining Sue, I push up onto my elbows, a small smile breaking through. "He is."

"Well then, congratulations, Mr. Plum. You survived, and sometimes that's the most we can ask for. Now, what are you guys doing Saturday? I have an idea."

WEIGHED down with Fifth Avenue shopping bags, and looking annoyingly refreshed, Faith walks through the door Friday evening and promptly kicks me out. "Pack your face masks, go to your apartment and get some sleep. You can come take Dyl to the program tomorrow but other than that, I don't want to see you back here until Monday afternoon."

I'd argued until I was blue in the face, but as I learned at a very early age, there is no winning against a determined Faith Plum. Taking her advice, I did as she said, I packed my masks, favorite bath oils, and some clothes, and headed to Chestnut Hill.

Driving well below the speed limit, I played no music, and despite the chill of the evening, had all the windows down, enjoying the cool night air on my face. I'd made Dyl and I some dinner, but had left before eating, so I ventured into enemy territory, passing Boston University to grab two Raising Canes's chicken sandwiches, some crinkle-cut fries, and a whole jug of sweet tea.

Guilt gnaws at my stomach as much as hunger does. I shouldn't feel so relieved to have a break, but I needed this. I've spent my first week at home alone with Dylan, and for the most part he's been happy. Somewhat surprisingly, I have been too. We had fun painting, Dylan paced the backyard while I pulled weeds, and hoped for the best as I planted the beets, peas and spinach seedlings we picked up from a local garden center. The park was visited more than once each day, and hours were spent scouring through Dylan's enormous DVD collection for some new musicals. A decision I slightly regretted after my fourth *Trying to Solve a Problem like Maria*.

So, while I wouldn't say we thrived, we more than survived.

A block out from my apartment, I pull up to a red light, close my eyes, let my head fall against the seat and let the gentle hum of traffic wash over me.

"We keeping you up, Doc?" *You've got to be fucking kidding me.* "I suppose it is past seven. That must be like midnight once you're over forty."

Without looking, I reply to the one person who calls me 'Doc', my tone as civilized as I can manage with a mouth full of fried potato. "Firstly, not forty, I was born this millennium, and I know book smarts aren't a traditional strength for your kind, but you do know I'm not a doctor, right?"

Cory's laugh is disturbingly arousing. "My kind? I dunno. From what I hear, you were once one of us sport loving plebeians, and look at you now? All doctored up in your all wheel drive BMW eating fancy chicken us mere mortals could only dream of."

Since the world's longest red light refuses to switch, I roll my head to the side and see Cory on the sidewalk, looking straight into my window. Damn. Flush-cheeked Cory in a sweat-soaked sleeveless tee, is a sight. Doing my best not to drool, I give a snide, "Why are you here?"

Smirking, he looks down, pinches his tee between his fingers and raises it, exposing an inch or two of tight, toned, glistening abdominal. "Jogging. But I think I've gone far enough. Can I grab a ride?" It's a rhetorical question. Before I can reply, he's skipping around the hood of the car, opening the door and sliding into the passenger seat, moist skin squelching against leather. "Light's green, by the way."

15

CORY

oc Plum's car is almost as nice as his ass. *And* that big, furry, manly chest. I know which one I'd rather take a ride on, though.

"You had practice tonight, didn't you?" James asks, eyes on me as I steal a greasy fry from his take-out bag. "Why are you out jogging?"

I got home from practice, studied for an hour, went to Green Line Ice for my first shift, then came home exhausted to find Mom crying. I couldn't handle it, so I ran.

"Not all of us are naturally hot like you. For me, it takes a lot of work." A dozen shades of gold and amber flash in James' eyes as he gives them an appropriate roll. "I'd ask what you're doing out, but I guess that's obvious." Looking for further distraction, I fish around in the bag. "Ooh, two chicken sandwiches. Why Mr. Plum, I do believe this is fate. They're my favorite." With a grunt, James reaches across the center console and snatches his dinner from my hand.

"Mine too. You want one?"

"I want something."

"Well, then. Why don't I turn around and drop you off. I've even got a coupon you can use."

"*Or* you can take me back to your place and we can split your buns."

It's tiny. Some may say insignificant. But the slight crinkle I see at the curve of James's lips feels like everything. "You really do think you're something, don't you?"

No.

"Cocky hockey players are so hot right now. I'm just giving the people what they want." When we slow to a halt at the next light, James seems to be at war with himself, hands tapping on the steering wheel, his head turning my way, gaze coasting up and down from chest to waist, then snapping back only to repeat the same pattern. I can't blame him. My red short-shorts are riding high.

"I'm not taking you to my old apartment," he says randomly. "That can't happen. You have to know that."

"Hey, I'm not the brightest, you said it yourself."

"That's not..." His tapping ceases, fingers instead gripping the wheel as though he's going to rip it from the dash. "It's wrong of me to mock your intelligence. From what I understand, you have a STEM-heavy course load and you're excelling."

Not any more. "Duh, of course I'm excelling. I wear glasses. I'm obviously a nerdy brainiac." James lets his gaze shift to my eyes, his own narrowing. It's fleeting, but electrifying.

"Even at this age, you still get that nonsense? Please tell me such childish taunts don't bother you."

"Of course they don't." I aim to disguise my defensiveness but if James' expression is anything to go by, I failed.

"Good. Because it's ridiculous to let such stereotypical, superficial things define us."

"What, superficial things like sexy swimmers' bodies, with pretty pink nipples?"

Collapsing forward, he lets his head fall against the steering wheel. "Yes. Things like that." There's a hint of a blush rising from the collar of his polo, and I am mad for it. It's so much fun watching him squirm that I don't mind the silence that descends as we take off again.

He must though, as without looking, he reaches for the touchscreen media display and taps randomly at the screen. Despite my best efforts, I know so little about him that the prospect of learning something as insignificant as the music he plays in his car is almost enough to give me a semi. Until some lame-ass country music fills the void.

"Please tell me you're not some secret gay redneck, because if that's the case, you can let me out here."

Several horns blare from behind us as James slams on the breaks, bringing us to a screeching halt. Before I can react he's leaning over me, fingers brushing the bare skin of my thighs as he reaches to open the door.

"On your way then."

"So it's true? You're one of them? A red voting redneck?" Jame's lips purse and his cheeks puff. I think he's going to blow and not in the way I'd hoped.

"Mr. Malkovich. Weren't we just speaking about the dangers in believing stereotypes? Not that I need to explain myself to you ... again ... but this is Mickey Guyton. A beautiful young country artist, who happens to be an outspoken liberal. Like me. Even if she wasn't, I would never accuse her, or anyone, of bigotry based on their music genre alone." With a nod, he motions towards the door. "Good night."

"But—"

"Good. Night." His cheeks are red now, but it's not caused by modesty. Stubbornly, I grip the edge of my seat. If he wants me out, he has to toss me out.

"No. I'm not going anywhere. For starters, I don't know where we are. What if it's not safe? How would you live with yourself if I was to be murdered?"

"We're a block from school and you're fast. I'm sure you can out run any killer that happens to be roaming Chestnut Hill this time of night."

"What if I trip?"

"Well, you better check your laces and make sure that you don't."

"What if—" Before I can think of another lame reason to not get out of this car, my phone rings in my pocket. Saved by the bell. Holding my right arm out, index finger raised, I grab my phone with my left, accidentally switching it to speaker as I do.

"Cory," Cherry screams. "What the hell is wrong with you? Who the fuck runs out on their crying mother?" Suddenly, James and I's roles are reversed. I can't get out of the car fast enough and he's gripping my arm to keep me in. "Did you know? Have you known all along?"

"No? I didn't know. I mean, no, I don't know. What am I supposed to know?"

"The mortgage, Cory. Mom took out a double mortgage a few years ago, and she's fallen behind. The bank is going to take the house."

"Whose house?"

"Whose house? What, you think she's crying over the Three fucking Bears' house? Our house, you idiot. They're taking our house."

"I'M TERRIBLE WITH PEOPLE, may well be a hypochondriac, and I can't drive stick." Is the first full sentence spoken between us since James kindly offered to drive me home. "This isn't my car. I can't drive stick because I never learned." Becomes the second.

"What?"

"This is Faith's. I drive a 1997 Honda that's currently sitting in our garage after refusing to start for the third day in a row. Faith let me take this, and she's going to use my dad's car that I can't drive because–"

"Because you can't drive stick."

"Exactly." Raising my gaze from the immaculately clean floor, I shift in my seat to face James and find him studying me earnestly. "The business I was training in, that I had just invested in and was planning to take over, went broke. There were some .... many ... accusations against the owner. I wasn't aware of any of them until it was too late and I lost everything."

I try and fail to return the compassion in James's expression. "That still doesn't explain the friends thing. Or why you can't drive stick."

With a wink, he taps against his temple. "Or maybe it does."

Agitation itches under my skin, not because he's implying he's dumb when clearly he's not, but because of the conversation we had in his office. "So what you told me about your brother and your apartment, that was a lie?" He shakes his head, a forced smile curving his lips.

"No. Two things can be true at the same time. It's a long story, but the condensed version is that within a year, I lost my partner, my job, then my dad who was not only an incredible man, but the carer of his son, my brother, Dylan. It's been a shit time, and I'm not trying to say my life is worse than yours, rather that there's no shame in having money troubles. Particularly when they've come about through no fault of your own. Occasionally even when they are."

Hyperaware that James, who rarely speaks of anything at practice outside that of his role, has opened the door here, allowing me a tiny peek inside. I know I should leave it at that. But the same curiosity that killed the cat seems determined to finish me off, too. "Why does your brother need a carer? Is he sick?"

"No, he's not sick. He has a significant intellectual disability, and profound autism. He used to attend an amazing day program four days a week, but when Dad died we lost insurance coverage, and we've been fighting red tape to get it back. Since Faith earns a ridiculous amount more than me, she works full-time and I'm home with Dyl the days we can't afford any outside support."

"Oh." *God I am such an asshole.* I have no idea what to say so I go for the first thing that pops into my head. "I've blocked everyone I've ever hooked up with on the apps. My loser dad, who could be dead for all I know, used to tell Mom he was taking me to the rink for peewee hockey, but he'd actually leave me in the car while he visited his *girlfriends.* When Mom confronted him, he didn't even bother excusing his cheating, instead he focused on me and said it didn't make a difference if he took me to the rink or not because midgets, who can't see the puck, can't play hockey."

"Shit, kid."

I'm not a kid. I think to myself before allowing the word vomit to run again. "They didn't know I could hear them, but I could obviously, and from that day on I swore I would make it to the NHL."

"And you did." We pull up at my house with its faded paint and crooked screen door. After putting the car into park, James takes it in, then turns to me with a grin that twitches his mustache and lights his whole face. He looks so much younger when he smiles. He really is beautiful.

"Yeah." I huff. "But at what cost?"

I t's Saturday morning, I've got a coffee in my hand, I've had a full night's sleep, and I'm on my way to pick up Maria, Sue and Dylan,who's apparently been awake since five a.m.

Despite the fact that we're heading to an activity designed for them, I am the one freaking out. Not only because I'll be doing something I haven't done in years, but because of certain conversations in the dark.

The defeated frame of Cory Malkovich version number four has occupied an abnormal space in my mind since somberly climbing out of my car, and moping through that wonky front door.

Over the years, I've listened to more than enough of my sister's psychoanalytical blabbering for me to consider myself a quasi-expert, but any idiot could recognize why the kid changes personas like I do socks. He's so desperate for approval, so keen to prove his dad wrong, and his mom right, mean-spirited teasing or lighthearted chirps about his height or glasses are taken in the same manner. They all hurt. They all twist the dagger that one of the people, who is supposed to love him the most, inserted.

All in all, I've a feeling that our conversation got us closer to the core of each other than anyone outside our immediate family has been for a very, very long time. I'm yet to decide if that's a good thing or not. Nor do I have time to do so, because when I pull up to the curb in front of our place, four smiling faces are eager, ready and waiting to go.

"We don't have to be there for an hour." I remind Faith,

who's too busy helping Dylan into the back to answer. Sue and Maria climb in beside him, then Faith joins me up front.

"I know we don't have to be there for an hour—"

"Just said that."

"But the guys are ready, and Sue and I figured that's a good thing, because they can take the time to explore, make themselves comfortable and you know, explore. I think that's imperative. Do you? I do ... Do you?"

Pressing my lips together to stop my smile, I place my hand on Faith's and give it a squeeze. "Faithy, Sweetheart. Are you nervous by any chance?"

"No," she says.

"Yes," Sue says. "She's also had four coffees in thirty minutes."

Eyes wide, I let out a loud whistle. "Okay then, nothing for you when we stop at Starbucks on the way."

"Starbucks, no! Do we have to? I'll smell it and then I'll be done."

"Yes we have too. I have yet to have my minimum caffeine hit, and there is no way in hell I am doing this sober."

BRADY BASSE really does smile all the time.

At first I was skeptical of that. No one can be that happy. Especially someone who was so recently deprived of their hockey dreams. But now that I'm getting to know him, my wariness has dimmed to a mild distrust.

As expected, we are the first to arrive at Green Line Ice and Brady—his dimpled cheeks, and booming laugh—are on the ice placing cones. It's Dylan's excitable clap that alerts him to our presence, and that smile expands. "Yes! Dude! You made it, I'm stoked." I'm not exactly sure which of us dudes he's referring to, but my coffee has kicked in, his enthusiasm is contagious and I wave like an idiot regardless. "Lotte, Cory," he bellows over his shoulder. "We have our first guests."

Ooh dear God.

Like I've taken a bullet straight to the chest, my arm drops to my side and the rest of me almost goes with it. Cory fucking Malkovich, the man I can seemingly not escape, comes strutting in from an office, the woman I now know to be Lotte—former Bears captain Noah Petterson's fiancee—following not long after.

There's not one part of me that can bear looking at Cory right now, so I focus on the blonde I have no inappropriate sexual attraction to. Surprisingly, it's not a chore. There is simply no other way to describe her but adorable. Her blonde locks are piled on the top of her head in a high pony Ariana Grande would be proud to call her own. The cutest plaid skirt and pink sweater I've ever seen covers her tiny frame, and her eyes are so big and wide, it's almost comical. From what I've been told, Lotte is part owner of this rink, and started inclusive skate and hockey programs for kids a few months back. This is their first such class for adults. I have no clue why the hell Cory, wearing a beanie he has no right looking so hot in, is here and quite frankly I don't care.

I really. Truly. Don't.

Not one bit.

There's only four participants in this first session and they and their families arrive at the same time that Lotte and what's-his-face make it to where we are sitting.

Shit I'm sitting. I didn't even realize.

Lined up before us are skates, four adult-sized skate training stands, some skate sleighs, grips, a collection of fidget and sensory toys piled into a basket, and Cory in obscenely tight athletic pants. I don't need to look at him to know he's smirking at me. I can sense it.

"Welcome everyone," Brady says, of course with a grin. "I'm Brady. This is Lotte, and this is Cory. Who's ready to have some fun?"

"I'm ready to leave," I mutter. "Does that count?" Faith, who's sliding off the seat to help Dylan into his skates, whacks me in the calf. "Ow, what was that for?"

"You know exactly what it was for. Stop being a whiny bitch and help me."

Brady hears this, and barks out such a rough cough of laughter, I fear he may choke on his tongue. "Faith!"

"You hear what I have to put up with, Brady?" I pout. "She's spending too much time around you hockey boys. Anyone would think you're a bad influence."

"I'm sure I can handle the Bears. After all, I survived you and your flow in our teens." In my periphery I see Cory's jaw drop as he trips onto the ice, righting himself just before he face plants. Until now, Brady and the coaching team have been the only ones to know I'm an ex-player. Guess the secret's out.

It takes longer than one might imagine to get Dyl's skates on, partly because of fitting his AFO's, ankle and foot orthotics, and partly because he's so excited. Though he hasn't been in months, he always loved skating and time hasn't seemed to have dulled his enthusiasm. There was a time where I used to bring him along with me to practice, but when I quit playing, I couldn't handle being at the rink. Once again, it fell to Dad who stepped in, instinctively knowing what he needed to do.

I'd kill for a sliver of that intuition right now.

Within a second of Dylan's helmet being fitted, he's off, knocking Faith to her ass in his bounding toward the gate.

Shit.

We should have divided and conquered. I should have got my own on while Faith helped Dyl. "It's our first time." Faith reminds me as I drop to a knee, cursing under my breath as I struggle with my laces. "Next time we'll know." Panic surges, Dylan, or someone else could get hurt and it will be my fault. But when I raise my eyes I see my freak out may be premature.

At center ice, smack-bang on the face-off spot is Cory and my big brother, holding hands, spinning in slow clockwise circles. In silence we watch and wave, Faith clinging to my leg like I'm the only thing telling her this is real. "Always clockwise," she eventually giggles, wiping a tear from her cheek. "Look at him. He's so happy. I think he's humming every time you wave to him."

She's right. He is. Dylan's smile is wide and contagious, as is Cory's. I'm not sure how long I squat on the floor watching them, but enough time has passed for Lotte, Brady, and the three other skaters to have joined them. They're not who I can't take my eyes from though. On their next pass, Cory shoots me a cheeky wink.

My heart does a slow, painful clench.

Oh dear.

"Why Doc. Plum. I do believe you've been keeping secrets." Exhausted but not yet willing to leave the ice, Dylan happily piled his long legs into the skate sled I'm pushing, snuggling beneath the blanket, while the ever cheeky Cory glides backwards alongside us. He's tried to get me alone several times over the course of the morning, and I've avoided each attempt like I would a sex talk from my Nanna. "You used to play hockey?"

Ignoring his scent, which today for some reason is giving fresh raspberries *and* mint, I nod. "I did, yes. A long, long, long, time ago." This confirmation has Cory practically levitating. "And I wasn't keeping secrets, it just seemed irrelevant."

"Irrelevant? How could hockey ever be irrelevant? That's like saying Spider-Man's web slinging is insignificant."

The mask of indifference I struggle to maintain around this infuriatingly likable man, slips. "Careful, Mr. Malkovich. Your inner nerd is showing."

"I know." He grins. "Just giving you the authentic experience you seemed to enjoy it last night." Noticing Dylan raising, opening and closing his hand, I come to a gentle stop and pass the water bottle sitting in the holder down to him.

"He does that when he's thirsty?" Cory asks.

"Yep, it's that for *drink*, and he'll tap his chin when he's hungry."

"Hungry and thirsty," he says, repeating the gestures. "Thirsty, hey Dyl. Ya know, I get that feeling a lot around your bro."

Ignoring his flirting, I point my right index finger and poke it into my left palm. "And this one, means toilet."

Back at the handles, we set off again albeit a little haphazardly as I use one hand to dab the perspiration building on my brow.

Not an impending anxiety attack. Or fatal heart infliction, I remind myself. It's the too close presence of a certain blonde. "About that, last night I mean. How were things when you got home? Did you have the chance to talk to your mom?"

"Nope. She was asleep, or pretending to be, and she was gone before I woke up. Pops, my grandpa, basically lives with us, but he's suddenly taken a vow of silence. My sister Cherry's as clueless as I am and Billie is a baby and can't talk."

"Billie is Cherry's daughter, and she's the one that called to check on you?" Much to Dylan's delight, Cory nudges me from the sleigh handles, and pushes off on another lap of the rink.

"He is. It was, and yeah, she's my twin sister."

"I have a sister!" *You're a fucking idiot.*

Doing an impressive job of suppressing his laughter, Cory simply smirks, and points to Faith. "I know. I've met her. Many times. You've met mine too. At O'Reilly's, actually. In the parking lot."

"That was your sister? But you—"

"Called her sweetheart? Yeah. Your affection for Faithy inspired me. And hey, you can't blame a guy for trying to make another guy jealous now, can you?"

It's perhaps for the best that Dylan chooses this moment, as I ride the precipice of return flirting, to declare he wants out of the sled. Discontent humming can quickly escalate so I nod towards the bench, and follow Cory who gets the message and leads us off the ice.

I'm incredibly impressed, and to be honest, kind of turned on by Cory's obvious talent for working with people. He oozes empathy and there's been no hint of patronization in his conversations with those he's supporting. I have questions a plenty concerning how he came to work here, and regarding his family, but none of it's verbalized because Faith stops before us and gets to work un-bundling Dyl from the blanket he's cocooned in.

"How was that, Dyl?" she asks as the first skate thuds to the ground. "I can't believe how long you lasted. Would you like to come back next week?" Pleased to almost be free, he rocks back and forth in his seat, eyes bright as he nods.

"You held up much better than your brother did," Cory

adds. "I thought we might have to roll you out of the sled and lift him in." Dylan and Faith find this hilarious of course, but in truth he's not far off the mark.

"Skating is harder than I remember. The ice is, too. My ass is killing me." It's out before I can stop it. There's some gentle snorting, and no one says anything, but if Cory's right eyebrow goes any higher, it'll be the first inhabitant of Mars.

Even though Dylan wanted out of the sled, he also doesn't want to walk, so after a mad dash to Faith's car, I return with the wheelchair we carry for such an emergency. The three Green Line staff help us carry our things back out, Lotte and Brady helping load the trunk while Faith and Sue help Maria, and Cory assists me to transfer Dyl from the chair into the backseat. Once that's accomplished, everyone seems suitably exhausted.

"Thank you for being our first clients," squeaks Lotte, who's clearly fatigued but also beaming and bouncing on the balls of her toes. "The grant we've received allows each participant ten free sessions, so we hope you'll all be back for lots more fun."

"And if you're ever interested in a private session, let me know," Cory whispers, foot tapping against mine. "Maybe I can help loosen those glutes."

"How slutty a short can I get away with at an official team event? I mean, Coach did mention Speedos, but I'm pretty sure he was joking." Wiping the drool from Billie's chin, Cherry looks me up and down, her disapproving scowl rendering reply unnecessary, yet unstoppable.

"Not that slutty." She holds Billie with one arm, and wriggles on her stomach to the now substantial pile of clothes littering my bed, digs around, and pulls out the red pair of Adidas shorts James saw me jogging in. The ones I bought purely because Harry Styles was wearing a pair on Instagram. "Try these."

"Can't. Wore them the other day."

"Who cares. No one will remember. Besides, the vertical stripes might make your legs look longer."

I should probably be insulted by that, but her point is valid. Ducking into the bathroom, I slide the yellow pair off and slip on the red. Dammit she was right.

"You were right," I confess, even though feeding her massive ego is never a good thing. "Look at these stems. Trust Harry to deliver an elongation revelation."

"Harry and me. Hey, that's got a nice ring to it. Also, speaking of rings, imagine if you and Plum got married, and me and his sister got married. We could have a double wedding." I stop flexing my calves in the mirror and lock eyes with Cherry.

"Okay, so let's grab that thought, and dissect it a little. One, I am never, ever going to get married. Two, James and I aren't fucking, or dating, yet alone engaged, and thirdly, last time I checked, you weren't queer."

"True, but if anyone could make me consider it, an intelligent, sexy blonde like Faith Plum could."

"Wait?" I drop the crop sleeveless tee I'm holding to my chest. "How do you even know what she looks like?"

"Ahh, there's this little thing called the internet. And phones have these apps, and you can find and stalk people like professors and plump-assed physiotherapists via them."

Oh good lord.

"Please tell me you didn't follow and like."

"Okay, I didn't."

"You did, didn't you?"

"Little bit, yeah."

"Cherry!" Sweeping her daughter off the bed, she's halfway out of my room, laughing like a possessed hyena when the heavy thud of the front door silences us both. Mom has been going AWOL anytime she suspects Cherry and I will be home. Everywhere you look, lies evidence she's been here, meals cooked and packed in the fridge, laundry folder atop the dryer, notes to say Miffy's been walked, but neither Cherry or I have laid eyes on her since news of the mortgage debacle broke.

Last night, we set a trap for her bringing Pops in as an unknowing accomplice. I told him I had to be at the Bears car wash by eight, and Cherry had a shift starting at nine. Worked like a charm. She may abandon her grown children, but never Billie.

As quiet as Cherry and I can be, we sneak down stairs, me tossing on my cropped tee as I go, Cherry plastering a hand over her mouth to stem her giggles. For a beat or two, all is quiet, then distinct Mom sounds drift up from the kitchen. "Remember, it could be Pops," Cherry warns. "No jump scares. We don't want him dropping dead on us."

"It's not Pops," I whisper. "Listen, she's humming ABBA. Pops hates ABBA."

Cherry freezes. "How do you recognize ABBA after like two bars and from here?"

"Hello!" I pop my hip and poke at my exposed belly button. "Feel free to apply stereotypes in this instance."

We make it to the kitchen just as Mom hits the bridge of *Honey Honey.*

Called it.

"Play it cool, sis. We don't want to scare her off. She may be old but she's quick and close to the back door."

"Right." Cherry nods, placing Billie in her baby-jail. About three seconds later, she leaps through the archway screaming, "MOMWHERETHEFUCKHAVEYOUBEEN?" The poor woman drops her still steaming cup of coffee and does indeed make a break for the door. I'm younger and faster, and beat her there. Cherry remains where she is, so now she's trapped.

"We know you're a proud, independent woman, but we also know about the mortgage," I say.

"And we want to help," adds Cherry. "But you have to be honest and tell us everything."

We say with perfect twin synchronicity that makes me cringe. Looking eerily similar to a meerkat, Mom's head twitches back and forth between us, before she deflates and collapses onto a stool. In all my life I think I've seen Mom cry maybe five times, so when tears descend down her cheeks, the same happens on mine.

"Your dad left me with so much debt. Every month for years I had to decide what bill I could afford, but the longer I took to pay things off, the more interest accrued. Eventually I couldn't keep up, so I found a mortgage broker on Craigslist. I'd never heard of balloon payments. I didn't understand and now ... I just never wanted you to know."

Cherry and I crowd around, then fold over her like petals closing over a bloom at dusk. "We can help you Mom. You just have to let us. If you hadn't been hiding you'd know I got a job and—"

"No." With surprising strength, she pushes us off her and stands. "That's enough. Next year you'll be gone and I'll have no say in what you do. But this year you're mine, and you have school and hockey, and that's it. No job."

I fold my arms over my chest. "Sorry to muff your huff, but I really like what I'm doing and even if I wasn't getting paid, I'd work as a volunteer."

"Pfft," Cherry scoffs, "wonder why."

"No volunteering either." I jump a little as Mom slaps her palm onto the bench top. "School and hockey. That's it."

"Um, hello. What about me? Can I quit too?"

"Cherry," I whine. "I think you're forgetting the point here. We're supposed to be chipping in, not mooching even more."

"Oh, right. Forgot, sorry." Cherry's stupidity is enough to have a little light emerge in Mom's downcast expression.

"I've made many mistakes in my time, but you two idiots are the best of them."

The hint of resignation makes that the best backhanded compliment I've ever received. It would be so easy to take that opening, and slap the puck home, but years of experience has taught me the wisdom in holding out for the right time to shoot.

"Can this idiot make you some breakfast?" Until now she's been avoiding my gaze, but she looks at me then, really takes me in for the first time since we ambushed her, and every speck of color in her face drains. "Cory, what in the hell are you wearing? God help me our Lord and Savior, is this what you're doing now? Is this your job? You're some kind of male gigolo?"

"Ma!" Caught somewhere between horror and hilarity, Cherry gasps but crosses her legs like she might pee her PJ's. Personally I find it too funny to be insulted ... maybe a bit of a compliment too. So once I stop laughing and regain the ability to breathe, I run my hands over my stomach and give my tight, exposed abs a slap.

"Hot right? The team car wash is today and we're slutting it up to bring in the male attracted gals, gays, and theys." And the gaze of a certain team physio I'm not sure will even be there.

If the curled lip is anything to go by, Mom's still not impressed. "And Coach Harris knows about this?"

"About the car wash, yes. That was his idea. The skin show? That's all me."

"I massively underestimated how many people have dirty cars. Do you think they're just here for us?"

"They are, I think I like it. I mean I feel cheap, but in a good way."

"I never expected the filth in the driver's minds would be far more disgusting than the grime stuck to their tires."

"I fucking love this!"

Lucas. Evan. Elliot. Sam. Me.

Five young men in their prime. Five grossly different attitudes to life.

The sun is shining. The birds are chirping. And there's a line of cars two blocks long waiting to be washed. Most cleaning equipment was dispensed within the first twenty minutes, with all customers choosing the top priced Man-wash over the regular sponge variety.

"If we do this every weekend, we'll get three grand in no time. Hell, we might even make it today." Lucas and Sam's eyes widen as they both give me a high five. I think it's because of my brilliant off the cuff math, but it's not.

"Cubby, look who's here." The jubilation spreading on Sam's face has me spinning as though I'm on ice. It's going to be Cherry. I know it.

But it's not. It's another of my favorite fruits. James Plum in a navy tee that stretches delectably across his broad chest, and shorts that would cover my knees, but on him sit sinfully high on his tanned, muscular thighs. And not just any shorts, they're pale blue, almost white velvet shorts for what's essentially a water sport. He's either feeling very brave, stupid or flirtatious. A million scenarios and positions I would like to see those legs in are playing in my mind when Sam and Lucas' reactions block them out.

"Hey, why did you point James out to me like that?"

"Like what?" Lucas replies coyly.

"Like he was the last empty life raft on the Titanic and—"

"And you wanna ride him?" Sam finishes. This time, I dodge their gleeful high fives, because *what the fuck?*

Deciding to say just that, I do. "What the fuck?" I hiss, teeth gritted. "What are you even talking about? I do not want to ride—"

"He's behind you."

"—James, hey. So glad you could make it." *Yeah, 'cause you're running the show, you dick.* I nervously attempt to push up glasses I'm not wearing, and change to running my hands through my hair at the last second. This man has me twisted.

"Looks like you've stirred quite the hornets nest." He slides his sunglasses down his nose, critically eyeing Sam whose abs are currently scrubbing over the front window of a Volkswagen Beetle.

"Traffic's backed up for miles." Those eyes then turn to me, and I can practically feel the heat singeing the hair from my body. My shorts are wet, really wet and possibly a little see-through. I'm wearing black boxer briefs beneath them, but still. Not a lot is left to the imagination. When his gaze makes its way back to my face, it lingers on the lips I just happen to be biting. "And I think I know why."

I should not have come here. I definitely shouldn't have worn these shorts, and I super extra triple shouldn't have let my eyes navigate Cory's wet body like Columbus did the Atlantic.

I already can't stop thinking about slash jerking off in the shower, in bed, and regrettably behind my locked office door while thinking of him. If things keep going the way they are, I'm going to be severely dehydrated and have crippling RSI.

Oh, and no job.

Why did I listen to Faith? "You need to be part of the team." She insisted. "I saw how much you enjoyed talking with Brady and Cory. Put yourself out there, get to know them. You can't lock yourself up in the basement forever."

With the thoughts of a certain young winger I've been having of late, isolated in a dungeon is exactly where I deserve to be.

I'm a staff member in a position of trust. Cory is a student. This ... whatever this fantasy is, it can't happen. Yet still, I find myself protective, maybe even jealous of the female hands reaching from windows, roaming his stomach, their eyes ogling those nipples pressed against the glass, wet and juicy.

I have been known to become obsessive, going through periods of fixation with songs, or a movie—Hairspray for example—and occasionally people. Not to a weird stalker extent or anything, it all stays in my head. But yeah. It can be problematic. Like it was with Brandon. Distance from that relationship has left me wondering if I was truly in love, or if he was just another fixation. A costly one at that.

Watching Cory now, what I feel, feels different.

Physicality has a lot to do with my admiration. As do his hockey skills, because there's nothing more attractive than a man confident in his abilities, and on the ice, Captain Cory is confidence-personified. But the overwhelming issue, the most complex complication is far more difficult to ignore.

I like that he's figuring himself out and I'm willing to take chances in that process.

I like that he's open to new things.

I like his tenacity.

I like his ridiculous wardrobe.

I like him.

Worse than that I care about him. After I took him home, sleep evaded me 'til the wee hours. The plight of his family consumed my thoughts. Hockey is an expensive sport. One I gave away to spare my family the burden of cost, but I could only do that because I overheard my dad. Cory's never been given that chance to do the same or even chip in, which in truth is both a blessing and a curse. As much as it would have helped his family, I would hate to see him face a decision like I did. Would hate to see the world deprived of his talent.

Perhaps the situation isn't as dire as his sister made out. He seems happy enough today. Then again, I've the feeling even with the weight of the world on his shoulders, Cory would stand taller than ever, like the load was nothing more than a mere feather.

I like that, too.

"You going to stand around looking pretty or are you going to help?"

I jump, but can't stop my smile from spreading. Maintaining my Mr. Grumpy persona around this team is becoming harder and harder.

"Morning, Brady." Turning to greet him, I come face to face with not only Brady, but his partners Quinn and Troye.

"Plummy, you've met Quinny, but this is Troye." Troye commands my hand as Brady continues. "James is Faith's brother and the Bear's new student physio." On the best of days meeting a colleague's partner can be daunting, but I've got two for one, one being a NHL rookie, the other my boss's daughter. I hope the fuck Cory doesn't come over here. I don't think I'm strong enough to take in that belly button under so much scrutiny. So yeah, I perform the perfunctory handshake then freeze. Thankfully, of the three people before me, Brady seems the most introverted and practically Miley Cyrus compared to me.

"Dad never shuts up about you and your magic hands, James. Apparently his shoulder hasn't felt so good since he was a rookie."

Under the gaze of six intensely focused eyes, I drop my head and nod. "It's all in the stretching."

"Don't be so modest. Plummy." I roll my eyes at Brady's nick name. "He's a muscle relaxation demon. I've never seen someone so flexible. Used to be a goalie, too."

"Is that so? Always been a big fan of flexible goalies." Smirks Troye before sending a heated look and wink, I'm almost embarrassed to witness Brady, who the innuendo seems lost on.

"Hey, we should see if Noah and Shane are on for a little three-on-three." He beams. "Shit that would be great."

"Yeah. Maybe." While I force a smile, the entirety of my digestive system clenches. A bit of three-on-three does sound fun. A lot if I'm honest. But it's also a terrifying prospect for someone with my level of introversion. It's been years since I played, or since I've spent that amount of time with anyone other than family or colleagues.

Can I be personable for that long? Then there's the … Hmm. Sweat forms on my brow as I self-consciously pat my soft belly. Maybe I could get there early and change before anyone else arrives.

"You okay, Doc?" A freezing cold palm belonging to the last person I need close right now, comes to rest on my forearm, fingers softly tracing a prominent vein. "You look like you're going to be sick."

I feel like it too. "I'm fine. Just skipped breakfast."

"Oh, wait here." With one last caress he jogs over to a pile of backpacks and bags that must belong to the team. When he finds his, a deep red with a pattern similar to that of cobwebs, and jogs back a little awkwardly, body tilting to the right. "I didn't know if we'd get a chance to eat, so I packed some snacks." He unzips the bag, and the reason for his wonky run becomes clear. Inside he has at least a dozen bananas, some protein bars, Gatorade and an assortment of nut snack-packs. Inspecting the collection, Brady chuckles and elbows Troye.

"See what I mean about a natural leader?"

"I do," he replied. "Knew you had it in ya, Cub. This is some A-grade, Noah-level shit."

Adorable is the only word that could describe the blush coloring Cory's cheeks as I pencil in another admirable quality, humility. "The NHL is going to gobble you up." As Brady and Troye continue to heap praise up his ass, it's clear he's as comfortable with attention as I am.

"How is that? The NHL I mean. Even as good as you are, it must be quite the leap from college," I ask Troye while taking a banana and Gatorade from Cory who beams like he just handed me my first born not a snack. That glee, me asking a question, and how fiercely I need to provide a distraction for Cory all taking me by surprise. I really wanted to ask how the team handled his queer, poly-relationship, but it's probably too much for our first meeting.

Considering his reply, Troye's eyes dart to Brady then Quinn, and it takes me a second to grasp why. Brady too, was destined for the big time before repeat concussions last season stole it away. That one look, and the smile and nod Brady offers in reply, conveys so much about their love. It's sweet, I think to myself. Kind of makes me sick.

"Fast," he says eventually. "A scrimmage is as intense as a Bears game, and the pressure you feel the second you slip that jersey on takes some getting used to. Thankfully I'm fucking brilliant, so it's nothing I can't handle."

Opening his own drink, Cory rolls his eyes. "So modest, too."

"Don't pretend you don't love, and miss it, Cubs. But I'm sure having Brades and James around is consolation enough to soothe the wound."

Wait. What?

As though he's thinking the same, Cory looks between us, then over his shoulder, yelling, "What? Oh, yep. Coming," to the no one who called him. With my brain still computing, I'm unable to think, and escape that fast, 'cause again … What? Does Brady, ipso-facto Troye and the rest of Boston know the almost thing Cory and I had? Has Cory got a thing for Brady? Are those shorts, that belly flash. All that flittering around posing in the gym not for my benefit?

That would be a good thing, I remind myself. How it should be.

The light sheen of perspiration dotting my brow upgrades to a torrential downpour blinding me.

Brady, at least I think it's Brady, edges closer, his blurred face scanning over mine. "Don't listen to Troye, Plummy. Cory's not interested in me."

"Or me. He's not interested in me," I insist a little too earnestly. "Why would you think that? That seems highly improbable. Why? Has he said that?"

Even blurred vision can't hide the, yeah right, expression Troye's hitting me with. "Whatever you say, Plummy."

It would be wise of me to shut the fuck up and leave it at that, so naturally. I don't.

"I do say. I am a staff member. Cory is a student. Anything between us would be highly inappropriate." Troye snorts, huffs and makes several other grunt-like noises.

"Look, I know we just met but trust me, anything worth anything is inappropriate."

A light misting of water lands on my shoulder, drawing my gaze to the latest car rolling up to be washed. Evan is waving, guiding them into position as though he's directing a 747 not a Jeep. Cory's beside him, bending forward at the waist, mouth open swallowing the water flooding in from the hose poised at his lips. I know full-well this is for show. A literal thirst trap designed to fill the tip jar that's been upgraded to a bucket. And it's working. His audience, a carload full of squealing college girls, are lapping it up.

As am I.

Lust shoots down my spine, pitching a tent in shorts. These shorts aren't built to shelter. There's a bucket beside me, so I snatch it up and hold it over my … situation.

"See what I mean." Troye smirks. "Appropriateness is highly overrated."

Disregarding the smirked looks he, Quinn and Brady send me each time I'm within a foots radius of Cory, I linger at the car wash like a bad smell of absolutely no use until the very last bumper is buffed.

"Thanks for helping out." Rosy-cheeked and wet from head to toe, Cory looking like every wet dream I'll have from here on in, has found his way to my side.

"Fairly certain you would have managed without me. I filled your bucket—I mean the buckets. I filled the ... Shit." Cory grins like I just handed him the Stanley Cup.

"And you looked so good doing it. I'm very impressed with your hose handling." In another totally unwarranted thirst trap, he then runs his hand through his soaked hair, shakes the water from his hand and grabs his phone from his backpack, fingers flying over the screen.

"Hot date waiting?" I ask nosily.

"Pfft. Nope. Not really interested in dating right now."

"No?"

Brow cocked, he grins again. "No. I'm ordering an Uber."

That should be it. I should wish him a good day and walk away, but instead I find myself tapping his foot with my own and opening my damn mouth. "Want a ride home? Maybe we can grab some food."

"Yeah?"

"Yeah, why not?" There's a million *why-not's* forming a cue in my mind, but as I seem to do so often around this man, I pay them no attention. "Better to use that money on filling your belly than someone else's gas tank."

Cory wets his lips and slides his phone into his pocket. "Since you're so heavily invested in filling things today, let's do it, Doc."

Rolling my eyes, I nod in the direction of my car and get moving, the stupidity of this decision sinking in with each step. Cory falls into step beside me, working hard to keep up with my longer strides. "Why the uber?" I ask, choosing a safe subject. "No electricity at home to charge the beast?" The second it's out I regret it. *They're having money issues, idiot. Way to taunt him.*

"No power issues, just sister ones … well, technically car ones. Hers has been playing up since I drove it to Canada, so she took mine because it's my fault, and she didn't want to take my baby niece to daycare in an Uber." I stop mid-step, causing Cory, who was so close, to slam into me.

"You have a baby niece?"

"I do. Well, technically she's a toddler not a baby, but yeah. She'll always be my Baby Billie."

"Huh." My feet decide to move again, but my brain is still stuck calculating. Cory's twenty-one. At what age does a baby become a toddler?

"If that constipated face is you doing the math, she was nineteen." I feel my cheeks heat

"Sorry, it's none of my business."

"It's not, no. But it's no secret either. Cherry had been in love with the same boy since she was twelve. Derek was a few years older than her, but his family left town when she was fifteen. He moved back when she was old enough, and they got back together straight away. They were really happy … until she told him she was pregnant."

We reach my car and he folds his surprisingly long legs into the passenger seat. Slumping his head against the seat he turns to face me.

"Didn't take it well?"

"No he didn't. Neither did his wife. The one he already had a kid with." His clear outrage when he thought Dylan was my son, suddenly makes sense.

"Shit."

"Yeah, shit."

We drive in silence until Cory points out a small Italian place a block or two from his family home. "You won't find better pasta anywhere in Boston."

Great. A sit-down meal. I should be insisting on a quick drive-thru burger—In 'n' Out—in more ways than one.

"Italian sounds good."

I *talian sounds good.*

As we scour the menu in the near-empty restaurant, James's expression says otherwise. Perhaps it's the romantic mood lighting, or the instrumental jazz that's causing those adorable frown lines to pop. Either way, I'm not mad about it.

"What are you in the mood for?" I ask, hoping his answer aligns with what I want. A special something that's definitely not an option.

"Arrabbiata, I think," he replies without lifting his eyes. "You?"

"Well suck me sideways. I was thinking the same. I love a bit of heat." James rolls his eyes for at least the tenth time today. "They'll get stuck at the back of your head if you keep doing that." He's reaching for the hand made bread that Gwen, my favorite waitress, left us, but pauses and scowls. "Doing what?"

"Rolling your eyes, all sassy-like when I'm flirty."

"You're being flirty? Sorry I hadn't noticed."

Flailing dramatically, I clutch at my chest, while also accidentally on purpose rubbing my leg against the inside of his. "You're brutal, Doc. I like it." *I like you.* "Maybe I'll have to try a little harder."

"Maybe you will."

"Ready to order, gentlemen?" Gwen, the cock-blocker, who's suddenly not my favorite, smiles down at me.

"I'll—"

"Hmm hmm." Clearing his throat, James places a hand over

mine, pointing to the menu with the other. It's such a masculine, dominating move and my dick likes it. "We'll both have the Arrabbiata, and maybe a serve of Zuppam and truffle-parmigiano fries to share."

"Excellent, and can I get you something else to drink?"

"Just water?" Hand still holding mine, he checks for consent with a look he has no right delivering in public. Or, maybe it's just a normal glance, and I'm kind of obsessed. Either way, I nod, and am lucky to manage that. With his whole face, and warm leg against mine, his hand, his ... him. Fuck, it's too much.

Gwen takes the menus and heads to the kitchen, leaving me reeling, swooning and realizing, this is no hook-up. This could be something real.

James is a man. A real man. And right now in his presence, I feel every bit the kid he insists on calling me.

I am in way over my head.

WE SAT in that restaurant for two hours, just shooting shit about family, comics and hockey. I've never been so turned on by conversation, or watching someone eat.

Now I'm back in reality. Back to pretending it's not the gaze of James and James alone I feel, as Coach Harris paces before us, face shifting between pride and annoyance.

I wish it was just me and James again. That he was about to chew me out instead of Coach.

"Boys, I'm not sure how you managed it, or if I approve of the methods, but with one Sunday and a lot of skin, you raised more than double the target." A stick tapping chant of NO MORE SUNDAYS, echoes around the rink, but such is the power of our leader, silenced falls on the rise of a single hand. "Not so fast." Merriment turns to fear, the sound of twenty smiles dropping to pouts almost deafening.

Coach pulled me aside when I arrived, so I know what's coming.

They're right to sulk.

"I expected the fundraising effort to take longer, and because I'm fucking brilliant, I'd already planned ahead."

"What does that mean?" Trent says, 'cause he's a dick who never shuts up.

"What it means, Hoffman, is I've got you for one more Sunday"

Trent's fists clench and doubling over like he was just sucker-punched in the guts is a tad dramatic. "This is bullshit." Okay, so he's a dumb, pathetic dick. Just as I suspected.

Coach outright ignores Trent's flailing, and continues, "Right, so, one more Sunday means more money for charity, which, despite what some think, is always a good thing. Now, warm up, ladies, then pair off for some two-man passing, let's go."

Behind me, Trent is losing his tiny mind. "I hate that guy. How is him underestimating us our problem?"

I shrug. "Just lucky, I guess."

"Yeah?" Falling behind, he presses his palm into my spine and shoves. "Well as long as you know you're never getting lucky with me, you little cocksucker."

I'm able to steady myself, and mean to shove him right back, But before I can, Lucas is holding me back, and Sam's in Trent's face. "What did you say, Hoffman?"

"You heard me, *Sammy*. I called your little boyfriend a cock-sucker." Ducking his head around Sam's wide frame, he glares, hate coloring his eyes. "Or does he prefer Fairy?" His crew of D-men idiots group around him, and I fear this is going to spiral out of control. I need to be the one to end it. I'm the captain. But for some reason, my voice, and nerve fails me. "Deny it all you like, *Cubby*. But we all saw your little outfit yesterday. No straight dude dresses like that."

Once again, it's Sam, who's as much a fighter as I am seven foot tall, who defends me when I can't. "You've seen Cory at O'Reilly's. The bunnies love him. He's not gay." He protests, fists bunching Trent's jersey beneath his chin. "But even if he was, so the fuck what? Doesn't mean he'd be interested in your dumb ass."

Three short, sharp whistles ring out, and James' baritone

voice then Hulk-like frame steps in, pulling the boys apart as easy as he would do two slices of bread. "We got a problem here, gentlemen?"

"No problem," I rush to answer, ignoring the daggers Sam and Lucas are shooting my way. "Sam was just helping Trent with his pads. They got a little twisted."

"Okay then. Now that they're un-twisted, get to center ice. Go," he snaps, when no one moves. There's no way he's buying that, but he nods and skates away regardless, Trent and cronies shadowing.

Sam gives me a nudge with his shoulder. "Just ignore him. We know you're not a—"

"Not a, what?" I snap, stupidly misdirecting my contempt. "Not a queer. A poof? Well what if I was? Would you be so quick to defend me then?"

"Yeah, I would, because it's no ones' business but yours, and because you're my captain, and my friend. At least I hope you are."

"What he said." Lucas nods, before shrinking under James' distant glare and skating toward him. For a physio, he's pretty fucking terrifying. And I'm pretty fucking confused.

"Since when have you, frat-boy-jock Sam, the most popular sophomore on campus, considered me a friend?" Sure he's friendly enough here at practice, and the few times we've hung at O'Reilly's. But there's a big difference between teammates and friends. Then it hits me. "This 'cause of my sister, isn't it? You were flirting with her—"

"No!" He blushes. "No. I mean, yes, I was flirting with her 'cause she's hot, but no, I didn't do that because of her. I like you, is all. You're cool, Cubs."

"Me?"

"Bro, is there someone else here?" Checking over each shoulder, he laughs. "Yeah you. Why is that so hard for you to believe?"

"Because literally no one, not ever, has ever said, implied or thought that."

"That's not true," he counters. "Lucas thinks the ice he skates on flows from your ass."

"That's because Lucas is as big a dork as me."

Sam laughs again, recapturing the attention of James, whose furrowed brows give a silent, shut the fuck up and get out here, look. One that Sam hears too.

"Looks like we're a team, Cubs," he says, nodding towards the pairs already shooting, then holding out his gloved fist. "Buddies?"

"Buddies."

MAYBE IT WAS the knowledge that I had a friend or two on the team looking out for me; the constant heat of James' gaze; or the stupidity of my showboating to keep it, but even for me, someone who loves hockey and practice even on the shittiest of days, today was extra fun. Sam and Lucas shadowed me, making sure their bodies were always between Trent's and my own, but when Coach pulled them aside to work on their edge work, he struck.

Not satisfied with chirping as we competed during the final scrimmage, the asshat decided to check me into the boards. Aiming to protect my head, which was down over the puck, I had just enough time to slightly twist, allowing my shoulder, rather than my neck, to take the brunt of the impact. It worked, so I don't have a concussion, but the radiating pain is so intense, I can hardly raise my arm to tug my jersey over my head.

"You right, Cubs? I could feel that shoulder crack over here." Sam's watching, eyes assessing.

"Yep. I'm good."

I'm not good. No part of this is good. I should most definitely get it looked at, but the thing is, it will be James' hands checking me over. James' hands oiling me up and rubbing me down, potentially while Coach White watches on. While my inner slut insists he is the best thing that's ever happened, there's an annoying voice of reason, the anti-slut, that's drowning him out.

Sam, Lucas, Brady and Troye. They're all on to me. Coach White can't be next.

I genuinely thought I could flirt my way back into James' bed without anyone noticing.

I was wrong.

It won't stop me of course. I'm no quitter. It just means I have to play my legs a little close to my chest, instead of laying them on his table, and spreading them wide.

Cards, I mean. Cards. Not legs.

As though summoned by my pain, James approaches, the stiff cotton of his pants fighting to contain those thick thighs as he ducks in front of me. "You okay?"

"Better now you're here?" I wink. My cockiness lasts about two seconds, because I try taking off my jersey again, and almost puke.

"You're hurt." It's a statement. Not a question and so gruffly announced I can't help but laugh.

"You seem personally offended by that."

"Not at all. I'm just curious as to why you wouldn't tell someone. Even if you're not comfortable coming to me, you need–"

"Why wouldn't I be comfortable coming to you?"

Slowly, like speaking to me is pure agony, he groans and runs a hand over his face. "Because of our ... history," he says, voice low. Sexy. "You're not comfortable with me working on you."

"Is that so?" I try again to tug my jersey off, but pain spears along the top of my shoulder, and collar bone then up into my neck. "Hockey players are infamously hesitant to declare themselves injured. Maybe I'm just a dumb jock who doesn't want to miss any ice time?"

"I think we both know you're not dumb."

"Aww, thanks, Plummy."

"What is dumb," he continues, cheeks flushed, "is hoping pain goes away when simple treatments could ensure it will, and prevent it getting worse."

In my periphery I see Brady counseling his proteges Nurse and Larsson. As goalies quite often are, they're the last to undress, everyone else already being in the showers. How Brady dealt with, or didn't, deal with his injuries altered the course of his future. I don't want that. And with Mom struggling financially the way she is, *we* can't afford it either.

I drop my head, roll my shoulder and wince as pain slices through me. "It feels weird. Kind of numb and tingly, but it hurts. Bad."

"And when did it start?"

"When Hoffman boarded me. Straight away it felt like my arm was pushed down, or further inside me."

Palms flat on his thighs, James pushes to stand. "That doesn't sound dumb, but it does sound like it needs investigating. Coach White's gone, so..." He then reaches out, offering me his right hand, to my uninjured left. "Will you let me help?"

I want to take his hand, like really, really badly, but something's stopping me. Leaning forward, I whisper, "It's a matter of trust."

James snorts and squats again. "Okay, Billy Joel."

"Who?"

"Nothing," he huffs, blush spreading down his neck. "Looking the way you do, I forget you're a kid sometimes." I can tell he regrets it as soon as he's said it, and the air between us thickens as a result.

"I'm not a kid."

"You don't trust me, then?" he counters.

"I do trust you, Jamie. I just don't trust myself."

F aith is the only one I've ever tolerated calling me Jamie. I don't like it. Never have and thought I never would, but seeing the word form and roll from Cory's sassy mouth, almost had me flopping face first into the floor. Doc was one thing. But him. Saying Jamie?

Yeah. That's hot.

Throughout the six years it's taken me to complete my training, I've seen and worked on dozens of attractive, near-naked men. None of them have prompted the visceral reaction Cory Malkovich doing nothing but sitting on the edge of my table, legs innocently swinging, has.

Hard as stone and struggling to breathe, all I can think of is an episode of Friends. Phoebe, a massage therapist, loses control of her unyielding desire, bends down and bites the plump ass of her client. Never in my life have I identified more with a straight woman.

I feel you, Pheebs. I feel you.

"Is there a problem, Doc?"

Yes. You. Inhaling through puffed cheeks, I raise my gaze stopping just short of meeting my off-limits patients'. "Nope, not at all. Just giving that ice a little time to reduce any swelling, and the heating to warm the room up." Liar. "Does your movement feel any freer?" Grimacing, Cory gives his shoulder a slight forward roll.

"It does, a little yeah."

"Good. Well, let's get that shirt off and have a look." The words are out there, but my feet aren't listening.

After way too long, Cory gives a huffed laugh. "I'm no medical expert, but I think you need to come closer to do that."

"I do. Yeah. It's just."

"You don't trust yourself either?" There's two ways to go here. One, be the dismissive jerk that comes so easily. Or two, be the person Cory has an uncanny ability to draw out of me.

"Little bit, yeah."

Caught off-guard by my confession, Cory's brows raise and his teeth sink into that bottom lip I keep picturing smeared in last night's white pasta sauce. "Well, I trust you, remember? So we're all good."

Nodding, I release another ridiculously large breath and edge forward. Honestly you'd think there was a crocodile waiting for me, not a young athlete I'm treating. "Do you think you're able to remove your jersey?" His eyes say no but he moves his hands to the hem and attempts to lift, managing to raise it only slightly before wincing. Placing my hand on his wrist, I hold him still.

"I can help lift it over your head, but you'd still have to raise your arm. Or—"

"Or you could tear it off with your teeth. Just rip into me like you did that bread last night." Rolling my eyes, I tilt my head to the side.

"Or I could cut it." Mel, the Bears equipment manager won't be happy, but there's no alternative. After searching high and low all I can find is blunt scissors used mainly for cutting dressing. They're useless against the thicker knit fabric of the jersey, and with an exasperated grunt, I give up on them maybe an inch or two in.

Perhaps sensing what's about to happen, Cory watches me silently, knuckles white as he grips the edge of the bed.

Praying for strength, I grit my teeth, fist the fabric on either side of the cut, and tear.

"Jamie, oh God."

"Please don't say, Jamie. Not now. Not like that."

His upper body, still beading in sweat, smelling of man, is so fucking perfect I'm forced to close my eyes before I do something stupid like suck those pretty pink nipples. Blind, I run my hands up, over his abs. Feel every rise and fall of his ribs. Trace the lines of his collarbone and then slip my fingers beneath the fabric and slide it from his shoulders. I don't let go of him though, I just stand there, head low in shame. I'm hard. So fucking hard I think I may faint.

"Look at me, Jamie. Please, open your eyes." Instead of scolding him as I should, I do as he asked, blinking away my blurred vision until I'm staring at Cory's crotch.

He's hard too.

"It feels really good when you touch me, Jamie. Please don't stop."

"I won't," I choke out, voice thick with desire, "but not because you asked me too, but because this is my job. Touching you is my job."

"And you're so good at it. It feels better already."

Christ, this is awful. Just so bloody horrible.

"Good. That's good." I force my lips to say. "Can, uh. Can you show me where it hurts?"

"Here," he says, immediately snatching my hand. For a split second I panic, thinking I know exactly what I'm going to be cupping. But as he has so often, Cory takes me by surprise, placing my flattened palm to his chest. Right over his heart, then laying his hand atop it. "Whenever you're near me my heart races. Can you feel it?"

"I can," I mumble, because I can. I feel the heavy, rapid beat in every one of my fingertips. "Mine is the same."

"Show me." Before I can reply, Cory tightens his hold on me and shifts our joined hands to my right pectoral. "Wow. It's hammering." He smirks. "Tell me, Jamie. Is that pulsing organ the only one I affect?"

"You know you're incredibly corny for someone your age."

"Horny, too, but that's probably to be expected with a man like you wedged between my thighs."

"I'm not—" I pause, look down and shit, I am. In fact, in this position, if Cory wanted, he would wrap his legs around my waist and frot against me until our hard cocks explode. "I need to check your shoulder." It's a reminder for me more than him.

"Fuck my shoulder."

In one swift move, my hand is disregarded, my shirt is clenched and Cory is pulling me down onto his lips. "Jamie."

"Oh, God." I cup my hand around the back of his neck, tightening my hold until I feel my nails dig into his flesh. His fingers are caressing down over my shirt, rucking it up and fiddling with my belt.

"I want to suck you off, Jamie. Please, I can't stop thinking about it."

I should say no. I should step back, walk out of here and never come back. But the whoosh of leather sliding through cotton loops, and the metal clang of my belt buckle hitting the floor knocks any good sense from my mind.

All I can think of is him. All I need is release.

"Fuck, Cubby," I groan, lips ghosting over his while he's sliding off the bed and pushing me back against the wall. "The door. I need to lock ... lock the door."

"Stay there." Releasing his hold, Cory strides across the room, turns the lock and stalks toward me, eyes roaming. before he kisses me one more time, filthy and raw. I never want it to end and whine when he pulls away.

Then drops to his knees. My pants and boxers follow and fuck. It's been so long, so damn long since I've had a man's mouth on me. So long since I've had a tongue working me over, that I almost blow the second he licks the pre-cum from my tip. As warm, wetness wraps around me, I weave my hands into his hair and grip.

"Yes," he moans. "Fuck, yes."

His eyes never leave my face as he deep-throats me, cheeks hollowing out 'til my dick hits the back of his throat, where he contracts again and again.

"Jesus Christ." Inhaling through my nose, I let my head fall back against the wall and thrust, my movements agonizingly slow in respect of my size. Cory, it appears, cares not for such things as consideration and pace. The hand he had resting on my thigh shifts to cup my ass and pull me in. Hard. It's all the permission I need. Every ounce of doubt and stress and tension see my hips pistoning.

There's nothing pretty or romantic here. It's just a sloppy and wet mess of want. A cut and dry race to the end. "I need this," I huff. "I need to fill your pretty mouth."

Gagging, blinking away the tears clinging to his lashes, Cory hums and groans, sucking so hard my kidneys may shoot into his mouth before my cum does. Still watching me, he groans again and palms his cock. The thought of him wanking as he gets me off is all it takes. I tug on his hair in warning but all he does is takes me deeper, constricting more and I spill inside him, the sounds of him swallowing and slurping extending my release. I've never come so much so fast. Or wanted to do it again so quickly.

I watch Cory lick me from tip to base, catching every last drop of cum before letting my softening cock fall from his lips, pressing his face between my thighs and balls and inhaling. "You smell so fucking amazing, James."

"Everything about you is amazing." I blush at my sappiness, but I mean it. Cory Malkovich is nothing like I expected but everything I need.

I just blew the man of my dreams. I'd say it's one of the best days of my life if I hadn't come in my pants like a pimple-faced virgin.

Actually, fuck that. It's definitely the best day of my life, and has given birth to daydreams of a future I never thought I wanted. Cozy dates in tiny restaurants. Holding hands. Hot sex and cuddles after. Okay, I'm getting a little carried away, but how could I not? I'm high as a kite on cloud almost 69. Nothing can ruin this.

"Oh fuck. Oh fuck this is bad."

Okay, maybe *something* could.

I glance up to James, and yep, he looks like he might pass out. His frown is next level. He's freaking out and I need to fix it. "Really, really, really bad."

"But did bad ever feel so good?" I run my hands up over his thick calves. "I like it, James. A lot. This could be a whole new persona for me. Bad Cubby." The twitch at edges of his lips relaxes the knot that frowny face formed in my stomach. "Which means I have to do that again. I need to see that come face at least once more." Climbing off the floor, and onto James' lap, I run my hands over his chest. He moans as my tongue swipes over his bottom lip, then bites my own when I try to pull away.

"Whatboutyou." His words slur together and I feel my cheeks glow like the tip of the Eiffel fucking Tower. *I did that,* I think to myself. *I sucked him stupid.*

"No need. I blew two seconds after you started fucking my

mouth. That was intense, Doc. I'm impressed." His blush deepens and I can't stop myself from tracing his cheek with my thumb. He really is gorgeous.

Unable to resist, I pull him into me for another kiss, clinging onto his neck when he attempts to pull back, a loose smile-the kind I've never seen-softening his face.

I could get used to this.

It's temporary though, and I see the second it clicks, that all *this*, the impressive belt removal, the groping, the squeezing of ass, the current gripping for dear life, has been done with one hand.

"Christ, Cory. Your fucking shoulder."

"It's fine, see." Fighting hard not to wince, I jiggle my arm. "Still there."

"I could have hurt you. Exacerbated the injury."

"But you didn't. In fact, I can't feel a thing." His brows, relaxed a beat ago furrow, and desperation sinks deep into my bones. I know enough of James to understand any dereliction of his duties will send him running to the hills faster than anything else will.

"You will. I haven't even assessed you. Tested your range of movement. This ... this is ... this is why I should never have taken advantage."

Now it's me pulling back. Me who's pissed. "Taken advantage? Who says you've taken advantage of me? Right now there's two of us that know about this and I sure as fuck don't feel a victim here."

"Not the point." Before I can blink, James has his pants up and is furiously scrubbing his hands in the basin, foam halfway up his forearms and splattering over the mirror before him. "If you still trust me, up on the table. If not, I'll go get Coach White." As he speaks, his eyes remain glued to the bubbles sliding down the drain.

"Of course I still trust you. There's no one I trust more."

"Probably not a good idea, Kid."

"I'm not a fucking kid."

"Dammit, don't you think I know that?" Clenching his fists, Jamie glares at me in the reflection and for a second I fear he's going to punch and shatter the glass. Instead he turns and almost tears the paper towel dispenser from the wall. "You think I don't see what kind of man you are? That I don't stay awake at night wanting to do to you what you just did to me?"

I slide off the table I'd just mounted and position myself between James and the door. No way he's escaping. "So we both want the same thing. What's the problem?"

"The problem is, I have two semesters to finish my training and I need to finish it, Cory. I have a family. Responsibilities. Debt coming out of my ass."

"I get that, I do. But why does that mean there can't be a few hundred thousand little mes coming out of your ass at the same time?" Eyes darting between mine, he looks confused, frustrated. As second later his expression switches to one of shock and he barks out a loud, unexpected laugh.

"That's freaking disgusting."

"True though."

It's as he chuckles, I notice what I didn't before. The dark circles marring the skin below his lashes. He looks defeated and suddenly tired. And I feel like shit for adding to his stress. Facing me, James takes a few steps back, turns and all but collapses onto the bed.

Keep your distance, I tell myself. *That's the wise thing to do.* But nobody has ever called me a genius. The intrusive thoughts, the need to touch that tingles the very tips of my fingers has feet thoughtlessly moving 'til I'm back by his side, shoulders and thighs pressed together. "I'm a student, yes. I know it complicates things, but I like you, Jamie. And even though you're hairy and old as fuck—"

"You know, I don't really like the Jamie thing, and I'm barely three years older."

"Whatever, Grampa. As I was saying, I'm more attracted to you than I have been to anyone ... ever. This time next year, if not sooner, I'll be in Canada. So I'm not asking for your hand in marriage here. Just time for some more discreet dinners, and laughs and a lot more coming."

Puffing out his cheeks, something he seems to do as often as he rolls his eyes, he turns slightly then exhales, slow and shaken. "I like you too."

"You do?" I'm caught off-guard, because that's not what I expected. Nor is the edging sideways until our legs squish. Or the hand landing on my thigh, fingers splaying until they cover its entire width. He starts and stops a few times before finally settling on what to say.

"I do. A lot actually. But if life has taught me anything, it's that the old adage, you can't always get what you want, is true. I already feel like I'm trapped in a life I don't want to be mine, and I'm not tying you to a sinking ship. You have too much to look forward to."

Whoa. No one should look or sound this sad so soon after a blow job.

"You may not know this," I say, fingers absentmindedly twirling through the dark hair on his leg, "but in the Marvel Universe there's this concept of the life raft. Mr. Fantastic, Spider-Man, Thor, Captain Marvel, Doctor Strange, and a few others are always on board, and no matter what cataclysmic event occurs, those on the raft will always survive and rebuild. Admittedly, I'm not quite at their level. But I am surprisingly buoyant. Maybe you could try hanging on to me for a little while. See if we can ride the waves together."

Looking slightly less pained, James raises his hand to cup my face, thumb caressing my jaw. His expression is tender, almost *loving*. "Did anyone ever tell you you're a complete nerd?"

I LEFT that treatment room with a suspected grade-one AC joint injury, the taste of James still on my tongue, and enough hope of future hook-ups with my sexy doc to override any pain. Completing the mix of glorious and bad was Coach Harris. He was so pissed at Trent for his overenthusiastic boarding he suspended him from training with the team for a week. For someone like me, that lives and breathes hockey, that would be devastating. For Trent, it was laughable. He couldn't have given a shit and ended up spending a week living it up in NYC.

So no Trent was a major up, but it was all down hill from

there, and further confirmation of my belief that when life feels to good to be true, it's about to fuck you over.

James' original diagnosis of a grade-one AC joint injury was confirmed with scans the next day, and after consulting with the Mounties trainers, Coach White and James gave me the bad news. "We're probably being over cautious, Cubby," White said, empathy warming his tone. "But the Mounties want to make sure you're fully healed before hitting the ice again. We'll keep up the cardio and James will work on some stretching, but—"

"How long?"

"Three weeks, no ice time."

Yup. Devastating.

Twenty-one days meant I'd only be back two weeks before our first game. Today marks the end of week two. I've not laid a hand, or tongue, on James. I can't skate. I've spent three shifts at Green Line assisting from the sidelines, unable to do my job fully, I can't help out Mom around the house like I usually do, and I am climbing the fucking walls.

"What good is a captain who watches on from the bench? He may as well not even be here." Shit attitudes like this aren't helping.

After a really, really, really deep breath, I unclench my fists and respond, "I may not be able to skate, *Trent*. But I can show the freshman the benefits of dedicating to a solid recovery program." I don't actually know if I believe this, but it sounds good. "I can also not be a dick. You should try it sometime." That I do believe. Wholeheartedly.

A rowdy round of Ooooos sees Trent rage-o-meter go from zero to one hundred. "I thought you liked dicks. In fact, I heard you more than love them. I heard you're gagging for them." The team falls silent. All you can hear is the steam erupting from my ears. Or maybe I'm just imagining that.

On my behalf, Sam and Lucas go on the offensive which is great, because I'm too busy being stuck in my own head. Trent's constant gay slurs could be random jabs by a homophobic loser, or he could be onto my secret.

The question is how? I've been super careful at school, making sure I don't hook-up with anyone from BC. And I've not so much as blinked at another guy in the locker room, *which* has been particularly easy because none of the team do it for me, *because* I don't want to fuck every guy that moves, despite what assholes like Hoffman think.

Wait.

Hoffman.

The Mounties.

McKinney.

Our little closet hook-up.

Connor fucking Hoffman.

Fucking fuck.

Panicked and needing confirmation, I toss the iPad I was using to record set play drills onto the bench. It slips off, because of course it does, and lands with a crack on the concrete floor, drawing all eyes to me and the sprint I've broken into. "Look at him run," Trent wheezes with laughter. "Some fucking leader."

Leaving his continued chirps in my wake, I again leave my defense to my teammates and high-tail it to the locker room. Seconds later, my phone is in my hands, and I'm unblocking Nate McKinney's number.

Surprisingly, he answers on the first ring.

"Cory?"

"McKinney, hey. Yeah, it's me, Cory. Sorry to call out of the blue like this but–"

"I thought I must have put your number in wrong," he says excitedly. "Don't be sorry. I'm not. I think about you a lot. All the time, actually. "

Fuck.

"Ahh, that's nice, but I'm seeing someone right now." I wish. "So I'm sorry but I'm just calling to ask you something."

"Oh. Oh, well, okay then. What can I do you for?" He laughs like he's the first person to come up with that, and I remind myself to re-block this number as soon as the call is over.

"Haha, great. Yeah, hey did you tell anyone about our little ... meeting in the cupboard?"

"What? No way, bro. Of course not." There's a long pause, and then. "I mean, well, actually I did tell my cousin, but he's cool. He wouldn't snitch."

"Your cousin named Connor Hoffman?"

"Dude." He laughs. "Did you slip and crack your pretty head? Of course it's Connor Hoffman. Know any others?"

My balls drop to my toes, ready to be ground into dust Fuck. Fuck. Fuck. Fuck.

Hunched over, I toss my phone and try to breathe, the banana I ate mid-training tries to claw its way back out my mouth. Trent Hoffman is going to push me from the closet. Yes, judging by Sam and Lucas' taunting at the car wash, my ass has been sticking out and waving around a lot more than I thought, and also yes, I shouldn't have to hide or be afraid.

But I am.

This is my decision. It's my God damn right to choose when, and to whom I come out too.

In no universe, no timeline or dimension will I let that fucking asshole take that away from me.

Boys. You still awake?

SAM

Ahoy, captain oh, captain. What's up.

LUCAS

Awake but don't want to be.

I know it's late, but can I interest either of you in a beer.

SAM

O'Reilly's?

I'm home with Billie, can you come here? Need some advice.

LUCAS

Who's Billie?

My baby niece

SAM

Wait. Whoa. Wait. You're asking us for advice, to come to your house and you have a niece? Who the fuck is this and what have you done to Cubby?

Haha smartass. Can you come or not? I have beer and nachos.

SAM

And a baby. Be there in 10

LUCAS

Dude, nachos. Make it 5

Not five, but thirty minutes later, I've confirmed that yes, O'Reilly's wasn't a prank. I do indeed wear glasses whenever I'm not with the team, Lucas is neck deep in a pile of cheesy corn chips, and Sam has Billie, who I hadn't been able to settle after her last bottle, bouncing happily on his hip.

Slightly pissed that the kid whose umbilical cord I cut prefers a perfect stranger to me, I scowl and shove a quac-covered chip in my mouth.

"Your screen door's broken? Why don't you fix it?"

"Why are you so good with babies?" I counter, more comfortable with deflecting than answering with, *I tried but it needs to be replaced, and we can't afford a new one.*

With a nonchalant shoulder shrug he swipes a chip, chews and then replies, "I don't have any siblings, and there's no babies in the family, so it's not that. Must just be my natural charm."

"I have one sister. Shit," Lucas slaps his thigh, "a brother, I mean. Riley was assigned female at birth, but came out as trans last year and has just transitioned. I guess I'm still getting used to it." Coyly, he watches us for reaction, fingers digging into the arm of the sofa like he's waiting for a fight. To ease his nerves, I plop next to him and nudge his arm.

"He probably is, too."

"Yeah. It's been hard for him. Some of his friends have been dicks, but he has two friends that have been cool."

Butterflies with wings of lead swarm in my gut. The gay thing suddenly seems an easier mountain to climb than the friend thing. "Can I count on that, too? Having two cool friends?"

Lucas's mouth falls open. "You're trans, too? Shit I thought you were just going to tell us you fucked Plum."

"I'm not trans, dick. I'm gay. And I didn't fuck James, either … I mean I kind of did but—"

"I fucking knew it! You look at him as though it's pitch black, and he's a light switch you're busting to *turn on.*" Dancing eyebrows Sam is so excited, for a second I think he's about to toss my niece in the air, but he settles for a fist pump and light jig that has Billie giggling. Never laughs like that for me, the freaking traitor. "Hand it over, Lucas."

Groaning, Lucas fishes a twenty from his pocket and slaps it in Sam's palms.

"You guys were betting on me? Is it really that obvious?"

"Dude, no offense, but last year, off the ice I could have forgotten you existed."

"Wow, Sam. How could I possibly be offended by that?"

"Wait. You didn't let me finish," he says, biting back laughter. "So yeah, once I remembered you were on the team, I thought you were an uptight ass ... wait ... and *then* magically when Plum shows up, voila! You were like a peacock finally letting those gay as fuck tail-feathers fly. It's beautiful, Bro."

Lucas buries his shaking head in his hands. "I think what the idiot is trying to say is you've come out of your shell since James arrived, and that the way you want to bone him is totally obvious. Can't say I agree with all of it, since I wasn't here, but yeah, I think that's the point."

"A hundred percent my point." Sam nods. "And we're absolutely your friends. As such, we should celebrate. Who's up for O'Reilly's?" I point towards the baby currently sucking on one of his black ringlets, eyes finally falling closed. "Oh, yeah."

As quietly as I can, I slide from the sofa, take Billie from Sam's arms and head upstairs. "Besides, there's more I need to talk to you about. James has shoved me into the friend zone, so there's that, and then Trent."

"Ugh, I hate that guy," Sam whispers.

"Me too. Let me put this little gal to bed and I'll make you hate him even more."

When I make it back to the lounge, the nacho plate is empty, Sam has found and cracked open two beers, and Lucas is curled up on the sofa, snuggled beneath a blanket, lost deeper to sleep than the baby upstairs.

"Poor little guy was tuckered out. Beer?" Sam holds the bottle out to me then nods to the empty space beside him. "You feeling better?" he asks when I take the beer, and drop onto the cushions.

"When was I ... worse?"

"You looked like you were going to puke when me and the Sandman came in."

"Yeah well. Confirming friendship then coming out is a lot for an introvert like me."

For some reason, that provokes a hefty snort. "Dude, I dunno if you know this about me, but I'm kind of popular. That means I know, and have to deal with a shit ton of people. And in my experience I can assure you that you, my friend, are awkward as fuck, definitely an over thinker and anxious. But an introvert, no way."

I take a sip of my beer. "You're just full of compliments tonight, aren't you?"

"I live to give." Mirroring me, he takes a sip from his, then another, and I think that might be it. But no. "You like people. Maybe even need them, and leading the team energizes you. You're an extrovert. Just a shy one."

"Aren't those things mutually exclusive?"

"Nope. A true introvert is mostly okay being alone. You seem to hate it, and do it more out of anxiety than anything." I narrow my eyes.

"When did you become such a people expert?"

"Told ya. I'm a big deal. I also take psychology. Analyzing people is my jam."

"Okay then, Mr. Expert." Nudging his arm, I sit up a little straighter. "Analyze this. A certain spoiled brat team mate—"

"Trent."

"Trent." I nod. "Knows I'm gay, and seems to be set on outing me. Do I tell Coach? Handle it with my fists? Or beat him to the punch and tell the team?"

Sam downs the rest of his beer in one go, then leans to place it on the coffee table. "Cubs, you won't even wear your glasses in front of the team. Are you comfortable with coming out?"

"If you'd have asked me that a month ago, I would have said no, but something's changed."

"Would that something be a certain Bear with a surname that rhymes with bum?"

"Maybe. I've been a bit of a slut this summer and it's been *so* great. I thought that was what I wanted, you know? Casual hook-ups to figure out what I liked. But now I'm not so sure. Hypo-thetically, if I did meet someone I was really into, if his name perhaps did rhyme with bum, I'd want them to watch me play, and come out to O'Reilly's after a win. I'd want to hold their hand and kiss them without looking over my shoulder. I don't want to hide who I am."

Unexpectedly, I'm pulled into a full man-hug, back slaps, noogies and spilled beer included. "Then I say it's time to cue Diana Ross, Cubby, 'cause baby, you're coming out."

A smile I couldn't stop if I tried, spreads as I picture every-thing I just expressed happening with James. And maybe a little bit because of fucking over Trent.

"Yeah. Yeah, I think I am."

"MAY AS WELL GO the whole hog."

An off-key chorus of *Pink Pony Club*, the team's latest pump-up song, bounces off the walls as I linger outside the locker room. On a normal day I would have been the first inside, already having showered and changed before anyone else arrived. Today's tardiness is deliberate ... and a tiny bit the consequence of freaking the fuck out in the parking lot, and once as I stormed Coach's office to alert him of my plans.

"Do you want me to act surprised?" he asked when I told him. "Or shocked? Because as you may recall, my daughter is in a poly-amorous relationship with two bisexual men. Nothing shocks me anymore."

It was a slight come down, but hopefully the team will give me a bit of the fuss I'm lowkey craving.

If the gay thing doesn't do it, I'm also wearing my glasses, my hair is in its natural floppy form, and Cherry, who was way too excited by this, forced me into wearing my *Sweat* tour t-shirt too. *Give them a little visual aid,* she whispered.

Like Chappel is doing for the boys, I take a fortifying breath, give myself one last pep talk, and take a step towards my destiny.

"You're wearing your glasses." Foot mid-air, I pause. My favorite gruff and grumbly voice now all I hear. "Forget to refill your prescription again?"

"James." I squeak. "What are you doing here?"

"I work here, remember?" He looks me up and down. "What are *you* doing here? And by here and you, I mean why are *you* dressed as *you* while being *here*?"

It takes a minute to process that, because James is leaning against the wall beside me, but when I do, my chest puffs with pride. "I know it's lame and no big deal, but I'm being me. The real me. Glasses, gay and geek."

"It is a big deal. You look good. I'd almost say life raft worthy." A rare, breathtakingly beautiful smile lights his face, before he glances over his shoulder, then hooks his little finger around mine.

HE'S HOLDING MY FUCKING PINKIE.

It's fleeting. Over before I can pull out my phone and capture it, but even if nothing physical ever happens again between James and I, this is a touch, a moment, I will never forget.

"Good luck, Kid."

"Thanks, Jamie."

Hovering by the entry opposite Coach Harris, I fight with all my might to keep my face neutral. This kid, and I use the term affectionately, this fucking kid amazes me. Pride is blooming where it has no absolutely zero right to bloom, as are other emotions I dare not probe too deeply.

I know he's dumbing this down by saying it's nothing to wear the thick glasses and fluffy hair, but to me and every other kid that was bullied and shrank themselves down because of it, coming out not only as gay, but as the real Cory, before a group of young men that are part of a community known for past toxic traits, is a feat of Herculean magnitude.

Voice steady and calm. Face teetering on the edge of green, he speaks from the heart. Perhaps Brady and Troye had already greased the wheel, but this is an almost entirely new team to the one they came out to last season. Even so, fresh faces and old, sit and listen to their captain reveal the real him.

"I know it may seem weird for some of you, but I just want to remind you that I am still me, the same guy who washed cars with you last week, who consistently beats your sorry asses in speed races, and can check you into the boards as hard as a guy twice my size. Oh, and finally, please don't worry about me hitting on you, 'cause you're all ugly as fuck and I wouldn't touch any of you even if we were the last men on earth."

Smelly socks, tape balls and anything else within reach rains down over Cory, who's taking a bow on the bench in front of his stall. The whole team, bar a moody looking Hoffman, joins in.

It's entirely too adorable, and I resign myself to smile.

"That boy grossly underestimates his likableness, and ability to lead," Harris says, pride evident in his tone. "He'll be a NHL captain one day."

"You don't think the gay thing will hinder him?"

David crosses his arms over his chest, eyes suspicious. "No, but I take it you do?"

"I think we both know the pro hockey world isn't always pro-pride."

"True, but guys like that punk Becker are laying the foundations. Maybe Cory can be the one to cement the change."

For some reason I find myself matching Harris' pose. Arms crossed over chest, right foot over left. "You know what, I think you might be right. If anyone can do it. Cory can."

Watching as his team embraces him one by one, I get a little misty-eyed, and the fluttering of my heart has me roughly clearing my throat and standing like there's a stick up my ass. Like they've all just scored the winning goal, they empty out of the room, fist bumping Coach and I as they go. Cory is last, the grin on his face full and deserved. Coach follows the team leaving Cory and I to walk down the chute side by side.

"Ya did good, Cubby. Take it easy on the ice, okay. It's your first skate. Work into it slowly."

"Sure thing, Doc."

Hitting the ice, the smirk-wink combo he tosses me over his shoulder is damn near pornographic. Pity I can't kiss it off his face the way my lips are tingling to do.

As though he'd missed a day, not three weeks, Cory glides effortlessly towards the goals, slowing to give his young goalies a helmet tap, before continuing his warm up laps. He really is the most talented skater I've seen, edge work I could only dream of and a burst of speed as impressive as anyone in the NHL. It's his eyes that have my gut twisting, though. Pure joy lighting the navy blue to glittering turquoise.

Brady appears at my side, expression as solemn as I've seen. "You shouldn't look so sad watching someone have so much fun. Do you miss it?"

My stock standard answer is there, ready to roll off my

tongue. But after what Cubby just did... "For years I rarely thought about it. But now ... yeah, Yeah, I do." I look down at my soft belly and give it a tap. "I think my body does, too." One look at the down turn of his lips, and I know the answer to my question before I've asked it. "What about you?"

"Shit yeah. Every day I wake up and look forward to practice. Then I remember. Sometimes I think the Docs may have got it wrong, 'cause I feel so good." He smiles. "But later that night after hours under the lights here or at Green Line, my head hurts so bad I can hardly open my eyes. I loved hockey, but I love Quinny and Troye more. One more game isn't worth the risk."

"You're a lucky man. Some of us never find the perfect person for us, and you found two of them."

"It's because of the troll." He nods, face serious despite the pink haired troll he's just pulled from his pocket and shoved in my face. "Princess Poppy is my good luck charm. I wouldn't have them if it wasn't for her. Maybe you should get one. Might help you find Mr. Right."

My eyes immediately find Cory who's on the opposite side of the rink, head tossed back in laughter. A bubble of something indescribable inflates in my chest. If things were different. I think before catching myself.

"I don't think I need any help with that."

"Not interested, or already found him?"

Giving him a nudge, I turn from Brady and head back to my office. "More ... not going to happen."

"They're not all so easy, you know."

"Easy? I never said he was easy. Who said he was easy? I never said he was easy." Yeah. Not feeling guilty at all.

"James, chill. I didn't mean to imply you hadn't worked hard on him. The way he relaxes for you and doesn't fight it, is great. He's always been so tight for me. He's almost the perfect patient for you."

Jesus Christ. Play dumb. Play dumb.

"Who are we talking about?"

Coach White, assistant coach, my supervisor who could finish my career before it starts, laughs and nudges me with his bony elbow. "You know, you seemed pretty uptight when you started, but you're a funny guy. Maybe that's why the boys respond to you."

"No, you were right, I am uptight. Boring as fuck too, and not much of a people person to be honest."

"What ever you say, Plummy."

"Not you ..." He's off, chuckling to himself before I can *bin* this damn Plummy thing. I should think myself lucky. For the third time today I have been caught watching Cory. I have to get my shit together.

"I see you watching me, Doc," Cory chirps, before taking off like he's on wheels, puck on the end of his blade and he switches between fore and backhand, wrong foots two defense men and taps the puck between Larsson's pads.

What a freaking show off.

"Filthy shot!" Brady hollers from behind the net, before positioning himself next to his goalie. "Nice moves, Captain."

Nice indeed.

Thoroughly annoyed with myself, and the fact that seemingly everyone in a ten mile radius is in the mood for conversation, I abandon the rink and head to the close confines of my office.

This thing with Cory is spiraling out of control as rapidly as he can pick up speed on the ice. On first meeting any feelings I had for him were neatly contained below the belt, but their gradual descent up is ... not okay. I can't shut him out and avoid him. Can't be with him in any romantic sense and definitely can't let things get physical again. I also can't deny that I like him as a person and feel, I hate to say it, happy when I'm with him. I haven't had much of that in recent years and I'm not particularly interested in letting it slip through my hands.

A further five people stop me on the way back to solitude, so once I've grabbed a soda from the closest vending machine, I close the door and collapse back into my chair, more than a little peopled out and ready to return to my basement and weighted blanket.

Tomorrow is day at home with Dylan, which means we have our usual routine to stick to. Park in the morning. Snack time when we get home. Maybe then some art, music 'til lunch, another re-watch of Hairspray, before an afternoon walk and dinner prep. Once Faith gets home it will be eating, bathing, Dyl's bed routine, then lumbering down the stairs and collapsing into my own.

Though hardly thrilling, the comfort of knowing what to expect in my day is as soothing to Dyl as it is to me. Had you told me that a day mostly alone with my brother would be a comfort, not an overwhelming burden of responsibility, I'd have never believed it. Unless we have a bad day. Though, there have been less of those since Manny was back on board, but still it's me and I am not the ... paternal not the word. Adequate? I need to find a word for not up to Dad's standards.

The man was a saint. Something I am not, nor will ever be. Even Faith comes closer than me, and she is what many have described as colder than a polar bear's asshole.

Feeling kind of sweaty, anxious and short of breath, I rub my hand over my chest. "Not a fish. Not a fish."

To compliment my breathing, I open my laptop in search of distraction. Perhaps the monotony of paperwork will stave off an imminent panic attack or unexpected heart failure.

I hope.

Instead of digging into course paperwork like I need too, find myself opening a blank word document and titling it—

Pros and Cons of life rafts.

Cons

1. Age of ship.
2. Conflict of interest between ship and ship owner
3. Ships heading in different directions
4. This sailor's unsuccessful navigation of past
   stormy seas

After staring at the flashing cursor for twenty minutes, I move on.

Pros

1. Everything, other than above.

"Fuck. I am so fucked."

This is getting me no where. But I still don't feel like doing any work.

Fanfiction time.

It's been weeks since I've loaded a new chapter onto Wattpad. Perhaps some superhero smut will clear the cobwebs, so to speak. The chapter was particularly spicy, the first time sex between Spidey and Hulk.

Sipping from my Pepsi I read the last few paragraphs, just to reacquaint myself. It's stock standard for the most part. Well, as stock standard as what is essentially copyright infringing porn can be.

"You should take that suit off, Peter. Let me see what lies beneath."

Quivering, Spider-Man tears his suit from his body, and throws himself against Hulk's massive frame, running his hands up and down the wide expanse of his muscular back, climbing him like a tree to taste his lips and whisper,

"I want to straddle your thick neck. Watch you suck my dick while you go town on my nipples 'til I blow my load all over that furry green chest. Then, I'll return the favor."

Holy shit.

Clearing my desk in a single leap, I don't run, so much as sprint from my office back out onto the rink, my internal maniacal laughter suppressed only because of where I am. Two things happen simultaneously as I approach. One: Coach blows his whistle and announces the end of practice. Two: Cory turns and our eyes lock.

"What?" he mouths, gaze shifting between my eyes and the stupid grin I can't conceal as he skates closer.

"Malkovich," I say as gruffly as I can. "I need to check the strapping on that shoulder. See how it held up."

"Sure thing." He nods to Lucas and Sam who trail closely behind him, then steps off the ice and follows me through the rabbits' warren of barren corridors to the treatment room. Facing the door as it clicks shut, I feel Cory's warm breath on my neck.

"Do you for-reals need to check my shoulder, or was this just a ruse to get me alone."

"If you don't want me to call you kid, never say for-reals again."

He huffs a laugh, steps closer and places a kiss to the back of my neck. Turning to face him, I place my hand on his chest pads and push him back towards the bed. "You've been a naughty boy, Cory. You need to be punished."

"What did I do?" There's a slight panic in his voice I find disturbingly hot.

"Hmm, I'm not sure if I can trust you. Perhaps I need to see the real you. I think you should take that suit off and let me see what lies beneath."

Cory is by no means stupid, but I swear to the God of Thunder I can hear his brain chewing the words. Eyes alight with mischief and hunger, slowly dull as he finally digests it.

"Wait."

"Oh my God. You've read *Love Comes in Green*."

Sitting on the edge of his desk, biceps popping in the doctor's scrubs he occasionally wears, James huffs out an unimpressed, "No." Then adds, "I wouldn't read that rubbish."

I'm struggling here. "Okay, then how—"

"I write it."

"You're BosSyd2001?"

"I am." He nods. "Normally I would deny such an allegation, but since you have plagiarized my work for the purposes of seduction, I feel like I need to stake my claim."

I almost come in my cup. "Stake your claim on me?"

"On my intellectual property," he corrects.

"Oh. Well that's disappointing. I was getting a bit excited thinking what you were going to do to me. A light spanking seems just."

James huffs out a laugh, which gives me enough confidence to squish in next to him, tapping his foot with my own. I may be imagining it, but even through my pads, I can feel the heat of his leg against mine, and I really, really wish we were both naked on top of this desk, not fully-clothed perched on its edge. "That little speech of yours was quite something. I'm really proud of you."

"You are?" I beam like an absolute dork.

"I am. It's not an easy thing to do, and something I never did. Not to my team, anyway."

"What about your family?"

James puffs his cheeks and shifts a little closer. "Well, when I was seven I told my beautiful Mom I was going to marry Captain America, and I used to steal all of Faith's Bieber posters. Coming out wasn't necessary. What about you?"

"Kind of the same. I thought it would rock their world but Mom busted me making out with my Tom Wilson pic in my room, the thing she was most disappointed with was that it was Tom Wilson and not a B's player." James releases a cute little ... giggle, I guess you could call it, and I expect the conversation to stay on the same path, but he stops laughing suddenly and grips my hand tighter.

"Cory, every time I see, or think about you, I also think how wrong it is. But life seems to keep throwing us together, and making it feel right. I'm not quite sure what to do about that."

"You know, Spidey once said, *no man can win every battle, but no man should fall without a struggle.*"

"So we can't win, but we're also destined to fight and–"

"Fall," I whisper, eyes glued to Jame's lips. For a second, as he leans in, I think he's going to kiss me, so I let my eyes fall closed. His breath ghosts over my cheek, then his lips do too.

"I would love nothing more than to wipe this desk clean, lay you out and have my way with you."

"Why do I feel like there's something coming that's not you, or me, but a but."

His hand tightens over mine, little finger caressing my knuckles. "But. I can't. Should circumstances be different–"

"But they're not."

"No. They're not." Pinkies linked together, we sigh in unison. "The other day at dinner, I told you that I liked you, and I meant it. Being around you makes me happy, and I want you in my life. For now, I can only offer you friendship. I'm not sure if that would be of interest to you, but–"

"It would be," I pretty much yell in his face. "It is, I mean. It sucks, but I get it. Like you said you have responsibilities and I have school and hockey. I don't want to be without you, so if friends is all we can have then friends it is." For now.

Leaning into each other, fingers still twisted, we fall into a comfortable silence that lasts both too long, and not nearly long enough.

"I really do need to check that strapping."

I raise my arm and glance to my non-existent watch, earning another precious chuckle. "Five minutes of friendship and you're already trying to get me naked. I'm shocked and appalled ... and turned on."

When James shakes his head and pushes off from the desk, I somehow manage to swallow the pitiful cry of, don't stop touching me, but only just. "Ha ha, smartass. Now shut up and get that gear off."

MY SHOULDER HELD up well after my first week of light training, which means I'll be back at full strength just in time for our first practice game against Harvard next week. We only have two or three between other New England teams, but they're a great opportunity to wear our new away jerseys, all white with maroon bands, and to test out our new lines, new goalies, and new opponents.

One of them being Hoffman. With little-to-no warning, and undoubtedly aided by a generous Daddy's provided donation, the asshole transferred to Harvard. It's a true gift from the gods, in my humble opinion, but it does leave our defensive pairings with little time to restructure.

Enter James Plum.

So, I knew he used to play in goal, but I had no idea of the hockey brain lurking beneath those curls. Apparently, neither did Brady. "I came early and found this, watching that."

The *this* is James working with Brody, Bailey, Dean and Robbie, the remaining defenseman. The *that* is the smile James sports and he drops into a near perfect butterfly.

"What the hell's going on? Is every clock I own wrong?" We both jump at Coach's voice, with Brady going straight on the defensive.

"Nothing! I mean, I couldn't sleep so I came in early to use the gym. They were already here." Brady points to the boys crowded around the net. "James wanted to help out, but didn't want to bother you when you've got so much on. Dean said he texted them all last night, and as suspected, he texts slower than your grandpa." Having shared those Grindr exchanges with James, I can say this is not always true. Wisely, I decide to keep my mouth shut.

Hand slipping beneath his cap to scratch his head, Coach nods. "Well I'll be. Look at that footwork."

"I know!" I add a little too enthusiastically. "He's bloody brilliant."

"A smile wouldn't hurt, though. Do I look that grumpy?" he adds, right as James pinches the bridge of his nose, the antics of the easily distracted boys starting to grate.

Normally he looks, and sounds, a hundred times more pissed, but I'm not touching that with a ten foot pole. Poor Brady, though, is in the unenviable position of not only being an employee, but an almost son-in-law. "'Course not. Coach. You always seem … ah, not grumpy."

Somehow Coach seems placated by this, and minutes pass by with grunts and hums of approval as our only communication. It's me who breaks the silence, nudging Brady's foot when he fails to respond the first time. "Brades, did James ever say why he quit?"

"What? Oh, yeah, nah he's never told me. What about you, Coach?"

"Something about his family," he replies, focus never shifting from the ice where James just gloved a stinging one-timer. "Not exactly sure what. Shame though. If he can move like that after all these years, imagine what he'd be like fully fit and in his prime." I'm fairly certain my imaging that would lead to me breaking the all-time, non-stop jerking off record, so I try very hard not to.

That becomes more difficult when James, tired of his protege's shenanigans, calls it quits and skates our way, cheeks flushed red, and a determined glint in his eye. "Any one of you could have stepped in to help me out, you know."

"Where's the fun in that?" Coach huffs. "It's not often I get gifted with someone who's as good with his hands." While I erupt into the loudest coughing fit ever coughed, Brady slaps my back and Coach continues, eyeing me suspiciously. "What was I saying? Yes, who's so gifted in so many ways. Physiotherapy, car washing, hockey skills. What's next James? You going to whip us up a six course meal?"

"You're too generous, and I can assure you that's where the talent stops." It's said with a pointed look towards me. One in which I raise my brows too, hoping to convey, *I didn't say anything*, with my eyes. "I hope you don't mind me working with the boys. I'm not trying to usurp you. Just wanted to give them a goalie's perspective of screening."

"And how did they go? Think any of it sunk in?"

"Yeah." He nods, taking the water bottle he'd rested on the boards, squirting it directly into his mouth, swallowing, then licking off a drip beading on his bottom lips. Not that I'm noticing. "In the first twenty minutes I'd say most of it did. After that, well, let's say my deaf cat Cleo would have picked more up. That didn't help." He points to the opposite side of the rink where, what the fuck? My sister and her bestie Chloe, who—unlike Cherry—is a student here, are watching on.

"Isn't that your sister?" Brady asks, adding. "How did you not see her?" I can hardly say my eye balls were otherwise engaged, but they were.

"I haven't put my contacts in yet." Everyone here knows I wouldn't even see them if that was true, and I don't hang around for them to tell me that. Instead I break into a sprint and do a lap around the boards. "What are you doing here? The womb, home, O'Reilly's? Must you infiltrate every area of my life?"

"Settle Gretel. Chloe's sister plays the women's team, remember? We came to see her but I thought I'd pop in and say hi to my favorite bro." Cherry leans around me to scan the ice. "Is Sam here?" I slap my palm onto the crown of her head and twist it to face me.

"Not yet, but he will be. Shame you'll be gone. Goodbye."

"But I just—"

"Goodbye, Cherry."

"Hi, Cherry." I do the worst possible thing I could do, look at James while in my sister's presence. He's back on the ice, leaning against the gate looking like every one of my God damn dreams. "We haven't officially met. I'm James, James Plum."

"Of course you are." Flashing a nauseating smile, she steps around me and skips to stand beside him. "I didn't know you played. You look very dashing all kitted out. Doesn't he, Cory?"

My eyes fall closed. "I hate you. Please shut up."

To my surprise, James doesn't run, or skate, for the hill, but laughs and blushes and it's way too adorable. "Mind if I steal your brother for a minute? I need to tape his shoulder before he starts."

"You need to take his shirt off to do that, right?"

Shoot me now.

"I do. But there's nothing to concern yourself with. I'm somewhat of a professional."

"At clothes removal?"

"That, and physiotherapy."

"So clothes removal, and rubbing your oiled hands all over—"

"What the hell is going on here?" Inserting myself between them, I squeal like a very man-like banshee. "Are you flirting with him, or just trying to embarrass me?"

Cherry ducks around me again and shoots a wink at James. "Well it started as embarrassing you. The flirting was organic, 'cause I get it, bro. I get it."

"Oh my God." Refusing to even look at her, or Chloe who is laughing like a hyena, I stomp away. "James, if I don't die on the way, I'll meet you in the treatment room. Cherry, Chloe. Go to hell."

"Love you too, little buddy. Don't forget to use the step if you can't reach the table."

Cory's breath ghosts over my neck and the sliver of collarbone my polo exposed. I pretend I don't feel it or the resulting dick twitch. Best I make some attempt at conversation. What's a topic that would turn me off?

I know.

"Your sister is quite something." I'm standing at the end of the bench, a distractingly shirtless Cory's sitting on. He turns to face me, but I'm too quick. Grabbing his head and shoulder, I hold him in place. He fights it, he really wants to make eye contact, but I want, no need, the opposite more. With a huff he resigns and goes back to facing the basin.

"As a half Aussie, shouldn't you say, she's a top notch sheila —owww." I'm not sure if I've taken some skin with it, or if it's the reminder of his sibling, but Cory winces as I peel the tape from his shoulder.

"No one but seventy year old men or bogans trying to be retro-edgy say Sheila. Now stop being a baby, and sit."

"What's a bogan? Also, you're the one who started talking."

"That's true. But I presumed that a gifted athlete such as yourself would have mastered talking and not moving at the same time. Now, sit still and answer the question. The bogan talk can wait, Cubby." I know he's as much of a fan of Cubby, as I am Jamie. But again like me, I think we're both warming to it when coming from each other. My suspicion is confirmed when he sits up as though I've shoved a stick up his ass. "Good boy."

"Fuck." He reaches his left arm over and slap his hand over

mine. "If you want us to be locked in the friend zone, good boying me is going to make that very difficult."

"Noted." Giving his shoulder a squeeze, I slide my hand, and the rest of me, as far as I can get in. Which isn't far.

This clinical white treatment room, sparsely furnished with a table, small desk I can barely fit behind, a series of stainless steel draws and cabinets and basin with a small mirror hanging over it, suddenly feels so crowded I can hardly breathe. That's where I linger, by that basin, and though half of his face is reflected back at me, it's enough to see the wicked smile I'm equally desperate to ignore and to kiss off.

Perhaps if you stop flirting, he will stop looking at you like he wants to eat you alive.

Clearing my voice, I try to steer the conversation back to safe territory. "So, your sister."

"My *sister ...*" he sighs, "is indeed *something*. She's had to be. Derek, that was her boyfriend, broke her heart so thoroughly she's not been with anyone since. Not seriously anyway."

"I can't imagine she'd have much time for it, what with Billie, school and now nursing. Her determination and work ethic is admirable."

"It's exhausting, and I've only watched on from the sidelines."

"I dunno, Cub. From what I've heard, you've done plenty."

"Yeah. Maybe. Not enough, though. For her, or for Ma." There's a soul crushing familiarity in his tone, and I know exactly what it's borne of. Inadequacy. An emotional state I have resided in for many a year. Being so fluent in its language, I want to delve deeper. Offer reassurance, support and understanding.

The urge to do so sees my fingers tingle with the need to hug him. But I can't. It's selfish as fuck, but letting myself become more emotionally attached than I already am is a diabolically bad idea.

Stomach churning, I decide it's time to deflect again.

Closing the drawer with a sharp thrust of my hips, I turn to face him, gaze still avoiding those mischievous blue orbs as I begin testing his range of movement. "I'm glad to see you wearing your glasses around your teammates. How does it feel? Have they responded appropriately?"

"Feels good, once they got over the whole, *hey Clarke, are you sure you don't have x-ray vision jokes*, they've been good, too."

"And with the ... ahh ..."

"Gay stuff?"

"Yeah, that."

"They've been great. Actually mostly great. One or two have avoided me in the change rooms, but that's their problem, not mine."

"That's a very mature attitude. I'm proud of you." And we're back to emotion. Fuck I am terrible at this. "So, how's the movement felt today? No swelling that you've noticed?"

"Not in my shoulder, no."

"Really?"

"Hey." He arches his brows and slides those fucking glasses down his nose, sitting it right on the freckle covered tip. "You leave an opening that wide, I'm going to slip right on in."

Rolling my eyes, I inhale, puff my cheeks and sigh. Using the time to mentally erase the image of Cory on his knees for me in this very room. "Jesus Christ, kid. You're not going to make this easy, are you?"

"Nope."

With Cory's eyes following the movement, my lips drop back into their naturally grumpy frown and the most awkward silence known to our generation takes hold.

"This will get easier, right?" he says eventually, voice pained. "The whole us being friends thing."

In truth I have no freaking idea, but wanting something, has to count for something, too. "Of course it will. If we want it too, and I think we both do. There's no pressure though. We can just keep it as colleagues if it's too weird."

"Nope. Na-uh. You're not getting rid of me that easily. We're buds who just happen to have had each other's dicks in our mouths, and still wanna bone, but don't. Simple."

"Simple." I nod again 'cause it's all I can seem to do. "Shoulder looks good." He jumps a little, like he just realized I've been manipulating his arm the whole time, while he's been zoned in on my 'stache. "Give it some ice when you get home and it should be fine."

It's official. The little nerd has got under my skin.

Due to his injury, he's not at practice much, and when he is, I'm working on his shoulder with Coach White breathing down my neck. All this means we haven't seen much of each other, and I miss him. Like a lot. It's unhealthy to think about him and his over the top, ridiculous flirting or the ludicrous, insufferable crap that flies from his mouth. That's why I need this friendship thing —the one I am demanding because I'm a selfish jerk—to work.

With that in mind, it's quite possible that this is the most autistic thing I've ever done, and coming from a man who has to practice smiling in a mirror, that's really saying something.

I've just googled how to make friends.

I started with, *what do boy friends do?* As in two separate words, boy and friend, and that led me to many links, of many boys doing many things I don't believe count as friendship. Then I tried, *what do mates do?* That was slightly more successful, but still, no. Only after adding platonic and group of, did I find anything useful.

Unsurprisingly, attending sporting events seems to be the most popular friend-adjacent activity, so that's what I've settled on.

Sport. Since I'd rather chew on my own face off than watch football, basketball, or baseball, hockey it is.

Only friends or not, obviously, we can't go to a Bears game. Northwestern is playing out of town, I hate Harvard so that leaves Boston University tonight—even if it means out of myself as a BU alumni, but that's a price I'm willing to pay. I want— need—to show Cory that we can work as just friends, and this, according to google, is the only way to do it. Before doubt can overwhelm me and I change my mind, I book two tickets, snagging some great seats, then close the laptop that's sitting on my chest.

Now to work up the courage to ask him. Blindly feeling around beside me, I find my phone twisted up in my sheets and raise it so slowly you'd think it was radioactive.

"Just call him you dick."

I hang up, call back, hang up and call back three times. Before I can get to phone, he's calling me.

"Jamie, what is it? What's wrong?"

"Oh, hey. Hey, Cory, Nothing. Why do you presume something is wrong?"

"Ahh, because you called and hung up like a hundred times."

"Oh, you can see that?"

As what I just said kicks in, he gives the cutest *'you idiot' l*augh, that's laughing at me without laughing *at* me. "Yeah, Grampa. These newfangled phones can do that. Now tell me what's got you in a panic.

"Willyoucometoahockeygamewithmetonight?" It's one word, and screamed. He gets it though, and I get an immediate—

"Yes, James, yes. I'd love too. What time?"

Ignoring the instant chub hearing, "yes, James yes," has inspired, I pull the phone from my ear, and glance at the time "Can pick you up in an hour?"

"Done."

"Great. Oh, and Cubby, just to reaffirm, this is a friends hanging out thing, not a—"

"Date. Got it. See you soon, babe."

"You can't seriously be wearing that?" Cory is standing at the open passenger-side door, abs fully exposed and perhaps dusted in glitter, with one of his slutty little cropped tanks, low slung baggie jeans and chunky white runners I just know a pair of crisp white tube socks slid inside of.

"Duh, I have a jacket." The jacket he holds out looks like something that would fit an American Girl doll, but it is technically a jacket. "What's wrong, *friend*?" He smirks as he deposits is round ass into the seat, then slides his glasses down his nose to stare at me above them. "Don't you like my outfit?"

"No, it's the opposite and you know it. That's why you wore it."

"Dunno what you're talking about." Buckling his belt, he flutters his lashes innocently. "We're just two hot friends, heading to a hot hockey game in enemy territory. Why is that, by the way. Coach ask you to do some recon?"

"No, not at all. Faith was home, Dylan is super chill, and I just felt like getting out."

"Fair enough. *And* just to make sure, we haven't seen much of each other this week, so it has nothing to do with missing me?"

"What? No way. Absolutely not. That's crazy. Didn't even enter my mind one bit. Nope."

"Well that is very convincing. Glad you cleared that up," he says, slapping my thigh.

"Cubby."

"Yes, Jamie?"

"My leg?" I glance down at his hand. The one lingering on my thigh and slowly edging up.

"Oh. That was not deliberate. Absolutely not. That's crazy. Didn't even enter my mind one bit. Nope."

"Excellent. Glad we could clear that up ..."

"Cubby," I repeat a moment later.

"Yes, James."

"Your hand. It's still on my thing."

"Annd you're telling me this *because*?"

"Move it Cubby, Jesus." I laugh so hard, I cry and I'm so glad I did this. After moving like a sloth, Cory does remove his hand and we make it to Agganis Arena without any further inappropriate touching. There's plenty of inappropriate comments, but yeah, hands stay on the correct side of the vehicle.

Braving the rival crowd, Cory awkwardly pulls the collar up on the puffer coat and slaps on hit Boston B's hat, backwards of course.

"You think that will keep the adoring fans at bay?"

"Should do. Works great at school." I must admit he's right. Glasses and cap on, he really does look like a different person.

The first thing we do once we get inside is hit the concession stands. Cory orders enough food for an entire team, and I stick to some nachos—just cheese, and a Pepsi. Anything more will upset my stomach. It's churning, and my skin itches, the lights and crowd and noise reeking havoc on my nerves already. I do love this game, but why must it be held in a nightclub?

We make it to our seat, I dump all the food I'm carrying and sigh in relief when my ass hits the hard plastic. In silence, Cory watches me from the corner of his eye, hand gently patting mine reassuringly when my own twitches nervously at my side. Unlike the groping in the car it's non-sexual and appreciated.

"Great spot." He eventually mumbles around a bite of his hot dog. "When did you order the tickets?"

"Ahh, I've had them for a couple of weeks." I lie. "Ryan was going to come with me but he canceled."

The dog is dropped back into it's cardboard tray, sauce and pickles sliding off with a plop. "Ryan? That dick from O'Reilly's?"

"Yeah, I mean no. He's not a dick, but he's the guy from O'Reilly's."

"Huh." Cory picks up the dog again, letting the bun drop and just taking the wiener in his hand. Eyes locked on mine, he deep throats it, then slides it back over his lips, sauce free. Biting a chunk off the end, he shoots me a wink and I shift in my seat to cover the ... situation brewing. "The tip's my favorite bit."

"Stop it."

"Stop what?" He smiles, doing the exact thing again. "I'm just eating."

Thankfully, the lights drop and if I squint enough I can pretend I don't see him treating that thing like I want him to do to my dick. "Just friends." I tell myself. "Just friends."

"Are you talking about fish, again?"

"No. Just reminding myself something important."

"Sounds boring. Ryan does too."

My eyes roll of their own accord. "Ryan is not boring." Ryan is kind of boring. "What's your issue with him, anyway?" I ask, leaning in to his ear so he can hear me over the announcements.

"No issue. Just looking out for my friend. I know a dud when I see one."

"All those years staring in the mirror really paid off, huh?"

Chuckling under his breath as we stand again for the national anthem, one defiled by Cory's erotic hot dog consumption that I cannot take my eyes off no matter how hard I try.

"We should do this more often," he yells over the cheering as the teams line up.

"What, eat food porno style?"

"No, but now that you mention in that too. Hang out, I mean. At the hockey or whatever. I don't get to do that very often. Still not sure why you're at a BU game though. Is Ryan-the-dud a fan?"

"No I am. I went to school here."

"You what!" He coughs, almost choking. "You went to BU? Does Coach know?"

"Yes he knows. It's called a resume, Cory."

"Well I am shocked and disappointed that you've been keeping this from me the whole time." Eyes narrowed, glassed a little fogged, he shoves a handful of popcorn into his mouth. "Talk about sleeping with the enemy."

"Lucky we're just friends who don't sleep together then."

"Yeah. Lucky. For you. A Bulldogs fan could never keep up."

Again, I can't help but laugh. "You're ridiculous, you know that right? And what about Troye Becker? He used to play with BU. You telling me you wouldn't go there?" My stomach drops at the mere thought.

"Moot point. He's taken and as we've discussed, I don't do cheaters."

"Good—"

"Having said that," he interrupts. "Should Brady be up for a three-way, then I would need to reassess."

"What about Quinn?" I huff, stupidly jealous even though I bought this up.

"She can watch. Or if she must get involved, I guess I could throw a few moves in. Not like I haven't been with girls before."

"Did you like that? Being with girls."

"Loved it so much so I decided I was gay." With a wink, he flicks my pouting lip with his thumb. It makes me unnaturally happy. As does the image my mind conjures of his riding my chest as I sucked on that very same thumb. My dick really likes that. "I much prefer older, hairier grumpy men. Ooh, especially fastidious ones with big dicks and mustaches. They're my fave." I'm tempted to reply that cheeky, glassing wearing short-ass twinks are mine, but I decide against it. My dick couldn't take his come back.

Instead I shove a handful of dry, twenty dollar corn chips in my mouth.

"Speaking of home," he says out of nowhere.

"Which we weren't."

"Would you like to come over for dinner. As friends. You can meet Billie and Mom ... as friends."

In no Marvel multiverse should the offer be accepted.

"As friends?" I stupidly confirm. "Just friends."

"Of course." He nods this time. "Nothing romantic or sexual at all. Eww. Gross."

Say no. Say no. Say no.

"Sure." *IDIOT.* "But I can't tomorrow. Faith's got some grading to do so I'm solo with Dylan."

"Oh, well why don't I come hang out with you guys then? Dyl loves me. Maybe I can cook? I make a killer mac and cheese."

I bite down on my lip, trying to think of a believable excuse, something that's really hard to do when I don't want there to be one. Cory at my house means my usual routine will be mostly unaffected, while also ensuring emotional chaos.

Fuck it.

"Mac and cheese sounds great. I'll text you my address."

Idiot.

Always up for some dramatics, Faith is loitering on the staircase that leads down to my dungeon, ducking so she can see me rather than actually come down like a normal person. Still, so intense is her glare, I feel it burn against my flesh from across the room. "Do you think it's a good idea? I mean, I know you're the master of this ..." she pauses, undoubtedly trying to come up with a polite description for my living quarters, before settling on, "... expansive domain, but should a student really be partaking in visitations?"

Probably not.

"What, like the kind you made with Brady?"

"That was different," she huffs. "I was concerned about Brady's well-being."

"Yeah, well, I'm concerned about Cubby's. Honestly, Faithy. You're making this into something it's not. He's coming for dinner. No harm, no foul."

"No harm. No foul? Wow, you really are immersing yourself into the sporting world, aren't you."

Suddenly I feel a headache brewing, I drop the book I was trying to read, and pinch the bridge of my nose. "I'm working as a physiotherapist for a hockey team, Faith. Sport is kind of relevant. Don't you think?"

"I do too, but you don't see me tossing around hockey phraseology."

"Actually, the origins of no harm no foul are rooted in basketball." There's nothing Faith hates more than being corrected, and as expected, this sees her clomping down the stairs.

"Oh, if that's the case, should I expect a seven-foot-three point specialist to join us tomorrow?" She's beside me now, a distinct air of judgement in her tone.

"Look. The kid has—"

"Kid? What is he, three years younger than you?"

Using my long limbs to my advantage, I hold out my arm, palm facing out in the universal 'talk to the hand'. "The *kid*, has just come out as gay, and a dork to his team mates, his family is facing some significant money troubles, and between hockey, school and Green Line, he's working his ass off twenty-four-seven, all while neck deep in an identity crisis. I thought a break from all *that* was required for his .... what did you call it? Well-being?" As expected, Faith fires back in an instant and makes it about her.

"Why have I, the Bears consulting psychologist, not been made aware of any of this?"

"I can't be certain, but you can, you can come across as a little ... unapproachable at times." Rearing back, a gasp of horror is released before she wills herself back to her usual steely expression. "Yeah, that's it. That's exactly what I'm talking about. You show a flash of humanity, of Faith, and then bam, gone. Back to Dr. Plum." There's no retort this time. Just my sister who seems ten years younger than she did seconds ago.

"I think we're both guilty of that, James. One could say it's hereditary."

"One could. But one could also want that to be different." With pushing off the mattress, I sit up and tap the space next to me. Inspecting my bedding, Faith screws up her nose before hesitantly perching herself beside me. It looks like she's sitting on barbed wire, but I decide not to point that out. "Remember what you said to me before the car wash, *'You need to be part of the team. You can't lock yourself up in the basement forever.'* Well, I figured you were right. I never used to be like this. When I was a kid, all I wanted was to have friends and be part of the team. To be accepted. When I quit playing, I gave up that part of me too. It was easier to think I was above it all, but my neck is sore from looking down on everyone. I'm tired of shallow connections that peter out because I won't give anything back. I want more."

After an uncomfortable silence, Faith nudges me with her elbow. "I must say, looking down our noses at people has been one of the common binds between us. Don't lose it entirely. Also, I've seen the way you look at Cory. You want friendship, but you want *him*, too."

I wrap my arm around Faith's shoulder and pull her closer. "Totally irrelevant. We do like each other, a lot. But we know where things stand. It's friendship. That's all."

"If you say so."

We share as affectionate a hug as both of us will allow, Faith's stammered breaths indicating she's more emotional than she's willing to let on. She's done this a few times lately. Been on the verge of tears before stubbornly clawing her way out of it. Like me, she's hardly had time to process Dad's death.

"Are you okay, Sweetheart?" I ask, pressing a kiss to the top of her head like Dad used to.

"Of course I am. Just tired is all." With one last snuggle, she peels herself from me and marches back to the stairs. "You sure you're going to be alright with Dyl and dinner?"

"Thank you for the cynicism, but yes. Me and my friend will be fine."

Now at the top of the staircase, she ducks again so I can see her face. "Great." She smirks. "Dyl's in the lounge watching telly so I'm going to start grading now. Make sure you and your *friend* keep it down." Strewn haphazardly across the floor, Dylan, Cleo and I are mid-Jenga when the doorbell rings. The ding sees Cleo hiss as though possessed, and zip to the safety atop his scratching post. Happily humming, Dylan's up before I am, his huge feet knocking the tower he's been focused on for the last thirty minutes. Technically that means I won, and because I'm pathetic, the small victory brings with it an irrepressible smile. One that has nothing at all to do with who's waiting on the other side of the door.

I hear Cory's voice before I see him, my heart reacting before my brain does, swelling when his perfectly excited, yet gentle, tone hits. "Dylan, my man."

Faith has taken Dylan to the last two sessions at Green Line and it seems I've missed a lot more than skating. When I make it to the door, the duo are mid side to side-up high-down low-hi five-handshake. Bespectacled Cory in all his glory, is running his hand through his windswept hair, and Dylan is bouncing on his toes, with a smile as big as I've seen since we lost Dad. My chest squeezes again.

Before I can invite our gray sweats and Bears hoodie wearing guest in, Dyl tightens his grip on the hand he hadn't released and pulls his apparent bestie inside. "Maria will be gutted," I mumble, trying not to sound as giddy as I feel while Cory is pulled down to our puzzle setup on the floor.

"Wait. Maria? From the skate program?" he asks, looking up at me through his lashes in a most un-friend like manner.

"The very one. If you ask her, not only are they best friends, but she's the love of his life. He may be too busy to pay her the appropriate attention while skating, but they see each other twice most days. Kisses a plenty, hand holding, the works." Using my socked foot, I tap their still joined fingers. "She's quite possessive. Wouldn't like this at all."

"Dylan, you dog." Cory holds out his free hand for the obligatory hockey celly fist bump. Not once in all my time spent with Dylan have I seen him do this. A high five, sure. The odd hand shake that always has him giggling. But the bump. Nope.

While I'm freaking out over that, Cory's begun chirping my brother, boasting over his Jenga skills and rubbishing Dylan's. It's a remarkably normal thing for a hockey player to do. I've not met one what wasn't an overly competitive fucker and Cory is not different. What is different is Cory teasing Dylan. There are very few people who converse with him like a *regular* twenty some-thing. Yes, he may like what many consider childish things, and not be able to verbalize his needs and desires, but he is still a grown man.

And my brother.

Despite my best efforts to ward them off, heavy tears roll down my cheeks. "Shit," I mutter, wiping my face with the back of my hand. "Guess we better get started on dinner."

"Oh, I forgot," Cory says around the tongue that's poking

from the side of his mouth, "No need to cook. Ma refused to let me come empty handed, and didn't want you to get food poisoning, so she made a huge pot of mac and cheese. I put it down by the door when Dyl accosted me—ahh, fuck it." The *fuck it* is directed at the pile or wooden bricks crashing to the ground. Dylan wins again.

"You'll have to lift your trash talk if you're going to beat him." Hiding my embarrassing face, I scurry to the door, bend and retrieve the gigantic Tupperware bowl covered in tin foil.

"Mom couldn't find the top," Cory says as I lift the makeshift lid and take a sniff.

"Smells good."

"It is good. Really good. And my favorite. Man, I'm going to miss her cooking when I go to Montreal." I*'m going to miss you when you go to Montreal.*

I scold myself for the thought. It's far too soon into our acquaintance for such foolish things.

"Right, well I'll go chuck this in the microwave. Make yourself at home."

Scurrying to the kitchen, I peel off the tinfoil and pop it in the trash, take out some plates and cutlery, and line them up on the counter. Cory ate his body weight in pasta at that little Italian place, and I'm fairly certain he could polish most of this off himself. With that I give him the lion's share, and Dylan—who is still happy squealing—gets a fair chunk, too. Since I'm suddenly all floppy in the stomach, I take what's left. Probably best not to feed those butterflies that have taken flight in there.

"Make sure you thank your mom for me," I call. "It was a lovely thing to do for strangers."

"You're hardly strangers. I've told her all about you and your magic hands. Any details I left out, Cherry made up."

He talked about me to his mom?

At this point, I could probably use my rapidly rising body heat to warm the food and get it done quicker and without the added radiation. *Calm the fuck down.* It's a concept easier said than done, because fuck oysters. Having Cory in my family home. Hearing the obscenely stunning man with stunning slutty little glasses that I'm unfairly attracted to, being so natural and kind with my brother, telling his mom about me, is surely the most potent aphrodisiac in human existence.

I'M PLEASANTLY FULL, maybe a little tipsy too after polishing off an incredible South Australian Red. Dylan has more creamy white sauce on his face then is currently digesting in his stomach, and Cory. Well, Cory is freaking adorable.

Better add me being a little bit of a goner to tipsy.

Right now, Cory's with Dyl in his room, sitting on the edge of the bed as Dylan smooths his fingers over his face in swirling, swoopy motions. Dad always said touch was Dylan's love language, and this routine had been in place since Dyl was a kid. The tradition has passed down to me or Faith since his death, but it's a strict family thing. Never have I seen him touch any of his support staff like this. Not even his favorite Manny.

Humming gently as he goes, he traces the line of Cory's chin, then up and over his cheekbones, nose then circles his eyes. A multitude of emotions churn inside me. Grief being the least pleasant. I miss my dad. Like, a lot.

My first reaction to this scene was to call him over and give him shit with something along the lines of, "Get a load of this, Old man. You've been replaced with a younger model." Then I remember. With the rampant change that's transpired over the last few months, moments like these fracture the shell of denial I've crafted around me. Piece after piece has fallen away. I'm doing my best to hold the remainder together, but I'm struggling, and I don't know if I'm ready to face the world without its protection.

Alongside the grief, sits resentment. Not for dad or Dylan, or Cory. But for ASD.

At times like this, I fucking hate the autism that makes my life uncomfortable, and awkward, but traps and locks away so many parts of my brother. When I was first diagnosed, I can remember well meaning therapists telling me it and the obsessive tendencies that sometimes crippled me, were my superpower.

What a fucking joke.

I didn't want a super power. I wanted to feel normal. To not get stuck on the same things for hours, or freak out in class when I was overstimulated, or not have a total breakdown if my teacher was away and we had a sub. I was tired of being the only kid in class not invited to parties. Even with all that, at least I could somewhat express what was happening or what had upset me. Dyl can't even do that.

I'm desperate to know what his thought process is as he traces the lines of Cory's cute upturned nose. Why this? Why the face? As far as we know he has no vision issues, but maybe he does. Is this his way of studying features he can't fully make out? Is it sensory? Does he enjoy the soft skin versus the hard bone structure, or is it completely random? Did he just do it one night, find some kind of comfort, so it became another of the many idiosyncrasies that make Dyl, Dyl?

Maybe one day I will, but for now, it's added to the mysteries of Dylan list, and I try to stop analyzing and focus more on the innocence of the moment. Something made easier when Dyl finds a ticklish spot on Cory's neck, just below his ear. Eyes crinkled as he squirms, the rough and tumble hockey player reduced to a giggling, squirming mess that has me thinking things I really shouldn't.

Like my feet have taken root in the timber floor, I stand watch unable to look away until Dylan can no longer blink away his sleepiness. Hands dropping to the sheets, he tucks them neatly beneath his pillow and his eyes fall closed. Even then Cory remains by his side, waiting until Dyl's breathing slows and evens out before whispering, "Good night, Dyl."

It's so bloody sweet I swear I can hear my heart sigh.

Visions of this very scene becoming a daily occurrence meet a hasty end when Cory, misty-eyed, and back lit by a nightlight, turns and smiles. He's so fucking beautiful it hurts to look at him. *He's also on the team.* I remind myself, while simultaneously making a mental note of that ticklish spot, just in case things should ever change between us.

They won't, though. They can't.

But a guy can dream.

Lost in thought, I don't notice Cubby stand and walk my way, but I do feel the press of his body against mine. There was no reason for me to, though. Yes I'm currently leaning against the door frame, blocking his exit. But no. He did not have to slide into the space between me and the timber, showcasing the height and weight difference that keeps me awake at night. Nor did he have to look up at me through his lashes. Lashes that are beaded with moisture.

"That was amazing," he whispers, wiping the threatening tears with the back of his hand, "does he always do that? If felt like … sacred. Like a blessing almost." Even in the dim light, I see the blush color his face. "God, that sounds so corny."

Before I can stop it, the one hand I can move decides to move in his direction, cupping his jaw, and wiping the one stray tear rolling down his cheek. "It doesn't sound corny. It is a blessing of sorts. Dylan touching you like that means he loves you."

Rising to his tip toes, Cory leans into the warmth of my palm. It's overwhelming, the desire I feel to wrap him up in my arms. To drop my head, to allow my lips to find his. To taste him. To make him mine.

Glasses fogging a little, he takes a stuttering breath. "And what does you touching me like *this* say?"

"It says I understand where Dylan is coming from. And that for now, maybe I need to leave it at that."

I gnoring the emotional near kiss that is potentially the sexiest thing that has—and likely will—ever happen to me, James and I are pressed together on his sofa, paying little to no attention to the Avengers movie on his TV. Snacking on a charcuterie board, I sip the fancy pants red wine James insists is delicious, but really tastes like vinegar, and try not to wince. Each time I've leaned forward for another cracker, I've *accidentally* slipped closer. We're now so close I feel the brush of every single James Plum leg hair against my skin and I fucking love it.

"So, do you know what torture Coach has planned for us Sunday, and are you coming to witness, or inflict it?"

Swirling his glass, James tilts his head side to side like he's silently weighing up the pros and cons of answering. "Do I know? Yes. Am I coming to witness? No." The hope inside me deflates like a balloon. Tomorrow he'll be at Green Line for Dylan's program, and if he was to show Sunday, I would have seen James everyday this week.

Despite that, and the almost constant inner chatter reminding me James, his mustache and I can only be friends, I can't stop wanting more. More of him on the ice. More nights like this. More ... him.

We're so far beyond infatuation, now, it's not funny. I've gone from several random hook-ups a week, to not even looking at other guys. Every time I close my eyes I see the big, broad hairy chest, glistening with cum and sweat, which means I jerk off constantly—twice before I came here—and for the first time in my life, I'm finding myself picturing a future where hockey is not my everything.

It's terrifying, yet addictive. Basically, I'm just a bag of skin, bones and want.

Realizing I haven't replied, 'cause now I'm thinking about his chest again, the best I can come up with is, "The boys will be disappointed."

"They'll survive," he scoffs. "Besides, with what Coach and Quinn have planned, you'll be so swamped, no one would notice if I was there."

"Pretty sure all of Boston could show up and I could still pick you out of the crowd." Oh, shit. "Because you're so hot and tall." Shit "heywannashowmeyourroom?" SHIT!

Blushing but polite enough to not laugh at my word vomit, James rises to his feet, then holds out his hand, fingers wiggling impatiently. "Come on then. I'll give you the grand tour. Should take all of five minutes, then you can get out of here. It's your last Friday night before the season starts. You should be out on a date with some young buck, not stuck here with an old man and his cold cuts."

If I didn't l know any better, I'd swear James was angling for a compliment, *and* fishing to see if I'm dating. Lucky for him, I'm easy to hook. "I'm not really dating right now, and even if I was, I like my men like you like your wine, vintage." I take his hand and let him pull me from the sofa.

"That mouth of yours is going to get you into trouble one day, Kid."

"Hope so."

Muttering 'Jesus Christ' as he goes, James leads me into the kitchen, flicks on a light switch, then swings open a door he has to duck to go though. "Wow, you really do live in a basement. I thought you were kidding with the whole dungeon thing."

"Nope. As big as this place is, there's only three bedrooms. Neither Faith or I were keen on sleeping in Dad's room, Dylan would never leave his room, and I would never let Faith sleep down here. Besides, having all this," stepping from the stairs onto what looks like a painted concrete floor, he swings his arms out wide to indicate *all this,* then points to a white chipped paint door, "with my own entrance and all, let's me delude myself I'm still somewhat independent."

"It's fucking freezing."

"That it is."

"And ... is that a civil war costume hanging from your ceiling?"

"It is." Now, as a man who collects Spider-Man figurines, I have no right mocking someone else's hobbies. But there's not a damn thing in this world that could stop my laughter.

"James Plum, are you a re-enactor?"

"Good lord, no." He blushes. "My dad was, though. That's his favorite unionist outfit. He'd just picked it up from the dry cleaner the day he died ... which wasn't down here," he clarifies, guessing my immediate thought correctly. "He was thoughtful, *and* stubborn enough to drive himself and Dylan to the hospital before he ... you know." James' huffed laugh is as painful to watch as I suspect it is to feel. "Bloody old fool."

"Was he old? Like, you're only in your early twenties, so he could have been quite young still."

"He was still young, I guess," he says after a trademark puff-cheeked exhale. "I mean he was fifty-four, but fit as a Mallee Bull and twice as dangerous, as they'd say back home. Didn't like doctors, though. Maybe if he hadn't canceled all the checkups Faith used to book for him, he'd still be here." In a few short strides, he makes it to his unmade bed and plops himself down. I follow, of course, sitting way too close and unable to shift my gaze from his beautiful sad eyes. "But he was always putting Dylan first, you know. Didn't matter how many times we reminded him that *he* had to be okay for Dylan to be. All he wanted was Dylan safe and happy and Dylan was always safest and happiest when he was with Dad. He loved him so much."

"He loves you, too. When he's skating he looks at you all the time, and he has this happy little hum he does when you wave at him. It's really sweet." *You're really sweet. You're incredible.* I think while swallowing down the emotion that has me verging on tears before the man who's grieving.

"Faith told me that, too. It's nice. I always have the feeling I'm fucking everything up. I'm broke, think I'm having a heart attack on the daily, and this might sound horrible, but this isn't exactly the life I had planned. And I don't just mean caring for Dyl, I mean this." Again his arms reach out to encompass *this*. Only thing is, I'm not so close to him, his hand slaps against my pec and I'm quick to capture, and hold it to me. Certain he can feel the thundering of my heart, I expect him to pull away but he doesn't. If anything he slides his fingers a touch, like he's caressing the soft cotton of my shirt. "Do you think I'm horrible?"

"No, I think you're extraordinary. Your mustache is quite something, too." He chuckles then takes me further by surprise when he rests his head on my shoulder.

"I'm glad that we're friends. And that you're here. I've always found it hard to relate and connect to people, but for some reason," he pauses, and I feel the heavy rise and fall of his chest, "It's an unfamiliar phenomenon to me. Feeling seen, and safe to be me."

"Because you are safe, James. You can trust me. I promise."

"BEING *FRIENDS* WITH JAMES, might actually kill me."

I've just left another painfully exhilarating morning at Green Line with James, Dylan and the rest of the crew, and have me, Lucas and Sam at Beanz and Bookz. Thanks to Lotte and Quinn working here, the once nerd epicenter of campus is now *the* place to be. Its upgraded clientele meant I never set foot inside, but Sam is a coffee snob and won't accept a cup from anywhere else. It's still an odd feeling to sit amongst my peers as me, not some stylized version of who I think I should be.

"Last night, I had to pinch my thigh, and picture Cherry humiliating me to stop from getting a boner, as he poured his heart out to me with his head on my shoulder. And watching him skate and laugh today was almost as bad."

Blushing, Nate rubs his hand over his neck. "Man, picturing your sister would not work for me."

"Please don't," I say, the acid in my empty stomach tickling my tonsils. "I need to eat." As though she's listening, the waitress who's been eye-fucking us since we walked in, swings by to take our order. Blossoming under her attention, Sam and Lucas both order the post-game protein pack Lotte added to the menu in honor of Noah. It's a turkey and avocado sandwich on whole-grain, topped off with an almond milk smoothie full of fruit, and protein powder. It would be my choice too, but since I'm low on funds, I stick with just the smoothie. Sam nudges my arm.

"Thought you were hungry?"

"I am. But I'm also poor." I toss the menu onto the table top and sigh. "You know what pisses me off? Rich assholes like Trent who can not only buy the whole menu, they can buy their way into Harvard." Lucas huffs in agreement, but Sam's lingering blush is reinvigorated.

"Not defending him *at all*, but not all people that come from money are like that."

"Everyone I know is," Lucas adds, ripping open and shooting every ketchup packet within reach.

"Well, I'm not."

Beginning to feel awkward as fuck, I shift in my seat. "You're not what? Rich?"

"No, I am rich. Or my parents are at least. I mean that I come from money, even older money than Trent, and I'm not a jerk. Maybe that's 'cause only my dad is my real dad, and not my mum. It's like the snobbery has been diluted somehow."

Lucas's red stained mouth falls open. "There's a lot to unpack there, dude. But let's start with how rich are we talking? Millionaires?"

Sam nods, then blushes, then switches to a head shake. "Nah, nothing like that. Just every day extra comfortable."

In what I suspect may be permanent, my brows furrow. "I don't get why you seem embarrassed by that?"

"I do," Lucas scoffs. "Why the heck do you make me drive all the time? I never said anything, 'cause I figured you couldn't afford gas. But here you are, Lord Richie Rich Money Bags, with enough loot to buy the whole damn gas station."

Un-knitting my expression, I wave off Lucas, and tap Sam's

hand to get his attention back on me. "Well, I guess you're the exception to the rule. Rich, kind … and cheap as fuck."

"Ha-ha. Just don't tell anyone, alright. People treat you differently when they think you're cashed up, and I don't want that. I just want people to like me for me."

"They do. And I will. So we have a deal then. We won't tell anyone about you and your gold-plated toilets, and you don't tell anyone about me, James and my boners."

A very warm, very *not* Sam or Lucas-sized hand lands on my shoulder. "About you and who now?"

R egret slithers through my veins like a snake through wet grass. How? How could I be so stupid?

"Can I speak to you in private, please?" Giving Cory no time to reply, I fist the collar of his tee and yank him to his feet.

"Sure thing, Doc." He squirms in my grip but also looks like he's enjoying it.

This does nothing to soothe my tempter. Bursting through the Beanz and Book door, I stride to the empty alley beside the building and roughly reacquaint him to the ground.

"Please. Please do not tell me you told Lucas and Sam about our ... encounter?

He smiles. He fucking smiles. "It's *encounters*. And, okay."

"Okay, what?"

"Okay, I won't tell you."

Pretty sure I know the answer already, but I stupidly ask, "You won't tell me because you never told them?"

"Technically I didn't. They guessed, and I accidentally elaborated it. So really, I was just respecting your request for me not to tell you I told them."

This. This very exchange is the exact reason I don't like people. Exhaling so loudly I scare away pigeons picking crumbs at my feet, I begin to pace. "Cory. Do you remember the discussion we had right at the beginning of my placement. I asked you, very respectfully, to keep what happened between us, between us. And what you said in my room last night. That I could trust you?"

"I do. You can, and I did. Only Sam, and Lucas know."

"And Cherry, I presume after her performance at the rink?"

"Yes. Cherry too. Oh, and maybe Brady ... but that's it. I swear." The zero dollar balance on my bank account the day I started this job flashes before my eyes. "I know you're angry but you don't need to worry. They're my friends. I trust them. You can, too."

Before I can stop myself, I swoop in and grasp Cory by the throat, pinning him against the wall. "Like I trusted you?"

"I'm sorry." He coughs, eyes wide. Begging. "Please, I don't have friends. I was just excited and got carried away. Please. I need you to be my friend, too. Please, don't be angry with me, Jamie." He thinks I'm angry, and I am. I'm furious. Just not at him.

I release my grip, stumble back and grasp my head in both hands. The dull thud of an impending migraine forcing my eyes closed. "We're not friends. We're not anything."

As I walk away, unable to look at him, I speak over my shoulder, not slowing my pace. "Coach White will take care of your treatment from now on. Please just stay away from me."

WHY I MUST CONTINUOUSLY SHOOT myself in the foot, I don't know.

I successfully avoided Cory at Green Line yesterday, by bravely faking a stomach ailment and making Faith go alone. She came home early though, and busted me elbow deep in salsa, guac, and chips. That meant when Brady called this morning asking if I could help out at the dunk tank Coach and Quinn have set up, Faith stole my phone from my hand and replied with a hearty YES, on my behalf. I would rather staple my face to the wall than be here, but Brady is just so damn lovely, and was so excited to raise funds for Dylan's Green Line program, I couldn't say no.

That and Faith made me.

Now I find myself in a life guard outfit, face to face with Cory who, like the rest of his teammates, is wearing nothing more than a rubber ducky clad Speedo and a smile. Not to be outdone, Quinn is wearing some sparkly maroon booty shorts and a cropped tee.

"Coach is sticking to the sex sells side of charity work, I see."

"It's a bit much, isn't it." Brady blushes as Sam bends over in front of him to retrieve a quarter stuck in the grass. "Can't blame Coach for this one, though. The budgie smugglers were Quinny's idea."

"And it was a brilliant one, too. Look at the line." Smugly, she nods to the admittedly impressive queue. "Gals, gays and theys know what they want, and predictably, what they want is some drenched, hot hockey boys."

This is a fact I cannot dispute since I am one of the aforementioned gays. Anger towards Cory rages deep in my soul, but apparently not hot enough to burn off my desire. He looks unfairly beautiful. Blue eyes glistening in the sun. Those pretty nipples peaked from the chill of the morning. Tan lines lingering from his Montreal summer, peeking out from the baby blue material barely covering his ample cheeks.

Fuck I hate my life.

"Okay James, since you're the tallest who's not my boyfriend that I want next to me, you'll be stationed at the tank. Your job is to fish anyone out should they need help, and cheat by hitting the knobby, target thing when people miss. Remember what we're here for. We want wet hockey boys, people. No person shall leave this place dry."

I do not need to ask why she chose to say, person and not player. We all know what she meant to imply. Brady knows it so bad his cheeks are redder than my Baywatch inspired shorts. The thought of being so close to Cory as he perches that ass on the tiny seat is nauseating. "Are you sure there's nothing else I can do? Maybe I can be the ticket seller?"

"Nope. You're the pool boy and that's final." There's no bother protesting. Brady has spoken of Quinn enough for me to know she always gets her way.

Resigned to my fate, I head in the direction of the tank. We're positioned on the grassy knoll outside Conte Arena, and while wet hockey players may be the main draw, there's also a few dodgy-looking concession stands and a Ferris Wheel that looks one loose screw away from toppling. Shoddy workmanship has failed to stem the flow of attendees. The still mild Fall weather has ensured a bevy of scantily-clad bodies are everywhere, to the point that it feels as though eighty percent of students living on campus are here. Of course the one person I want to avoid is all I see, hands swinging idly at his side as he waits for me at my post.

"Can I help you with something?" With little tolerance for any Speedo related shenanigans, the ... well, rudeness of my tone is reflected on Cory's face. He looks wounded. And so he should.

"Oh, umm. I was just wondering if you're feeling better? Faith said you had the squirts. I wasn't sure what that was at first, and kind of wish I still didn't."

Fucking Faith.

"I'm fine, thank you. Nothing contagious you need to worry about." I attempt to move away but Cory grabs my elbow and pulls me to a stop. In all honesty I could probably drag him along the grass behind me if I wanted too, but something tells me he'd get off on it. He does let go when I stare so intensely at his fingers, so intensely they may ignite.

"Wait, Jamie. I was hoping we might be able to talk," he says, forcing his pout into a weak smile. "I need to apologize."

"Nothing to apologize for. You've said what you needed to say ... to apparently everyone you've ever met in your life, and I've said all I needed to say to you. Now, if you'll excuse me, I have some dunking to do."

Instead of leaving as I'd hope, he lingers. "Maybe I could help?"

"You are helping. You're in a tiny pair of togs. You're going to get wet. That's it. That's all you have to do."

"What are togs?"

I'm not sure who gave her a whistle, but I'm grateful Quinn's incessant tooting steals Cory's attention, and redirects my gaze from the patch of grass I was staring at rather than him.

"Hello, everyone," she yells unnecessarily into a megaphone, deafening those unfortunate enough to be within five meters. "Welcome to the first annual Wet Bear Parade!"

"Annual?" Mutter several of the players, apparently hearing this for the first time.

"We're going to get started now, so Bears players I need you lined up over by Coach Plum, and dunkers, check your tickets. When your number is called, please come and stand here by me and our handsome ball boy, Brady." A round of wolf whistles and jeers follow, and Brady, who looks like he wants to run, makes the poor choice to bend and grab a handful of balls to avoid the attention.

"Nice balls, Brades," is screamed by at least a dozen people.

"Nice ass," by a dozen more.

Quinn eventually restores some kind of order and the first ticket holder is called to action. "Number one, come on down!"

Number one is a bubbly blonde wearing a cropped 'I love hockey boys' tee that barely covers her ample breasts, while up first on the hot seat is Sam. Lucas, Jesse, Reece and Tom jostle to take his place, and I'm forced to remind them that the blonde is here to dunk them, not date them.

"Yeah well, I'd like to take the chance," Tom says.

"Go for it, Spits." Sam, who's looking out into the swarm of people, moves to the side. Following his line of vision, I see why.

"She's very pretty," I say, helping Tom onto the tiny metal seat not made for hockey size asses, and nodding toward Cherry while Cory's twin sister, who's holding a ticket and nervously bouncing on her feet.

"Pretty is an insult. She's stunning." Runs in the family, I don't say. "I'd really like to ask her out, but..." his voice trails off as Cory pushes through the pack to stand at his bud's side.

"Who do you want to ask out—"

"Okay, everyone," Quinn calls, saving Sam from certain death. "Up first we have sexy junior, and center, Tom Swallows!"

"SPITS, SPITS, SPITS," the team chants, much to Tom's mortification and Quinn's chagrin.

"Yes, thank you boys. Katie, are you ready?" Katie, the hot blonde that's set the boys alight, takes a ball from Brady, holds it aloft then takes a very professional-looking pitcher stance. Winding up, she lets rip a fastball that smacks straight into the center of the target, sending the crowd into a frenzy, and Tom straight into the freezing water with a hilariously fading, *oh fuuuccckk.*

I'd presumed my station was fairly pointless, but the shocking burst of cold seems to startle Tom, and most of the boys that follow. Which means by the time Cory is up, I'm freaking exhausted, as wet as the players and understanding why Quinn had me wear such a thin white tee.

"You tits look amazing in a wet shirt, by the way." Perched on the edge of the seat, he smirks down at me, and winks. His own tits look quite glorious, but I haven't noticed that at all.

"Yeah, well fuck you." Much to the disappointment of Cherry who has let countless people go before her to be able to take aim at her brother, my temper won't wait for her ball toss. With an open palm I slam that fucker, sending Cory into the water with a manly squeal. Because he wasn't seated properly he makes the biggest splash of the day. I am as wet as he is but that squeal and his expression of shock was totally worth it. "Sorry I slipped. Tim, can you help Malkovich from the tank? I'm on break."

After my impromptu and apparently successful recent practice sessions with the D-Men, Coach Harris asked me to act as a temporary defensive coach. The team don't have one at present, the last being called up to the NHL, and it's an area where they really do need work. It's a big deal, a sign that maybe they're considering keeping me around once my placement is done. It's also a bump-up in wage, something the Bears technically aren't required to pay, and as much as I'll deny it to anyone who asks, something I really enjoy.

It does take me away from Dylan another day per week though, but the extra money in my pocket means we can afford another support worker to join Dyl's team. Sue, a recommendation of Manny's, started this morning. Faith's taken a leave day to show her the ropes and let her and Dyl get acquainted, and all seems to be going well if Faith's increasingly vitriolic replies to my admittedly frequent texts are anything to go by.

> FAITH
>
> I know you have been home with Dylan a lot over the last few months, and I know you love your routine. But James Alexander Plum, I swear to God, I will give you a free and horridly painful circumcision if you message me one more time.

Nothing gets my phone out of my hand like the threat of barbaric surgery.

In truth, today's preoccupation with Dylan and whether or

not Faith knows how to put on his AFO's, what angle he likes his toast cut on, where she can find his misplaced fidget spinners, and how long it takes to walk to the park we've been to approximately three thousand times, may be a distraction.

On the disgustingly loud and jovial bus trip to Harvard, Cory is in the seat before me, blonde hair bouncing, and smelling of bubble gum, because whichever God hates me more made it the only free spot. Several times he's turned to speak, smile, or stare at me and each time I've pretended to be so consumed by the scenery, I've not noticed. Obviously I have, his reflection looking back at me in the window both the 'cause and cure to my distress.

The anger I felt at the coffee shop has not waned, or even dulled after the dunking. It's intensified. I'm so bloody mad, and hurt, and embarrassed. I've known this man for a handful of weeks. The remorse over becoming physical, and his betrayal seems disproportionate. But then again, my attraction too and affection for him far exceed anything I've felt previously.

Maybe that's why it hurts.

Of course that's why it hurts.

Anxiously, I rub at my tight chest. "Brady, tell me again why we all have to take the bus when the arena we're playing in is ..." I pause to look at my watch, "perhaps twenty minutes away from BC?"

"Team spirit."

"Are we talking Nirvana here, or do you expect me to believe piling a group of giant, grown men stuffed into ill-fitting suits, into an admittedly lovely bus, encourages bonding?"

Brady pops his second ear bud out, and gives me a dimpled grin. "You're extra salty today. Get out of the wrong side of the bed?"

"Since my shitty bed in our even shittier basement is jammed against a wall, I'm going to say no. Saltiness is just a delightful personality trait."

"Yeah, but it's normally like ... chicken salt. Flavorsome and kind of sweet, not just dry your mouth out straight up salt from the ocean. Or that fancy pink stuff. Hey, you're Aussie. Do you remember chicken salt? Shit I miss it."

As Brady continues to ramble about Australian condiments,

I zone out. Thankfully, we've been traveling for seventeen minutes, so the rant lasts only three more and we're pulling into the exalted grounds of Harvard.

"You speak all fancy like, Doc Plum. Is this where you went to school?" Sam, who I've also been ignoring, asks. I can't pretend I don't hear him now, as Brady is staring at me, waiting for my response too. I don't need to look, to know Cory is also.

"No."

"Oh. Well, where did you go?"

I really don't want to tell them it was BU. They'll tear me apart limb from limb, and I really need them to be a physio.

"School. Hey, look." I point out the window. "Cheerleaders." I'm not even lying. Beside the bus parking zone, a gaggle of pompom touting girls barely dressed in hot pants and tight, cropped jerseys, are shaking their wares for all to see. Every head on the bus bar three, mine, Brady's and Cory's turn, so it's almost a perfect distraction.

"You're into girls? Why aren't you looking?" I ask Brady.

"What's the point? None of them can pull off short-shorts like Quinny ... or Troye. " He blushes at the last bit, then leans forward. "Don't tell Troye I said that. I mean it's true, but don't tell him."

My narrowed eyes accidentally dart to Cory. "Don't worry, *Brady. I* can keep a secret." It's petty and pathetic, but man, it feels good too. As I stand, I see him and Brady exchange glances. No doubt the latter will know everything that happened before I step outside.

HALFWAY THROUGH THE SECOND PERIOD, I'm seriously wondering why any human would subject themselves to a career in coaching. I'm fairly certain the jam and cheese sandwich Dylan and Faith made for me is capable of carrying out my instructions better than this defensive unit is.

"Do they deliberately do the exact opposite of what you tell them, or is that just a happy coincidence?"

Coach Harris and White share a patronizing laugh, then slap me on the back in unison. "Bit of both. Welcome to coaching," Harris says, the maniacal smile receding as Nurse knocks the puck back into play rather than gloving it. Fortunately Cory is there to clear the puck from the zone, but it's called as icing. That means a face-off and we've lost more than we've won. The ref tosses Sam after he must blink too aggressively, and I watch, teeth biting into the flesh around my nails, as Cory takes his place.

Face to face, the size difference between he and his opponent, Parker, is almost identical to that between us. Why that, and his stern face of determination has me breaking into a light sweat is better left unexamined.

As too is my exuberant reaction when he wins, and taps the puck back to Lucas, the growing friendship and connection that saw Cubby blurt our secret evident. They can read each other. Trust each other and a twinge of jealousy that has nothing to do with sex, sparks inside me.

Other than Ryan, I have no friends. Cory was someone I felt like I could be *me* around. Grumpiness didn't deter him. If anything he seemed to like it. He's a dork like me, read my fic, and instead of giving me shit for writing such absolute trash, he used it to up his game in the bedroom.

The way that turned me on is yet another thing I'll be leaving well alone. Then there's those slutty little glasses. Why do they have to be so ... slutty? I snort a laugh as I picture him, sans specs, reading the upside down menu at O'Reilly's, then rub my chest to ease the pang that memory creates.

Christ. It's only been a week, and I miss him. Or maybe, it's the wasted potential, the loss of what we never really had, that stings.

Either way I have to get over it. I'm too bitter and jaded to let the trust Cory is building with his team be rebuilt between us.

Turning my attention back to the game, I feign the deserved enthusiasm. Ignore Coach Harris' chewing and do my job. We end up winning the game, but only because Harvard's latest recruit, Trent, gave us two power plays, then kindly earned an assist on the match winner. Old habits die hard I guess, as Cory fooled the twit into passing the puck to him in front of an open net. With a flick of the wrist he snuck it above the goalie's right glove. It was a beautiful goal. Cheeky, but beautiful. Quite like the man who scored it.

"See what Trent did?" I say to my huddled up D-men in the locker room. "Don't do that."

Bailey, who is an absolute smartass, wipes the non-existent tears from his eyes. "Truly inspirational, Coach Plummy."

"That's why I get paid the big bucks." After ensuring my boys did play well, and the potential of forming a brick wall defense is there, I send them off to the showers, and sulk back out to the ice.

The Zamboni is already doing its thing, scraping, refreezing, resurfacing. My skin itches with the need to get out there. Fucking up a fresh surface was always one of my favorite things.

"You did good today, Plummy." I roll my eyes but can't stop my lips from twitching into a smile.

"You've got the boys saying that now, Basse. Thanks for that."

"You're welcome." He slaps me on the shoulder then mirrors my pose, gripping and leaning against the boards, knuckles almost white. "How did you enjoy your first time? Was it everything you dreamed?"

"It was. Thank you for being so gentle."

"Bet Trent's teammates aren't being too gentle with him. I can't believe he fell for Cubby's tricks."

Feeling a sudden headache coming on, I release my grip on the boards, and pinch the bridge of my nose. "He can be quite persuasive."

"So I've heard."

I am not touching that with a ten foot pole. Instead I knock Brady's foot with my own. "Hey, it was your first game too. How are you holding up?"

Skewing his lips to the side, he takes a second before answering. "Not as bad as I thought it was going to be. I missed it, but seeing how far Nurse has come in preseason was kind of satisfying." His face then transforms into a blushed smile brighter than the arena lights above us. "That helped, too." He points to the approaching Troye and Quinn, the latter holding a sign in front of her stomach.

GOALIE COACHES DO IT BETTER

"Did her father see that?"

"Nah," he laughs, blush intensifying. "She only held it up once he hit the rooms. She's a risk-taker, but she's not stupid."

Quinn breaks into a sprint then jumps into Brady's arms, while Troye looks like he's fighting hard not to do the same. "You did so well, baby." She swoons. "Didn't he Troye?"

"He did." He nods, biting his lip. "You stood still, barked orders, then paced up and down like a perfect little soldier boy. Maybe when we get home you can blow my—"

"Troye!" Groaning, Brady buries his face into his hands. "Not here."

"What? I was going to say, bugle. Get your mind out of the gutter, Basse." His head then swivels, smirk intensifying as an unimpressed Coach Harris appears. "Good win, Dad."

Coach mutters something about punks under his breath, then turns to me. "Ah. I was wondering where half of my coaching staff went to. Should have guessed. Quinny, you are to hockey players what flames are to moths." I'm not quite sure if he's joking and don't particularly feel like hanging around to find out.

"Sorry 'bout that, Coach. Did you need something?"

"Yes, Malkovich is complaining about his shoulder. Can you have a look for me?"

"Coach White is treating him now, Sir."

"Coach White has his hands full with Nurse and his groin."

"I bet he has," snorts Troye, who is again ignored.

"Besides, you've done a great job on his treatment. No point switching now." He then pops a piece of gum in his mouth and motions down the race. "Off you trot, Plummy."

The urge to argue is so strong I almost choke on the words, but without saying. "I can't touch him because I'm angry that he told people he blew me. Or even better, please don't make me, 'cause I want to fuck him," there is no way to justify my refusal.

Instead I nod, turn and sulk away to my certain doom.

I scored the winning goal. Duped Trent into handing it to me, and, for my first full game back, the shoulder has held up really well, and could honestly do with a little ice and rest.

So yes, there is sweet fuck all wrong with me. I require no treatment. No taping.

What I *am* sorely in need of is Doc Plum anywhere in my vicinity, but preferably looming over me with his hands anywhere on my body.

Or inside me. I'm not fussy.

All week he's looked through me like I'm a sheet of glass, and I can't take it a second longer.

He has to forgive me. I have to make him see that I'm sorry.

Jamie is good at his job. Great even. Which means he's going to take one look at me and know nothing is wrong. I have to work quickly. Since he's a writer, I figured the written word might have more luck in winning him over.

I look down at the note I scribbled on a take out napkin I found in my bag, and wince.

JAMES. IT'S ONLY BEEN A WEEK, AND I'VE SEEN YOU ALMOST EVERY DAY, BUT I MISS YOU. IF I COULD GO BACK IN TIME AND NOT SAY ANYTHING ABOUT US I WOULD, BUT I CAN'T. I UNDERSTAND WHY YOU'RE MAD. AND HOW MUCH YOU HAVE TO RISK, AND IF YOU GIVE ME A SECOND CHANCE AT FRIENDSHIP, I SWEAR I WON'T LET YOU DOWN.

Like you said, life seems to keep tossing (no pun
intended) us together. I'd really like the opportunity to find out why.
Yours, Cubby

The Yours at the end is risky and deliberate. James doesn't have a lot of people in his life. I want him to know he has me. In whatever form he wants.

When the door finally swings open, and the face and body that keep me awake at night saunters through it, I lose my breath. He's so fucking handsome.

"Even after you dunked me, you're still angry." I don't want that to be the first thing I say, but it is.

"I'm not angry."

"Your face, your mustache in particular, says otherwise. It twitches when you're pissed, and that thing is jumping around like a coked-up squirrel." He talks all snooty too, but I decide to leave that out for fear he may implode. Adorably, he purses his lips. I think it's an attempt to control the quiver.

"My mustache does not twitch, and I am not angry. One has to care to remain affected by another's betrayal, and since I don't, I'm not." After dropping his satchel bag by the bed, he washes and dries his hands at the tiny basin he dwarfs, moves the row of stainless steel draws holding medical supplies and pulls out some tape and scissors, I think he's done. He is not. "If I was angry I might have spent hours pondering how you could risk my career so thoughtlessly, or how out of all the people you could discuss things you promised never to discuss, you chose your teammates. The people I have to work with and treat everyday." James turns and approaches, eyes trained to the floor, which is disappointing since I've already removed my gear in the hopes the nips might win him over before I needed the note. A roll of tape is deposited beside me and he stands between my spread legs. He smells amazing. It's agony. "But I haven't. Not a single moment."

Twitching must be contagious, as maintaining a solemn expression is killing me. "Glad to hear it, Jamie."

Eye's falling shut, he does the other thing I've noticed him doing a lot, a slow puffed cheek inhale, then exhalation. "Good."

"Great."

"Okay then."

In silence, he takes hold of me and manipulates my shoulder, testing its range of movement. It's the wrong shoulder, but I don't correct him 'cause he's got the cutest frowny face on and he's touching me, and that's all that really matters. "How does that feel? No pain?"

"Feels great. Movement feels like nothing happened. I think you've cured me, Doc." His eyes close again, and I'm treated to another puffed cheek breath.

"I'm on the wrong arm aren't I?"

"Yep. But in all honesty, there's nothing wrong with the other one, either."

"For fuck's sake, Cory." The roll of tape is picked up and tossed across the room. "I have other people to treat, you know. My humble job may be an insignificant joke to a big time, soon to be NHL-er like you, but this is my life, not some childish game."

"I know that, and it's not insignificant. You're not insig—" I stop short, knowing there is nothing I can say that will break through his stubbornness. Since he's now hunched over the basin again, gripping the bridge of his nose like his brain might explode out his nostrils, I slip off the bed. With the note in my trembling hand, I pad over to the door and drop it into his open bag, saying a little prayer he reads it before it's tossed. "I just ... I miss you, and this was the only way I knew you'd see me. It won't happen again."

CARRYING the weight of the world on my perfectly healthy shoulders, I stumble through the still broken door and collapse onto the sofa. Miffy's there as usual, barking at me like I don't feed her scraps from my plate at every meal. Despite the jovial mood after a great win, the ride back to campus blew chunks. James refused to acknowledge me once again and I got stuck sitting next to Kyle Larsson, whose motion sickness had him vomiting three times in a twenty minute trip.

"Is that you, Cory?" Mom calls from the kitchen a second before she appears, Billie on her hip tugging at the strings on the front of her apron.

"Hey, Ma. Your Royal Cutie," I reply, not raising my head. Plopping Billie on the carpet near her ever-growing pile of toys, she squishes into the tiny free space, rustles my hair then presses a kiss to the top of my head. "You're spreading yourself thin, my boy. School, hockey, that job. It's too much."

"It's not, Ma. I swear I'm fine. First game back always hits hard." Which is true. Not quite this hard, but hard. "Besides, I like working at Green Line. Brady and Lotte are amazing and the clients are so much fun. It's good for me. And after this weekend, I'll have enough wages to pay half this month's mortgage. We'll catch up in no time."

"It's not right." She tuts, shaking her head. "Children shouldn't be taking on a mother's responsibility."

I roll to my side, and grasp Ma's hands. "We're your children, but we're not children, Ma. You've worked your ass off for years to pay for my hockey and for Cherry's school, it's about time we gave you something back other than a headache. Now, will you tell me how far behind you are." Smiling, she kisses me again, this time on the only part of my forehead that's accessible.

"No, but you're a good boy, Cory. Now come and eat. I made you mac and cheese."

"With chicken and bacon?"

"With extra chicken and enough bacon to clog all of your arteries. There's garlic bread, too." Before she can slide away, I wriggle my hands free and wrap them around her. She feels thinner than usual, frail, even. So much so I'm conscious not to squeeze her too tight.

"See, that's why me and Cherry want to help. You're the best."

With a grunt, she stands. "I am pretty amazing."

I beat her over to Billie and carry her back into the kitchen, sliding her roly-poly legs into her highchair where she immediately starts smooshing her pasta between her equally chubby fingers. My stomach rumbles as Ma fills a bowl with pasta then slides a whole plate of cheesy bread before me, watching as I shovel it into my mouth. "Something else is wrong. You're not eating."

"I literally have my mouth full," I mutter around a chuck of chicken. "How am I not eating?"

"You're slower than normal. Tell me what's wrong. I know there's something. Billie does too. Don't you, Bill?" I turn to my left. Billie's currently licking the sauce from the tray in front of her, blonde locks trailing behind tongue.

"Yeah. She looks super stressed."

"She's comfort-eating. Now tell me."

Knowing full well she's distracting me from the money thing, but also that she could hound me over this for hours, days even, I yield. "There's this guy—"

Grasping her chest, she slides into the seat beside me. "There's a guy? There's never been a guy. I mean, there's a lot of them if the damn Grindr notifications and midnight disappearing acts are anything to go by, but there's never been a *guy* guy."

"You know that Grindr sound?"

"Don't be ridiculous, of course I do. When you first came out I heard it more than I heard my own voice, now shut up and tell me about him."

A short on detail, long on whining retelling follows, Mom's face morphing between, *Aww*, *what the*, and *you didn't*. The overwhelming expression though is sympathy which makes me feel equally seen, sad and pathetic.

"Honestly, I had no idea. I can't believe you never told me you were getting teased at school, or that you felt so insecure you arrived early to practice, just to change. And why?" She grabs my chin and shakes my head. "Look at this face! Glasses or no glasses, ten feet tall or five, you're so cute I could eat you up. What put that notion into your head?"

How do I reply to that?

I don't know what caused *it*. Was it the lifetime of being the smallest in every grade? Of being the last one picked in sports even though I was often the best. Of being a target. Was it a faulty

I'd seen the news, knew inflation was up which meant interest rates would go north with it, but I've had my head so far up my ass lately, I didn't do the math 'til now. Now that I'm at the checkout of our grocery store, overwhelmed, overstimulated, with a credit card that's been declined. The store is crowded, and some electrical issue has only one register open, and the checkout operator looks as though she may cry.

"I can try it again sir, but it's not working. Do you have another card?"

"No, I don't have another bloody card. Would I have had you try that ten times if I did?"

"Don't be angry at her," says one of the many assholes in line behind us acting like assholes do, staring and tutting. This one dressed head to toe in Red Sox gear. "It's not her fault."

I'm not angry, I think to myself, because now I can't fucking speak. *I'm … suffocating. Drowning. Every fiber of my body on the verge of exploding because every sound in this building is over amplified.*

Hoping one may magically appear, I check my satchel for the hundredth time, this time pulling everything out and dumping it on the conveyor belt. I do normally carry a second bank card, Faith's, after something similar to this happened one day, but with Dylan screaming alongside me. There's a drink bottle, a few stray almonds, my keys, some treatment plans and a napkin that seems to have some kind of note on it. The same jerk that yelled at me for yelling, pipes up again before I can read it. "For God's father figure? The church's blatant homophobia mixing with my own internalized version, and the fear of being me caused me to live in for years? All I know *is* that I hated me before I could learn which me I was, and after a summer spent fucking everything that moved, seeking approval from random faces then rejecting them before I could get rejected, I finally see it.

That James has helped me see *it.*

The *it* being that I don't need to be who people want or expect me to be. That I am okay with me. Just as I am.

What a shame I had to lose something I wanted, but never really had, to see it.

sake, man. Just admit you're a loser, put the shopping back, go. I got a game to get to."

Pain shoots through my chest, sweat dripping into my brow as I try and shove everything back in my bag before I become the six-foot-five loser someone live streams crying in Wegman's. And that's what I want to do. I want to collapse to the ground and cry if I don't drop dead of a heart attack first.

Not a fish. Not a fish. Not a fish.

"Doc Plum?"

Oh dear God.

There's only a handful of people on the planet that call me that. One I can rule out instantly. Actually, make that two. It's not Cory, I'd know that voice anywhere, and there's no accent so it's not Brady either. Daring to look, I raise my eyes and find the soft smiling face of Sam. "Are you okay? Do you need help?"

"He needs someone to pay for his shopping, that's what he needs," Red Sox adds. I really hate that guy.

Before I can process what's happening, Sam rests a steadying hand on my shoulder, and fishes his phone from his pocket with the other. "I got it, Doc." With a tap he's paid, is loading my shopping back into my cart, and wheeling towards the exit. After muttering another apology, I take off after him, humiliated, grateful and dreading the questions I know he must have. It takes longer than I expect for them to come, which is good as my brain is too congested with anxiety over how this must look, of what he must think of me, to let anything else exist.

Looking too scared to speak, Sam is patiently waiting for me to load the groceries into the trunk, hand annoyingly tapping on the roof rack. I crack before he does, the first words I offer him after showing such kindness become, "Must you do that?"

"Do what?" He follows the direction of my death stare, and his hand stills. "Oh, sorry." His crestfallen expression leaves me feeling like an even bigger tit than I already do, but I can't deny the relief I feel with out the tappity tap tap. "So." He forces a smile. "That was—"

"Rude." I take a beat or two longer than I'd hope to get the rest out, Sam's big green orbs never leaving mine, but eventually I manage to add, "I'm so sorry. I'm autistic, and embarrassed and ... broke."

"You don't need to apologize. I had a cousin who was on the spectrum. I kind of figured what was happening." My mind catches on '*was on the spectrum*'. Dear God don't let him be a 'we cured him with Vitamin A and protein-person'. "He passed away a few years ago."

"Shit. I'm really sorry to hear that."

"Yeah. It was hard, but he had been really sick for a long time, so at least he's not in pain anymore." He gives the car one more tap, then snatches his hand away. "Sorry. Ah, do you need a hand with anything else before I go?"

"No. No I don't."

"Okay then. Well, see you at practice." With a wave he strolls away like he didn't just step in and save my day. I watch him go, noticing he passes all the cars parked before the store.

"Did you walk here? Do you want a ride?" I yell as he waits to cross the street.

"Yeah. Cool, thanks." Face lighting up, he jogs back to the car, waiting at the passenger side door while I return the cart.

"Great. So you're heading back to your dorm? You share with Lucas, right?" I ask when I pull from the curb. "How's that? Playing together, living together."

"Most of our classes are together, too. And it's fine. He's cool. Pretty quiet, and obsessed with his girl, Hannah. A lot of people expect things from me, but he's not one of them."

"Why?"

"Why do people expect things from me?"

"Yeah."

"Oh, my family is loaded. Those that know love to take advantage of it. It's kind of my fault though," he shrugs, knuckles tapping against the window, "I was kind of shy as a kid. Money helped me buy things. Buy friends, I guess. So yeah, that's why I like Lucas. He was my friend before he knew I was Samuel Bailey. Son of media magnates Eloise and Bronson Bailey. Cory, too." He raises his brows as he says Cory's name. I notice and he notices me noticing. "You shouldn't be mad at him. He never told us about you, we guessed and to be fair, you make it pretty obvious that you like him. So, in a way it's kinda your fault."

"Oh really? I'm not quite sure what you think you saw, but I do not like *Cory*."

"He likes you. A lot. He's been miserable since—" Enraged that Cory has again spoken to Sam about our non-existent relationship, I go to jump in. Sam's not having a bar of it, though. Neither is the stop gesturing hand he's shoved into my field of vision.

"He never said anything, but again, it's obvious something changed, and since whatever happened between you happened, he's been miserable. If you want to be with Cory just be with him, Lucas and I won't say anything. And what, you have a few months left with the Bears before you're qualified? Just control those hungry eyes of yours and you keep it on the DL. Easy. "

"I'm not having this discussion with you."

"Maybe it doesn't have to be a discussion. Maybe you just need to listen."

"Well, maybe you need to tell me your address so I can get you the hell out of my car." My tone is gruff, and I'm not sure if I meant it to be. Either way Sam doesn't seem to mind. That same easy smile is back.

"You know, on second thoughts, I don't feel like going home. I might go see my cousin. It's on the way. Could you drop me off there?"

"As long as you say nothing else about you know what, then fine. Lead the way."

"Are you dicking with me?" I pull up to the curb and slam the car into park. "I mean seriously, this isn't funny. How did you get this address?"

"This address." Sam taps the damn window again and I'm a second from losing it.

"No, the address you haven't guided me too, and that we're

not sitting in front of. Yes this address. This is my apartment building." *Or it was.*

"No way! My cousin lives here... well she has a place here. I'm probably here, hiding from the world, more than she is. Bit of a globetrotter. Small world, hey."

"Frighteningly."

"She's on 3A. What about you?"

"3C."

"No way. You're freaking neighbors. How awesome is Mrs.T? Great cookies."

"Well I did think she was great, but that was before I heard about the cookies I've been missing out on."

Unclipping his belt, Sam chuckles, then pauses, hand on door. "Wait. 3C's for sale. This is a great building. Why are you leaving?"

"It is a great building. I love it. But remember how you just paid for my groceries, which, by the way, I am very grateful and fully paying you back for? Yeah. That's why."

"Oh. Shit. That sucks."

"It does indeed suck."

Lips skewed to the side, Sam nods. "You know Cory's family has money trouble too. It's really sad. You've met his sister Cherry, right? She's hot."

My head is spinning from the sudden change in both Sam's countenance and expression. I guess a pretty young woman can do that to some pretty young men. "I have met Cherry. We spoke about her at the dunk tank, remember? She seems like a handful."

"Yeah." He sighs wistfully, settling back into the seat.

"Sam."

"Yeah," he repeats.

"I need you to get out of the car, now." Like he's been shocked back to life he jumps in his seat and opens the door.

"Oh, yeah. Sorry about that. And don't worry about paying me back. If you must, make a donation to charity. I don't need it. See ya later, Doc." With that he slips from the car and jogs towards the building. My building. My home.

Knowing at least my bed and my weighted blanket is on the horizon, I sigh, shove my crappy car into drive, and go.

"DYLAN, want to help me make dinner?" Responding with a hum, he practically leaps from the sofa, and I congratulate myself on a perfect afternoon. We've been to the park, watched a movie and the credits are rolling right when I need to start food prep.

"What do you feel like tonight? I was thinking some fancy omelets." The words have hardly left my mouth and Dylan is floating around the kitchen, humming while gathering ingredients. There's definitely an omelet in the making, but then he adds bananas, chocolate chips and baking powder to the collection and I know what he's after. "Omelets and pancakes?"

It is times like this that I am more fascinated by autism than frustrated. Dylan struggles with many daily functions, especially those requiring fine motor skills, but slap an apron on him and put him before a mixing bowl, and he's a Great British Bake Off contestant.

Dyl gets busy mixing up his favorite, and while he does that I bitch to him, like he holds the solution to all my problems.

"You remember Cory, the Jenga guy?" Dyl's whole face lights up on hearing Cory's name, then I picture the face touching and get *all* the feels again. "Yeah, him. Well, turns out he told his friends about us, even though he said he wouldn't. I got mad of course, 'cause I'm a grouchy piece of shit, and now I feel bad 'cause I really like him. It just feels like ... unfair. You know?"

Rocking back and forth, Dyl holds up his eggs. "Shit sorry, mate. I forgot cracking these bad boys is my job." Once they've been added to the dry ingredients, Dyl adds double the chocolate needed and the banana he's mashed already and then the milk. None of it's measured, but seconds later he has a perfectly smooth batter and is holding it out to me, eyes darting between his bowl and mine. "Why is yours not done," written all over his face. Like with the eggs, I'll handle the cooking. Not because

Dylan's not capable, but because he has a fear of the naked flame on the gas stove top.

Grabbing two frying pans from the pot drawer, I put them on the heat, and toss in some butter. "Big?" I ask, holding out my clenched right hand, "or little." Repeating the same on the left. As expected, Dyl taps my right fist. "Good choice, dude."

Since I haven't even cracked my eggs yet, I decide to stick with the pancakes. It's not the healthiest dinner, but Faith's not here to judge, and it's still better than a greasy take away.

I give myself a little pat on the back for a perfect first pour and wait for the bubbles. "This kid on the team, Sam. He thinks I've been too hard on your pal, but I'm not so sure. Theoretically I get where he's coming from. I may not give a shit about fitting in, but Cory does. Spilling the tea was like some kind of ritualistic, bonding experience. Sam also says Cory told him he really likes me, so that's nice. But also not because he shouldn't like me 'cause nothing can happen. It's just a fucking mess and so bloody typical. Why does the first guy I've been into for an eternity have to be out of reach?"

I'm daydreaming now, picturing Cory's face and staring out the window by the stove, when Dylan shoves me. "Oh, shit. Sorry mate." I flip the pancake that was seconds from burning and give a half smile to my brother.

"I know this is for the best. Being friends was never going to work, but I miss him, Dyl. Is that weird?" In response, Dyl holds out a plate that's as empty as I feel. "Here ya go bud. Thanks, for listening."

I've only just poured more batter into the pan, when several loud thumps echo up the stairs and through the open doorway. "What the hell is that?" Cleo is turning circles at my feet, so it's not her knocking over my stick collection again. Turning off the heat, I mosey over to the entrance to my dungeon, heat rate accelerating with each step, and stick my head into the darkness. "Turn the light on dick." I lean back, flick the switch then peer in again. For a second there's nothing, but then three more bangs ring out.

Holy shit, someone is trying to break in through my door.

P ounding so heavily against the door, I may knock it down, kind of defeats the purpose of bypassing the front and sneaking to James' basement entry, but do I stop? No.

There's no cars in the drive so I'm not even sure if he's home, but I just saw Faith in the library, so at least I know she's not here. And for some reason, my brain memorized Dyl's routine when I was over for dinner, so I know they should almost be sitting down to eat.

Despite the incessant pounding of my fists, there's no sign of James. Deciding to give it one more go then try the front like a normal person, I give three more hard knocks, the sigh of relief when the light flicks on. One of the blinds is open, so I can see James' bed, a book lying atop a pair of neatly folded pajamas sitting by his pillow, as does a teddy bear I definitely didn't see on the grand tour. Why that bear makes my chest squeeze so hard, I don't know.

I do know James is going to be pissed, though. Me knocking his door down is diametrically opposed to his 'stay the fuck away from me' request. I'm just about to try again when his adorable grumpy-ass face pops into the window.

"Cory? What the fuck?" He disappears again then the door is flung open, light spilling out into the garden. Wearing Ugg boots on his feet, sweats, a Boston B's jersey, and brandishing a hockey stick as a weapon, he places one hand on the opposite door jam, blocking the door with his massive frame. It's so fucking adorable I can't stop myself from smiling.

"Hey, James. Sorry—"

"Hey James. Hey James? What the hell, Cory. You almost knock my door down in the middle of the night after I explicitly told you to stay away, then give me, *Hey James.*"

Not sure why he did my voice like the Fat Comptroller from Thomas the Tank Engine, but it's best not to mention that now. Can't seem to stop myself saying this, though. "The middle of the night? It's not even seven."

It's quite possible this will be my last night on earth.

"Did you come here to give me shit, or is there something you want? You've got seconds to tell me or this stick is going to become very closely acquainted with your prostate and your tonsils."

Protectively, my butt-hole clenches around itself. "I'm sorry. I don't know why I said that. I do need to talk to you about something really intense, and I didn't have anyone else to talk to. Actually I did, but I wanted to talk to you."

"Why me?"

Yeah, Cory. Why him? "The truth is I don't know why. I just ... I mean, I want to talk to you all the time." James inhales, and tilts his head to the side, like a big, burly puppy. When he says nothing, I add, "But especially now."

There's every chance he's going to step back and slam the door in my face, and I'm readying myself for that, while hoping to god that's not how this goes. When he doesn't, I inch closer.

"It's the bank. They've foreclosed. They're taking Mom's house." James' eyes soften before my own.

"Dylan and I are making pancakes for dinner. You hungry?"

JAMES' gaze flicks back and forth between me and his plate. Ignoring it, I shovel another fluffy into my mouth and smile. His expression has been fixed since Dylan pulled out a seat and pushed me into it. Obviously he's not comfortable with me being here, but why ask me inside to eat if you're just going to sit and glare at me? We haven't got to why I'm here yet, and despite the awkwardness, it's a bit of a relief. Staring or no staring, a semi-peaceful family meal is what I need right now.

I'm not family, of course, but still.

"These are great, Dyl. You'll have to give me the recipe."

"There isn't one," James replies gruffly. "He does it all from memory. I've tried to jot it down as he goes, but they taste like rubber whenever I've tried." Again he studies me, eyes narrowed and slightly twitching. It's unnerving to say the least. If he's going to yell at me, I'd rather just get it done with.

Maybe I should just ask what the deal is. Clearing my throat, I do just that.

"Apart from the whole you not wanting me here thing, is there something wrong? You keep looking at me like I've shot your puppy."

"That's Dad's chair." Words explode from his chest in a gulp of air like he's been held underwater. "He hasn't let anyone sit there since Dad died. Not me. Not Faith. Not even Cleo."

I almost tread on the aforementioned cat as I leap to my feet. "I'm so sorry. I'll move."

"No!" James reaches over the table and manages to snag the hem of my shirt and hold me in place. "Please, you don't have to. It's just a shock. He's …" James pauses, eyes beading with tears, "for every meal for almost six months, he's watched the chair like he's waiting for Dad to walk in. And the face thing, the touching. That's always been reserved for me, Faith and Dad. That's it. Then here you come, meeting him what? A couple of times, and he just lets you in. He has the most pure, beautiful heart, and he trusts you. That means something to me, Cub."

I gasp so loud it should be embarrassing. "You called me, Cub. You haven't done that since—"

I don't have the chance to finish that sentence. James stands, fists more of my shirt and drags me onto his body. "You mean something to me." Trembling, he rests his forehead against mine. With three deep, shattered breaths, I inhale his always fresh, clean, man scent that's mixed with maple syrup and bacon to create the most heavenly thing any nostril has ever smelled. "You came here to talk to me about your family. I've been rude. I'm sorry. I was just ... Will you stay? I just have to do Dyl's routine, and then maybe we can talk."

"No," I say way too quickly resulting in James' pretty pout emerging.

"Oh. Sorry I—"

"No, no, I mean, yes. How about I stay, we do the routine together, and *then* we talk."

Exhaling slowly, he smiles. "Yeah." Then nods, before placing a kiss on my nose that feels so intimate I shiver. "Together. That sounds perfect."

I'M ESSENTIALLY A PROFESSIONAL ATHLETE, but by the time Dylan is snoozing, I'm tempted to roll him out of bed and snuggle in the warm spot he leaves behind.

"Fuck, Jamie," I say as we descend the first set of stairs, pass through the kitchen, then down again to the basement. "I'm starting to understand why you look so grumpy all the time. You're not moody, you're exhausted."

"I'm choosing to take that as a compliment." Pulling me down with him, he flops onto the tiny sofa pushed up against the wall. There's no lights on down here other than a tiny almost nightlight plugged in at the foot of the stairs, meaning like the nose kiss, it's insanely intimate.

Trying to ignore the press of his thigh against mine, I focus on one of the points we need to talk through. "I'm really sorry for just turning up like this."

"No you're not." He snorts.

"Yeah, you're right. I'm not. But I am sorry for talking about you to Lucas and Sam." James places his hand on my knee and squeezes. Prior to this moment, I'd not realized there was nerve running directly from kneecap to dick, but hey, you learn something new everyday.

"I know you are. Forget about that now. Tell me what's happening with the house."

The load just being in James and Dylan's presence had lifted, returns tenfold.

"When Mom, or Grandpa actually, first told us about the mortgage problem, Mom made it sound like it was a new thing. But it's been dragging on for almost a year. Legal proceedings had already begun, and yeah. There's nothing we can do. The house will be sold at auction in two weeks."

"Two weeks? That's it? You have to just pack up your life and be gone in two weeks."

"No, the auction is in two weeks. We have to be out in nine days."

James flops against the back of the sofa.

"That's ... shit Cub that sucks. I'm so sorry. What are you going to do?"

"Well that's what I wanted to talk to you about. The plan was always for me to finish college and go straight into the NHL, but maybe they could play me in the AHL for a bit. I don't really care, I just need money."

"Cory. Please don't tell me you're thinking what I think you're thinking."

"Are you thinking I was thinking of asking my agent to reach out to Montreal if they would be interested in calling me up now?"

"Yeah, nah, that's not happening. No fucking way am I letting that happen."

"You're not letting that happen?" I'm feigning insult but, damn, possessive Jamie is hot.

"Damn straight I'm not. You can't just leave. What about m ... school? What about ... School?"

He was totally going to say *me* then, but I let it slide 'cause his 'stache is twitching so hard it may fall off.

"Fuck school. Mom has lost everything because of me and hockey. I have years to finish my degree once I retire, but Mom and Cherry and Billie need a roof over their heads now. If Montreal won't take me, I'm quitting hockey and school and getting a job."

James folds forward rubbing his hands over his face. "I get

what you're saying, but, wait." In a flash he's on his feet pacing the room before me. "It's perfect. It's just sitting there empty."

"What's empty?"

"My apartment, Cubby. That big fancy three bedder that I sucked you …" He blushes, "well, you know the one. It's empty. You and your family can move into my apartment. You can stay as long as you need. You don't have to leave me."

A perfect solution, even if it's temporary, is being handed to me on a silver platter. I should be calling Mom and Cherry, jumping for freaking joy. But I'm incapable of movement, my brain snagged on six words, *you don't have to leave me.*

WE'VE BEEN SITTING on the couch for potentially hours. Talking about nothing and everything, but especially comics, his ideas for the next chapter of Love Comes in Green. All in all, the last few hours have confirmed what I've long suspected.

I'm falling for him.

I've also been arguing with him. He won the battle over me calling off my agent, but this one I am determined to win.

"You can't let us live in your apartment for nothing?"

"Why can't I? It's empty. May as well be … not empty."

"It's too generous. Mom will never go for it. We have to pay a fair rent and I think the only way for us to do that is for me to start playing in Canada or be working full time."

Not for the first time, Jamie grumbles under his breath and pinches the bridge of his nose. "I never did tell you why I quit playing, did I?" That one sentence has his uncharacteristically relaxed body returning to its normally tense state.

"No, and you don't have to, either, if it makes you uncomfortable." I nod to his hands, both now clenching against his thighs.

"It does, but I think it will help you understand why this is important to me. Yes, I'm being selfish because I don't want you to go, but I also don't want you to have the same regrets I did."

"Okay then. Tell me."

He clears his throat maybe three times, then takes a deep, shaken breath that shifts both our bodies. "I loved hockey, Cory. Like. I loved it. When I was a kid I never fit in. I was always on the outside. Always struggling to be accepted 'cause I just didn't know how to be like the others. I didn't smile like they did. I didn't understand why they were smiling in the first place. Dad was great, he taught me how to read expressions, and showed me that sometimes people did things that were the opposite of what they felt, like laughing when they are scared or intimidated, or crying when they are happy. Anyway, when Mom died, and we moved back to the States, one of the first things he did was enroll me and Dyl in hockey. Dylan was in an all abilities league and I was in peewee. I was weird, the biggest and worst skater, so they shoved me in goals and kind of ignored me."

"Pfft. That's mean. And dumb. Goalies are amazing skaters."

"They are. And I became one, really quickly. For the first time ever I was good at something. I didn't feel awkward or out of place. When I stopped a goal, I got head taps from the other kids and then at the end, I got the goalie cuddles and head taps. I loved it, Cubs."

Fuck. His eyes are glistening with tears, and I want to hug him so badly. I can see on his face he needs to get this out, though, so instead of reaching out, I tuck my hands beneath my thighs and press them into the cushion. "So, what changed?"

"Money did. As you know, hockey is expensive. Having a child with disabilities is too, especially with our fucked up medical system. Then there was Faith the super brainiac, who was going to college when all her friends were Juniors. Her age meant it was hard for her to get more than a partial scholarship. I was fifteen, I knew things were tight but I didn't know how tight, 'til I heard Dad on the phone one day. He was talking to Mom's sister, my Aunt Dianne, about selling his burial plot. The one next to my mom. He was crying so heavily it was hard to make out everything he was saying but I heard Dylan, insurance, college and hockey. Dylan needed to be cared for. Faith had to go to school. I didn't need hockey."

And that's it. I can sit on my hands no more. I pull them free and proceed to flap them around my head in ridiculous outrage.

"So what, you just quit?"

"Yup. That night at dinner I had a meltdown that was essentially a tantrum. Told Dad I hated hockey, and was only playing to please him. To top it off, I sprinkled in a little of the homophobic taunts so casually tossed around the locker room. He wanted me to fight. To keep playing, but I convinced him quitting was what I wanted."

"Jesus, Jamie. That really blows."

He breaks in to an unexpected laugh then turns to face me. "It really did, kid. But it had to be done. Regret, loving and missing something so wholeheartedly while simultaneously knowing it was the right thing to do, is a cruel kind of pain I never want you to experience. So, you will move in to my apartment. You will pay for whatever utilities you can. And you will finish school."

"I will, will I?"

"Yes. You will." He shifts closer, cupping my face in his strong hand and brushing his nose against mine. "And do you know what else you'll do?"

"Does it have something to do with the way you're touching me?"

"Yup." He nods. "You're going to kiss me."

"I want to fuck, James."

"I want that, too." Swiftly he stands, plucking me off the sofa like I weigh nothing, and holding me to him like I mean everything. The desperate slut I am, I wrap my legs around his waist, and begin rolling my hips, seeking out the friction we both need more than air. "You're so beautiful," he sighs, lips pressed against mine in an exchange of air more than a kiss. "I've never felt like this about anyone."

"Me either, Jamie."

He groans, thrusting into me. "Fuck I love it when you call me Jamie."

"Jamie," I repeat. "My Jamie."

Over the last few weeks, the fractured pieces of who I thought I was, wanted to be, and had to be, have begun slotting back into place. But this, the way Jamie kisses me now, needy and deep like the next moment he has with me may be his last, binds them all together.

Here. Now. With Jamie. I am whole. I am me.

Lips only parting so I can pull his jersey over his head, he carries me to his bed, tosses me down then crawls over me on all fours, hard dick straining to be freed, dragging along my legs. Pausing when our cocks are aligned, he rolls against me then hooks his fingers beneath the waist band of my sweats.

"Can I?"

"Fuck, yes. Take them off. Fucking burn them, just get me

naked." With a chuckle he tugs them and my briefs down, then shifts around to do the same with his own.

Had I known this was to be the outcome of my visits I'd have worn a sexy jock or silky thong. *Next time.* I think to myself. Because there will be next time. I don't care if we have to exist in the shadows, I am never letting the light this man's touch ignites in me dull again.

"Cory." Hovering above me, Jamie smiles then proceeds to kiss down my neck, focusing on a spot just below my ear that has me writhing and giggling like a fool. "Have you read any other sex scenes in my fic?"

"All of them." I sigh, barely able to respond at all.

"What's your favorite?"

Every scene is my favorite. James's fic is the hottest I've read, but there is one chapter in particular I keep going back to time and time again. I pull away from his lips, not because I want to, but because I won't be able to speak if he keeps kissing my neck like that. "My absolute favorite is when Spidey and Hulk have just defeated the Green Goblin in his apartment, and Spidey bends Hulk over, pins his hands behind his back and fucks him to oblivion. The thought of that big body of his taking it hard and raw from behind, fuck, it kills me every time."

"Do it to me, then," he says, reaching to his nightstand, he retrieves condoms and lube, then rolls onto his back beside me. "Fuck me into the mattress."

"You want me to fuck you?"

"I do. I'm a big greedy bottom, Cubby. Feed me."

"Jesus, James." As quickly as I can, I make my move, switching positions so I'm on top, hands roaming over his big, hairy chest. "Fuck I've dreamed about this every night for weeks."

"Me too."

Though the plan remains for me to fuck Jamie until next Tuesday, I also want to take my time doing it. Leaning down, I kiss his lips, his nose, ears, and chest before returning to his mouth. Gripping my neck, he holds me in place, lavishing my tongue with his own. His lips are soft. Hungry and bitey, too. We stay there, making out and frotting against each other, dicks leaking.

"I want to come with you inside me," he moans, "and if we keep doing this that's not going to happen."

"Can I prep you, or do you prefer?"

"You. I want you to get me ready." A shiver of excitement rolls down my spine. This is really happening.

Beginning with tracing his tattoo with my tongue, I trail down, kissing a line over his soft belly, giving special attention to the area around his belly button before dropping lower and taking him into my mouth. He bucks beneath me.

"Jesus, Cub."

I laugh, taking him deep, hollowing out my cheeks as I reach for the condom. I pop back off to slip on the condom before my hands are slippery with lube, then grease those bad boys up. "I'll do my best to open you, without making you come, but I also won't stop if you're close. Whether it's with my fingers in your ass or my dick, I want to watch you fall apart, Jamie. That's all that matters for now."

I don't wait for a reply before slipping between his spread legs, sucking the head of his cock between my lips and sliding my finger back to find and press against his hole.

I'm watching his reactions so intently I see the moment his breathing changes, slowing. Deepening. Those years of yoga and Pilates shine through. He's so relaxed, my finger slips right in and I'm able to add a second with little to no resistance. He's writhing beneath me. Sweating and mumbling, that relaxed state flies out the window when the pad of my finger brushes over his prostate. Once again, he bucks beneath me.

"Am I going to have to pin your arms behind your back? Tie you to the bed, maybe."

"Whatever you want," he grunts as my finger pokes that spot again. Laughing, I keep working him open, delighting in how responsive he is and totally getting off on the power trip that is having this big, *hulking* man quivering beneath me. He groans when I pull out, raising his head to eye me pleadingly. Holding up the lube bottle is all he needs to bring relief, and to let his head fall back against the pillow.

"You're really good at this," he mutters when I'm three

fingers deep and scissoring. "And I really like it, but, ahh fuck. I'm ready, Cory. Please, I'm ready."

I know he is. He was ready a few minutes ago, but the heat of his body, the tightness, the rush of making him melt to my touch has been too enjoyable to stop. I do though, gently sucking him in, rolling my tongue over his slit to gather the pooling pre-cum as I withdraw. The second my fingers are free, he rolls to his stomach, and freely places his hands behind his back.

"Such a good, big boy," I praise, then smack his ass so hard I leave a welt I kiss away. I'm painfully hard, not having touched myself once while prepping for fear of coming too soon. I feel the same nerves again as I take hold of James' wrists and press down on his back. He arches beautifully, that insane ass taunting me.

"Are you ready for me, Jamie?"

"Yes. I need you."

"And you have me." With that I press inside him. "Holy fucking fucks," I groan, stopping and folding over him before I'm even halfway in. "Jesus, you feel incredible. I just need to stop a sec." I take the opportunity to tighten my grip on his wrists and kiss his back, running my tongue over his spine, then back up, fisting his hair in my hand and pulling him onto my lips. I kiss him until I feel the heat low in my belly, give one last tug on his hair, then release him. There's no more delays after that. Back up on my knees, I feed my cock into his impossibly tight, wet hole until my pelvis is flush against his, feeling him adjust around me, I begin to rock. "Tell me if it's too much."

"It will never be," he groans, voice muffled. "I can't deny it anymore. I want it all. All of you."

"Jamie." I lose control, hips pistoning, I fuck into him so hard, I think the headboard may smash through the wall, as I call his name again and again. "Jamie. Jamie. Jamie." I slap his ass, lean down and sink my teeth into his back, tightening my hold on his wrists. It's desperate. The sounds and smell of sex and sweat are so potent I will never forget it. As hot and as perfect as this is, one thing is missing.

"Need to see you," I pant, releasing my hold of him. "Turn over, Jamie, please. I need to see your face when you come."

He groans, deep, rough like my big bear that he is when I pull out, and rolls to his back without complaint. Before I can enter him again, he sits up, grabs the back of my neck and tugs me into a kiss. "You're incredible."

"Because you are."

Bodies slick with sweat, emotions running high, we break apart. Longing to feel his tight wetness, I slide right back inside him. The pleasure, the bliss of fucking into him now tenfold that I can see his face. How his teeth sink into his full bottom lip. His mustache twitches. His eyes, and their golden glow burning brighter than ever, and solely focused on me.

Greedy for touch, I place my hands on his chest, dig my fingers into his flesh and unleash. I'm pounding him so hard, pegging his prostate with each thrust he comes without warning or touch, squirting all over his stomach and chest and sending me over the edge with him. I need to see us together. Need to paint him, mark him with my release. I pull out, and rip off the condom just in time for the first burst of hot cum to land on that delicious chest. He groans with each spurt, eyes fixed on my dick as pulse after pulse coats him.

Despite the cum coating his skin, I collapse against him, my stomach swirling with sentiments I can't express. This man. This beautiful man who's kissing my head, and stroking my back so tenderly. Who has offered me his home. Is risking so much for me.

Fuck I am so gone.

And the best part is, I think he is equally lost in me.

I press off his chest enough to see his face. "I've never—"

He cuts me off with a kiss I feel in the deepest part of my soul. "Me either."

Tendrils of light reach through my ill-fitting blinds, caress my cheeks and wake me. As consciousness blooms, I realize I'm smiling. And naked. And not alone.

Cory stayed the whole night.

Now that the overwhelming emotion and pent-up desire has been released, I should perhaps be panicking. Jumping from the bed, shaking Cory awake and demanding he leave. But there's not a shred of anxiety within me. Not a bit. Only certainty that this is it. That *we* are right. No matter how wrong it may be. So instead of tossing the beautiful man, who's wrapped around me like a tortilla on a burrito, face cutely tucked into the crook of my neck, out, I pull him closer. Breathe him in, and fall back to sleep, for once, let me have something for me.

"Jamie, what the fuck?"

And there's the panic.

Dislodging the warm body lying perfectly still atop me, I leap from bed then remember I'm naked. "Jesus, Jamie. Put some freaking clothes on. You too!" Faith demands. I think she thinks she's pointing at Cory, but she's blinded by the hand she slapped over her face, so she's aimed more at a barren wall to the right of us.

"Calm down, Faith." I laugh, picking up and slipping on my

jersey. Predictably, she does not calm, and that may be because she's copped another eyeful as she squints between her parted fingers. My top barely covers my junk, so I reach for my sweats and yank them on too.

"Calm down? Calm down? You're naked in bed with a twenty year old student. A–"

"I'm twenty-one next week," Cory adds, before shrinking back into the corner he'd retreated to.

"Your birthday is next week?" I ask, smiling ear to ear. "We should do something—"

"JAMIE!" Faith is shrieking now. I've never heard her voice reach these heights. "Listen to yourself. He's on the team. This is going to cost you your job."

"I won't let it."

"I know it will," Cory and I reply in unison, then freeze. Faith does too, so we just stare at each other like morons until Cory breaks the stalemate.

"What do you mean, you know it will. No one has to know, Jamie. We can keep it a secret until I leave and—"

"You're right," I interrupt, as I make my way back to bed, back to Cory, who without hesitation, wriggles closer and leans into my side. "We *will* have to keep it between us, Cub. But I'm not waiting until you go to Canada. There's a month left of my placement, and once that's done we can ... you know. Do. Us. ... If that's what you want of course."

"It is what I want." Eagerly grabbing my wrist, he threads his fingers between mine then raises our joined hands to his lips, placing a sweet kiss. "I mean I don't want to hide at all, but a month is nothing. A month is—"

"A freaking joke!" *Fuck.* I pretty much jump into Cory's lap, I'd totally forgotten Faith was here. "Are you kidding me? You honestly think you'll be able to stay on the down low for weeks? And what, you're just going to lie to everyone until then, and expect me to do the same?"

"Please, Faith." Releasing Cory once more, I slide from the bed and edge closer to my sister. "I've been really unhappy for a really long time. Just give us a month. One month to sort this out. And I promise, should things go astray, and we get busted,

I'll take the heat and make it known you knew nothing. I'll protect you. I swear."

"Excuse me, Jamie, if I don't take your promises to the bank. Not so long ago you promised me nothing was happening between the two of you, and here you are. Sneaking him into your room."

"Don't be angry at James, Professor," Cory pleads. "This is the first time, and James didn't sneak me in. I was really upset last night. My family is losing our home, and I needed someone to talk to. Jamie helped me. A lot."

"Yeah, he helped you right out of your clothes into his bed. Very charitable of you, James." Hands on hips, she's about to release another tirade when a series of thuds from upstairs steal her focus. "Great. Dylan's up and I'm totally out of routine now."

"We can help." Bending, I retrieve Cory's clothes from the floor and toss them his way. "Dylan loves Cory. You can get ready and we'll take care of Dyl until Manny gets here."

"Damn straight you will." She's off before I can add anything further, stomping up the stairs like a two hundred pound ogre. "Bet you're ass we're talking about this later, James. And as for you, Mr. Malkovich. See you in class."

And poof! The second the door closes, that calmness I handled that with vanishes. It's done. Gone. Finito. "Holy shit, we're fucked." Gasping for air, I grasp my chest. The one that's about to fracture from the intensity of my pounding heart. This is really it. I really am a goner.

"Hey. Hey, James, It's okay. Baby it's okay." I flinch at Corey's touch. The way his hands so tenderly caresses my hair, over my neck and down my back, sounds like coarse sandpaper over timber pumped through a megaphone, but fuck it, I'd die if he stopped touching me. "We're going to figure this out. I'm not going anywhere."

"I … I can't lose you, Cub."

"That's good then, 'cause you're not going too. Just breathe for me baby. Just breathe."

WHEN I WAS TEN, I stole a packet of Milk Duds from a concession stand at our school fair. I didn't even like Milk Duds all that much, but for some reason that yellow box called to me.

I felt so guilty, I was sick in the stomach and couldn't bear to eat them. On our way back to the car, Dad busted me sneaking them into my B's backpack. Grabbing me by the scruff of my shirt, I was promptly dragged back to the stand and forced to make a confession.

It was mortifying. Would never hold up in court, due to the coercion techniques of my six-feet-four dad, and the worker seemed more pissed off that my stuttered, long-winded apology was delaying his lunch break, rather than he was at my thievery.

A similar feeling of guilt and shame washes over me when I get to the rink thirty minutes late, and Coach Harris is waiting for me in my office. 'Cause of course he is.

"Morning, Coach." I try with all my might to keep my voice as neutral and dull as it normally is but I can hear a tremble I hope he doesn't. "Sorry that I'm late. Manny was, and it's a bit of a chain reaction then. You need me for something? How's the family?"

Super chill.

"Family is fine, thanks for asking. Don't worry about being late, and I do, yeah." He taps a stack of papers before him. "Take a seat, we need to have a chat." Oh dear fucking Lord. While pondering if I could out run him, I move behind my desk, but sit on the edge rather than sliding into my chair. Faster getaway and all.

"Chat away."

He knows something is off, he's chewing at a reduced rate and eyeing me suspiciously. "You alright? You seem kind of … nervous."

"I have diarrhea. Terrible, terrible diarrhea."

Wincing, he shifts uncomfortably in his seat, using his feet to wheel further away. "Should you be here? I was going to use you on the ice today. Stuck in the net fully padded up is not the place to be when you have …" He waves his hand before him.

"Diarrhea." I offer. "I have … diarrhea."

"Yes. So you said." After clearing his throat, I think to hide his smile more than anything, he continues, "We've been impressed with you James. I wasn't sure at first, but the superiority complex you seemed to bring with you has dissolved. The boys respect you, you have a great hockey brain, and are a natural coach. We haven't made this public yet, but it's likely Dale White will be moving to the AHL next season, and I'd like to offer his position."

Holy shit. He keeps talking but I'm not listening. All I can think about is the man I left in my bed this morning, and the prospect of either hiding what we have for an entire season, breaking it off, or turning down this opportunity. Something I thought I was prepared to do when it was a hypothetical. But now. Now?

"You want me to be Assistant Coach and Trainer? Full time?"

"I do." He nods, adding yet another piece of gum to his mouth. "As long as you survive the diarrhea."

"Wow."

There's a knock on my door , and Cory's head pops through, his smile fading when he sees my expression. "Hey coaches, sorry to interrupt, but Mom insisted—" The chance for Cory to complete his sentence is stolen by the appearance of his mother, his sister and a baby I presume is Billie.

"Mr. Plum. Cory told us about your offer." Unlike her son, Deirdre Malkovich doesn't knock, or even wait to barge in. Eyes, red and puffy, tears are streaming down her face, she wears a stained apron over her clothes like she's heard the news and just dragged him out of the kitchen and into the car. "It's so generous. So kind. But I insist we pay a fair rent."

"Rent?" Harris rises from his seat. "What are we talking about here?"

"Mom," Cherry says, forcing her way between her mom and the desk, she looks like she may leap to get to me. "We're interrupting something. Why don't we take Billie out to the rink, and let Cory speak with his coaches?" It's a question, but she doesn't wait for a reply, before she hooks her arm into her mom's and yanks her out into the hall.

"Why do I think there's something going on here I need to know about, and that will give me a headache?"

"Because there is something you need to know about, though it shouldn't be pain-inducing. Quite the opposite actually since this something will be keeping your best player on your team." Coach's eyebrows rise and his chewing picks up in pace.

"My family is being evicted," Cory blurts. "Well, technically not evicted as we aren't renting, but we're being foreclosed on. I was thinking of contacting Montreal and heading up north early, if they'd have me, that is. Just to earn the money to buy Mom's house back from the bank, or find her another."

"So I offered them my apartment," I finish. "I've been trying to sell it for some time. It's sitting empty. Has three bedrooms. Seemed like the perfect solution."

Nodding, Coach's eye roams between us. "It's a very generous offer indeed. I didn't realize you two were so close."

"We've become friendly." It's a version of the truth. The only one I'm free to give anyway. "We're both complete dorks at heart and I guess we kind of bonded."

"Superhero buddies." Cory offers, so damn cutely I can't hide my grin.

"Yes, quite. But honestly, Coach. I would offer the same to anyone on the team. It's the right thing to do. For Cory's family, the team, and for me. The Malkovich's will be paying rent, which will help cover the mortgage I've been struggling to do alone. It's a win, win."

"We don't want it to seem like you're playing favorites, James but it's an honorable thing to do. I'll get in touch with the legal team, and have them draw up some type of lease that specifies this is done under the knowledge of us, but without our endorsement. Situations like this can become messy. I have to protect the team, and the college."

"Absolutely. Great idea and this is all above board, Coach." I can't look at Cory, though I can feel his gaze burning into me. "All above board."

After the sweet, but over the top gratitude Mom and Cherry laid on James, it's surprising he's still speaking to me. Giving me a rim job in the backseat of his car feels like a minor miracle.

Determined to keep his word to Faith, all of our hook-ups, and there's been a lot of them, have taken place either in a car, at his apartment as we *prepare* it to be moved into, and once in a stairway on campus—poor judgment but oh so hot.

As is this. It's dark out, convenient since we're parked in the empty parking lot of a Home Depot. It's a ridiculously tight space for a full grown man and a giant, but by God are we making it work. My face is buried into the faux leather seat, and James' face is between my cheeks. That damn mustache brings me to the breaking point. Taylor Swift is blasting through the speakers, the car vibrating with the heavy bass of *I Did Something Bad,* while James does the very same to me.

"Don't you ever shave that thing, Jimmy. I'm going to paint your back seat."

Thrusting his tongue deeper inside me, he tightens his grip on my ass cheeks and moans. He loves me calling him Jimmy. And eating my ass. "So good, Jimmy. So good." When he growls this time, the vibration does me in.

I buckle beneath him, almost convulsing and spilling all over his seat. "James, fuck you're going to be the death of me." He doesn't stop, just laughs and delves deeper and deeper before sliding his finger in to abuse the gland his tongue can't reach. I feel him jerking himself as he does, and it's that mental image plus the renewed stimulation in my ass that sees me come again.

"Cory, fuck I'm coming too." The hottest back shot ever splashes on my sweat-soaked skin and I collapse, James falling on top of me. The weight of him delicious.

"Holy shit, that's never happened before," I pant. "Actually I didn't even know it was possible."

"Ne meither." He huffs a laugh, lips peppering me with kisses. "I mean me neither. Fuck, I think my brain just blew out my dick." Suddenly his laughter stops and his stills. "Next time, I think we should go for three."

"I agree."

"Can you even breathe right now?"

"Nope. It's the best." James laughs again, his body jiggling as he lifts off me and sits on his haunches as much as he can, and for the fiftieth time this week, I count my blessings. "You know, when I first met you, I would never have expected you to write filthy fan fiction, say things like, I think my brain just blew out my dick, and laugh because your cum-soaked body was suffocating me. You're quite the dirty old bastard once you drop the snooty Frasier act."

"I'm surprised you even watched Frasier."

"Why, because I'm just a kid?"

"No, because it's too high brow. You seem like more of a Dumb and Dumber guy."

"Hey!" I sit up and slap his sticky chest. "None of the dumb jock stereotypes, please. You know I'm smart as fuck. After a rough start I've worked my way up to the highest grades in your sister's class. And she hates me, so that's even more incredible."

The joyfulness in James' expression melts away. "She doesn't hate you, Cub."

"Pitt. I think she does. Even Brady thinks so."

"Brady said that?"

"He did. And don't worry. I haven't spoken to him, or anyone about us. He's just picking up the vibe your big sis is laying down."

James' face falls further as he reaches for one of the wet wipes he's started keeping in the car since we started fucking in it. "Sorry," he says, as he effortlessly flips me over and starts cleaning. "She's stressed with all this insurance crap, pissed with me because of the position I've put her in, and I get it. She shouldn't be taking it out on you, though."

"Did you do what I suggested? Tell her we weren't seeing each other anymore?"

"I tried but she called me out straight away. I'm smiling too much to not be having sex, apparently."

I should probably feel bad that James is having a hard time with his sister because of me. But it's hard to focus on that when I hear he's smiling all the time because of me, too.

"I make you smile?" I coo.

"Shut up." He snorts, then tosses the dirty wipe in my face. "You know you do."

"You make me smile too. Even when you toss cum rags at me."

"Never say that again, Cory."

"I will if you ever stop smiling."

"Deal."

I'm contemplating round two when my phone rings. It's in the pocket of my jeans, buried somewhere on the floor, and by the time I find it, it's stopped. It starts again immediately and worry sets in as James finds then hands it to me. "It's Coach."

"Shit." I take a breath and answer while trying not to laugh. James has slapped his hand over his mouth to keep quiet and it's so freaking cute it's not funny.

"Hey Coach. How you doing this fine evening?"

"Fine, Cory. Thanks for asking so formally. You sound like a fucking butler."

"Yeah, sorry. I always get a bit nervous when you call."

"Good to know. Listen, I was talking to your mother today, had an idea to run by her." I sit up so straight, so fast, my head spins.

"You talked to my mom?"

"I did. I knew it must be close to the time you have to move out of your home, and I wanted to lend a hand. I have one last Sunday of slave labor up my sleeve and I've decided to use it to help your family. Come Sunday morning, the team will be at your place seven sharp. If you have any ... private items you don't want your teammates to see, I suggest you pack them securely before we arrive."

Several private items only me and my prostate have been introduced to recently, spring to mind. "Thanks for the heads up, Coach. And for helping us move. It's unexpected and so appreciated."

"Yeah, yeah, I'm a Goddamn saint. See you at practice, Captain."

Sitting next to Brady, one of my favorite people, in my favorite class, sports psych, has been the highlight of this term.

At least it was. "Do you want me to talk to her? There's got to be a reason why she's so ... um." His face screws up as he searches for the right words.

"Why she hates me all of a sudden?"

Exhaling, he makes a sound similar to a horse and nods. "I was looking for a better way to say it, but yeah. She does seem to hate you."

It would take all of five words, I slept with her brother, to explain her sudden dislike of my fave, but I promised Jamie that I wouldn't talk to anyone about us and I *have* to keep my word. I'm desperate for whatever this is between us to last. Even when I go to Canada, as hard as it will be, I need James in my life.

It feels like every second we spend together, I understand him better. Despite his grumpy, snooty outer shell, when he lets his guard down and shows who he really is, the guy's a Goddamn delight. He's so fucking funny, would do anything for those he loves, and he has a really big dick.

I lean over my desk to shield my face from the professor. "You know what it might be? I talked to James about the house stuff, and the coming out stuff. And the friend stuff too. Maybe she's put out that I didn't come to her."

Brady shoves his hand in his pocket, and I know he's rubbing the hair of that damn troll. It helps him think. "That doesn't seem very Faith-like. She genuinely wants the best for the team and as long as you've reached out for help, I don't think she would mind who you went to."

"Mr. Malkovich, is my lecture interrupting your conversation?"

Wincing, I raise my head, and come face to stomach with Professor Plum.

"Actually I was talking," Brady cuts in. "Sorry about that."

"There's no need for you to cover for him, Brady. After all, Mr. Malkovich will be twenty-one this week. I'm sure he's big and brave enough to fight his own battles. I'll see you in my office after class."

"But I have practice."

"Well, you better not drag your feet then." Brady begins to speak, but is silenced by a remarkably similar death stare to the one I've received from her brother.

The rest of our lecture drags, and when Plum dismisses us, I rush to beat from the lecture theater to make sure I beat her to her office. Even though I'm about to get my ass handed to me, I can't stop smiling. I haven't been back here for weeks, not since I was stalking Jamie while eating alone. It's sad to look back and think how lonely I was then, but brilliant to compare it to now.

Lost in the daydream that relaxation provokes, I didn't hear Faith approach. "Did you run here?"

"No, of course not." I totally did. As though she sees my lie, she rolls her eyes and pulls open the door.

"Come with me, Cory."

"Okay."

The door to her office isn't even closed before she starts. "I know you're young, and that it can take years for people to come into themselves, but I don't think you know yourself enough to be considering a relationship of the nature that James needs."

Well, okay then. "Ah, no offense, Professor, but you don't even know me."

"Do you know you?" she counters immediately, her steely gaze fixed on the chair I think she wants me to drop into. I stay standing, though. It's much easier to run that way.

"What the fuck does that mean? Of course I do."

"Ah, okay. Sure thing, Ken."

"Ken? What ... what the hell is happening right now?" I glance around the room like someone's coming to help me. There is no one of course. I'm in this alone.

"What's happening is that I'm concerned about my family. What's happening is me calling you out for changing your personalities like Ken doll changes his outfits, hockey Ken, school Ken, Grindr Ken. I could go on. My brother believes you're this sweet, caring, dorky guy who's amazing with and bonding with Dylan, something that happens rarely. What I'm concerned about is that guy being just another costume and my brother's being hurt when you tire of wearing it."

Wow. That stings. I take a minute, slow my breathing and try really damn hard not to become defensive. "Faith, and yes, I am calling you Faith because what we're talking about here has nothing to do with my education and everything to do with what happens in my personal time. You're one hundred percent right. I was like that. I absolutely was and have no shame in admitting that." Moving to sit behind her desk, Faith scoffs and I can practically see the words, I knew it, written on her face.

"But you're also way off. I *did* feel the need to be what people wanted or expected me to be. I hid my glasses, my sexuality. I wore my hair different, was generally ashamed of being me, and trying to be everything I'm not. But then I met James, who helped me see that I'm just a guy who wants nothing more, and deserves nothing less than to feel safe enough to come out. Not only as gay, but as himself. Only a special man can provoke that kind of introspection, Faith, and that's exactly what Jamie, the man I've fallen for, is."

Faith looks at me blankly, her right eye lid twitching.

I may have broken her.

"You've fallen for him?" she whispers. "It's not just ... fucking?"

"No. It's not just fucking. I mean it started like that, and it is out of this world, but no. It's not just that. I want to be with him, Faith. I wouldn't be risking so much, if I felt any less."

"Did you ever consider that it's easy to take that risk, when you're not the one in danger of losing everything."

Bile rises in my throat. "What do you mean?"

"What I mean is, this *relationship* isn't putting your career, and future livelihood at risk, but it does for James. I'm sure he's told you about his past. If the truth comes out, he could lose everything all over again, Cory."

"But it won't," I argue. "He won't."

"But he could. So I have to ask, if you care as much as you say you do. If you're really falling for him, why would you put him in such a precarious position?"

"I ... I ..."

Fuck.

I swear I have been staring so intensely at my phone screen, time is sliding backwards. Faith and I have been waiting on a rep from our insurance company. That alone is tedious, but I'm busting to get out of here for another reason too. It's Cory's Birthday weekend and I still need to get his gift. With the rest of my week booked solid, this afternoon is my only chance.

I'm just about to send out a search party for Jennifer, the customer care consultant—loosest use of the term ever—at AWP Insurance, when she waltzes in, sitting behind her desk with no formal acknowledgment of her lateness or our presence.

"Another month or so and we should have everything sorted." Proudly, she taps the manila folder sitting before her, the one I'm beginning to suspect she hasn't opened since Dad passed away.

Mirroring Jennifer's movements, Faith leans forward and taps the same folder in time with her words. "Another. Month. Is unacceptable."

"I agree, Mrs. Plum."

"Miss," Faith corrects with another tap.

"Sorry, I should have gathered you were unmarried." Before Faith can leap across the desk and strangle the care right out of Jennifer, I slap my hand over her knee.

"Like my sister said, Jenny—"

"Jennifer." She corrects, her forced smile firmly in place.

"Jennifer, sorry. A month is unworkable. We've been carrying the burden of Dylan's costs for almost six months. This is not only unethical, I believe it's unlawful. Insurance companies such as yours, mustn't deny coverage based on a pre-existing condition like autism."

"Of course we can't, and that's not what's happening here I assure you. Dylan's cover has not been declined, rather delayed. Your late father left no will. Legal proceedings take time. Knowing this, we've been generous enough to cover Dylan's medical costs even without full coverage. I can assure you, at the *end of the month*," she taps again, "things should be resolved."

"We need a little more than *should* this time, Jennifer," Faith says, practically levitating.

"Unfortunately, that's all I can offer right now."

Having had enough, Faith stands and slaps both hands on the timber top, the movement scattering papers. "That's not good enough."

Jennifer says nothing, just glances to the doorway where a buff guy in a suit is standing, and motions for him to come in. "Thank you for coming in today. David will see you out now."

"David can go get fuc–"

"Faith," I say, harsher than perhaps necessary, but she can't see the security guard strutting in like I can. "It's okay. We have to go now." By the time I've finished that sentence, the bruiser is beside me, looking like he's going to crack his knuckles any second.

"Great." Faith, who's now redder than my shorts at the dunk tank were, barks. "Call security on the people you're supposed to be helping. Excellent use of your resources." With that she shoves the manila folder onto the floor and storms out. "See ya next time, Jenny."

"I FOR REALS thought you were going to deck her."

"Never say for reals again ... And so did I for a second." Faith smiles at me. Actually smiles so I can see her teeth, and I'm so relieved I could almost cry. She's barely acknowledged my existence since walking in on Cory and I. The fact it's happened several times since, hasn't helped either. "I can't believe they can string this out for so long. Even with the advocacy groups help."

"I know, it's bullshit. But hopefully Jenny, Spawn of Satan, will pull through." A laugh is added to the smile and I feel like I've won the lotto.

Faith pulls out of the undercover parking lot into the busy traffic and I pull out my phone. Once I'm done shopping, and he's out of class, the birthday boy is coming over to the apartment. Unease prickles in my belly. He's canceled our last two meet-ups, and even when we have been alone, he's seemed ... distant. Playing it cool while around the team, and in public, is one thing, but something feels off.

Is the novelty of our clandestine affair already wearing off?

There's no waiting message, which is good, but I decide to fling him one just in case.

> It feels like forever since I touched you. Can't wait.

It goes to read immediately, so I sit and wait and stare at the screen, shielding it from the dappled light the passing oaks create for two blocks. But there's nothing. No 'can't wait to see you, too'. No thumbs up, no 'Get fucked.'

Nothing.

Huh.

"You'll crack the screen if you stare at it any harder."

"Huh," I say out loud this time.

"Your phone. You've stared at the thing for hours."

"Oh, yeah. I'm just trying to get hold of Cory. He's been hard to pin down the last few days. Maybe I should message him again, or do you think that would be too clingy. Shit. I'm coming off as clingy, aren't I? Fuck my chest hurts. Look at me, woman. Do you see clingy?"

"No, I see a hypochondriac who needs to breathe. I'm sure he's just busy with practice and his friends and class. Maybe it's a good thing to have a break. Maybe he's matured a little and realized the cost of this little game he's playing?"

Right. My hackles rise immediately. Faith's made it perfectly clear she is no fan of our relationship, but even so she's looking entirely too smug and self-satisfied for my liking. Sitting up ramrod straight, I lay my palms on the dash to stop myself from grabbing the wheel and pulling us over.

"What did you say to him, Faith?"

"Nothing ... that didn't need to be said."

"Faith!"

She smiles like the devil incarnate. "Yes?"

"Don't fucking smile at me. Tell me what you said to him."

"You're acting irrationally. This thing is going to fizzle out anyway. Cory has months left here and then he'll be in Canada and you'll be here with me and Dyl. It makes no sense to risk your career for a fling."

I'm so angry right now I'm seeing stars. "It's not a fling! I ... I ..." Shit. Do I love him? Is that even possible?

"Please don't try and tell me you love him." Tossing her head back, she barks out a laugh, each cackle grating on my last nerve. "Don't be ridiculous James. He's a boy. You call him Kid, for heaven's sake."

"He's like three years younger than me, and I use the term affectionately. Besides, who the fuck are you to judge any rela-tionships I have when you've never had one?" Her grip on the wheel turns white-knuckled.

"I'm not passing judgment, I'm making observations. You've known this ... man ... for a few months, and are stalling the sale of your apartment, moving him and his family in, jeopardizing your career ... none of it makes sense."

"You're right. It doesn't make sense. But maybe things don't always have to. Buying into Ferris Health Group made sense. Brandon made sense. Quitting the one thing I've ever loved made sense, and look how well all that worked out for me."

My lungs squeeze tight, pain shooting through my chest. I'm a stuttered heartbeat away from ripping open the door and rolling out onto the sidewalk to die, when Faith's hand lands on my leg. Bile rises in my throat and I shrink away for her touch. I don't want to look at her, or hear one more word. "Slow your breathing, Jamie."

"Don't call me that."

"Fine, slow your breathing please, James Samuel Plum."

"Don't tell me what to do."

Faith mumbles something under her breath but I can't decipher it because I'm too busy dying. Cubby has delivered me the first sprinkles of happiness I've felt in a long time. I'm happier at work. Coping better with the demands of caring for Dylan and actually looking forward to getting out of bed in the morning. I know it's not permanent, but I'm not ready for it to be taken away from me yet, either.

Sweat stings my eyes and my lips start to tingle when I picture Cory and Dylan together. If he's done with me Dyl's going to be heartbroken, he's already so attached. What was I thinking, introducing them? How the hell have I been charged with being responsible for another human, when I can't even handle this?

And Cory's present. I haven't got his present.

"Jamie." Warm hands cup my face. "Jamie, please. You have to slow your breathing." I open my eyes and Faith is there, my car door is open and we're at the side of the road, dust still settling from her rush to pull over. "Please. You're scaring me."

"Trying," I blubber. "Sorry." Role modeling slow, deep breaths, Faith edges closer until she's almost in my lap.

"You have nothing to be sorry for, Jamie. This is on me. I've overstepped. Again. Everything will be okay, I promise. Just breathe with me."

WHEN I WAKE, I'm sitting in the passenger seat, before an unfamiliar house, in an unfamiliar street. Unfortunately, the dull thud and mental fatigue clouding my thoughts are known all too well.

"Lucky, I was just about to leave." I roll my head to the left and blink, then blink again. I'm definitely in Faith's car, but that's definitely not Faith staring back at me. It's a bit of a mind fuck. "Chip?" In his lap is a bag of corn chips. Unable to find any words, I shake my head.

"Are you feeling better? Faith said you sleep like the dead after a panic attack, and she wasn't kidding. Your ability to sleep through Mr. Daugherty's excessively loud, nosey-ass lawn mowing is quite impressive."

The blinking and staring continues until eventually I manage to utter, "Is this your house?"

"'Til this weekend it is, yeah."

"It's nice. The door's wonky though."

"It is. I was going to fix it before we left, but fuck em." For some reason, that makes me laugh. Like a lot. Tears run down my cheeks and Cory joins in. I'm not even sure if he knows why.

"I'm sorry I've been avoiding you," he says once the hilarity subsides. "I freaked myself out a little."

I wipe the moisture from my cheeks. "I think someone might have given you a shove in the right, or wrong, direction."

"Maybe. But she was kind of right."

"Why don't you tell me what she said, then I can tell you if I agree." Cory gives me the run down and by the time he does, I'm both exhausted and pissed off. "She had no right to say any of that to you, Cub. This is my life. My decision."

"Like it was your decision to quit hockey?"

"Exactly."

Doe-eyed, Cory looks up at me, the half smile on his lips unreasonably cute. "I don't want you to regret me like you regret your past."

"I don't think it's possible to regret anything when it comes to you. Actually that's a lie." Pausing, I take his hand in mine and press a kiss to the inside of his palm. "There is something that would 'cause me considerable remorse ... not spending every possible moment with you while I can."

"I don't want you to lose everything because of me."

"And you are everything to me, so it looks like I'm set."

There's a lot more I'd like to say, three little words the meaning of which far outweigh their size, in particular. But perhaps that's best left for now. Like me, Cory seems to be contemplating his next words. The wide-eyed expression lingering while he chews the lips I wouldn't mind tasting about now.

"James, I—"

"Yoo-hoo boys!"

The fuck!

Grumbling, I gaze around Cory and see Cory's mom twinkling her fingers at me like I'm five. Next to her and looking decidedly less enthused, is Faith. Seeing her moody face doesn't console me after missing the tea Cory was about to spill, but it does help.

"Why don't you come inside and eat? I made cake."

Unless it's the one attached to Cory's long legs, cake is the last thing I want right now. I'm exhausted, my head is pounding and I need to get Cory wrapped around me stat. But his mom looks so hopeful and Faith miserable, I nod and open the door. "What kind of cake are we talking?"

ot that it will be mine for much longer, but James and his sister are in my house. It's weird.

But great.

But weird.

It's also the longest period of time Mom has been tear-free all week, and no matter how awkward it feels to have my professor, sister of the dude I am fucking, and falling for in my kitchen, it's worth it.

Six and a half, the half being Billie, of us are crowded around our kitchen table. Billie's sucking Faith's hair and Grandpa, a man who has never left the state, is currently bombarding her with questions about Australia. Drop bears in particular.

"So you're telling me they don't exist?"

"That's what I'm telling you, Arthur, yes."

"And they're not koala bears, just koalas?"

"Correct." Billie coughs up a chunk of blonde locks that land with a wet slap against her. She looks close to vomiting, and her brother seems delighted by that. He's sat back and let her field the questions, enjoying every moment of her suffering. My very own bear wears a smile so sweet and pure it's taking all my strength not to drop in his lap. I'm feeling pretty damn good about now, then something happens to take that feeling to a whole new level. As Jamie laughs, his hand slips beneath the table. Finding mine, he links our pinkies together.

It's kind of become our thing, has me damn near purring like a kitten and I love it.

Like I love him.

It's come in so quickly I can't pinpoint the exact moment I went from falling to fallen, but I've landed on his furry chest and couldn't be any happier. I should probably be a little more stressed about our future, because Faith did make some valid points. How things will work out when there's a border separating us, and I'm under the NHL spotlight being the utmost. I'm oddly calm about it though.

Maybe this is what true happiness feels like.

In a desperate bid to change the subject, and de-saliva her hair Faith sips from her tea, finger raised like the Queen, eyes shifting to the moving boxes we're surrounded by.

"How's the packing coming along? Three adults and a baby—"

"Oh, I love that movie! We watched it with Grampa when we were kids," I interrupt a little too excitedly. "Come to think of it, Jamie, you've got that whole Tom Selleck mustache thing going on."

"He sure does." Mom winks, biting her lip and James' grip on my finger turns crippling.

"And on that nauseating note, Jamie, can you and the 'stache come help me with bringing some of my hockey gear down from the attic?"

"Sure thing." Frown fixed firmly in place, he releases his hold of me as he slides from the table.

"I'll help too!" Faith yells, moving to do the same.

"No, you stay here, sis." Jamie smirks. "You can tell Arthur all about the flying spiders."

Gramps lunges to hold Faith in place. "A flying spider? Is that a real thing?" Faith's ardent denial becomes background noise as I lead James from the kitchen. The state of the house is a little embarrassing, the carpet is worn, paint faded, but Jamie only has eyes for me as we ascend the stairs.

"Have you spent your whole life here?" he asks, taking my hand as soon as he feels confident no one is following.

"Yup. The hospital I was born in is five minutes away, my schools were all within walking distance and the first girl I kissed lives two doors down. This neighbourhood has been my home as much as this house has." We make it to the landing and I point towards my room, the puck and stick decorated CORY sign Mom made in her short-lived pottery era hanging on the door. "Want to see where the magic happens?"

"I thought the hockey gear had to go down stairs?"

"It does. Right after I go down on you."

EVERY TEENAGE FANTASY my gay little brain ever conjured is coming to life. Jamie has me pressed against my bedroom door, one massive hand pinning mine above my head as he tears at the button of my jeans with the other.

"Why did today have to be the one time you skipped the sweats." His gruff voice, warm breath and urgency weakens my knees.

"Laundry day. Thought I was safe. Didn't expect this." Each point is panted out as though I'm at the tail-end of a cardio session and not the beginning. With the button finally free, James tugs both jeans and briefs down my thighs and drops to his knees. My heart rate quadruples as he stares up at me.

"Leave the hands on the door and don't ever dodge my calls again, Kid." With that he slips the head my dick between his lips and hollows out his cheeks.

"Jesus Christ." Relief washes over me and my head smacks against the timber, the dull thud undoubtedly audible downstairs. I should probably be concerned that my entire family is directly beneath us, nothing but carpet and lime and plaster laying between us. But I'm too needy to care. It's only been a few days without his touch, but fuck. "I missed this. Missed you."

Humming, he rolls his tongue over my tip, swirling it through the pre-cum before sealing me whole. I hit the back of his throat and he does that thing he does, where he constricts in short sharp pulses that has me seeing stars in seconds.

"Fuck you ruin me."

Unable to follow his commands, I drop my arms and weave my hands through his hair, tugging as I begin to fuck his mouth.

The consequences are swift and brutal. James grunts, pulls off me with a pop and sits back on his feet. He's pissed and it's so fucking hot I almost come.

"Didn't I say hands off?"

"Yeah, but–"

He stands and grips my jaw, holding my face still as he leans in. "You've fucked me around the last few days Cory, and it's time face the consequences. Hands. Off." With an up nod he motions to the door and I follow, throwing my hands back to their original position. "That's my good little slut."

Holy shit.

Eyes falling closed, I almost collapse on top of him and he returns to his knees.

"This will be over real quick if you keep talking like that." He makes no reply, just tugs me a little to cup my ass cheeks and pull me back between his lips. "Fuck your mouth is incredible." It's hard to imagine anything feeling better than this. The tickle of the mustache, the soft plump lips, the warm slide of his tongue. He's doing the job my hips started, tugging me in and out, impaling himself, choking and gagging on my cock again and again. As hard as not touching him is, it's equally blissful handing over control. Letting him do with me what he wants. When he takes me even deeper, I whimper and beg. "Yes. Yes. Make me cum, my big boy." Heat shoots down my spine, pooling at the base of my dick, searing through my balls. "Coming."

Release is seconds away when James slips off, resting on his heels again and wiping his mouth and tear-stained cheeks with the back of his hand. As close as I was to coming, I now am to crying. "What are you doing? Why ... Why did you stop?"

"Punishment." It's said way too casually for how hopped up I am. "Edging. Making you suffer. You choose."

Before I can wail some more, he dives back in, this time sucking my balls into his mouth before replacing them with my dick. This delicious cruelty is repeated several times, and until I'm a sweaty, mumbling mess who's begging for release. "Jamie, I need to come."

His reddened eyes meet mine and he shakes his head while simultaneously sliding a finger into his mouth, caressing my dick before pulling it free and between my cheeks. "Beg." He grins at my whimper, and likely because he knows I can barely stand, and would say and do anything at this point.

"Please, Jamie," I whine like a bitch. "Please let me come." He nods, his finger breaches my hole and I explode, so hard and fast cum spills from Jamie's mouth, dribbling down his chin and neck.

Coughing and spluttering, he fists my shirts and drags me to the floor.

"You want me to?"

"I want you to clean up the mess you made." He runs his finger from collarbone to chin, collecting the glistening cum on the tip, before bringing it to my mouth. "Open."

I do of course, opening my mouth just enough for him to slide his finger inside and over my tongue. His expression is so heated, so erotic, I feel myself hardening again. "Now the rest."

Because I'm greedy and pathetic, and so far gone for this man, I act immediately, swirling, tracing the lines of his neck and jaw with my tongue, licking up every drop of cum, before claiming his mouth with mine.

It's bruising, messy, and laced with the love I feel growing by the second. By the time we break apart, I'm begging again, but this time it's for me to return the favor.

"Let me taste you, Jamie, please. I'll do anything."

My hands are in his hair, my mouth back on his as he nods his consent. A beat later I'm fumbling with the zips of his chinos, desperate to get my hands and mouth around his throbbing erection. "I'm going to make you feel so good, baby."

"You always do." Hard, weeping and bobbing expectantly, the soft skin of his fat, heavy dick caresses my palm. He's panting and sweating, so close to the edge that I can't help seeking a fraction of revenge for my edging.

"You really do have the most beautiful cock I've ever seen," I whisper, leisurely stroking him, and tapping him against my cheek. He looks pained now, so I yield. "Best tasting, too." I slip him into my waiting mouth, sliding my tongue up and down the thick vein traversing his length, then taking as much of him in as I can. After maybe three or four hearty sucks, he's gripping my head, fingers digging into my jaw, fucking into my mouth at a punishing pace then coming straight down my throat.

Sated, sticky and smiling, we collapse as one, star-fishing on the rug, pinkies linked between us.

All I can smell, see and think of is him ... and how I can make this feeling last forever.

I am in hell. Well, not *hell*, hell, there are worse places I could be, buried alive in a cheap, ugly coffin, stuck inside a cave filled with giant spiders, are a couple that spring to mind. But a party full of drunk college students is right up there with killer arachnids.

Just days before Cory celebrates his own day of birth, we're partying it up for Sam Bailey's.

On a Thursday, I might add.

Since Sam, who is apparently the most well liked person at Boston College, lives in a dorm room with Lucas, he's sweet talked a frat house into hosting. The place is packed to the rafters with a good portion of the student population, the team, of course, and the coaching staff, too. Wisely, they all left within the first hour, but my constant need to be around a certain sexy little winger, sees me lingering well after I should.

And, I will admit to no one, enjoying myself more than I expected. The music, an eclectic mix of nineties house and 2000's bangers, has my head bopping and my feet tapping, and I've even dressed up. My polo has been replaced with a loose, white linen shirt and these pleated and surprisingly comfy, wide leg pants Cory made me buy after seeing Henry Cavill rocking a similar pair. The way he drank me in when I picked him and Cherry up, was almost enough to make me feel confident.

For about twenty seconds.

Now, as the official *old weirdo* sitting on the sofa nursing a cup of tea, I've assigned myself the role of team shenanigans supervisor. I'm not delusional enough to think the boys aren't going to drink, but my presence may at least stop them from getting too messy. Plus from my comfy spot, I have a great prospect.

Cory, the boy who claimed to be an introvert, is currently on the coffee table, grinding between Quinn Harris and the birthday boy while wearing baggy jeans hanging below his ass, and a cropped sleeveless tee that barely covers his nipples. Cherry stands at their feet, jeering, wolf whistling and thrusting dollar bills their way.

Her antics aren't what holds my gaze, though. It's him. The sensual sway of his hips. The play of muscle beneath pale flesh, the contraction of those washboard abdominals my tongue is desperate to taste. Best of all, every time he raises his arms, I'm treated to a tantalizing glimpse of those pretty pink buds I need between my teeth, stat. It's hypnotic. So much so, I don't notice Brady flop onto the sofa beside me until he nudges me with his elbow. "Nice jugs."

"What?"

"The cup." With a nod he motions to the interesting boobs mug I was handed by one of the frat boys.

"Thanks." I cup my right pec and wink. "Molded off my own, and I threw on my own potter's wheel."

Brady nearly chokes on his tongue as a blush colors his face. "Really?"

"No Brady. We're in a frat house. It was the only tea holding vessel in the kitchen."

"Oh, yeah. Right, good one, Plummy." He laughs some more and sips from his flat looking beer. "I honestly thought frat parties like this only existed in teen movies."

"Yet here we are, two Aussies and a boob cup, mooching on the couch like true dropkicks."

Head collapsing onto my shoulder, Brady erupts into laughter. "Dropkick. Crap I haven't heard that for ages. Man, I miss footy."

"Me too," I reply, gaze not shifting off Cubby. "Thank God for VPN's, hey."

"True." I feel his eyes on me, then, in my periphery, I see him look towards the dancers. "Quinn's quite smitten with Cubby. I think maybe ... she's not the only one?"

And consider the spell broken.

Think quick, idiot. Think quick. I point towards the other dancer. "You think Sam's interested in Cory?"

"Ahh, no." He scoffs. "No, that's not who I meant." I hold my breath, waiting for the, *I meant you, idiot, b*ut maybe he notices the sudden rigidity in my posture, or the lack of breathing, because he moves on with a chuckle. "How are you enjoying your time with the Bears?"

Sighing in relief, I wriggle in my seat, body relaxing. Well, relaxed for me. "I was certain I'd have a heart attack within the first week, but the boys have grown on me, and the fixed nature of the hockey world suits my need for routine."

Brady nods thoughtfully. It's obvious he wants to ask more, but he's so kind, and empathetic he doesn't want to be nosy or overstep. "Do you think you'd hang around if Coach asked?" he asks eventually.

"As the favorite son-in-law, don't you already know the answer to that?"

"No, but I figured he's heading in that direction. I don't think he would have asked you to help out in defense otherwise."

I'm distracted when Cory does some kind of booty drop-bounce-thingy. "Do I what?"

"Do you think he will ask? Do you think you'd accept?"

"Oh." I blink away the vision before me, and turn to Brady. His smile is bigger than the boner my pants are reining in. "He has already, actually. I've partially accepted, 'cause yeah. It's a huge opportunity. But it's also a pretty full on gig, and I'm not sure I'll have the availability he needs with Dylan. Even when he goes back to his day services, he'll be home by four and someone needs to be there with him."

"One, that's awesome. About the chance of you staying. And two, is that what your dad did? Stayed home with Dyl?"

A wave of suppressed grief rolls over me. "He did, and he did a better job of it than I ever will. He was amazing, Brades. Everything he did had a reason, every moment an opportunity to learn. He was so determined to give Dylan the chance to live independently one day, he'd take an hour to do the dishes if it meant Dylan could inspect every plate, bowl and fork. Stack it just how he wanted, then pull it out and start again. I've tried to do the same, but I just don't have the patience. Even when I do, I don't have a fucking clue if I'm doing it right."

"To be fair, James, there's not many that would. Your dad sounds incredible, and was probably always worrying about what would happen when he was no longer around, like a lot of aging carers do. I think he'd be really proud of you and Faith."

"Maybe, but Dyls is our big brother. We didn't really have a choice."

"See, that's where you're wrong. You know Troye?"

"Troye the boy who looks at you and Quinn like you both created the earth?" He blushes again, and smiles so purely I can't help but glance at Cubby.

"Yeah, him. Well, his moms adopted him when he was a kid after his own parents ditched him. Blood means nothing. Blood can run. Showing up, being trustworthy, sacrificing part of your-self even when you're scared and exhausted, and don't know what the fuck you're doing. That's what you're doing. That's what makes a family." He then points to Lucas, who looks more uncomfortable here than me, as he snatches away the beer Sam recieved from the boob-mug giver. "A team, too. That's why I'm sure Coach will ask you to stay."

I can't help but wonder if sneaking around with Cubby outweighs all the positives Brady kindly appointed to me.

"Anyone ever tell you you're wise for a blonde jock?"

"Yup. Coach did yesterday, actually. I thought he was being sarcastic, but now you've backed him up I'll take it as the compli-ment he intended."

"Who are we complimenting?" Red-cheeked and puffing, Quinn slides between me and Brady, wrapping her arms around his neck, while Cory does the same—minus the snuggles—between me and the arm of the sofa.

"Obviously me and my dancing," he says with a wink directed squarely at me. "That's why we're here. Come dance with us."

"By us, do you mean them?" I point to Sam who has a new partner in Cherry.

"What the fuck?" Cory's up and dragging me with him before I can laugh as intended.

"She's a big girl, Cub. I'm sure she can handle herself." As I say that, she slides her hand around Sam's waist and pulls him closer. He reciprocates and they're now pressed so tightly together there's boob squishing involved.

"Yeah, well I'm sure she's had too much to drink, and that Sam is a great guy, but a complete slut with a big secret." Pulling up beside them like an agitated mom in a school pickup line, he greases Sam off while forcing himself between them. "Hey guys. Look. James is dancing."

I am not dancing. I am standing completely still. Arms crossed over chest. Frowning.

Seeing this, Cory's big eyes widen, and his head tilts, and his bottom lip drops. He's silently begging me to boogie and because I am a weak, uncoordinated fucking fool, who would do anything for this kid, I do. I have no idea what this noise is, and I'm a step or ten behind the beat, but my feet are stomping and my shoulders are shrugging and Cory is smiling.

He's not the only one.

"You are without a doubt the oldest twenty-something I've ever met, and I know Lotte."

"Thanks," I reply uselessly to Quinn, because her attention is already back on Brady who looks almost as awkward as I do while she gyrates against him. His unease is short lasting though, the open adoration of her expression, is eagerly reciprocated with one hand over smoothing over her ass, the other cupping her jaw. I can't take my eyes off them, and it's not in a creepy, *let's watch the hot couple make out,* way.

I'm envious.

Jealous.

Seething.

There's only one person in this room, in this world, that I want to look at, and touch and be looked at and touched by, and I can't.

We can't.

Perhaps thinking the same, Cubby abandons his cock-blocking and shimmies those pretty nipples my way, hands gripping my hips all too briefly to pull my ear to his lips. "I'm tired of hiding. I want that to be us," he whispers, beer breath not remotely unappealing. "You look so sexy, Jamie. I'm so hard for you. I can't wait to get you alone this weekend."

Trying to act unaffected when I'm quite the opposite, I clear my throat and smile.

"Me too."

Bouncing back to slot between Sam and Cherry, the six of us form a circle, laughter and off key lyrics to *Call Me Maybe* bouncing between us. But in my mind, all I hear Brady's words, *sacrificing part of yourself even when you're scared and exhausted, and don't know what the fuck you're doing. That's what you're doing. That's what makes a family. A team.*

The thing, the crop-top wearing person I want most would likely destroy my family *and* my team, but damn it if I can sacrifice us and walk away.

"Happy Birthday, Cub."

It's Friday morning. I've a slight hangover from Sam's party, and am dehydrated from Jamie draining my nuts after said party, but that's not why I'm playing hooky from class.

Since it's my birthday weekend, and we have no game, James has called in sick too, and we're spending two naked days at his apartment. Along with several dozen apologies, that's the fifth time he's repeated those words. "Promise you're not upset that I don't have a pressie for you?" he whispers again, lips ghosting over mine.

"Hearing you call it a pressie is pressie enough. Well, that and eating my ass out, sucking my dick and letting me fuck you in the shower. What more could a man ask for?"

"Something pretty and wrapped?"

"Well, your dick is pretty. Slip him in a condom and then he's wrapped, too." He gives me a slap on the chest.

"Haha. Very funny."

"I know. I'm hilarious. I'm also open to that, by the way."

"Open to what?" His kisses stall.

"To you … in a condom … in me."

"Oh." I catch a flash of color on his cheeks before he rolls from his side to belly, burying his face into his pillow. I take the chance, grabbing my phone from the bedside table and snapping a photo before he can stop me.

"What would happen if I wasn't?" It's muffled, but I'm ninety-nine percent sure that's what he said.

"You mean, if you weren't into topping?"

"Uh-huh," he almost hums, nodding with his pink face still hidden. So freaking cute. "I've done it, and even though I like to be quite dominant at times, topping just never felt natural to me. So yeah. What would you think?"

Matching his position, I roll onto my own stomach and run my hands through his soft brown curls, releasing a fresh burst of fruitiness. "I would think I never want you to do what you're not comfortable with. I would count myself lucky for having a big beast of a boyfriend that loves taking my dick up his ass, and I would be proud to have a man who's secure enough in his masculinity that he can admit he's a power bottom queen."

Slowly, he twists to face me, honey eyes wide as saucers. "Boyfriend?"

"That's what you took from that?" I laugh. "Yes, boyfriend. If you want that, too."

"You want to be my boyfriend?"

"Of course I do. You're like my favorite person. You're funny and grumpy. Sweet and caring. You've got a dick thick as a tree trunk. A mouth like a hoover and an ass so warm and tight I could come again right now just thinking about pushing into it. Who wouldn't want to carve their name into that?"

I have no time to react, before James rolls onto his back, sweeping me into his arms as he goes and sitting me on his hard dick, before pulling me down to lie flat atop him. As he did with his pillow, he buries his face into the crook of my neck and inhales. Moisture drips onto my neck, is he crying? I move to pull away and check, but he shakes his head and pins me to him. "I can't look at you right now. Just let me say this, okay?"

My stomach does an anguished, slow roll settling somewhere in my throat.

This is either going to be really, really great, like getting drafted to Montreal great. Or really, really bad. Like getting drafted to Toronto. There is no in between. "Okay."

Remaining silent and deathly still, I feel him inhale again, his cheeks puff, then his breath ghosts down my back as he exhales. "Cubby. I know because of work and Canada, we were going to keep things casual, but ... I think I might love you."

"I think I might love you, too." I pretty much yell back, as all air is squeezed from my lungs.

"You do?"

"I do. Actually, I don't think it. I know … Wait. Can you let me go for a sec? I want to see your face. And breathe."

"Shit, sorry." James relaxes his kung-fu grip and I push off his chest. Silver lines stain his flushed cheeks, and his lips are all pink and puffy.

"I know I love you. Honestly, I have for a while, but I was too afraid to say it out loud, in case you freaked out."

"Me. Freak out. Please, that never happens."

"You're right. I must be thinking about my other hypochondriac boyfriend who mutters, not a fish, not a fish, not a fish, under his breath almost every other day."

James' brow furrows as he scowls. A few months ago, I'd have shit myself if he looked at me like this. Now it just turns me on.

Actually, it probably would have back then, too.

"I've never really been in love before, but is it normal to make fun of your beloved's potentially fatal medical conditions?"

"Having never been in love before, I couldn't safely say. Wait. You brought this place with that Brandon dick. Didn't you love him?" He shakes his head and pulls me back down onto his chest. I go happily, cause, duh.

"At the time I thought I was, but now I know what it really feels like I think I was just comfortable. After I quit hockey, I was kind of depressed and isolated. Brandon helped me though that, and I was grateful. He was my friend. But I wouldn't have risked so much, and been willing to walk away from everything for him. Not the way I would for you."

The words, *come to Canada with me,* burn so severely against my tongue I fear smoke may soon billow from my ears. James could just as easily have a career there. We could get a place with a big enough yard for a winter-time rink. Maybe a dog that didn't hate me like Miffy, or an equally gender-confused cat like Cleo. We could make a life for ourselves. One where we didn't have to hide.

It could be perfect.

It will be perfect.

Hope balloons in my chest, but my move with me to Canada spiel, is paused by jiggling coming from beneath me, and James's full belly laugh. "Can you believe that?" he says, sounding miffed. "What a selfish prick. Expecting me to up and move to Florida weeks after we bought this place, *and* when I had Dyl, Faith and Dad here. He never got that we were a package deal, even before Dad was gone."

A package deal.

Relocating James is one thing. I would have zero problems with Faith and Dylan coming with us, and it could even be beneficial. The Canadian healthcare system shits all over ours. It could be perfect. But Faith is the youngest professor to be granted tenure at BC, and Dylan has Manny, and Maria and his routine. The short-lived hope bubble bursts. Looks like James has a habit of attracting selfish pricks.

Happy birthday to me.

WHILE JAMES IS SHOWERING, I potter around the kitchen, searching for plates to dish up the Chinese takeout we ordered for naked lunch. I've tried to keep my mood upbeat since the whole, Brandon wanted me to leave, bombshell but it's tough.

It's one p.m., which means we've had twelve hours together. Apparently that's more than enough to solidify that this is what I want. I want this to be permanent. I want to wake up with James every morning and go to bed with him at night. I want to lay in bed 'til noon, have sex in the shower, order shitty food and head back to bed.

I know that's not reality, but when our reality is harder to swallow than these dry-ass looking egg rolls, who needs it?

Giving up on the crockery, I grab some forks and spoons and am setting the food up on the table when James hollers, "Cory, where are you?"

"Kitchen," I yell back. "Food arrived." I smell his fresh, clean cologne seconds later he appears ... in a tee and sweats. Don't get me wrong. He looks fucking amazing. It's white and wet and really see through, but still. "What the hell, Plum? Naked weekend ring a bell?" Smirking, he looks down and pats his chest.

"Oh. I forgot. Maybe you should come and take it off me?" I don't think I have ever abandoned food so fast.

Moody or not, I'm on him in a flash, hands slipping beneath the hem, up over his ribs and tugging the damp cotton over his head. It hits the floor, and so does my chin.

"What did you do?"

"Can't lie, Cubs. That's not the reaction I was hoping for."

It takes what feels like a good few minutes of slack-jawed ogling, and pawing hands, before I can speak.

"You. You—"

"I carved you into my tree." He points to the haphazard

CORY'S BOFRIEND"

emblazoned across his pecs. "It's your present. I'm your present."

"You shaved Cory's Boyfriend into your chest hair?"

"I did ... You hate it, don't you. Shit, you're really going to hate this, then." Looping his fingers into his waistband, he pulls down his pants, letting them fall and pool at his feet. "My original plan had been to do the *boyfriend* thing here, but I stuffed up the B and just made it into a heart." Front and center in my favorite clump of dark hair ever is a J ♥ C.

Blushing again, he clears his throat. "I've never considered myself a romantic, and now I know why. I've mutilated my body. Have hair covering every inch of the bathroom, and I'm pretty sure I've spelled boyfriend wrong."

"You did. It says, bofrend."

"So, make that not good at spontaneous, romantic gestures, or shaving words into my chest hair via a mirror."

"You are good at it." I almost sob. "The romantic gesture bit espccially. I love it. I fucking love it almost as much as I love you." He beams. Literally fucking beams in a way I've never seen and steps closer.

"Happy birthday, baby."

It's already move-in day—five a.m. Sunday, to be exact, which means our time is almost up. Once Cory and his family move in, it's bye-bye secret apartment hook-ups, hello back seat of the car. Still fun. Just squishier.

Since we've only eaten and fucked all weekend, the fridge is barren, so I've ordered-in some breakfast from a deli around the corner. It's run by two Melbournites, and they do a mean Aussie Cafe brekkie. I've gone with an egg and bacon sandwich, and a couple of sneaky slices of avocado toast, that I'll be eating while standing because it feels like my ass is on fire. While Cory, who's drifted back to sleep, chose the traditional USA takeout—donuts and coffee. Pausing my doom scroll on my phone, I send a check-in message to Faith. She's finally finished her grading, and was kind enough to give me a break this weekend. Once that's done I get all creepy and watch Cory sleep, in particular, the steady rise and fall of his chest.

I should probably wake him. Coach and the rest of the boys will be here at seven, and we have to shower, change the bedding and open up some damn widows, 'cause this place smells more like a medieval whorehouse than a million dollar apartment. Thing is, he looks so cute all wrapped up in the duvet. I know our future is complicated, but he really is the most beautiful creature. How did I get so lucky?

A touch of melancholy hits as the door bell rings, signaling our last meal. "Cory. Mate, wake up. The food is here." After placing maybe twenty kisses to his perfect upturned nose, I slip from bed, toss on my sweats and head to the door.

Gaze on the carpet, I swing the door open and bend to pick up the bags ... that aren't there. What is, though, are pristine white Nikes that look eerily similar to the ones Coach Harris practically lives in.

"Morning, James. Worked up a sweat already, have we?"

"Coach!" Giving myself a head spin, I bolt upright, almost knocking him over in the process. He's early. Forty-five minutes early. Thank God I'm not naked.

Though, you'd think I was , if Coach's expression is anything by.

Slightly puzzled, I scratch my chest.

My shirtless chest.

The one with *Cory's bofrend* carved into it.

Oh dear.

In the blink of an eye, my boss has gone from his usual complexion to one redder than Mars, and it only intensifies as booming laughter from a dozen or so hockey boys fill the hall. While I tried hard to ignore how his fists have clenched, Coach shoots a glance in that direction then turns back to me.

"I'm trying very hard to not jump to conclusions right now, James." His voice, disturbingly calm and eerily similar to Hannibal Lecter, sends a chill to my very soul. "I think I deserve an explanation, but it'll have to wait. I'll hold these fools off for ten minutes and I suggest you, and anyone else who may be here, make yourselves decent." With that, he shakes his head and turns to walk away.

"Thanks, Coach."

"Don't ever call me that again."

Swallowing the rising sea of bile I feel like I'm drowning in, I close the door and fall against it, my forehead landing squarely on the peep hole, that had I used, may have averted this crisis. "Oww."

Rumination wastes valuable seconds and only ends when a ping on my phone coincides with a violent knocking on the door. Again. "Oww." This time it's the food for sure, the smell wafting under the door has my empty stomach rumbling. Pity there's no time to enjoy it. After surveying the hall for stray hockey players, I snatch the bag from the floor, let the door close once more, and make my way to the bedroom.

Cory, who's rather spectacularly naked and star-fished in the dead center of the bed, is still asleep. Nothing would make me happier than to slide in beside him and pretend our world wasn't about to implode, but I just don't have that luxury. It hits me then, as I rest my palm on the small of his back, that this may be the last time I get to see him like this, and a small part of my heart breaks away, becoming lost in that sea of nausea.

"Cub. Cub," I whisper, lightly shaking him despite the urgency of the situation. "I'm sorry mate, but you have to wake up."

"No," he grumbles, voice heavy from sleep. "You have to un-wake up."

"Can't I'm afraid. Coach is already here, Cub. He saw what's left of my chest hair. He knows. We've only got a few minutes before he brings the team up."

Cory is one of the fastest skaters I've seen, but nothing he's done on ice could compare to the way he moves out of that bed. "You're fucking with me," he scoffs disbelievingly while also whipping his briefs off the floor, and hopping into them. "You're not clutching your chest, or sweating, and I hear no screaming. He would definitely be screaming if he knew."

"See, I thought that too, but it was even worse. He was calm. Scarily so. Maybe that's why I am, too."

"Oh, we're fucked." Warranted panic ensues. Dressing as we go, we race around the apartment, tidying and opening windows before meeting back in the bedroom, red-faced and panting and not in a good way. "Maybe we can tell him it was just a joke? What rhymes with Bofrend. Kofend? Lofend? Weekend! We can say it was supposed to say Cory's weekend. 'Cause it's my birthday. It's perfect."

The sneaker I was sliding my foot into drops to the floor. "That is not perfect. It's quite possibly the stupidest thing I've ever heard."

"Yeah, I know. Shit. We're fucked." The wall-to-ceiling window that overlooks Chestnut Hill Reserve shakes as he slumps against it. Beholding such a beautiful man back lit by an equally beautiful backdrop is something I'd normally appreciate as one would art in a gallery, but now's not the time. Instead I take a mental picture, and lock it safely away for another day.

Cory seems to realize his position too and turns to peer outside. "Damn. No fire escape. How far up are we, do you think? Jumpable? Looks like it might be. I reckon I could—"

I wander over to the window, wrap my arms around his waist and drop my head against his shoulder. "You're not jumping, Kid. If you think Coach is going to kill me now, imagine what he'd do if I let his star player break every bone in his body." His body melts into mine as he sighs.

The chance to reply is stolen by the sound of a dozen or so brutish hockey players, and one frustrated Irish catholic woman pounding on the front door. "Cory it's the boys and your mom. I can't find my damn key, Honey. Let us in."

"Yeah, Honey." Chorus the idiots. "Let us in."

Turning in my arms, Cory stands on his tip toes and kisses me. It sweet and soft, and so fucking sad I could cry. "Whatever happens, even if I get kicked off the team, this weekend, and every thing that came before it, has been totally worth it."

Fuck, I hope he means that.

Pressing a kiss to the top of his head, before what may be the last on his lips. "I love you, Cub."

"I love you too, Jamie."

THE MOST AWKWARD moving day ever has come to a close. The team is finishing the last of the pizzas we had delivered. Everything has been carried in, set up and packed away with quite remarkable efficiency and a surprising lack of breakage.

What's not in tact though, is the relationship, perhaps friendship I built up with David Harris. The man has barely looked at me all day, and when he did I was met with a cold stare reminiscent of a great white shark. Cory has fared a little better. Harris has actually referred to him by name instead of grunting in his general vicinity. He's also made damn sure Cory and I were never left alone for more than a few seconds.

I miss him so much already it hurts. I'm not sure if that's romantic or sad.

Maybe it's both.

Either way it is what it is and now that the food is gone, and everything is in place, it's done. Billie's sleeping soundly in her cot. Deirdre is tucked up beneath a blanket on the sofa, and Cherry, well Cherry is making eyes at Sam as she has been all day.

"That's it boys," Coach declares as he crushes the last of the moving boxes. "Time to let the Malkovich's enjoy their new home."

"I don't know how to thank you, David. You too, boys," Deirdre says around a yawn as she attempts to unfold her self from her cocoon.

"Please, don't get up," he says, flashing her a smile I can't imagine receiving any time soon. "You've had to pack up your life in a week. You must be exhausted. I'm just glad we could help."

"Help you have. You're a wonderful man. Cory has been blessed to have you watch over, protect and mentor him."

On our way to the door, David pulls me and Cubby aside. "I want both of you in my office at nine tomorrow."

"We can do earlier if you like," Cory says with more enthusiasm than I can muster right now. "I'll be there at seven for training."

"No you won't," Harris mutters over his shoulder while marching to the door. "Consider yourself suspended."

"Suspended! How long for?"

"Let's give it a conservative, as long as it takes for me to look at you *and* not strangle you. How's that sound?"

Cory and I exchange side-eyed consolations. "Sounds perfect, Coach."

He walks out, and I linger, hoping to squeeze one more moment with Cory out of this lemon of a day. There's no hope though, not with David watching me like a hawk.

"See you tomorrow," Cubby says

"Tomorrow."

"You know I can't let you stay with the Bears, don't you?" Coach, I mean David says with a calmness once again that sends shivers up my spine.

Taking a sip of my coffee, I let the bitterness burn my throat and nod. "I do. Coach."

"Conducting a sexual relationship with a student, consensual or not, is an unforgivable sin, James."

"I know, Coach." His ire then turns to Cub, who's as white as the ice he glides so effortlessly upon.

"You too, Malkovich. The sky is the limit for both of you, but you in particular. Why would you toss it away for some ... torrid affair?"

"It's not an affair, Coach," Cory replies, his voice meek. "I fell in love with James, and he's fallen in love with me. We tried to keep it as friendship, but ..." he pauses to rub his hand down his face, "after everything you've been through with Quinn—"

Coach's fists pound into the table top. "Don't you dare compare your behavior to my daughter. Quinn is a good girl. She would never risk everything like this."

"But she did, Coach. Had you not been the man you are, she could have lost you, and your wife. Pretty sure that would have felt like everything to her."

Coach scowls, I can almost hear the man's blood boiling. Pushing off the table, he stands, fists clenched at his side. "Cory you will be suspended for two games and your captaincy of the Bears will be reviewed. Now go. Get out of my sight."

"No," Cory snaps. "I'm staying with James. This is on both of us. Me more than anyone since I'm the one that pursued him when he told me to leave it. He's helped me be a better person and player. He's helped me be me and you can't—"

"He can, Cub," I insert. "He's right. Don't make it any worse for you. It's okay, I promise. Just go and I'll meet you outside."

It's clear to all that he's not ready to submit so I add the one thing I know will get him there. "Make your mom proud. Go be with your team."

Slumping in his chair, he nods then slowly stands and exits, resembling a worn out sloth more than the elite athlete he is. The second the door clicks shit, Coach is on his feet, the palpable anger I expected from the get-go, raging.

"One snap and he's off. You have him well trained, don't you."

"That's not fair," I protest, trying and failing to keep my tone dispassionate.

"Isn't it? You're in a position of power and you took advantage."

"I disagree."

"Of course you do. Most predators would." I take a moment to absorb the impact of those words.

"You think I'm a predator?"

"If the shoe fits." He shrugs, his expression so cold I could hardly recognize him. "Now did your sister know about this?"

"No."

"Are you sure?"

"Yes."

"Then we're done here." I resist the urge to correct his posture and he bends at the waist, and hoists a box onto his desk. "Coach White cleared out your things, and completed all of your paperwork."

"Thank you Coach-David," I correct after a scalding glare.

"Don't thank me. Just get out of my sight."

Box in hand and heart in a million pieces, I slink through the corridors of Conte Arena. A million arguments race through my mind. I could have argued that technically, I too, am a student. That the balance of power between Cory and I is equally distributed. That he is a man and made this choice with a full and clear knowledge of what was at stake. But ultimately, I come to a decision I hate with every fiber of my being.

Cory deserves better than this. Better than a life spent with someone the world will undoubtedly view as his mentor does. As a predator.

As expected he's waiting for me in the parking lot at the rear of the complex, on what is an unfairly crisp and clear day. Leaning against my car that's parked squarely in front of the door I emerge from, he sweetly but unnecessarily waves and hollers, "James. Over here."

"I thought we could ride together," he says as I arrive by his side, open my squeaky car door and slide my belongings inside. "Maybe we could get some food?"

"Don't you have class?"

"I do, but I'm not going. This ... figuring out what we're going to do is more important."

"See, that's where you're wrong." I slam the door then turn to face him. "Harris will be watching every move you make, Cub. You have to go to class, and maintain your average and work your ass off to show him you deserve that captaincy."

"I will do all that. But Mom and Cherry are at work and I thought we could go home and talk and–"

"I'm not coming home with you, Cub," I say a little too curtly. "And before you ask, no you can't come home with me. Coach is right, I should never have let this happen. We can't do this anymore." The hurt in his eyes is more damaging than if I should stare directly at the sun above.

"But we're free now. We can be together. I'll help you find a placement. I ... I thought you loved me."

"I do love you. I love you with all my heart, Cub. That's why I have to let you go. It's your time. Your moment. Cubby Season, if you will. Your future lies here as the captain of this team and then in Montreal, and mine," I pause, sucking in a painfully sharp breath, "And mine is here with Dylan and Faith."

He throws himself into me. Arms sliding around my back. Legs wrapping around mine, hoisting himself up 'til his eyes are at my chin level, wide and staring up at me. I should remind him of where we are, of our audience. But I don't because I don't because I'm a selfish bitch and I can't let him go. Not quite yet.

"Then *I'll* quit. I don't want that future if you're not in it."

"You're not quitting, and you will want it in time."

Cory buries his face deep into my shoulder, and shakes his head. So fucking cute. "That's not true. All I want is you."

"I want you too, Kid. But you have to trust me on this. I've walked away from this world in order to please someone else, and the regret I felt soured me on the inside. I don't want that for you. I want you to take all this pain and passion and funnel it into your game. Kick ass this year. Take home the Hobey Baker and the Frozen Four, and do it knowing I'll be cheering you on through every damn second."

"I don't want that."

"You do. I know you do, and you do too."

He shakes his head again but makes no further argument and neither do I. Instead I grip him even tighter, kiss the top of his head and let myself feel the weight of him one last time.

I'm not sure how long we stay that way, but it comes to an end via the whispered words of Sam. "Boys, Coach was heading this way when I left. You might want to end this before he sees it and ends you."

"Thanks Sam," I say as politely as possible without lifting my head. Cory takes a different approach.

"Get fucked, Sam."

Laughter bubbles from me and I use the jiggle it causes to relax my hold and let Cory slide down my body. Hands still locked, he stares at me. Rivulets of tears descending his cheeks, and mine. He looks so fucking sad, and selfishly, I'm tempted to take it all back. To take him in my arms again and never let him go. But this is the right thing to do. I know it is. It's just really fucking hard.

Palms sticky with sweat, I make an attempt to slide my hand

from his and am almost successful, but he hooks his pinky and latches it around mine.

"Guys he's coming," Sam repeats, tapping me on the shoulder before making a hasty getaway.

Unable to summon the strength to look into his beautiful blue eyes again, I focus on our entwined fingers, the last part of us connected as I slide away.

"Goodbye, Cubby."

R outine. I hate that mother fucker. My brain, though. My brain thrives on it and suddenly in the space of twenty-four hours, the safe and predictable life I'd crafted for myself fell apart.

I have no job.

I have no ability to stop fucking crying.

I have no Cory.

The right thing was done. I know that, but tell that to my feet. The ones who can't stop pacing twenty-four-seven.

Or the tender skin around my nails that now bleeds as much as my heart that is shredded beyond repair.

Or Dylan, who can sense his Jamie isn't right, so he's not right.

Or Faith, who like me, is so thrown by the sudden change in all our lives she's more distressed, has retreated back in to herself and cried more each and every night than she did when we lost Dad.

Or my brain, that is obsessively picking apart and analyzing every micro-moment looking for one where is all went wrong, which is stupid and pointless because I know what moment was the very second I hoped for more. The second I said yes to becoming a Bear.

I don't want to be this person anymore. I don't want to think ... obsess over everything, or feel everything as intensely as I do. I don't want the supermarket lights to hurt my eyes and the sound of keys jingling, or a mysterious rattle somewhere within my vicinity, to drive me fucking insane.

I don't want to think about *him* all the fucking time.

Since Dad died, actually no, since Brandon left and the practice screwed me over, I've tried to pull myself together. To rise above it all. I have. But the weight if it all keeps sucking me back under.

I'm just done.

I've not spoken a word in weeks and begin to fear I my remain silent forever. I just don't know to find the words. Like my hope, they've just … vanished.

For someone like me, grumpy, rigid, controlling, second chances don't come around easily. Hell, first chances don't. And that's why this whole fucked up situation confirms my opinion on the cruelty of existence. A life, a universe that would dangle a perfect, pretty man before my eyes like a crystal spinning on a string. A man who was capable of loving all the parts of *me* reflected back to *him, all* the hidden evils even I couldn't, and then it take him away.

Yeah, that's not for me.

Six weeks later

"Jamie. You either have to find a new job, make up with, then have mind-blowing phone sex with Cory, gag, or—"

"Cory and I broke up, remember. That's exactly what you wanted me to do and I did it. You were right, I was wrong. I was stupid you were smart. He's gone, I'm here. Now leave me alone, Faith."

Mumbling under her breath, Faith throws my weighted blanket at my head. She misses 'cause she sucks. "No. I will not leave you alone. I love you. Dylan loves you and we need you. I'm sorry you're hurting but, yes, in the long run, I do believe this will be for the best."

"Okay, sure Doctor Plum. But since I'm kinda sleepy, do me a solid and wake me when that long run's over." I roll to my side and bury my face into the tiny gap between my mattress and the wall.

Crinkling beneath my pillow is the reason for my latest self-pitying slump. Doom scrolling as I attempted to sleep two, maybe three nights ago, I came across an article covering Cory's PR visit to Montreal. For some stupid reason, I printed a photo he looked particularly delicious in and studied every pixelated inch of it for hours.

Wasn't my wisest decision. Sadly, not my dumbest.

"Jamie, I know our life is not what we had planned, but it is our life. You are a vital part of it, so please, Jamie. Get up, have a shower, then come and have pancakes with Dyl and me. I can't miss work again today." Much to my relief, Faith clomps up the stairs, leaving me to wallow in my own filth. Just as I want.

Or maybe not.

Cunning as she is, she leaves the door to my dungeon open, meaning I can hear every clatter and clang she makes, and the squeal Dylan releases when Faith loudly pronounces I'm joining them for breakfast.

"That's right, Dyl. Jamie's finally coming. Thank you for pulling out his chair. I'm sure after three days, he's as excited to see you, as you are to see him." Dylan's happy clapping seals the guilt she absolutely intended me to feel. I may be able to ignore her, but Dylan is another matter.

After washing off my stink with the bare minimum effort, I dress in a ratty old tee and sweats, take one last look at Cory's pic, then tuck it back under my pillow before I kiss it again.

Dylan's smile is worth the herculean effort. As is the sight of him pulling out my chair. It is not my chair though. It's Dad's.

"You want me to sit in Dad's chair?" Dyl hums and taps the timber three times, as Faith slots between us, depositing a short stack covered in bacon and syrup. "He's been pointing at it for every meal. I thought it was the usual, where's Dad thing, but I guess not."

Teary-eyed, I stare at the seat that has been empty for months. It's just a chair, I tell myself, but all of us here, crowded around it know that's not true. Dyl taps it again, then scoots around the table to take his place beside me. "Okay, Dyl. I'll sit here."

"Excellent." Faith claps as she returns to the stove. "Since you're up, you'll be able to make it to your doctor's appointment."

Syrup drips down my arm as I drop the fork I'd just picked up. "What doctor's appointment?"

"The one I booked for you. Now hurry up and eat. You'll need to shower again before you leave. You smell like a dead rat."

"FAITH'S BEEN CONCERNED, but your blood work is fine, as is your ECG. Now, you can both ignore the grief and heartbreak over your dad, and your recent job loss and the breakup Faith told me about—"

"Faith has a big mouth, and I am not heartbroken—" I one hundred percent am.

"And you can devalue the work you're doing with Dylan all you like, James, but that multiplied by carer's burnout—which is real, before you say it—is enough to have anyone struggling to function."

I roll my eyes, and have the distinct impression Dr. John Lappin wants to sleep me on the back of the head in punishment.

One of my dad's best friends, he's been our family doctor since we returned to Boston, so I wouldn't put it past him. Not only for being sassy but because he's sick of me. I've been in his office at least once a week since ... since Cubby left.

"Dad cared for Dylan for years and he never burned anything other than every piece of toast or steak he cooked."

"You think so, do you?"

"I know so." Crossing my arms over my chest, I lay back on the stretcher like I'm in an emperor's robe, not just wearing a thin paper gown, boxers and socks.

In response, John tilts his head to the side, a slow smirk spreading as he scoots the wheely stool he's on over to his desk. Muttering under his breath, he searches through his drawers.

"Uh-huh. Here it is. Your dad had me keep this here for you and Faith because he knew there was a chance Dylan would be living at least part time with one or both of you one day." He wheels back to me then hands me a manila folder stuffed with crinkled papers. "As your physician and trusted friend, I hope you accept what I'm about to say in the loving and supportive, compassionate way that it's intended. You're a fucking hypochondriac pain in my ass James, as so was your dad. Read." The folder is thrust in my direction, a few papers flittering their way to the ground as I scramble to gather them while lying down.

"What are you talking about? Dad was the most mentally 'I got my shit together' kind of guy I ever knew. Also, should I be seeing this? Medical records are confidential, John."

"I've been a doctor longer than you've been alive, but thank you for the patronization, *James*," he says, delivering the whack to the head I've been expecting. "Most of these aren't medical records, and for those that are, in there you'll see I have your dad's written consent to share."

Juggling papers between my right hand and elbow, I use my left hand to push myself up into a seated position. "Dad really wanted me to see these?"

"He did, Son. I'll give you a moment to read through them. Just call if you need me, I'll be in the next office making a call."

Leaving me metaphorically lodged between happiness and crapping my pants I open the folder and take out a fist full of what look like handwritten letters. The first being dated maybe six months after Mom died.

John,

Thank you for helping me with the property hunt. I can't tell you how much it means to me to know the house is in a great school district, and that it and the yard will be safe for the kids.

In your last letter you expressed such

implicit confidence in my ability to do this all alone, but I really think you've made a gross overestimation.

Everyday, it feels like another piece of my heart has broken off and floated away. Faith spends her days telling me she's fine, and her nights crying because she thinks I can't hear her. Jamie has not ability to hide his emotions and just cries all the time, and Dylan keeps sitting beside or pointing to Heather's chair like he's waiting for her to come home.

I don't know how she did it, John. How did she manage all three kids, and school and their appointments and Dyl's meltdowns and medications? I genuinely fear I'm screwing up so badly, they'll be taken off me or I'll drop dead from a heart attack and leave them orphaned.

Come to think of it, this pain in my chest, and shortness of breath is truly troublesome. Perhaps when we arrive, you can give me a full work over?

Christopher

Good lord, he's me.

Tears fill my eyes and I continue to read, but only fall when I find one email dated back when I quit hockey.

He insists he doesn't want to play this

season, but I know he's quit for Faith and Dylan.

For me.

I'm so damn proud of Jamie, and I want to tell him he doesn't need to sacrifice what he loves. That somehow, I'll find a way for the burden of it all not to land on his shoulders. But it breaks my heart to admit to you that I can't, John. Even with your generous offer of assistance. I'm drowning in debt, there's more out of pockets for Dylan's supports everyday, and hockey, while it's hie's dream, just isn't an essential right now.

All Heather and I wanted is for them to be happy and in love like we were, and to have successful careers. He's only a kid and I've already failed him. I'm failing them all.

I can only hope he will forgive me one day.

A SIMILAR THEME runs through each thing I read. Dad was just as overwhelmed as I was. And not just when we were kids. There's notes here, copies of emails and texts that show Dad struggling to get help for Dylan. Evidence of his quest to grant Dylan the right of independence. Records of almost monthly medical tests, searching for answers to what ailed him, and notes John left insisting he was healthy. It was anxiety. He was burnt out right to the end of his life and I never knew.

A knock on the door draws my eyes from an application Dad had made for Dylan to receive funding for an independent living complex designed for adults with autism. It's a place I know well, Dyl has stayed there for respite weekends several times. He loves it and poor Dad had all but begged for permanent funding five times and each was rejected.

"Fuck I hate this," I sob, wiping my cheek with the sleeve of my hoodie. "I wish he was still here, John. I'd tell him he never failed me, or Faith or Dyl."

"He knew that in the end, I think Jamie. He was so proud of Faith becoming a professor and of you for pivoting to study physiotherapy."

"I'm glad he got to see some of his wishes fulfilled before I went and fucked everything up."

"You didn't fuck everything up. You just fell for the right person at the wrong time. He'd still be proud of you, Jamie. He wanted you to be happy in every aspect of your life, and that includes your love life."

I rub my chest, my tattoo almost burning beneath my fingers.

Balance, playing through my mind over and over.

I need to right myself. To find some balance. To make Dad proud, and I think I know where to start. Crinkling, my gown slips from my shoulder as I roll from the bed and start dressing.

"Please don't talk about my love life, not only because it's weird, but because I'm done with that shit. I have no time for men, especially not now that I have a mission."

"Ten minutes ago, you thought you were on your death bed, now you're off on a quest? Are there eight other members of your fellowship hiding in here?"

"No, and yes. I can't do much about a boyfriend when the only one I want is out of reach, but I'm getting my job back, and I'm getting Dyl into that place, John. I swear."

Connor Hoffman. Connor fucking Hoffman is the first face I see when I'm lead into the Mountie's change rooms. With everything that's happened over the last few months, I'd forgotten about him, his admittedly hot cousin, and his asshole brother. Thankfully, I'm certain it would go both ways. He's a big deal in the NHL. I am not. There's every chance he won't remember who I am. Or that I hooked up with his cousin in a cupboard the second last time I was here.

Bent over tying his laces as we enter, he looks up when he hears Gary, the equipment manager's heavy Québécois accent. "Cory Malkovich," Connor says, adding a double finger gun. "They call you Cubby, right? Great to see you again, man." Ahh fuck it. "You're here early? Nate's not coming 'til next month."

"Yeah, I know. He messaged me this week." Which is true. After running into each other during the finals, I've struck up a friendship with him and his boyfriend, Tom. Going as far to have an apartment in the same building as them.

Accepting Connor's outstretched hand, I shake it and try really hard not to wince. The dude's a beast. "I had nothing keeping me in Boston, so I thought I'd come up early and get a jump start. Congrats on a great start to the playoffs." In truth, the second I was off the NCAA ice, Coach Parker called me up. Obviously I've not played, but I have with the Missiles, The Mountie's AHL team.

"Thanks, dude. Going well so far. Looking forward to having you with us next time." With an up-nod, he sits again and goes back to his laces. I really want to ask him about Trent. With what I remember from last year's development camp, and this re-introduction, Connor is nothing like his brother. He knows his cousin is queer, and hasn't made a fuss. Maybe I'll have nothing to worry about.

Following Gary, who politely waited as I spoke to his team's star winger, I slide my phone from my pocket just enough for a discreet check. Brady, Sam, and Lucas are flying in this afternoon to help me move into my apartment.

I've been in Montreal since the Bears second consecutive Frozen Four win in April. Like I said to Connor, I had nothing to keep me there and everything to escape. James and I have only spoken twice since our split. Once when he returned some of the things I'd left at his place. And again when he sold his apartment —thankfully to a private investor who was happy to keep us as tenants, even with an increased rent. Both times felt like a dagger being reinserted into my heart, that was then twisted then left to rust.

Time has helped me see maybe it was the right thing to do, but nothing can takeaway the pain. James helped form who I am, and that's the kind of love you just never get over.

Pretty sure that's why the boys are coming to help me settle in. As witnesses to the mess I became, and the arbitrators of my somewhat resurrection, they deserve to enjoy a taste of my success. I've got the whole weekend planned. Limo transfers too and from the airport. A fancy dinner tonight at one of Montreal's best restaurants. A private, guided tour tomorrow, Cirque du Soleil tickets, *and* whatever cheap crap I can think of in between 'cause I am broke.

"Coach tells me you've got some pretty fancy accommodation over in The Village?" I can't help but note Gary's raised eyebrows as he points me towards a long hallway I think leads to the administrative area. After Nate made me aware of it, renting in The Village, a suburb also referred to as, "The Gay Village," was as deliberate a move as chasing Jamie was, and one I hope to also come to love. Since I'm not quite sure of the reception I'll receive as one of a few openly gay players in the league, I thought I would at least pick a neighborhood where I knew I'd be accepted. "You rooming with any of the other rookies, or … a friend?" Nate, I know he's thinking.

"Nope. Just me. Back home in Boston I was living with my mom, my sister and a toddler."

"Oui, je comprends."

"That's … you understand, right?"

"Yes, oui. Well done, Cory. You're learning to speak French?"

"Trying. It's a lot more difficult than I imagined it would be. Probably should have started the second I got drafted, but with school and practice, I never seemed to have time."

"Never mind. You seem like a smart boy. You'll pick it up. Now, would you like to see the most important part of the complex?"

"The rink?"

"Non, la cantine."

BACK IN MY APARTMENT, I sit on my balcony, in my egg chair with an iced coffee, a copy of a smutty MM romance Cherry insisted I read. Instead of taking in the view of downtown Montreal, reading, I'm scrolling through the photo gallery on my phone. Something I've found myself doing a lot over the last few months.

With every snap I see of that last weekend Jamie and I spent together, my heart breaks a little more.

I need to get over him. I know I do. But right now, I want nothing more than to somehow melt into the screen of my phone and go back in time. To that version of me. To sweet kisses, lazy breakfasts, Jamie lying beside me with his face buried into his pillow, to me buried inside him.

Had I known we were dancing on the edge, that the very next day we would tumble off and never recover, I would have taken more photos. But for now I have four, like my old number at the Bears. I stare at them so often, I could draw them from memory at will. They are tattooed in my brain, like Jamie is on my heart, and I will treasure them, as I do our time together, 'til the very day that I die.

After way too long, and way too much moodiness, I book a ride, slide my phone back into my pocket and leave my unread book on the seat, and head inside. The boys' flight will land in two hours. I was planning on meeting them here, but as nice as it is, I need to get out of this box of an apartment.

Changing out of sweats and the Bears hoodie I almost live in, I slide into the latest suit I had made in preparation of the season to come. It's dark navy with a lighter blue-check, the tailor who dresses several of my future teammates, claims they favor. It's fancy as shit, but to make it me I pair it with runners and a cropped tee. With a buzz I'm alerted to Uber's arrival and the sadness that's weighing me down lifts, just a smidge. Grabbing the handmade sign I'd planned to hang in the kitchen, I head down stairs, messaging our group chat as I go.

> Can't wait to see you boys.

Sam must have been staring at his phone as he replies straight away.

SAM

> You too, Cubby. I've been feeling short of late.
> Being around you again will give me a much
> needed ego boost.

"Fucking asshole." I scoff, much to the ire of the driver who eyes me in the rear view mirror. "Oh, not you. My friend," I say, holding my phone aloft. He mutters something incomprehensible and I think French then returns his focus back to the road.

> Hate to tell you Sammy, but they have magic
> water up here and I'm now seven foot.

SAM

> Cory Malkovich, Montreal's blond Hulk. I can
> see the headlines now.

Hulk.

The word alone is enough to end my short-lived happiness. Comics, fanfics, anything superhero related have been erased from my life. I can't think of them without thinking of James, and to my already obsessively thinking of him isn't healthy. Adding in a sex scene he's written, that we acted out, would not help.

It's there though, now. That thought, that compulsion, burrowing deeper into my mind as the traffic all but grinds to a halt.

One look couldn't hurt. Right?

Wattpad is opened for the first time in months and my favorite fic, Love Comes in Green is accidentally the first I check for updates.

There's been six chapters added since my last reading.

Six. That's one for each month we've been apart. Surely it's a coincidence but hey, a guy can dream.

The first chapter was posted three days after I moved in to what was then James' apartment. The most recent chapter just three days ago. Unable to help myself I click on and open the last.

At first all seems normal, villains reeking havoc, cities being destroyed. It's as great an escape from reality as it always was, witty, sexy and warm just like its creator. But then...

> *No matter the victories. No matter the vindication.*
>   *Regret is the poison surging through my veins,*
>   *pushing me to become more isolated. More*
>   *bitter.*
> *For a time I believed his fate had been altered.*
>   *That perhaps I was not destined to walk this*
>   *world alone.*
> *But alas, I was mistaken.*
> *My hero. My savior. My love. My heart. All*
>   *forfeited to a future I will have no part in.*
> *Peace comes in waves of clarity.*
> *I was right. I was noble.*
> *But still, I am forever trapped in once upon a time.*
> *In the past.*

> *So no. Love does not come in green. It dies in flames*
> *of maroon and gold, and drowns in frozen*
> *ponds of ice.*

Holy shit.

I can feel his pain through the screen. In my heart. In truth it's been there all along, but this has rolled the stone from the tomb, and ripped the fatal wound right back open.

Closing Wattpad, I do what I told myself I never would.

Jamie, I miss you.

Not five minutes later, my phone buzzes.

JAMIE

Miss you too, kid.

GRATEFUL TO BE AN ATHLETE, I make it to the airport with only five minutes before the boys' flight lands. It was not part of the plan. Nor was almost decapitating several hapless passersby with my sign as I race toward the gate.

I'm here as they make their way through the crowd though, sign held high above my head, a semi-forced smile on my lips. Having heard from Jamie for the first time in months is bitter-sweet but, my friends have watched me wallow in self-pity for just as long. They've come all this way to see me. I can pretend to be living the dream for a few days.

Suddenly, it's not so hard to fake it 'til I make it. As you would expect with someone so tall, it's Brady I see first, looking every bit the Aussie surfer with his blonde locks reaching chin length. Lucas is next, standing on his tip toes to see over the crowd and guide Sam, who's not looking where he's going but at his phone with a suspiciously pleased smirk on his face, by the sleeve of his tee.

I know for sure that Brady's seen me, when his cheeks turn the color of my old jersey, my welcome sign hitting the mark.

Flounder, Bailey and Basse.

Welcome to Montreal Morality Rehabilitation Center

Lucas and Sam seem to find it hilarious. Brades not so much.

"What the hell, Cubby. This is another country, you know. They might think we're deviants and deport us." This is said as he hugs me so tightly I can barely breathe.

"We're already through customs, bro," Sam adds, who picks me up and whirls me around as though I'm his long lost love and he's just returned from war, the second Brady releases me. Lucas is quiet as usual, smiling while his head pivots back and forth between me and the terminal behind us.

"You okay, Lucas?" I ask as I get his version of a hug, a one armed bro-slap.

"Yeah, of course. Just have that feeling like I left something behind." He starts patting himself down, running through his mental checklist in whispers. "Phone, wallet. Passport. Yeah. Definitely missing something." Sam grabs him by the shoulders and spins him around.

"Hey you're right. It's your carry-on. You must have left in the plane, you dick."

"Shit, Lucas." Bending, I rifle through the small collection of bags the boys dropped at my feet. Two smaller ones have Brady's name tag, and the larger Sam's. "Is it all you brought with you? Quick, run back and see if the flight crew have it." I'm just about to push him back into the throng when a shadow looms overhead.

"Don't panic, Kid. I've got it."

O nly the back of his head and strong, defined curve of his shoulders are visible, but already, something inside me has healed.

The anxiety that's ruled so much of my life, rears its ugly head. You have no idea if he's moved on, if he's been dating, or hooking-up. He won't want you anymore. He's going to be a star. You are nothing.

During my several meltdowns in the days leading up to our flight, my travel mates ensured me none of what I desperately needed to be untrue, was, and the truths I was clinging to, needed more than air, were. Cory's not seeing anyone. Not even hooking-up. Has been miserable. Talks about me all the time.

The fear lingers, maybe his old insecurities have resurfaced. Maybe the contacts are back in. The DL lifestyle back on. That's why receiving that text as we were beginning our descent felt like fate. Those four such tiny words, *Jamie I miss you*, telling me what felt like a massive risk, wasn't so risky at all.

"Jamie?" he says, with not a minuscule amount of movement in his body.

"Hey, Cub."

In one move he turns and leaps, legs wrapping around my waist, arms around my neck. His face is buried into the crook of my neck, instantly dampening my shoulders. I flinch, because in truth, it's a little triggering. The last time he made such a move was when we were saying goodbye.

"But ... I sent you a message."

"You did."

"You were already on the plane." It's a statement, not a question. One that deserves a sincere, considerate response.

"I was. Good sleuthing, Kid. Glad to see all the book smarts you picked up in college haven't been wasted." Rattling with laughter, he pulls his head from its hidey-hole and flashes me a smile that takes my breath away.

"Please don't make me say goodbye again. I don't think I could take it."

"That's one word I won't ever ask you to repeat, Cub. Not if I can help it, anyway."

"How about moist? I hate that, too."

"Fine. Moist and goodbye. Got any others you'd like to add, or can I kiss you now?"

"Kiss, please." The words still linger on his lips as mine crash into his.

"We'll leave you to it," someone in the background says, but I have no interest in learning who. I'm too consumed by the man in my arms and love in my heart.

And to be honest, the hot hockey butt beneath my fingers.

"I read your fic," he says when we come up for air. "It was—"

"A cry for help?"

Giving his head a cute little tilt side to side, he winces. "A little yeah, but a beautiful one."

"Speaking of beautiful." Leaning in, I seal my lips over his and groan. Fuck I've missed this. He's so soft and warm, and so fucking sexy, and I'm so relieved I wore a tight pair of jeans, 'cause I was mayor of Boner City right now. His hands leave their position around my neck, and weave up through my hair. I've not had it cut, or shaved, since Cory left, and the way he's tugging on the ringlets nestled around my ears, he's a fan of the hermit look.

"Want you," he pants, gasping for air before his tongue pushes past my lips again, caressing my tongue with his own. "Missed you." I'm hard, so fucking hard and so fucking aware of where we are. It's hard to care though, when my skin is a buzz and Cory rolls his hips, pressing his own erection against my stomach.

Pulling my lips from his, I journey down his neck and bite

that sweet spot below his ear soliciting a greedy whimper I need to hear in a more private setting.

"Jamie," he says, swallowing heavily. "I think we'll be arrested if we don't stop."

"I don't care as long as you're there."

"You will. Eventually. If we stop now at least we can start again when we get home. No other inmates named Billy-Bob watching, either." Chuckling, I drop my head against his shoulder.

"Just stay on me for a second." I slip my hand between us and palm my aching cock. "Actually, better make that five minutes."

Shaking his head, he presses one more kiss to my lips then slides off me and straightens his suit. Once happy he looks less disheveled, he looks up at me and smiles.

"Hi."

"Hi yourself. Nice suit. Love the tie."

"Nice beard."

"Wanna come home with me?"

Bending, I slide my arm around his waist and pull him against me where he belongs. "Abso-fucking-lutely."

"So, Jamie. Boys. Whose idea was this?" The five of us are spread out in the back of the limo, Lucas and Sam are halfway through a bottle of sparkling wine I'm hoping is complementary, Brady is texting someone, Quinn, Troye or both, judging by his smile, and Cory is tucked into my lap. A position I don't plan on letting him leave any time soon.

"You won't believe this," I scoff, scratching the bridge of my nose. "But Faith did."

"You're right. I don't believe it." Everyone laughs but me. Amongst the many memories to torture me through each night, the little chat Faith had with Cory, then recounted to me, has been one of the most haunting memories of our time together. Time and time again, those, if you love him let him go, barbs were the things that kept me awake. I can't imagine how painful it must have felt to have my sister toss them at his feet, only for me to do it too.

"She's my fiercest critic, ardent defender and teller of truths. The day I graduated, she hugged me, gave me a kiss on the cheek then passed me a Canadian work visa application."

"She did not."

"She did. I think she'd reached her 'sobbing gay brother listening to droopy ballads' limit." Cory holds me a little tighter.

"You were sobbing?"

"I was. Losing a lot of hair, too." Proudly I stroke my beard. "That might have had more to do with it than the tears, actually."

Suddenly, Cory jumps then fists my shirt. "Dylan! What about Dylan?" There's genuine distress in his voice which makes me love him even more.

"Dylan's doing great. The advocacy group finally helped us get the insurance sorted and my dad's doctor helped him get a placement in this amazing community house. Dad's goal was always to have Dylan live with some kind of independence, and now he can. He has his own little apartment with a kitchen, so he's supported to cook his own meals. There's a staff room attached for sleepovers, and a shared garden with these net swings he's mad for. When he moved in we took him shopping and he picked out his furniture, and the best part is, Maria moved in, too. They're neighbors. He's so happy, Cub. It's Dad's dream come true."

"Dylan's too, I think."

"I hope so. At first I felt guilty, and was worried that people would think we were locking him away in some ... institution. And he can't express how he's feeling, you know. What if he hated it and just wanted to come home, but couldn't tell us. Anyway, we did two months of weekend trials, and by the last one, he didn't want to leave. He really does seem happy."

"And he still comes to Green Line. Best skater on the ice," Brady adds, before turning and tapping on the tinted glass dividing us from our driver. "Hey, mate," he attempts to whisper. "Can you do us a favor and take us to Hyatt Place?" The driver nods his affirmation and slides the glass back up.

"*Why* are we going there?" Cory asks.

"It's where me, Lucas and Sam are staying."

"You're what? I thought—"

Blushing, he points between James and I. "You thought we were going to sleep in the same apartment as you two?"

"Yeah. No thanks." Sam nods to Lucas for backup.

"We wanted to stay with you, Cubby. But when James relented and came along we booked a room each. Brady can send his filthy messages to Troye and Quinn, Sam can send his to– Oww. Absolutely no one," he adds after Sam kicks his thigh. "And yeah. I too will message no one 'cause why would anyone want me?"

Sam's sheepish grin doesn't go unnoticed by anyone. Among a litany of worries over my unsolicited migration, will Cory be single? Still interested? Hate the beard? This secret between Sam and me has created the most fear.

I want Cory and I to have a fresh start. One that's open and honest. All pucks on the ice, if you will. But Sam's sworn me to secrecy. Bailed me out. I can't break his confidence. Thankfully, even though he's clearly covering something up, Cub's too excited over the prospect of alone time with me to bother digging.

"We've got an hour before dinner. Tour later. Fuck me now," is my reply to the offer of Cubby showing me around his apartment.

"Deal."

With little regard for his need for oxygen, or the cost of that sexy suit, I fist the tie hanging loosely around his neck, and drag him inside, throwing that lithe, but muscular body up against the wall and tearing open his shirt.

"Those fucking nipples," I groan, taking them into my mouth one after the other, licking, biting 'til he's writhing. "So fucking sweet." He's collected enough to use the time wisely, though, blindly popping the button of my jeans, and tugging them down.

"As much as I want you to take your time and taste every inch of me, I also need to be inside you yesterday."

"I vote for that, too and came prepared."

There's a full length mirror on the wall opposite me, a final chance to check yourself before you wreck yourself with bad fashion. Also to show what your man has shoved inside his ass.

Busy hands still. "You wore a plug on a plane?"

"Sounds like the porn version of a movie I've seen."

"Jamie!"

"I did." I laugh. "Not the whole flight, that would be weird. I popped it in when I went to the bathroom. Not an easy feat when you're my size."

Behind his fogged up glasses, Cory's eyes, more beautiful a blue than my mind pictured a million times, narrow. "Pretty confident I'd take you back, hey?"

"Are you taking me back? I feel like it's the other way round, but we've got time to battle that out."

"A lifetime."

"Exactly."

CORY

NHL training is so far above what I was doing in Boston, it's not funny. It's also fucking amazing. The season hasn't even started, but Nate and I have been working with a private coach and the Mounties team to make sure we hit the ice running. Or skating.

My body is capable of things I would never have expected. I'm lifting more. Bulking up. Definitely eating more. Skating faster. I'm also deeper in love than I ever felt possible. Feeling Jamie trusting me more and more with his authentic self. Just as I did, and still do, with him, has altered how I see myself.

I truly feel like a man. One deserving of him.

Because of his masking, I don't think I realized the impact his autism had on his day to day living until he moved in. Even though he's loving his work for a NFP working with adults and kids with autism, it's been a tough transition.

The grief he had been too busy to acknowledge hit hard, and watching him struggle through it was heartbreaking and eye opening. Boston, his home and the center of so many of the routines he'd built his life around, is gone. As are the people. It's clear to see how much he misses Faith and Dylan, but the pain of absence is made easier by knowing they are both thriving.

Bit by bit, day by day, we're making new routines. Creating

new traditions and fucking like rabbits. We've made some friends, too. Tom, Nate McKinney's boyfriend being one of them. He's older and grumpier, and hates people even more than Jamie claims to. They're perfect for each other.

Just like Spidey and Hulk are.

Just like Jamie and me are.

THREE MONTHS LATER

JAMES

"Tell me this, Kid. How is it that I'm more nervous than you?" Looking drop-dead gorgeous in the new suit he had to have made after I tore him out of the last one, Cory turns to face me.

"Superior intellect. Good looks. Skills. Should I go on?"

"Nope, I think you covered everything. Oh, except massive ego."

"Oui."

With a chuckle, and the slight dick-twitch that happens whenever he speaks French, I pull into the Mounties player's parking area and take the first spot I can find. "There's probably not many NHL'ers being dropped off for their first game by their boyfriend, but fuck it. Maybe we can make it cool."

"Tom's driving Nate, and calling it cool instantly makes it uncool."

"Says the guy wearing Spider-Man briefs."

Turning off the ignition, I slump back in my seat, rolling my head to take in the sight before me. "I'm really proud of you. You know that, right."

"I do. And I'm really proud of you, too."

"Pfft, what for?" I scoff. "Having only three freak-outs before we left the building, or pulling over to vomit on the drive here?"

Cory leans over, presses a kiss to my lips and hooks his pinkie into mine. "Yep. For all of that, and for picking yourself up, dusting yourself off, and climbing right back in beside me. For agreeing to sit with the WAG's even though I know you'll hate every second of it," he pauses, looks me up and down hungrily, "For wearing my jersey and for letting me fuck you in it when I get home."

"Pretty sure I'll be thanking you for the last one." Cupping his jaw in my hand, I kiss him, pouring every ounce of belief and love I can into it. When I pull away, he stares up at me through tear stained lashes, doe-eyed and perfect.

"I love you, Jamie."

"I love you, too, Cubby. Now go get 'em."

Book Four Bonus

Bunny Season was book 1.
Kitty Season book 2.
Cubby Season book 3.
Hmmm. I wonder which season will be next?
(Not playing. I genuinely don't know.)

CHERRY

I t's an odd thing to both cherish and rue the day you met someone.

The guy approaching me now, looking like one of the grassy knoll stoners in the nineties classic, *Clueless*, is not likely to evoke such a dilemma.

"Hey sweet thang." He reaches out and rubs the black ruffle of my dress between his fingers. "You new here? Haven't seen you arou–"

"I have a kid."

"Have a good night." And with that, he's off faster than he wanted to free *me* of my panties.

Called it.

This is why I don't date. I can smell *them* a mile away, and by *them* I mean fuck boys. It's a recently developed gift, one I only wish I had at fifteen. And seventeen. And let's not forget nineteen. Nineteen was a doozy. They all were I guess since it was the same guy.

Derek. The—cherish and rue—guy.

As a teenage single mom, I shouldn't cast aspersions, but his name alone should have been a raging douche alarm.

Without meeting and falling for him, I wouldn't have my precious girl. But I also wouldn't have been robbed of my innocence, forced to learned the cruel reality of love, at way too young an age. Nor would I possess a hole in my heart so all consuming, not even the love of my beautiful Billie can heal it.

Speaking of heels.

"Cherry. Was this loser hassling you?"

"No more than you are. Now back off, Cory. You're clumsy as fuck, and cramping my style." The unfocused eyes of my brother stare back at me, mistrust oozing from their edges as he squints. He's not drunk, the dick just refuses to wear his glasses around his team mates. In the few minutes we've been at O'Reilly's—Boston College's local bar—he's tripped twice and tried to order a drink from a cardboard cutout of a leprechaun.

"I'm cramping your style? You're the one who begged me to come."

'Cause he's right, I follow him to the hockey player-filled table, slide in after him and toss my arm around his neck. "And I'm grateful you caved. It's nice to be young, dumb and carefree. Thanks for letting me live as you do for a few hours."

"I'm not carefree. Or dumb," he huffs, snatching and pretending to study a menu from the center of the table. "You're right, only a complete genius who definitely doesn't need glasses, would studiously read an upside down menu."

"Hey," he whispers, "ix-nay on the glassesay."

"Are you trying on pig-Latin? Is that what's happening right now?" His pure embarrassment only makes me laugh harder when I shouldn't. Cory is the captain of the BC'S hockey team, cute—duh, 'cause he looks like me—is fun to be around, and he's an amazing player. The problem is he's also a massive nerd, who wears coke-bottle glasses, reads comics, and is more than a little insecure about it. *Little* being the operative word. I'm five-seven, many consider me tallish, but at the same height, Cory is on the shorter side. Especially when it comes to hockey players. He was nervous as all hell coming here tonight, but since I needed it as much as he did, I may have bullied him into it. What I didn't do, was suggest he go without either glasses or contacts.

Observing our banter is rich asshole-party boy Trent. I've met the pompous ass a few times via my bestie Chloe, and he reminds me so much of Dereck, my skin crawls at the sight of him.

"Cubby," he sneers. "You finally landed a babe. Well done, little man." *Yep,* I hate him.

"I'm his sister, moron."

Nodding as he gulps the last of his beer, Trent fixes his seedy eyes on mine. "Makes sense. Such a short-ass could never pull such a hottie. I'm Trent." He winks.

"Right. Yeah, we've met before."

"'Course we have. Can I get you a drink?"

"No thanks. I'd rather not be roofied."

Cory and I share a high five, and another dickwad sitting beside Trent, snorts then burps right in my face. As the stench of stale beer and nuts wafts, Brady—former Bears player and now assistant coach—flicks his straw wrapper in the belcher's direction.

"Have some manners, Nurse. You're in public. Not the locker room." He then turns to me, his trademark blush firmly fixed in place. "Hi Cherry, sorry about that."

"You've got nothing to apologize for, Brades. Some apes just can't be taught no matter how skillful a teacher."

Trent and his pals huff in unison and depart. "Let's get a drink, boys."

I don't let it drop though, not while they're still in earshot. "Isn't that right, Cory? ... Cory?" Turning to my brother, I find him peeking out from behind the still upside down menu. "Hello! Earth to Cory."

"What?" Briefly, he blinks up at me then continues to squint across the room. Following his gaze, I spot a big beefy guy with a mustache, who's exactly Cory's type.

What in the gay drama have I stumbled into?

My heart races with excitement. I've not seen Cory in action since he came out, but have been living vicariously though his Grindr notifications. "You know, if you wore your glasses, you could actually see the fuzzy figure you're watching like a freak, is also staring at you."

"I know that. What I don't know is who he's with, and why he's touching him."

"Who's touching what now?" Spinning in his seat, Brady repeats my movement. "Oh, James." He smiles and waves to this James, causing Cory to slide deeper beneath the table. "Dunno who he's with. Maybe it's a date. Cub, come say hi and find out."

"Nope. No thanks. I'll stay here and keep an eye on things.

You go but don't tell him I saw him. Not that he'll care, but don't
"

Slightly bemused Brady slips from the table and heads over to this James. "Okay. I'll say hi for you."

"No, don't!" Cory yells to his back. "Shit." Brady approaches James, shakes his hands, then points our way. "Are they looking at me? What's he saying?"

"For fuck's sake, Cory, how am I supposed to know." Having suspected Cory would need them, I pull his nerd frames from my tiny bag, and slide them onto his face, accidentally on purpose poking him in the nostril, eye and ear in the process. "Here put these on you damn fool. Then maybe you can tell me who the hottie we're ogling is."

"Nice glasses, Cap. They suit you." A voice so low and rough I feel it mark my skin, draws my gaze off my twin brother and onto someone, something, far more enticing—a set of alarmingly deep gray eyes on a gorgeous face. "Who are we ogling?"

Heat rushes to my cheeks, and I feel my eyelashes flutter on their own accord. "Why you, of course."

Popping a straw into his mouth, Mr. Hot chews it slowly, his gaze raking over me, before tossing me a wink that's sexy, not vulgar. "Knew it. Hi, I'm Sam."

"Hey, I'm—"

"Cherry. Our fearless leader's twin sister. Knew that, too." Plucking the straw from his lips, he reaches a ridiculously long arm over the table, picks up my hand and presses a soft kiss against my knuckles. His overtly sexual confidence should render it nauseating. But those eyes, blue...gray? I can't quite tell. That smile and that slight southern twang, make it the sexist move I've ever experienced.

I feel naked. Exposed. I both love and hate it.

Unsurprisingly, Cory fails to appreciate our obvious chemistry. "Hands off, Bailey. Sisters are off limits. You and your Mr. Smooth act can go ... take off." Flicking my braid over my shoulder, I squish closer to my baby bro and snuggle against him.

"Aww, you're so protective of me, bro. And you have such a way with words. Especially *off*. I've got another one for you. Stop being such a jerk *off*. Sam was just being polite. Weren't you Sam?"

"Sure was, Mam."

"Please," Cory scoffs. "I've seen you pull that kissy-hand move at least a dozen times."

"Maybe so, Cubs. But how many of those girls do you see me leaving with?"

With a huff, Cory begins to reply to this teammate, but I cut him off. "Probably none if he went in blind like he has tonight." My zinger earns me another high five, this time from Sam, the skin-on-skin contact resulting in a far different feeling coursing through my veins than the prior one did.

Instant lust.

It's a rare thing for me to experience. I've numbed that side of me since Billie was born. Feeling it once more is as terrifying as it is thrilling.

Even though I've had a longstanding man embargo in place, I'd very much like to explore the latter of those emotions, but the night turns to shit before I can. Trent, his crew, a few stray puck bunnies and their hideous attitudes, fill our tables empty seats, take one look at Cubby with his glasses on, and all howl with laughter. "Since when did Chicken Little play Hockey?"

"Chicken Little is close, but I think it's giving more ... Stuart Little."

On and on they go. Some of it's harmless, good natured chirping, but Trent in particular, consistently takes it too far. If it's not Cory's glasses, its his love of superheros, his height and his precocity of leaving alone.

As Brady and Sam do their best to rein in the crew of morons, Cory shifts in his seat, his gaze drifting from the table out to the parking lot where James is still chatting to his friend. In all honesty, I'm not even sure if he's listening. My overprotective ass could be getting more worked up over this than he is.

Either way, I get why my lil bro has been so hesitant being around these ... people. The eagerness I felt to be out with those my own age, and the flirtation Sam inspired, withers up like my mom's homemade soda bread. I'm seconds from losing my shit, when Mustache James and his date leave, and Cory decides he's had enough, too. Coincidence? I think not.

"Let's go, Cherry." With a short sharp smile and up-nod to Brady and Sam, he waves to the twats, then makes for the exit. I do the same, waving to the two decent humans, but offering no such courtesies to the others, choosing instead to give them a up close view of my two middle fingers.

"Cherry, wait!" Sam leaps to his feet before I've made it a few steps. "Could I get your number? I thought ... I mean I'd like to ask if we could go out sometime?"

YES! FUCK YES!

"I'd like that too, Sam, but I don't think so." LOSER. "I'm not really dating right now. I have work and ... stuff." Instantly, guilt eats at the lining of my belly. Referring to my girl as 'stuff', is not okay, but even though I can't date him, I hate the thought of him judging me the way so many others do. "But, my friend Chloe is on the Bears women's team. Maybe I'll see you round the rink?"

I don't know him well to say for sure, but he seems disappointed, the dimple popping smile he flashes forced. "Yeah. For sure, Cherry. See you round."

ACKNOWLEDGMENTS

I love these boys so much, and this book was a dream to write.
Thank you so much to all that have supported me through the
process, especially my family, and my amazing street team. Love
you guys.
EJ you're the best. Belinda, Olivia, Emma and Devon for all your
advice.
My beta Aleshia, and my gorgeous editor Callie, I can never thank
you enough.

And finally to my absurdly talented cover designer Luy, thank
you for all your hardwork and excitement.
xo
Bindi

ABOUT THE AUTHOR

Bindi Kennedy lives in Melbourne, Australia with her husband, two eternally embarrassed daughters, and the true loves of her life, her fur babies. She loves potatoes, hates balloons, and has an unhealthy obsession with Scottish Highlanders in kilts.

When she's not adding a heartfelt twist to her fun, flirty and spicy romcoms, Bindi can be found reading, or listening to Taylor Swift...probably while crying.

Also by Bindi Kennedy

Green Line Ice

College Hockey Romcoms

Bunny Season

Kitty Season

West Village Series

Four interconnected, standalone romcoms set between NYC and Australia.

Rules in Love

Secrets in Love

Lost in Love

Trouble in Love

The sweetest Christmas novella ever.

Kisses Cuddles Christmas & You